Based on a True Story

ROLL OF THE DICE

Original Story

Written

by

Joseph A Cangemi

ISBN: 1-4196-6496-4
ISBN-13: 978-1419664960

Visit www.booksurge.com to order additional copies.

ROLL OF THE DICE

≈

JOSEPH A. CANGEMI

For Gloria

Who gave me my start in the real world, and gently, but
forcefully, pushed me to strive for excellence and reach out
for new heights. She's my friend, my wife, my mentor, and
my lover. She's a great girl and one more fine woman.

CHAPTER 1
NEW YORK, DECEMBER 11, 1925
6:05 A.M.

"By God, this is one hell of a snowstorm!" Jules Salarno
said. He had grown up in Naples Italy, and had never witnessed
anything as violent as this. The morning sky had been suddenly
deleted by enormous clouds and looked like a sheet of murky ice.
The gusts of wind made a landscape of large mountains against the
neglected brown stone apartment buildings and streets. Jules, his
mother and father came to America eleven years ago and rented a
two bedroom flat in the lower east side of Manhattan. Jules's
mother had two boys born in New York since then.

Jules tightened the wool scarf around his face, held his
fedora with one hand and struggled along the trash infested
sidewalk embracing the buildings. Then a striking blast of
hurricane-like wind whipped him aside into a telephone pole. He
wrapped one arm around the pole with all his strength and watched
the empty street turn into massive drifts of cotton candy. It was
so cold, the air made his lungs burn. He bravely managed to creep
along stepping over half-empty trash cans and rancid garbage. The
wailing wind caused his hearing to have a ring. His eyes came
across a clattering door of an abandoned grocery store. He

thought, God, I gotta warm up before pieces of my body start
breakin' off. I'm goin' in, who's gonna know. He yanked the door
open. Suddenly, hundreds of rats ran off everywhere. Jules
bolted back a bit but rats didn't scare him too much, he had an
unusual relationship with them; a new recipe he contrived for his
scam. A glowing street light helped him to see inside. He eyes
studied the dilapidated room. There were broken boxes of oatmeal
and flour and sacks of wheat and empty cans of fruit and broken
wine jugs and large barrels, some standing, some on their side
rocking and creaking. Snow and wind blew in the store from a
broken window on the wall nearest to the alley forming a mound of
snow over empty wood boxes and debris. A large rat skimmed across
his torn snow boots, and he instinctively gave it a swift kick. It
smashed against an empty barrel and ran off. "Jeez-us!" He
shouted, "How close can ya get! When I'm ready to put ya ta work,
I'll call on ya, till then, watch where yer steppin'!!" The large
front window had been boarded up at one time, only the top quarter
and lower half had endured the weather, anybody could look in the
place. A blast of wind howled and made the loose boards shudder
and rap against the window scaring Jules half to death. He looked
outside, and thought, I gotta get out this weird place, it's
givin' me the creeps. The wind and snow blew around so bad, Jules
could hardly see. Jules thought, sheeeit, is the City of New York
gonna survive er wha'? Smiley better show, he's suppose to meet

me at seven at Shrap's Pub, he better be there, what's a little snow. He's gonna love the "Mickey Mouse" con I came up with. I won't tell him everything until we're through pulling it off. This way he'll know what to do for the next con. I can see his face now after we pull it off, he'll gag aroun' a bit then spill his guts out all over the place. He laughed as he rubbed his hands together.

The lower east side of Manhattan was a poverty stricken area, a place where poor Italians and Jews and Irish and Germans migrated. It was a melting pot for poor immigrants from all over the world. The lower east side was a exciting crazy place of push-carts and beggars and peddlers and gambling joints and whores all aroun'. And Jules's favorite cigar store, where he learned to bet on the horses, play the numbers, just about anything. Wild-eyed dreamers populated New York City and Jules was one of them. Anxiety overwhelmed him. He had to make a decision--would he meet with the boys at 10:00 a.m. to pull off the big heist or do his own thing. He thought about it. This was not just an ordinary day. Today was special. It was his birthday.

Fifteen.

Jules Salarno was fifteen.

Christ, the boys are gonna have a fit if I don't show, he thought. He knew he was a bright boy, and age had certainly never held him back. I'm gonna get my mama and brothers outa this rat

hole jungle, Jules thought, and it's gonna be my way. The
visibility cleared a bit, and a snow removal gang passed by in a
truck plowing snow and spreading sand. They were the only ones
out in this storm. Jules had a good feeling about pulling off his
"Mickey Mouse" con he invented, this was more important than
meeting with the gang. Not only that, the boys carried guns and
switchblades, and Jules didn't like that. Suddenly, a gust of
wind slammed the door shut, it flung open and closed again, this
time locking in place. Jules jumped, and yelled out, "What the!"
He looked in the direction of the banging door, "Oh Jesus, it's
only the stupid door, God, scared me off my feet--this rat hole's
makin' me nervous." A gallon wine jug fell off the shelf and
smashed to the floor, and a wine barrel rolled across the floor
hitting against another. He studied the area in the dim light
thinking it was a wino who came in through the broken window but
realized the wind blew the jug off the shelf and had made the
barrel roll. He turned around and looked out the window, and
thought, gotta get outa here, too spooky for me, I'm thawed out
enough. At that moment, another rat skimmed across the window sill
directly in front of Jules's eyes. He bolted back and thought,
Jesus, my little friends are getting bold nowadays, they tryin' to
tell me somethin' or wha'? Jules's eyes pierced into the rat's
eyes, it was at least ten and a half or eleven inches long. The
rat didn't move, it stared at Jules as if it was hypnotized.

"Are you hungry my little friend?" Jules said.

The rat was within arms reach. Slowly, Jules reached in his coat pocket and broke off a piece of bread he normally ate for breakfast, and cautiously lay it next to the rat. The rat took the bread and ran off. Jules took a few steps to the side not looking and walked into cobwebs. At the same time, his nose started to drip, it tickled but the cobwebs were not the place for Jules. He jumped away out of the clinging webs and quickly brushed them off then shook his head and coat wildly. He didn't like cobwebs, he thought spiders were in them, and spiders and snakes were not Jules's favorite friends. He wiped his nose with his worn wool glove, and thought, spiders, cobwebs, rats, I'm gettin' outa here, I'll warm up at Shrap's. Suddenly, he realized something. He slapped his forehead and looked astonished, and thought, that's it! The goddam rats! Hey, Jules baby, that's it! "Mickey Mouse"! My little friends here helped me make a decision! My mind's made up, I'm goin' for the "Mickey Mouse". Can ya beat that, all the while I'm in here, an' what do I see? Rats! Rats all over the place, rats walkin' across my feet, rats lookin' at me...had clues all aroun' me, well it's all together now. Screw the boys--no future, they're a bunch of losers. I'm gonna be rich. This really made my day--I know my "Mickey Mouse" con is gonna work. Sheeeit, I got it right from the rats themselves. Horses mouth, rats mouth, what's the difference, I got it-I got it, boy,

I feel like singin'--better not, might scare the rats away for good. At least now I'll be able to get mama the medicine she needs, food, clothes an' books for my brothers--it was meant to be to stop in this deserted store. I'm gonna call this place The Mickey Mouse House. He chuckled to himself, and looked at another rat staring him nearby, and said, "One thing's for sure little fella, my marks (victims of a con man) won't ever find out about my "Mickey Mouse" con. New York's gonna get a sting like they never had before--with your participation of course, so stick aroun' pal 'cause pretty soon yer gonna have all the cheese ya want." He danced his way out the door on his way to Shrap's Pub.

Jules Salarno was a handsome boy, tall and collar-length light brown hair, with startling dark warm brown eyes that were hypnotic and genuine. Pale skin. Short chin. His handsomeness was not perfect, but he was mesmerizing. His once-broken nose gave his looks the dangerous edge he needed. His fingers were long and strong. He walked erect and gallant. And had a light-hearted disposition and a soul filled with optimism.

Three years ago, Jules's father, a mason by trade, fell off a scaffold and broke both feet. He's been out of work ever since and became a violent alcoholic. He spent what little money he received on cheap wine and came home once in a while when he wanted something. He never had money to support his family, and he beat on Jules's mother then beat Jules with a barber strap until he

passed out. Jules's ailing mother through her husband out to
never see him again. But the old man sneaked in the flat from
time to time, and when he did, Jules got a beating worst than
before. Jules had the last of the whippings hopefully. He had
made up his mind and was determined to get his mother and two
younger brothers, Peter (9) and JoJo (7) away from this purgatory.

Jules thought, God, where's the time go? I was eleven years
old when we moved to Manhattan. Sheeeit, seems like yesterday.
When I got off that banana boat, I thought I died and went to
heaven. Well, it hasn't been quite like that, more like a bad
dream. MaMa 'n my brothers are gonna start feelin' a whole lot
better now that I'm gonna be makin' some bucks. My ultimate dream
is to invent a sting of some kind where the apple (victim) will
not ever find out he was a rube (victim). I'm gonna rob from the
rich and help the poor people too. The Big Store (any confidence
game requiring a fake front in a card game , gambling den,
bookmaking parlor; also called "joint", "the store," or "the big
con") is what I'm goin' for. I'll figure how to do it. The "Mickey
Mouse" is small time but it'll pull me through for now. I'll have
a few bucks to do what I have to do for my mama an' brothers--
after that I'm gonna have big bucks. He believed in his dream
with all his heart and had never dreamt or thought of anything
else. His mother and brothers were his main concern.

When he left for Shrap's Pub, he thought of his best friend,

Smiley O'Brian. Jules had planned to meet with him at 7:a.m.
sharp. Shrap's Pub was their hang-out. It was a bitter cold walk
to Shrap's Pub. He passed the "Dancing Academy" where gentlemen
could hire a private dancer for more than dancing lessons,
gambling joints and a few winos--who carried their own heat. He
finally made it to Shrap's Pub and knocked on the gated door. A
short fat man hurried to the door, and unlocked it.

"Hey Jules, what you doin' out in weather like deesa? Come,
come inside, you look like icea cream." Louie said.

"Could be worse, Louie baby, know what I mean?"

"Boy, oh boy, you make joke early. Go, go now, sit down-sit
down, I gotta make coffee before Shrap come in. In five minutes,
you gonna have Louie's besta brew." He patted Jules on his
shoulder and quickly shuffled back in the kitchen.

Louie was five feet, two inches. Two hundred-thirty pounds,
and smelled like burned garlic. When he walked, he'd shuffle
along at a fast pace that made his large belly bounce around like
a tub of jello.

Jules took off his torn snow boots, left them on the mat at
the front door, and walked to the back of the room to his usual
table near the phone booth. The room hadn't warmed up yet; it was
60 or 65 degrees. He sat down leaving his black fedora and
oversized coat on then put his tattered gloves in his pocket.
Jeez-us, I can't wait to talk to Smiley, he thought. He looked at

the clock on the wall, it was 6:55. He thought, he better have
his ass here, I told him to be here at 7:00 sharp. If he want's ta
be in on the "Mickey Mouse", he's gonna have ta be on time. He
gave me his word. If he don't show, I'll find somebody dependable,
that's all--so he get's pissed, big deal--he has ta learn the
meaning of loyalty. He's been my best friend for seven years, I
don't know why I waste my time with the moron. He's stubborn,
impulsive an' is a sex addict on one hand, on the other he can be
a good grifter (con man). He's sharp, amusing and has a I.Q.
better than average. We'll see if he get's here on time, I know
him to well. He'll show alright, but he'll come through the front
door late, I'll bet on it. Bein' a thief is not right. Whatever
I steal, I'll give it back. I'm not going to rob just anybody, or
take food off their table unless they can afford to lose. Robin
Hood did it--so can I. He glanced at the clock again, it read
7:03, then he stared at the front door, and thought, I knew that
Irish moron wouldn't show on time. I've told him time an' time
again how important it is to be on time with appointments. I'm
gonna have to teach him a lesson. This is the last straw, the
lying bastard.

Jules picked up the daily newspaper Louie left on the table
and started reading. He heard the door open and looked up
thinking it was Smiley. It was the two bums Jules considered
hiring to get him a dozen of fresh dead rats a couple of days ago.

He felt sorry for them. The bums looked half frozen. They were
drunk and could hardly walk but managed to make it over to Jules's
table. The smell of alcohol filled the room with the familiar
stench of alcohol Jules's father had when he whipped him half to
death. He hated that smell and brought the newspaper up over his
eyes to avoid them.

The bearded one cleared his throat. "Well, we doin' business,
friend?"

Julie fanned the newspaper to clear the air. "I can't do it.
I'd like to do you boys a favor, but I told you two nights ago, I
found somebody else." He fanned the newspaper in the bearded ones
face.

"Listen friend," the bearded one said, "everythins got a
price, name yer own."

Jules raised his voice. "It's not that, I can't do it, that's
all--need a interpreter er wha!" He flipped over a page of the
paper and brought it up over his eyes.

The other fellow came over and stood there like a defendant
at a sentencing. He was a good looking fellow all right, and Jules
would have liked to have done them a favor.

"Two dozen fer two bucks," said the good looking one. He
quivered and waited for a reply.

Jules heated, looked in his desperate blood-shot eyes. "Don't
make me feel bad now, damn it!"

"But we can get ya all ya all the rats ya need--at's all we need is a chance, whatcha say?" Said the good looking one, in a humble voice.

"I don't know what kinda wine yer drinkin' but what I'm sayin' ain't gettin' through yer burned out brains. I'm tellin' ya for the last time, don't make me get up--ya never showed ta meet me last night, I don't do business with people that make promises and break 'em, would you?" Jules said heated.

The good looking one had a blank face, then replied, "S-sure, I do it all the time."

"I don't like liars either. Yer a has been pal, now get your stinkin' asses outa here before I get mad--get outa here, both of ya!"

"Is that a threat!" The bearded one asked, heated.

Jules's eyes pierced into the bearded one's bloodshot eyes, and said softly, "Definitely not--just a promise." Then harshly said, "Now get the fuck outa here!"

The two bums looked at each other for a moment, made a about face and ran out like cockroaches when the lights turn on.

Two or three minutes later, Smiley O'Brian came in. He looked like a snowman. He hurried to Jules's table, and stood there scratching his crotch. Jules lowered the paper then glanced at the clock. He turned to Smiley giving him a dirty look.

"You gave me yer word you'd be here at seven sharp, yer

twenty minutes late!" Jules said heated. He through the paper
across the table and stared at him waiting for one of his
magnificent excuses.

"Oh boy, it's gonna be one of those contrary mornings I see.
It never fails, I've never seen you in a good mood before you had
yer first cup of coffee. I mean, you're a likable meatball once
you get that caffeine down. I'd give my right arm to see you
change." He scratched his crotch again, and stood there.

"You got lotsa balls standin' there scratchin' away tellin'
me my shortcoming's. You should look at yourself an' ask: do I
know what loyalty is? Why do I always make up bizarre excuses?
Do people really believe me? How much longer will Jules put up
with my bullshit? Will Jules cut me in on the scam he invented?
I have ta learn to be honest to be respected. Work on those
things pal, an' maybe you'll amount ta something." Jules's eyes
studied Smiley's eyes and his body movements.

"You know Jules, you're absolutely right, I'll work on that,
promise. You've always been right helping me out. Can I sit down
or sit at the other table? I'm so cold I kin spit out ice cubes."

"As long as you sit across from me. Looks ta me ya sat on a
dirty jon at one of those sleazy joints ya hang aroun', probably
ya got the crabs."

"Crabs? Nah, it's the bleach in my underwear, I added to
much when I washed my whites, that's all." He sat down, pulled a

cigar from his breast pocket and put it between his teeth. He never lit it, just enjoyed the taste of the tobacco. On rare occasions he'd be without it.

"Hey Jules sweetheart, you aren't gonna believe this," Smiley said excitedly and laughing, "The funniest thing--just a while ago--before I got here--two winos--I mean, two real dummies, they were runnin' at full throttle down the street." He laughed harder than before," I mean, they were goin' some place in a hurry, till they realized a pile of trash cans was in front of 'em. One of 'em tried to stop, smashed into his pal, slipped on the ice, an' they go flyin' in this heap-a-shit--papers, garbage, all over the place. Holy Christ! A bunch a rats came from every direction outa there. I wanna tell ya, I haven't had a laugh like that since Lucky got caught gettin' laid in the park."

"You're a moron!" Jules said heated, "Don't try to butter me up with that bullshit story! You promised me, gave me your word you'd be here at seven sharp!"

"B-but--"

"There are no b-but's, Smiley. I've known you for seven years, pulled you outa jams not even your mother or 'ol man knew about--"

"Jeez-us Jules, have a heart will ya--I'm sorry-I'm--"

"I've heard those apologies long enough, get out of here, yer no friend. If you can still read, go to the library--look up the words, loyalty, respect an' ambition--I can think of a hundred more words, I'm not wastin' my time with a moron anymore."

Smiley took the cigar out of his mouth, and sat there dumbfounded.

Jules stood up, and said heated, "While you're at it, define the words, friendship, integrity and self-pity, that should keep ya busy for a month er two!"

Jules was teasing Smiley to see if he would stand up like a man and give him a good argument. Jules knew Smiley wasn't himself lately. He wanted his best friend to open up and tell him the problem he held within. Jules wanted to help Smiley, and this was the only way to do it.

Smiley raised his arms out and waved them about. "OK, ok, ok, ok, whadaya wanna know?"

Jules ignored Smiley completely, he turned and walked inside the phone booth; Shrap had it shipped from London; it was painted red with a wood accordion door and glass paned top. Jules closed the door, and dialed.

The room started to warm up. Smiley took his black knit hat off and stuffed it in his coat pocket, and thought, damn it, my big mouth, now he's really pissed off at me. I shoulda just said, I'm sorry. Wish I looked on the table to see if he had his coffee. Christ, he's a Mr. Hyde without that first cup. Once he has some caffeine, he turn's into a Dr. Jekyll, that's the guy I know.

Where's that goddam Louie! Hope he brings the coffee, grounds 'n all, I can care less right about now. But it sure as hell would be nice to have it before Jules gets off the phone. If he comes out before that, I'll just be a good boy 'n keep my trap shut. And if he think's I'm leaving this joint--I ain't going anyplace, damn it.

Smiley had light blond hair, cropped like an oarsman, clean and neatly in place and eyebrows perfectly matched his hair. His deep blue eyes were bloodshot and troubled. He had a well shaped nose, thin lips, and creamy skin that had a year-round reddish wind look. For a 17-year old, he looked 20 and he knew it. He was six feet tall and weighed 185 pounds. A molded smile appeared on his face ceaselessly. A small dimple became visible on his lower left cheek when he was depressed.

And today he was.

As he removed his Navy Pea jacket, his large hands got stuck in the tattered lining. He finally got it off and neatly hung it over the chair.

Louie came out of the kitchen and brought the coffee to the shaky table. He set Jules's mug down, and said, "Hey Smiley, I no hear you come in, you ana Jules gotta be coo-coo to come out ina weather like dis, no? Wait a minoot, I fix da table." He folded a few paper napkins and slipped them between the floor and table legs. It's alla fixed upa, now you no get sea sick." He giggled, sounding like a excited hyena.

"Thank's Louie my man, you're a sweetheart. I been meanin' to ask you, when you make love, do you giggle like that too?"

"No-no, I makea much-much more--like symphony." He giggled harder than before. I bring some coffee for you. Ifa you hold you breath, I come back before you letem out." He quickly shuffled off to the kitchen giggling as if he gave the funniest line of all time.

Louie hurried back to Smiley with a mug of coffee. "Here ya go gooda lookin' face. Maybe you want yer usual hash ana eggs ana my fresha Italiano toast? I got 'em in da oven now."

"Not now, Louie my friend, I'm waiting for Jules. I'll give a holler when we're ready."

"Justa holler loud whena you call, I gotta fix da frozen pipe ina back kitchen."

"You bet Louie, my man."

"I gotta do everyting over he. Dat Shrap, he no do nothin' aroun' he."

"Don't worry Louie, everything is temporary, remember that." He gave Louie's belly a brisk rubbing, and smiled.

"Ya, you right-you right. You a good boy, my friend. I go now, gotta fix em up." He walked off proudly knowing Smiley meant well.

Jules came back to the table and stood there looking at

Smiley. He thought, what am I gonna to do with this lonely guy?
Maybe I was to hard on him. I'll straighten things out.

Suddenly, the front door crashed open--it was Shrap. He was
eating a steaming loaf of Italian bread in one hand, and holding a
bottle of beer with the other. He never came in his Pub looking
like this. He wasn't exactly drunk, he looked as if he had a
terrible hangover. He stomped his feet on the floor, it left wet
snow all around. His high shined combat boots glimmered. Shrap
habitually wore a black felt fedora, dark glasses, navy blue
wrinkled slacks, and had a unlit cigarette behind his left ear at
all times. He was talking loudly to himself while chomping away
when he slipped on the wet floor and fell on his butt. This
didn't seem to bother him, he just sat there devouring the bread
and sipping his beer. He got up and mumbled and acted as if
nothing had happened. He was a broad, squat, powerful man, with
big loose hands. A red shaggy handlebar mustache. A chest like a
wine keg. Large feet. Tightly sprung. One would get the
impression that Shrap, could bound six feet straight up into the
air from a standing position.

Shrap took a big bite of bread leaving chunks of crust all
over the floor, and walked past the twelve bar stools to the back
of the room, then across to the phone booth, all the while staring
at Jules and Smiley. He walked by them with a slight wobble and
smelled like a brewery.

"You all right, Shrap?" Jules said.

Shrap walked around Jules's table and didn't say a word, he just continued walking slowly heading toward the jukebox in the corner near the front door. His eyes studied the place as he past ten tables then he stopped abruptly and stared at the jukebox. With the side of his combat boot he kicked it at a certain spot, and it played the tune "Dinky, Dinky Dee," sung by Jimmy Durante. He wobbled and turned and danced his way behind his aesthetic antique wood bar, then started wiping it down. He cared for it as if it was the only possession he owned.

Jules sat down and tasted his coffee while his eyes studied Smiley, and thought, look at him, don't look at me, no apology, nothin'. He sit's there watchin' Shrap wipin' down the bar like he never seen it done before, he's somethin' else. I'll ignore him, he's embarrassed an' tryin' to concoct the perfect story ta tell me. I know him better than his mother. He picked up the newspaper, and leafed through.

"How ya doin' Shrap ol' buddy?" Smiley yelled out.

Shrap didn't look up, he just said, "Feel as good as I look. An' quit yellin' fer Chris'sake, yer not in da fuckin' stadium ya know." He continued polishing and wiping down the bar unhurried.

In a loud voice, Shrap yelled out, "Hey Jules, Louie make da coffee yet?"

"Yeah, sure," Jules said. "We got ours. He probably didn't

hear ya come in...said something about a frozen pipe in the
kitchen."

"Hey Jules," Shrap yelled out again. "I'm lookin' for a
bartender, know somebody honest an' dependable?"

"I'll check aroun'--"

"He's right here in your presence Shrap, your's truly, Smiley
O'Brian himself, master of hosts and bartender of bartenders."

Jules gave Smiley a surprised look, and said, "Since when?
How about school?"

"I'm through with school. My last day was yesterday. I told
you a month ago that I've been contemplating on leaving the A-B-
C's 'n X-Y-Z's bullshit--I need the coins."

Smiley ignored Jules and dealt directly with Shrap.

"What's the deal Shrap, my future boss?"

Shrap kept his head down making a serious attempt cleaning
and polishing the bar. "I'll pay ya twelve bucks a week, six
days, ten-twelve hours a day, you keep da tips an tree square
meals. When can ya start?"

Smiley rubbed his hands together excitedly, and said,
"Monday. What time ya want me here, Shrapy baby?"

Shrap looked annoyed as he walked over to the table where
Smiley sat, he put his lips close to Smiley's ear and whispered,
heated, "Don't ever call me Shrapy baby again--my name is Shrap,
got dat! An' keep dis job under yer hat. Ya get paid in cash--get

it, boy? Be here at tree p.m. sharp--ya steal anytin, yer gonna
be limpin' fer a long time--an' dat means after you gid outa da
hospital, jus' like da udder guy I had, gid it, boy?!"

Smiley raised his arms and shook his hands, palms facing
Shrap and swallowed loudly. "You don't have to worry about me
stealing anything, Shrap, sir."

Shrap burped in Smiley's ear. "Ya, I know kid, da last
bartender said da same ting."

Shrap looked at Jules. "Whadaya tink? Ya consider pretty boy
here kin handle da job, or wha'?"

Jules looked at Smiley's hands for a moment. Smiley just sat
there with his fixed closed-mouth smile, tapping the table with
his fingers and he stared at Jules. Jules leaned over the table
and lightly grabbed Smiley's hand and looked at it. Then turned
and looked into Shrap's green bloodshot eyes, then back to
Smiley's hand, then back to Shrap, and said, "Well, with the big
hands an' long fingers pretty boy has, he should be able to handle
a few more drinks than the average bartender--with that, I leave a
toast to my pal, Smiley." Jules and Smiley lifted their coffee
mugs, and Jules said, "Here's to you and here's to me, and we
never disagree. But just in case we ever do, here's to me, and the
heck with you." They tapped their coffee mugs, tasted their coffee
and laughed.

Suddenly, Shrap backed off from the table, he looked as if he was about to explode, and yelled out, "Louie! He looked at the ceiling, "Louie! Where's my fuckin' coffee!"

Fifteen or twenty seconds later, Louie came bursting out from the kitchen looking as if he had been greasing a car. His red suspenders were falling from his shoulders, and his freshly pressed white shirt was wet and partly hanging out of his black shiny pants. He had a pot of coffee and quickly came to Jules's table and filled Jules's and Smiley's white chipped coffee mugs. He smelled like a old corroded steel pipe hand rubbed with garlic. Louie didn't look at Shrap, he just filled the two mugs.

"I'ma sorry I come out alla dirty likea dis, Shrapa have no consideration for me what I do aroun' he."

Shrap raised his arms to the ceiling, and shouted, "Jesus Christ! It's gonna be one a dose days!" He went to the back of the bar, and watched Louie. He stood there erect, arms crossed, stiff faced, and waited for him to bring his coffee.

Louie softly said to Jules, "Ifa Shrap was no my brother-in-law, maybe somebody shoot da buma." He turned toward the bar and walked slowly staring at Shrap, and shouted, "Rush, rush, hurry disa, hurry data--ma-fungoo."

"Louie, Louie, Louie," Shrap said softly, "why ya gettin' so emotional? I thought ya liked me a little bit. After all, if it wasn't fer me, ya wouldn't be workin' here." He slapped the bar with a powerful strike with both hands and shouted, "Now gimmie me fuckin' coffee!"

Louie gave Shrap a dirty look, poured the coffee in Shrap's personal shiny brass 35-millimeter shell casing mug. Louie spilled coffee from shaking with anger. Shrap instantly wiped the coffee from his immaculate bar.

"Jesus Christ! What a stupid fuck! I just got through cleanin'--you did dat on poipose, I know ya did! I don't know what my sister see's in ya--yer a scared little shit! Now gid outa my sight, go finish what ya were doin'!" Shrap yelled out.

Louie turned away and thought, what a shitaface. I no need dis bullashit, I fix his ass. Louie turned back and looked at Shrap, then slapped his personal coffee mug out of his hand. Shrap's mug flew across the room. Coffee scattered everywhere; the bar and whiskey bottles and ceiling and floor and smashed through the glass of the jukebox where it settled. Somehow, the jukebox started playing the tune, "Dinky, Dinky Dee," sung by Jimmy Durante. Shrap froze in his tracks, he looked dumbfounded. He looked as if he were a statue in the standing position with his hands pulling his hair out.

Louie felt good slapping that coffee out of Shrap's hand. It was long over due.

Louie shouted, "Whata kind a guy you are? You no say hello, you no say goodabye, you no say noting except Louie, fucka dis, hey Louie, fucka dat! Well, Fucka you too! Whena my two friends,

Jules ana Smiley, leave disa place today, I go too. How's dat, bigashot! End a story." Louie proudly shuffled off back to the kitchen.

"As long as we been comin' here, Louie an' Shrap been fightin', but not like this. Shrap's gonna be a tough guy to work for," Smiley said, scratching his crotch.

"That's the most logical thing you've said this mornin'. Whadaya gettin' second thoughts about working here?" Jules said.

Smiley looked at Shrap standing behind the bar looking sad, then back at Jules, and they broke out in laughter.

"No-no, I need the money. I can handle Shrap, you'll see. When you gonna clue me in on that con you've been workin' on?" Smiley said, excitedly.

Jules thought, I'll forgive Smiley, this time for being late, we've been friends too long. I'll straighten him out. "There's a minor detail I'm workin' on. I'll let ya know the score in a few minutes, relax-relax, I'm waiting for Izzy to show up at work. I called him a few minutes ago, he's not there yet."

"Is Izzy connected with this deal too, Jules?" Smiley asked curiously.

"I'd rather not say anything right now, just relax for Chris' sake will ya, you'll know what's happinin', you'll know." Jules pulled out his pocket watch and checked the time. "Izzy should be there in a few minutes."

"Well, that being the case," Smiley picked up his coffee mug, and said, "Here's to the con, and here's to you Jules, the brain behind the deal." Jules picked up his coffee mug, and together said, "Hear! Hear!" They clanked their coffee mugs and tasted their coffee.

I hope everything is okay with my pal Izzy, I can't do the "MICKEY MOUSE" without him. I'll wait a few more minutes. I need a partner to pull this off right. Can I depend on Smiley? Will he play the part? If he does, I can't tell him how the "MICKEY MOUSE" works until it's over. For the time being, I'll play it by ear. I know this con can easily be pulled-off, but it has to be done professionally, Jules thought.

CHAPTER 2

NEW YORK, DECEMBER 11, 1925

8:30 A.M.

Jules pulled his pocket watch out from his coat pocket. It was 8:30 and a good time to call Izzy. Jules got up and walked to the phone booth. He went inside, closed the door and dialed. On the fifth ring, he was about to hang up, but let it ring another time.

"Ahlow? Moyshe's Deli, can I help you?"

"Moyshe, it's me Jules, how are you?"

"Oh, Julius, haven't seen you in a while. I'm fine. Maria, she's soon to have a baby. Such a deal she make's of this. You want cold cuts maybe?"

"Not right now, I'll call back later. Izzy there?"

"Yes and No. Right now he's in the cellar getting something. He should be back anytime now."

"Tell him to call me as soon as he gets back. I'm at Shrap's, he has the number, okay Moyshe?"

"Sure, Julius, I won't forget."

"Say hello to your pretty wife. And tell her I said she's gonna have a beautiful girl this time. I have a feeling."

Moyshe laughed. "As long as it's healthy, we'll be thankful."

"Mazel Tov," Jules said.

"Okay Julius, be well."

Jules stepped out of the phone booth and walked over to the bar. As he walked, one of his wet shoes suddenly started to creak with every other step. He was sensitive about these things, so he initiated a limp to prevent the shoe from making this embarrassing sound. He leaned against the bar, looked up and studied the leaf-embossed metal ceiling; it was white at one time; it aged, a yellow stain from smoke and rust and peeling paint were all over. The eight circular hanging lights had a cloth shade around them and were frayed and discolored. He gazed at the hundreds of mirrored and lighted beer and whiskey advertising frames scattered on the walls, and thought, I'm gonna miss this place. Where else can I see a montage of promotions like this? He looked at the back corner wall next to the phone booth. The wall had a 8 X 10 inch wood framed picture of Eddie Cantor, the entertainer and a matching photo of Jan Peerce, the opera star, autographed to Shrap. They were the only objects that decorated the red 3 X 20 foot wall.

Smiley shouted, "Hey Jules, c'mon, your eggs 'n hash are here. C'mon, there gonna get cold."

"Okay, I'll be right there," Jules said, as he gestured boldly with his left hand. He thought, I'm gonna miss Louie, too.

As Jules approached his table, he limped ever so slightly so

as not to create the embarrassing creak from his wet shoe. Smiley
knew how sensitive Jules was about his appearance and all the
little things, so Smiley, jokingly poured on a little heat, after
all, both were accustomed to teasing each other from time to time.
Smiley looked down at Jules's wet shoes, and said, "Jeez-us,
what's with the limp, meatball? Wait! Don't tell me -- you bought
a new pair of snow boots and you didn't want to wear em cause you
need a new pair of shoes? No-no, that's not it -- I got it-I got
it -- Shrap asked you a question and you didn't want to answer and
you smiled an' said, why you wanna know?" He laughed so hard, he
pounded on the table, like he'd scored the winning point of the
last game of the football season and became the hero. Jules stood
behind his chair, nonchalantly took off his coat, placing it
neatly over the chair, rested both hands on the table, pierced
into Smiley's glassy bloodshot eyes, paused a moment and
leaned forward into Smiley's face.

Jules said softly, "I been meaning to tell you something
Irish, it's been on my mind for a long time." Jules stopped
talking. He backed off, sat down and had a sip of coffee.

Smiley had a confused look about him. "I-I don't under--"

"Never mind." Jules said harshly, "I've come to the
conclusion that this hangover you have don't wanna clear up, so
I'm not wasting my breath telling you a goddam thing."

Smiley shrugged his shoulders and acted like Jules hadn't

said a thing. He leaned over his plate of soft boiled eggs and
hash and stuffed his mouth with food as if he hadn't eaten in a
week. He pointed his fork at Jules, trying to say something. His
cheeks were bulging. He chewed, swallowed and mumbled something at
the same time.

"Whath the dealth?" Smiley chewed his food and swallowed. "I
mean, what's the deal? Sorry 'bout that." He drank some coffee to
wash down what was left in his mouth. You want to tell me about
the scam you invented right? That's what you wanna tell me."

Jules ate some hash and said softly, "Wrong. What a moron.
And quit pointing yer fork at me."

Smiley took a small bite from the Italian toast, chewed it
and swallowed. "Ahhh...wait a minute...yeah, I know what you're
gonna tell me, it's Sasha--yer fixin' me up with Sasha, right?"

"You're really sick, but seeing you're starting to sober up,
I'll tell ya what I'm thinkin." Jules leaned forward into Smiley's
face, and said loudly, "Don't be so concerned with your rights
that you forget your goddam manners!"

Smiley bolted back in his chair, both arms stretched out, his
palms facing Jules. "Ok-ok-ok, I'm sorry. This bad habit I fell
into has to stop--you gotta help me, Jules."

"I'll do the best I can, but you have to help yourself first.
And another thing, yer hangin' out with the wrong crowd. Yer like
a lost kid, an' ya been rattlin' on with your big mouth over the

past few months talkin' about things that don't make any sense--
look at yourself--go ahead, go look--I forgot what color yer eyes
are anymore. You been antsy, fidgety an' been acting like a idiot,
look at yerself, look in your eyes while yer at it--go ahead, if
you can see straight, dick-head!"

Jules thought, I know he's been drinking. I never said a
thing to him. He better talk to me and let it out, I'm not
pulling it out of him. He's gonna have to tell me like a man. I
know Smiley, inside 'n out. He'll tell me, I know he will.

Smiley got up from the table and looked in one of the
mirrored beer advertising frames on the wall next to him.

"Holy sheeeit! I didn't think I looked this bad."

"What!" Jules shouted out, "I don't believe yer being honest.
You gotta be blowin' yer top! He's gonna make it, I can see that."

Smiley sat down looking sad. He couldn't look into Jules's
eyes. He nervously tore a paper napkin into tiny pieces, dropping
them on the floor. He slowly lifted his head up, looked into
Jules's warm eyes, swallowed in hesitation and cleared his throat.

"I've been drinking, Jules. It's been a nightmare. You gotta
help me. If anybody can, I know you'll at least try, you have in
the past. I feel like a fool, Jules." Tears rolled down his face.

Jules felt sorry for Smiley, and talked to him affectionately
and with deep concern.

"You know Smiley, I always thought you had more intelligence

than the average kid on the block. It breaks my heart knowing
you've been messin' aroun' with the booze. I knew, but I didn't
say anything. I'm sorry. A best friend should always be there. I
failed in that part. I don't understand why you're doing this.
Being your best friend, I've always told it the way it is. It's
time I tell you again--yer feeling sorry for yourself, and if you
think you're gonna be a part of what I'm putting together, yer
mistaken. I need someone straight, someone with backbone and
ambition. What ever happened to that guy I once knew?"

Smiley wiped his tears with his hand. He thought, Christ,
will I ever straighten out? I can't let Jules down anymore, he
risked his neck getting me out of some shady deals. I'd be in the
can if it weren't for him. It only made sense to be honest with
him. He leaned forward, clasped his hands together, and in a
modest tone of voice, he said, "Remember last year when my ol' man
took off with that show dame? Left my mother 'n me a lousy twenty
bucks an' a letter sayin' that he had it livin' with a bitch an'
bastard son?"

"Yeah, what about it?"

"Well, six-seven months ago, I heard a rumor that my mother's
been screwin' half the studs in the city. Not only that, I found
gin bottles hidden all over the house. She became a boozer and I
heard her boyfriends sneakin' in the house--they'd party an'
screw night after night. I heard everything--I felt like I wanted

to kill the pervert bastard. I couldn't stand it anymore, so I
started drinkin' my mother's Gin. Then, last week I found a note
on my bed sayin' she was goin' away for a couplea weeks. She left
me fifty bucks an' said, don't worry--that's it, couldn't believe
it. Well, after that, I had it. I made up my mind, right there
an' then that I'm takin' off too. I quit school and been hangin'
out with a bunch of losers. I was out of it, Jules. I thought
about telling you, I couldn't--to ashamed. So, I guess were even.
We let each other down, didn't we? That shouldn't make you feel
so guilty now." Tears rolled down his face and he dropped his
head.

Jules squeezed Smiley's arm. "Everything will be alright. We
all go through some sort of suffering Smiley, in more ways than
one. It'll pass. Maybe it's a way we're put through a test to see
how strong we are and to gain wisdom. Life goes on. I'm here to
help you just like your here to help me." Jules raised his voice
and pinched Smiley's cheek. "Now pull yourself together Irish, or
you ain't gonna have another cup of Louie's great coffee!" He
smiled and hoped Smiley would laugh.

Smiley's dimple on his lower left cheek disappeared. Jules
knew Smiley was no longer depressed.

Smiley looked at Jules and started to smile then broke out in
laughter. Jules looked at Smiley with a serious face for a moment
then slapped his forehead and bursted out in laughter.

At that moment, the phone rang. Jules ran to the phone to answer.

"Yeah, Izzy, this you?"

"Hey Jules, it's me awright. I'll be here all day. Got yer order on ice. When ya comin'?"

"Be there in a half hour or so." He hung up, rubbed his hands together in excitement and went back to the table.

"What was that all about?" Smiley asked.

"Doesn't matter right now, I'll tell you later. Let's concentrate on you and what we're gonna do about solving this problem right here and now--where ya stayin'?"

"At my house. My mother won't be back for another week an' seein' I'm startin' work Monday, I'll have a chance to look aroun' an' find a bed." He gave Jules a look as if he knew what Jules was thinking. He held up his hands, palms toward Jules, shaking them. "Hold on, just hold on a second before ya say a thing. I know you like a book. I know what you're gonna say. I'm making you a promise--I'm through with the booze from this day forward--so help me God. I know I have to prove it to you Jules--I will."

Jules looked at him with a serious face, and said, "Okay Smiley, you'll have time to prove what you say. I want you here tonight at 6:30 sharp. Did you rent the clothes I told you to get?"

"Yes, shoes too. I have my own black socks, I have everything plus. Jeez, Jules, thanks, thanks for believing in me."

Somehow, Smiley spoke proper English suddenly. His attitude toward life now may have changed from resentment and militant and defeatist, to being a habitual easygoing individual like Jules.

Jules stood up, lay two dollars on the table, put his coat, scarf and hat on then pinched Smiley's cheek. "The chow is on me. You're gonna be just fine Smiley, my man. Tell Louie 'n Shrap, I said good-bye. See you at 6:30 sharp." He walked to the front door, slipped on his worn-out snow boots, wrapped his wool scarf tightly around his face and walked out.

CHAPTER 3

NEW YORK, DECEMBER 11, 1925

9:05 A.M.

He could not believe it. He battled the wind thinking the end
of the world is coming, but there was nothing he could do. Jules
thought, if I'm gonna be rich, there's a few sacrifices involved,
this is a big one. How long can it snow like this? Keep walkin'
Jules, you're almost there. He approached what appeared to be an
isolated grocery store. He paused a second and shook the snow off
his coat. An aura of poverty surrounded him. He knocked on the
door and Izzy came halfway out. Jules handed him a piece of paper
with money wrapped around it. Izzy was a year younger than Jules
and he stood six foot even. Skinny. Wore wire rimmed glasses.
Brown eyes. Freckled face. Strawberry curly hair. He looked like a
young Abraham Lincoln.

"What time ya comin' over with everything, Izzy?" Jules said.

"I'll be over yer place aroun' 1-1:15, is that okay with
you?"

"Yeah, sure." Jules waved good-bye. He ran to keep warm. As
he approached his broken-down brownstone building, he warily
looked around. When all was clear, he sprinted then slid on the
icy sidewalk; losing control, he fell and flew into a heap of

trash cans and got pinned underneath. Three or four rats skimmed across his face as they ran off in fright. Jules, scared to death, struggled to get out, but slid back into the pile, which caused more trash cans to tumble on him. More rats ran across his face and body; after a furious struggle, he managed to get out. He walked up the outside stairs, and continued up the flight of rickety stairs to his second floor flat. He tried to unlock the door, but his hands trembled so much that he couldn't. After a moment spent composing himself, holding the key with both hands, he unlocked the door and walked quietly to his room. The only sound he heard was his heart pounding at a high rhythmic pace. When he entered his bedroom, his two little brothers, Peter and JoJo, were asleep. Their mattresses were on the cold floor. The bedroom had no furniture except for orange crates that served as tables and shelves. A few old worn-out throw rugs covered the floor. The closet had a sheet for a door, but, remarkably, everything was tidy and orderly. Jules flopped on his mattress, and put both hands over his face as he remembered the rats swarming all over his body. He looked up at the window, and below the sill a long home made shelf contained Volumes of Socrates, Plato, and Sigmund Freud. He reads voraciously, and has several volumes of other challenging books.

Suddenly, Jules's drunken father appeared in the doorway of Jules's room, clasping a barber strap. He broke into the house

again somehow. His thin wrinkled face and bloodshot eyes were
full of hatred. Without warning the old man's 125-pound body
charged at the boy. Because Jules had been through this before,
he bolted back, his back to the wall. A dead silence hung in the
room as Jules's heart pounded; he backed across the wall and sunk
to the floor.

The old man staggered towards Jules and started whipping his
face and body. Peter and JoJo were awakened by the disorder and
cleared the room at first chance. They hid, crying, under their
Mama's bed in the other room. The raunchy smell of stale wine and
beer from his breath filled the room as he beat on Jules. A
whack, and another, and another, and another. The old man
screamed out like a raging maniac, completely out of control.

"You buma, I'm sick ana tired of support you...you no go to
school like you brothers...takea that," he whacked Jules again,
"ana that," and again. Jules escaped the last forceful stroke as
the strap hooked on to the wooden crucifix that was hanging on the
wall, and ripped it off. The strap somehow got hung up from the
large nail that extended from the wall, and the cross smashed the
old man in his evil face, causing him to lose his balance and
smash against the wall. He slowly dropped to the floor in a messy
puddle of blood, with the crucifix protruding from the left side
of his face.

A voice came from the other room, and Jules could hear his

upset Mama yelling, "PaPa, PaPa, you no good buma, whata you do
here! Get out! Go away from my sona, you no good drunka! Get outa
my house! Get outa!"

Jules tried to get up, but he couldn't; the only thing he was
able to do was crawl. He struggled to the doorway of his bedroom
when, suddenly, the old man was there again. Whack, whack, whack.
His bloody, foaming mouth drooled like a mad dog as he screamed.

"You no see my truck, you no see disa time, I fool you." He
laughed like a crazy man. Mama's voice got so strident that the
old man lurched into her room and punched her in the face. She
tried to get out of the bed and fell on the floor, mouth and nose
bleeding. She struggled to grab her walking cane, which rest on
the bed, and stopped him with a direct, smashing hit to his bloody
manic face. He dropped to the floor, motionless. Thinking that she
killed him, Mama cried. Peter and JoJo clung to each other as they
lay under the bed crying helplessly. Jules entered Mama's room.
Covered with blood, face red with hatred, he saw Mama on the
floor, crying and Papa getting ready to strike her once again. She
looked at her husband and cried out, "Why you do disa...you no
know whata you do. You come my house when you want someating. You
get nothing...now get out! Get out you buma!"

Jules couldn't take it any longer. He grabbed his father,
slapped him against the wall, opened the door, then kicked the
drunk down the stairs.

"You ever hurt Mama again, I'll have yer balls hangin' on a telephone pole with a big fuckin' nail, ya wino creep!"

The old man fell head over heels down the stairs to the landing. He was disoriented and groggy, but managed to get up and grab the half-open door. The hinge on the door broke, and down the front stairs he and the door both tumbled, smashing against the sidewalk into the rat-infested trash cans.

Jules was sick about throwing his father out. He just wanted him out, away from his Mama and him. Jules's body hurt all over, but he was more concerned with his ill mother. He stood at the top of the stairway looking down at the landing, tears in his eyes, and thought, who is he coming in here beatin' up Mama n me. I hate him-I hate him. He screamed in tears. "I have no father anymore. Yer dead as far as I'm concerned--dead! I'll see you in hell!" He walked to the hallway window and seen his father lay motionless across the pile of tumbled over trash cans, and thought, oh, God, what did I do to my father? I can't let him lay there an' suffer. No-no, leave him there, he'll just be back an' beat the livin' crap out of me an' Mama again. I have no father anymore--he's gone--finished--forever.

CHAPTER 4

NEW YORK, DECEMBER 11, 1925

10:40 A.M.

Mama lay on the floor crying and Peter wiped her bruises with a wet cloth. She held another cloth on her forehead, and JoJo brought in a basin of hot water. Jules, bruised and bleeding, entered the room then ran to his Mama on the floor and embraced her.

"JoJo," she screamed, "bringa fresh water for you brother, hurry-hurry, towels too, hurry upa." She looked and lightly touched Jules's face. "Oh my God, are you alla right my poor bambino?"

He looked at his sad faced Mama, "I'm okay Mama, Papa won't hurt you again, promise. I thought he was gonna kill ya. I hate him for what he did to you, I hate his guts."

Mama held Jules and rocked him. "Julius my son, everytinga gonna work out, you listen to Mama. C'mon, help Mama ina bed."

Jules picked up his 90 pound mama, put her in bed, and covered her with a quilted blanket. JoJo came back with a pan of water. Jules comforted her with a cold towel and wiped her bruises.

"Peter, get a glass of water for mama." Jules said. "And

the both of ya get ready for yer 11: o'clock class, yer gonna--"

"I'ma feel better now Julius, c'mon over he, I clean you up, forget about the boys for now." Mama said.

After removing Jules's shirt, Mama dipped a towel in the water. She gently washed his bruises while tears rolled down her face.

"God, look what Papa do to you. Hold still Julius, this no take long."

"Ooo, ouch, t-take it easy Mama, yer killin' me."

"Mama's sorry, hold still a little more."

In pain, Jules tried to be quiet, he didn't want his Mama to feel any more upset than she was.

"Guess what Mama?" Jules said.

"You gonna tell Mama you love me?"

"Oh Mama, I love you," He grabbed her hand and kissed it.

"No, it's not that. For dinner tonight, I'm makin' a surprise for ya."

"What you make for Mama?" She continued wiping his bruises.

Jules jumped away. "Ahhhh, ouch, jeez Mama, not so hard. It's a surprise...can't tell, besides, it wouldn't be a surprise if I told ya. You'll like it, I know ya will."

The boys peeked in the room as if they were avoiding Jules.

"Okay yooz guys, yer gonna be late for school, c'mon now, get yer butts movin', this ain't no holiday--move-move."

Jules's grammar was very good but he would lose it from time to time.

Peter looked at Jules sympathetically, "Do we have to go, Jules? Don't you think we should stay home and take care of you and Mama?"

JoJo put a word or two in, and said, "Yeah, I feel the same as Peter--besides, I'm really upset about you an' Mama an' everything. I'd like to help out too."

"Hey wise guys, are ya gonna get ready or do I have to dress both of ya?"

The boys respected and admired Jules, they hightailed it to their room to get dressed. Jules put another blanket over his Mama and kissed her forehead.

"Thanks Mama, go to sleep now, you'll feel better. I'll make sure the boys get off ta school."

"You a good boy, my sona." She closed her eyes.

Jules closed the door to Mama's room. He walked through the living room, which consisted of an aged red, yellow and green flowered Oriental rug, a small round dining room table and four tattered chairs. In the center of the table, a basket filled with fresh bananas and peaches and pears and apples and red grapes glistened from a beam of light coming from the only window in the room. A statue of the Blessed Virgin Mary on a small table with unlit candles and a large picture of Jesus Christ hanging on the

wall. When Jules entered his and the boys bedroom, Peter and JoJo
were dressed. They were eating a banana and tying their shoelaces
on their worn leather shoes.

"I'm goin' out tonight." Jules said. "When you two brains
come home from school, dinner will be on the stove stayin' warm.
Make sure Mama takes her pills, and clean up the place. I'm makin'
Mama's favorite sauce with meatballs an' veal. Save me some an'
make sure yer h--"

"Homework gets done." Peter and JoJo said simultaneously.

They looked at each other and laughed. The boys kissed Jules
good-bye.

"I'm doin' extra good in school today, Jules. This way I can
have an extra meatball. Make a bunch of 'em, see ya." JoJo said.

"You got it--git outa here."

Jules looked at his books, walked over to his bookshelf and
reached for his favorite, Socrates. Some of the books obstructed
the view of the alley but they were more important to him than the
scenery. In pain, he carefully sat down on an orange crate and
started to read. It was the only way Jules knew how to escape from
the real world.

It was 1:15 P.M., Jules lay on his side still reading. His
mattress on the floor had army blankets for a cover, and his
two pillows were rolled army blankets that had been tied with
burlap string. Suddenly, he heard three knocks on the kitchen

door. He got up easily, and walked to the door. In a soft voice,
he asked, "That you Izzy?"

"Yeah Jules. C'mon, let me in, I'm freezin'."

In his bare feet, and only wearing a pair of wool pants,
Jules unlocked the two bolts and removed a 2 x 4 that crossed the
warped door. He opened the door, and Izzy came in carrying a box
of groceries.

"Holy cow, Jules!" Izzy said loudly. "The ol' man got ya
pretty bad--Christ!"

"Shhhh, keep it down will ya, my Mama's sleepin'." He put his
hand over Izzy's mouth, and whispered loudly, "Shhh the mouth!"

"Jeez, sorry 'bout that, Jules. Those bruises--I-I never seen
you look so bad before. Maybe I can put some cream or something on
them for you, don't want to get an infection."

"Thank's Izzy, I'm all set. Put the groceries on the counter,
just talk real soft."

Izzy whispered, "Okay." He put the box on the counter, and
said, "That ol' man of your's is real bad. He even stole some food
in the store a couplea weeks ago. Moyshe caught him and let him
keep it but he can't come in the store anymore."

"Moyshe shoulda called the cops. I don't care anymore. He
beat my Mama for the last time. I'm takin' my Mama an' brothers
outa this rat hole as soon as I get a few bucks together. They
deserve a better place to live, I'll see to that."

"You'll do it Jules, I know you will. Is your mother ok?"

"Think her nose is broken, not sure. I gotta get her to a doctor as soon as I get some cash."

"I'll give it to you. Pay me back when you get it."

"That's real nice of you Izzy, but I'll be okay. You're a good friend. I'll never forget you."

"You've done it for me, Jules. I just want you to know I have a few bucks saved for a rainy day, and today is a rainy day as far as I'm concerned."

"You're a sweetheart, nobody has ever volunteered to help me like you have. I can tell you one thing, everything is fallin' in place. As far as our business deal, I want you to keep it between you an' me, is that clear?"

"You have my word, Jules." He shook Jules's hand.

"Okay Izzy. Wadya bring?"

"Everything on the list you gave me is here. I gave you a extra loaf of fresh bread, just out of the oven--on the house, and something just for you, in the newspaper wrapping. Their on ice too." He winked his eye at Jules, and Jules winked back. "Ok Jules my man, I have other deliveries, gotta run. Don't be shy pal, I'll always be around to help you. See ya."

"Thank's Izzy."

Jules put the groceries away, and started to prepare his special dinner for Mama. He hummed a tune and tasted the tomato

sauce while two large pots of water boiled. He chopped a hand full
of garlic, threw it in a pan and mixed it with the sausage and
veal then added a little wine. The smell left a taste of hunger
throughout the kitchen. When the sausage and veal was cooked, he
poured it in the sauce to let it simmer. A smile of contentment
lingered on his face. He knew his Mama would be thrilled with his
special dinner tonight. He unwraped the newspaper, took two rats
out, and cleaned them. Then he cut them in bite size pieces, and
boiled then until they were tender.

Later on, he cleaned up, got dressed, and hurried to meet
Smiley. This was the big night Jules had worked so hard for. His
"Mickey Mouse" scam was about to be performed.

CHAPTER 5

NEW YORK, DECEMBER 11, 1925

7:25 P.M.

Jules disguised himself with round wire-rimmed eyeglasses and a false mustache. He wore a black fedora, black camel hair overcoat, a conservative dark blue pin-stripe suite, white shirt with a red and dark blue striped tie, black shoes and socks. He looked like a business person. He rented everything except for the white shirt, that was the only thing he owned. Smiley was disguised with a false beard and round wire-rimmed glasses, he was equally dapper. He wore a dark brown fedora, a light brown cashmere overcoat, a navy blue double-breasted suit, white dress shirt with a solid burgundy tie, black shoes and socks. And as usual, a long unlit cigar protruded from his mouth. The twosome looked like successful business men. Jules had made reservations in advance. They walked into the classy La Trattoria Ristorante, and checked in their overcoats and fedoras. Jules greeted the maitre d' as if he knew him, and with a warm handshake, Jules slipped some folded cash into his palm. The maitre d' smiled and escorted the two to a table in the center of the room. Several people were eating and talking at the tables. After they ordered, Jules lit up a Camel cigarette and observed the crowd. Smiley, sitting like a big shot, chewed on his long cigar enjoying the lifestyle. After a few minutes, the waiter served two large bowls of minestrone soup at their table for starters. Jules took a slurp.

"Needs salt." Jules said softly.

"Mine's just right, Jules. The chef knows his stuff."

Jules leaned towards Smiley, and gave him a look that would frighten a mad-man, and said softly, "I want you to be especially aware of your English, understand?"

Smiley face reddened, and with a toothy, he nodded okay.

"Thank you indeed sir, I appreciate your concern."

Jules added a pinch of salt, held his palm over the bowl for a moment then stirred the soup. He tasted a spoonful. His tongue touched something that felt odd. He reached into his mouth and pulled the strange object out, and held the thing in front of Smiley.

"Jesus Christ! That looks like a rat leg!" Smiley said in a loud whisper. His face turned pale.

Looking down in horror at the leg, Jules jumped up, spilling soup and whatever was hidden at the bottom of the bowl--tiny rat feet--all over the table and his expensive shirt, the only one he owned. He clamped his mouth shut and pointed at the upturned bowl as he glanced excitedly around the room. Smiley felt as if he were about to vomit.

A waiter rushed to the table, stared at the rat parts, and quickly led Jules to the kitchen, away from the growing dinner crowd. Smiley sat at the table, hands crossed over his chest, feeling nauseated by the thought he ate a rat. Waiters surrounded him. Trying to help, but looked confused. Another waiter hurried from the kitchen, whispered something in one of the waiters ear, and rushed Smiley back to the kitchen with him. A waiter at the table called a bus boy, and the table was cleaned off and reset as if nothing had happened.

"What seems to be the problem, sir?" The owner asked Jules.

Jules stood there holding on to two waiters, and wiping sweat from his forehead. He looked like a upset customer who had eaten a rat.

"S-something in my soup...agggg...a rat...i-it's foot...ohh."

The owner glanced at his waiter, for confirmation, and got a grim nod.

"Ughhhh...ahhhhh...oh God...ughhhhhh...s-sorry...ooooahggg."

Smiley vomited on the waiter's pants and shoes.

The owner pulled a wad of cash out of his pocket and looked at Jules. "Here son, take this fifty. You and your friend can leave by the back door--I'd appreciate it if you both keep quiet about this incident." He looked at the waiters holding on to Jules and Smiley, and said, "Clean up these gentlemen before they leave."

After wiping off their clothes, a waiter brought Jules's and Smiley's overcoats and fedoras, and out the back door they went, the door locked behind them.

They high-tailed it down the alley, two newly solvent con artists making their first big score. It was hard to run, however, because Jules couldn't help laughing so hard. They pulled into an alcove, both puffing and out of breath. They sat back against a wall to take a rest, Jules still laughing. He reached in his pocket and removed a small packet of newspaper then unwraped it and scattered rat parts on Smiley's lap. Smiley bolted back and hit his head on a drain pipe attached to the building.

"Ouch! Jesus Christ! What the fuck! Are you crazy? Where'd you get the rat? You tryin' to make me sick again?" He vomited on the sidewalk.

Jules affectionately grabbed Smiley's arm, "Jesus, are you okay Irish? I didn't think you were gonna heave yer guts out over a few rat parts!"

Smiley thought, I don't know why I have such a weak stomach. Jules is a big teaser, he did that for a reason. Hey, now I get it, he slipped those rat parts in the soup--what a dummy I am. We made some cash tonight. Hot dog! That Jules is a genius, I feel better already. I want Jules to tell me about the scam. He should tell me anyway. Smiley started to laugh wildly. He looked at

Jules, and said, "I'm fine, meatball. The sight of those rat
parts got to me, that's all. I'm completely embarrassed."

"Don't worry, it can happen to anybody."

"Why didn't you tell me? I mean, you never made me aware of
how the deal worked?"

"I thought about it and decided to play it by ear. I wanted
to see you perform in a natural way, you know. You were perfect.
Now that you know what the Mickey Mouse is all about, that's all
you have to do is repeat everything you did exactly the same way.
Isn't it better to experience something cold turkey rather than be
told how to do it sometimes?"

"Yeah. You had me believing I ate a rat, you bastard. You did
good. Your a great actor. You should be in the movies. What a
con, great job well thought out. By the way, how'd I do? Did I
perform or did I perform?" He rolled his long cigar around his
mouth. He looked like a peacock with it's feathers all blossomed
out. He sat there with an endearing smile, and stared at Jules.

"Ya did a good job. I had to hold back from laughin'. I had
no idea what you were gonna do when the waiter came by the table
and looked at those rat parts all over the place."

Neither did I. If anything, I held back from heaving my guts
out but I wouldn't allow myself because I was to embarrassed with
all the people around. Jesus, I don't know how I did it, no shit."

"Well ya did, and I'm proud of ya."

"That's what I like to hear. Did you know I was the best actor in school? I was Jack, in Jack in the Beanstalk."

"You're a comedian, Irish. I thought I'd die when you chucked-up all over that poor waiter's pants an' shoes, that took the cake. If you really want to be a nice guy, you should send something to that waiter--maybe, pay for the dry cleaning of his pants you vomited on. It'll make you a better person."

"Good idea, Jules. I'll take care of that first thing in the morning. He'll appreciate it, I'm sure."

"Here's twenty-five bucks. The owner of the restaurant gave me fifty, not bad for a bowl of soup, huh?"

As Smiley reached for the money, Jules swiftly drew it behind his back, then brought it back to his face.

"You only get it if next time you look like you did on this con today...like you crawled from the morgue."

Both studied the money, stared at the rat parts, looked at each other, and then broke apart laughing.

Jules handed the cash to his friend, and with a big smile, Smiley grabbed it. Then, his grin gone, Smiley reached toward's a large dark spot on Jules's cheek.

Jules had tried to cover his bruises with some of Mama's makeup, but he'd wiped his eyes so many times during the laughter that the skin on his face revealed a painful rainbow of colors.

"The ol'man snuck in again?" Smiley asked.

Jules jerked his face back in pain. "It'll be the last time. The coward beat on my Mama, too. I wanted to kill the wino bastard when I seen him hit her. Something came over me and I threw the filthy bum out of the place. I don't know how I did it, I-I just seen her helpless on the floor and before I knew it, I jumped on the drunk to stop him from giving another blow to her. When I think about what I did to my father, I want to cry. I can't tell you how much it hurts me." Tears rolled down his face.

"Jeez Jules, I feel real bad for you, yer Mama too. It'll all work out, you'll see. Is your Mama alright? There's gotta be something I can do. Maybe I can come over your place an' tell a few funny stories to your Mama, seein' I'm a good performer an' all--I have some great lines, I can sing to her too!"

Jules laughed and looked at Smiley's serious face with his goofy expression.

"Thank's Smiley, ya sound like my Mama. Yer right, everything is gonna be fine--especially if you stay away from her. That's all she has to do is hear you sing, she'll never be well again!"

They laughed and hugged and laughed, tears rolled down their faces.

"Hey Jules, how would you like me to do an impression, like Hamlet, Romeo...or good ol' Jimmy Durante? I'm good. In fact I impersonate them so good, you won't believe your ears."
"No-no, the cops sure as hell will pick us up. But ya know, we've

been friends since we found out girls weren't boys, maybe you can do something helpful and meet me at 8 sharp tomorrow morning--the park, you know, where we usually sit an' bullshit."

"Yeah sure, okay, I'll be there. You goin' some place? Got a date? Do you have to leave right now?" Smiley said disappointed.

"My Mama. I wanna make sure she's alright. You did a good job tonight Smiley." He grabbed Smiley's shoulder, and shook it. "See ya bright an' early, pal."

"Yeah, okay Jules, see you at 8 sharp. Hope your Mama's feelin' better. And thank's, thank's for cuttin' me in on the "Mickey Mouse". Love ya--oh jeez, Jules, there's one more thing-- I'm only available for comedy and singing engagements on week- ends. Thought you wanted to know, in case you change your mind."

Jules waved good-bye and thought, what a crazy guy. All he needs is guidance and someone who cares. He'll be alright. It may take the rest of my life to get him on the right track, but I've been through much worse, I guess. I don't know who's crazier, him or me. He laughed. I feel great, kinda sore but I'll be ok. I hope Mama and the boys enjoyed that special dinner. I'm starved-- meatballs, veal and pasta, smothered in sauce, mmmmm, can't wait. Hope they left me enough.

By the time Jules got home, Mama and the boys were sound asleep. A candle flickered on the dining room table. A handmade birthday card made by Mama and the boys lay clearly in sight. He picked it up and read it:

Dear Jules,

Mama and your two brain brothers

enjoyed your special dinner. It was the best you've

ever made. Mama's nose is not broken. Mrs.

Covino came over and visited with Mama and said

rest and a little more of your special dinners would to the trick.

Happy Birthday, we love you.

Mama, Peter and JoJo   X X X

Jules thought, what a nice original birthday card but right
now, I'm hungry. He went to the kitchen and filled a dish with
meatballs, pork, veal and pasta and enjoyed his late night snack.
after he ate he cleaned the dishes, brushed his teeth and went to
bed. He lay in bed staring at the ceiling thinking of his favorite
hide-away on the rooftop, the place where he went to contemplate
when he couldn't sleep. He quietly slipped out of bed, pulled on
his pants and wool turtle-neck sweater, looked at the rented camel
hair coat and shoes and decided to put them on too.

Walking up two flights of rickety stairs, he noticed the
rooftop door was unlocked and slightly open; this was
unusual, because all the tenants knew that Mister Cavino, the
manager of the building, insisted that the door always be locked.
Mister Cavino had a year-round heated greenhouse that occupied

half the roof, and he always gave vegetables, herbs and ferns to all the tenants. Mister Cavino had built the greenhouse himself. It was made of wood and glass and as solid as Fort Knox. No one was allowed inside the greenhouse unless they had permission from Mister Covino. A large bent nail was the only lock on the door that led into the greenhouse, anybody could walk in. Most of the tenants respected Mister Covino's wishes and stayed out. Take an exception like Loretta Feinstershieb, for example. She lived with her mother and two brothers on the second floor of the building, on the opposite side from Jules's apartment. She was absolutely gorgeous.

Jules had tried to date her many times, but he would get the brush-off every time. She was three years older than him. She and a boyfriend frequently visited the greenhouse. She had several boyfriends, and frequently snuck in the place. They weren't picking tomatos either. Loretta may not have been the brightest girl around, but that didn't matter, Jules had dreamed about being with her. And of course, it bothered him to know that the older boys on the street bragged that she was a nymphomaniac and gave the best blow jobs around.

Jules walked alongside the greenhouse on his way to his favorite corner, paused a moment and looked into the dimly lighted greenhouse. He admired the plot of tomatos and the sections of stringbeans, cabbage and peppers. He walked past the parsley and dandelion sections and continued on past the herbs. He reached his favorite place near the ledge and looked up to the sky. The night was brisk and the stars were shining bright. He lit up a cigarette and thought, I can't get Loretta out of my mind tonight. I'm gonna knock on her door tomorrow and make another attempt to ask her out...I got a few bucks in my pocket an' can show her a good time. A few minutes later, he felt a soft touch of a hand on his shoulder. He turned around and Loretta was standing there. Her waist-length red hair blew in Jules's face and open mouth. He couldn't believe it and thought, I must be dreamin'. He took the strands of hair out of his mouth, they tasted like strawberries. He thought, this is not a dream, holy shit. Relax Jules, just be cool. Oh God, she's beautiful.

Loretta handed him a gift wrapped with green paper and red ribbon. She smiled, and said, "Hi Jules, happy birthday. This little gift is just for you."

"Aww, jeez Loretta, ya didn't have to do this. How'd ya know it was my birthday?"

Laughing quietly, she snuggled up to him, gently kissed his cheek, and brushed her hand through his hair.

"Jules, are you going to open it?"

Jules thought, I don't know why I'm so shy when it comes to receiving gifts. I'm starting to sweat and it's cold out here. He awkwardly tried to delay opening the gift.

"What are you doin' up here at this hour? It's almost one o'clock." Jules asked curiously. He was a nervous wreck.

She backed off and smiled. A slight breeze blew open her coat and revealed her naked body. Her large breasts were aching for attention. Her red pubic hair looked soft and eager to be touched. She covered herself and took the gift out of Jules's hand then grabbed his arm and led him to the greenhouse. Jules's heart pounded as he became aroused. When they reached the greenhouse door, Loretta gave Jules a sexy look.

"Go ahead lover, open it."

Jules pulled the bent nail out of the latch and opened the door.

"Make sure it's closed." Loretta said, then took him by the hand to a spring cot and mattress covered with five or six burlap bags. The smell of kerosine lingered in the air from the burners that kept the greenhouse at a warm temperature. They sat down on the squeaky cot and Loretta gave Jules a pleasing look.

"You can open the gift now Jules."

Jules tore the paper off in less than two seconds, and thought, I have a feeling tonight is gonna be a great experience. I'm trembling. Control yourself Jules. God, something good is gonna be happinin'...I'm gonna get laid or somethin'. My dream is comin' true, now what do I do? Play it by ear, that's it. Holy Christ, she's so beautiful.

Loretta touched his face, "You're in deep thought, Jules."

Jules shook his head. "Oh, I'm sorry. I've been thinkin' what a coincidence it is you being here. I-I thought of you just before you came up to me, a-and there you were--that's magic--better open this gift before it becomes obsolete." He smiled at her, and opened the envelope. I even get a card, how nice. Yer a sweetheart. Do you mind if I read this to you?"

"I don't mind, as long as you read it softly." She brushed her hand across his upper thigh. "Go ahead, I'm listening."

"O-oh, I-I'm kinda slow when it comes to these things." He pulled the card out of the envelope, and read:

Happy Birthday, May you always remember this special day.

Jules, for many years we've passed each other and just said hello. You've tried to talk to me but I always thought you were to young. I don't feel that way anymore. I want to make up for being so cold to you. I couldn't think of a better way to celebrate your birthday than to be with you.

Happy Birthday,

Loretta

"Jeez Loretta, what a nice thing to say. I-I'm lost for words." He kissed her softly on the lips. "Thank you."

"Do you forgive me, Birthday man?"

"Forgive you?"

"For being so cold to you through the years."

"Awwww, that was yesterday, today is what count's."

"You're so sweet. Why don't you open the box."

"Okay. But before I do, I'll be honest with you...I mean...I-I get these hot feelings, and I kinda tingle when it comes to these sorta things, know what I mean or not?"

"Yes, I guess so, but look what else is in there anyway."

Jules finally pulled open the gift, it was a pint of Jack Daniels.

"Loretta, how did you know this is my favorite?"

"Smiley told me all about you. Don't you dare say anything, promise?"

"No big deal. I won't say a thing, promise." Jules leaned over and kissed her lightly on the lips. "Okay kid, can you handle a blast of this stuff?"

"Thought you'd never ask." Loretta said sensually.

Jules opened the bottle and gave it to Loretta. She took down a mouthful, then Jules did, then she downed another, then he managed to secure one more swig, and then he set the bottle on the floor.

Loretta gave Jules a look which meant, take me, I'm ready, that's what he read anyway. He knew from reading what to do when it came to this sort of physical activity.

"Do you like my body, Jules?"

He put his arms around her and pulled her close, and thought, nothin' like the real thing. Whatever comes next is gotta be better.

The fragrance of strawberries and roses came off her skin. Her coat slipped off as she unbuttoned Jules's pants and opened them.

"Kiss me Jules, kiss me hard," she murmured urgently as her soft hands found his throbbing penis. She pulled his pants down with excitement, and drew them down to his thighs, his calves, his ankles. He pushed them off with his feet.

Breathing hard, she kissed his ear, then licked his neck. The feeling of her warm moist tongue sent chills down Jules's spine.

"Take your coat and sweater off Jules, hurry, I want to kiss and taste your body...ohhhh, you taste so good."

Jesus, she's driving me crazy, Jules thought. I never thought I could get this hard. He found a way to take his coat and sweater off without disturbing Loretta's magic rolling tongue. She pushed him back and found his penis. A feeling Jules never felt before suddenly sent messages to his brain; don't stop...don't stop... Then her hand gently held onto his balls and she lightly pulled and squeezed them. With her other hand, she took a firm grip of his penis and put it in her mouth gently sucking up and down slowly. "Mmmmmmm." Then she sucked harder and faster and faster until...

Jules screamed. "Ohhhhhh, God" A surge of sperm left Jules's body and Loretta sucked it out of him. Jules thought, this is the way I want to die, but first I have to make sure I come at least five more times. "Ohhhh, God, don't stop-don't stop, yer beautiful...so, so...beautiful...oh...baby-baby-baby."

She let go of his penis and kissed her way up to his chest. Then she wrapped her arms around him. With great care she helped him to push her down onto the cot. He cupped her breasts together and rolled his tongue across both nipples, then concentrated on just one. She moaned in rapture.

"Don't stop Jules," She murmured, "Roll your tongue around my nipples...harder...harder, that's it...ohhhhh Jules, don't stop-don't stop." She grabbed his head, held it firmly in place, and then pumped into his body, as her head pounded against the mattress. Both fell off the cot onto the tomato plants. She rolled Jules on his back and slowly kissed and rotated her warm tongue around his nipples.

"Do you like my tongue?" She asked urgently.

"Ohhhh, God, I love it...you're beautiful, beautiful, ohhh."

"Want more?"

"Don't stop, please don't stop...yer soooo terrific...ohhhhh, yer beautiful...absolutely beautiful."

"I love it Jules...I love your body...mmmmmmm."

He writhed with excitement. "I died Loretta, died and went to heaven, keep me there-keep me there, you got the magic." He thought, it's time to quit looking at those nude girl pictures.

She licked her way down to his stomach, passed his naval, and rolled him over onto the lettuce patch, then rolled him onto his back again into the soft fern, and found her way between his legs. Holding his throbbing penis with both hands, she rolled her tongue slowly around his balls to his thighs, then slowly back to his balls, all the while sucking and moaning. Loretta gradually reached the bottom of his penis and found her way to his circumcised head. She opened his thighs and pushed her head between them.

"I want to suck you again...it's so good." She murmured, "Mmmmmmm, I can't get enough, mmmmmm...it's so, so beautiful, mmmmmmmmm." Her tongue, like her fingers, were soft; she moved it slow, and knew exactly what to do.

Jules pumped away in her mouth, his body wet from perspiration. "I'm gonna die...that's okay...keep killin' me... love it...I love it...love it...love it, love it...oh, God... God...ohhhh God...

She stopped sucking and opened her thighs, then guided his penis into her warm wet body. She pumped a few times and moaned.

"Oh-oh-ohhhhhh Jules, I-I'm doing it-doing it...ohhhhh, yes-yes-yes...ohhhhhhhh, soooooo good...

Jules felt the world coming to an end, preparing for release, getting ready to explode. He held tightly to Loretta and pushed himself inside her as far as he could go. She wrapped her legs around him and squeezed him tightly.   "Ohhhh, God...I'm doing it again...oh-oh-ohhhhhhhh, Juuuuules."

And then it happened. The most exciting, throbbing, out-of-control feeling he'd ever experienced. He was coming!

And he was inside Loretta--a real female--his hand and some nude girl's picture had nothing to do with it.

CHAPTER 6

NEW YORK, DECEMBER 12, 1925

6:45 A.M.

Jules walked to the park. On his way, he thought about
Loretta, boy what a beautiful girl, body too. She could keep a
troop of soldiers out of trouble, that's for sure. I feel sorry
for her. Maybe she'll find a nice guy and have a family some day.
I had a great experience. In fact, it's the best birthday present
I ever had. Girls are really-really great.

When he got to the park, it was deserted. He dusted off the
snow on the bench and waited for Smiley. The morning was bleak and
it looked like snow would be falling soon. Jules heard a whistle
in the distant, it sounded like Smiley's.

The park was their favorite outside place. It overlooked the
Washington Bridge. It's tranquility and fresh air kept them apart
from the hustle and bustle.

Smiley trudged through the snow making his own tracks and
stopped about a car length away from Jules. He fell back into the
fluffy snow, extended his arms and legs, then moved them up and
down and side ways to form an angel. "Nothing like being alive,
huh, Jules? I haven't done this since I was a kid." He laughed and
asked Jules, "And how are you doin' today, my performing genius?

My Plato? My hero?"

Jules smiled. "Feel great, just great. It's nice to see you in such a good mood."

Smiley got up, and said, "Got a few bucks in the pocket, startin' work tomorrow, all I need to make things perfect is a real good piece of ass...outside of that, I'm ready for the world." He looked at Jules with his closed-mouth smile while scratching his privates. "Why you askin'?"

They laughed, then laughed harder than before.

"Whadaya think? I care, know what I mean? I mean, looking at you scratchin' yer nuts an' what little you got, I'm beginning to think you sat some place where you weren't suppose to." Jules said laughing. "You have real class scratchin' yourself like that, ya know?"

"Jeez, I didn't mean to embarrass you, but this itching is killin' me." He scratched his scrotum. "I couldn't sleep all night. I've been sratchin' myself like crazy an' don't know where to scratch first, my front or back!"

Jules laughed. "You got the crabs, moron!"

Smiley looked like he seen a ghost. "The crabs!...W-where... do they come from?"

"You mean to tell me that you don't know about the crabs? Everybody knows about crabs, c'mon, you're putting me on, right?" Jules said.

"W-well, I, ahh...yeah-yeah, I heard of them...they come from the Ocean, I never had 'em before. I heard garlic crabs are the best. There is something else I forgot to tell you."

"What might that be?"

"I'm just kiddin'. I'm so happy an' care-free, I wanted to see if I could fool you. I don't have the crabs, I was just practicing my acting abilities." He laughed and put his arm around Jules shoulders, and said, "Jules, I love you like a brother."

Jules thought, what a moron. He's so insecure, it's pathetic. God, give me strength."

"You're definitely something else, my Irish friend?"

"Whadaya mean?"

"Thank God, there's only one of you." Jules said softly as he slowly shook his head. "Anyway, just for making me believe you had the crabs, I'm taking you out to dinner tonight. We're gonna do another "Mickey Mouse", so get in the mood for some Irish stew."

A big smile covered Smiley's face. "And where preytell will we be having this scrumptious spread? Or shall I say dinnah, like the blue blood would say it, if you will."

"You are an absolute aristocrat. I insist you be at Shrap's at seven bells sharp--same evening dress--same script--you know, old chap." Jules said, having a little fun.

Smiley placed his hand on his chin, and said, "I have to say, my dear man, I can hardly wait for this extraordinary feast. I seem to procure an erection at the very thought."

Jules got up and placed his hand on Smiley's shoulder.

"And I insist that you conduct yourself in an appropriate
manner for this evening's event, my dear fellow, and all will go
well. You do comprehend my prayer, my fellow artist?"

Smiley bowed to Jules, then suddenly danced and hopped in a
circle of frenzy. "Woopie doo an' coochy due, were doin' the
"Mickey Mouse" an' eatin' too...coochy-coochy-coochy-coo. He
laughed, and fell in the snow.

Jules watched him and thought, he's crazy, an absolute child.
He's gotta get laid. He's so frustrated it's not funny anymore.
If he don't straighten out, I'm gonna tell him to see a shrink.

Jules shouted. "You've really blown your top this time,
c'mon, get up and quit making a fool out of yourself!"

"Awww, jeez, don't you ever have any fun? I mean, doesn't
this "Mickey Mouse" get you excited?"

"I can think of better ways to get excited, like gettin laid
an' eatin' a banana split at the same time!"

Smiley looked at Jules with a blank face. "Now that's what I
call adventurous. You're right, forgive my childish behavior, I
lost my head. I've gotta learn to be more serious."

"You do that. I gotta go. See you later." He started to walk
away, hesitated, and looked back at Smiley, and said, "Can I
depend on ya tonight?"

Smiley sat up in the snow and looked back at Jules. "Got my word Jules, Shrap's, seven sharp, in my all-in-all." He saluted.

Jules gave Smiley a smile and the finger, and walked away.

That evening, Jules and Smiley dressed in their rented clothes and made-up disguised faces, took a cab from Shrap's to Guilfoil's Track 14 restaurant near the main train depot. The "Mickey Mouse" performance was a success, and Jules received seventy dollars from the generous, owner. The two scam artists were escorted out the back door. Another successful sting had been carried out.

Unbeknown to Jules, Rocco DeLucca, the owner of DeLucca's Italian Restaurant (which is a front for his gambling spot), happened to be in Guilfoil's Track 14 enjoying dinner when he spotted the two grifters pulling off their con. He liked the scam and followed Jules and Smiley until they split up and went their separate ways. Rocco stopped Jules and told him that he watched his con, liked it and wanted Jules to visit with him at his restaurant. Jules was honored, because everyone knew "THE ROCK"-- he was the Don of the lower east side. He was respected.

The next morning, Jules walked to Rocco's restaurant. It was bitterly cold, and the wind whipped several trash cans over and rolled them down the street into parked cars. The streets were deserted except for a few tractor and trailers, and a snow plow leaving a mound of snow alongside parked cars. As he turned the corner, he noticed several cars parked in vacant lots and along the curbs on both sides. The street although dimly lit, was a productive wholesale district. The warehouses were opening for another day. The smell of wood and diesel fumes lingered in the air as tractor and trailers backed into the loading docks a half a block away. Jules looked up to the roof of a four-story building. Between the snow and blowing wind, he could barely make out the large red-flashing sign, that read: ROCCO'S ITALIAN RISTORANTE. Jules thought, maybe I caught a break. Christ, sure can use one. What am I gonna say? Awww, jeez, knock it off with the what's gonna happen bullshit, play it by ear and just say it the way it is like ya normally do. As Jules got closer to Rocco's, the rustic wood building looked like a converted warehouse very well kept. He approached the entrance. His knuckles almost made contact with the double wood door when, suddenly, the doors smashed open and two drunken men came barging out knocking Jules backwards. He fell over a bench and landed in a pile of snow. The men paid no attention or weren't even aware this happened, they just staggered on and laughed, arms over shoulders.

"Nice guys! Thank's a lot!" Jules shouted. They didn't hear a word. He got up, brushed off the snow, and went to the door again.

A brass plaque on the now-closed door had been partially covered with snow. He dusted it off with his hand, it read: "PRIVATE CLUB - MEMBERS ONLY.

He thought, heard all about this joint. Jesus, Mary an' Joey
baby, I don't believe The Rock himself want's to talk ta me! Ok
Jules, do what ya gotta do. He knocked hard four times, as if it
was an emergency.

A 300-pound, six foot bald doorman opened the door. He looked
like a wrestler who hadn't ever lost a match. He had cauliflower
ears, a full blond handlebar mustache, and gold capped upper
teeth. His arms were huge and bigger than Jules's thighs put
together.

"Whatcha want kid?" He asked, in a low brassy baritone voice.
He stood there and expanded his chest, then cracked his knuckles,
and waited for a reply.

Jules quivered from the sight of him. "Rocco, I'm here to see
Rocco. My name is Jules, he's expecting me."

"Yer names Mules? Is dat what you said?" He asked with a bad
attitude.

Jules thought, who is this brute anyway, what's he tryin' to
do, scare the shit outa me er somethin'? I'll just stand up to the
shit head. He looked at the brute dead in his eyes, and said,
"Listen big boy, I'm not here to raid the place, I said my name is
Jules, J-U-L-E-S, I have an appointment with The Rock, is that so
hard to grasp?"

The doorman backed off a bit looking dumbfounded. "Oh,
golly, I'm sorry Mr. Jules, I ain't trying to give ya a hard time,

jus' doin' ma job. Now I remember, Rock told me earlier he was expectin' a kid called Mr. Jules, you must be the kid, right?"

Jules stared at him, and thought, this gorilla musta bounced off his head when he was a kid. "That's right, I'm the guy The Rock is waitin' to see, alright."

"O-okay Mr. Jules, follow me if ya will."

Jules followed the doorman through the crowded barroom, up a flight of stairs to a second floor, where they were admitted by a cautious brawny doorman.

Suddenly, they were plunged into a room of chattering, clamoring people. This was a spot for card and crap games, a place immune from legal interference, a place where any sucker could play in the hope of winning. The room was smothered with cigarette and cigar smoke, and reeked with wine and whiskey. Jules followed the palooka through the fascinating room, past the roulette table, where the wheel was spinning and people were living it up. They continued on to a crammed crap table, and squeezed their way through, went past a blackjack table and another crap table, where someone scored it big time.

They finally got to the back of the room, and approached a red door marked PRIVATE.

The 300 pound doorman pressed the button on the wall, the door opened and they walked in the room. A stocky pocked-face Black doorman wearing a black patch over his right eye admitted them. The room inside was large, and had six round tables; five players and a dealer were seated at each one, playing poker. Six cashiers were busy cashing out and exchanging cash for chips in their caged-in cells on the back wall. A waiter served drinks at the tables. Standing in a corner, talking with a young little boy, was Rocco DeLucca.

Jules swallowed, his mouth suddenly felt waterless. There he is, my ace in the hole, The Don. God, what am I gonna say? Should I kiss his hand? Quit acting like a jerk, just shake his hand an' pretend he's your long lost Uncle--go ahead, be yerself for God's sake, he thought.

"Wait here." The 300 pound doorman took a few steps forward, and nodded his head at The Rock. The Rock nodded his head back. The 300 pound doorman stepped back to Jules, and said, "Stay right here, Rocco will call ya when he's ready." He walked away.

Rocco's eyes zeroed in on Jules and gestured with his right hand, to come forward. He was six feet, four inches. A scar crossed from his left eye over the nose, continued to the left side of the mouth, and ended at the bottom of his square cleft chin. He had a full head of slicked-back black hair and black bushy eyebrows with no hair separation in the center. Wide black eyes that would taunt a snake, a large crooked nose, and a dark greasy complexion.

The floor creaked as his 280-pound body walked into his

office. He bent over slightly, so his head cleared the top of the doorway, and pushed the half-closed door open with his right hand. His left forearm was missing; from the elbow down there was only a folded, empty sleeve. The door half-closed behind him.

Jules approached the office, he paused a moment, and stared at the name on the door: ROCCO DELUCCA. Jesus, this is it. I don't know what to expect. Well, go check it out Jules baby, he thought. He heard Rocco call out to him, "Hey, kida, whata you waita for...c'mon, c'mon, Rocco no bite you."

Jules gave the half-closed door a little push and it swung open then returning to it's half closed position. When he entered the large, neatly arranged room, he saw a big oak desk, an antique oak stocked bar, a large oil painting of a small olive grove in the mountains of Sicily, behind Rocco's desk, several wooden filing cabinets, framed pictures on the walls of Rocco posing with well known people, and two long tables piled with cash. Two bookkeepers were sitting at the tables, counting and recording the amounts in large thick books.

Jules reached out and shook Rocco's hand. "How are you sir?"

"Whata you see here today, it'sa between you ana me, capeech?"

Jules stood there in awe, trying not to show his emotions. He thought, I've never seen so much cash in my life. There must me enough cash there to buy all a New York--God!

"I ask you question, sona, but you no answer...Rocco say, what you see here today isa between you ana me, you can hear Rocco, no?"

"Oh, I'm sorry--I understand perfectly well, sir."

"Atsa good." Rocco said, smiling, and rocking in his chair. You no have to call me sir, everybody call me justa Rocco--datsa my name. Sit down-sit down, we talk." He pulled out a stogy from a wooden box on his desk, licked it up and down, then put it between his stained teeth. The 8-year old boy came in with a glass of red wine on a tray, and placed it on Rocco's desk.

Rocco pinched the boys cheek, and said, "At'sa good boy. Dis is my sona, Mario. Hey Mario, say hello to Jules."

Mario walked up to Jules, reached out and shook Jules's hand.

"Nice to meet you, Jules." He had a big toothy smile and held a firm grip on Jules's hand while he shook it.

"I've seen you around, Jules." Mario kept shaking Jules's hand.

"Me?" Jules looked around then back to Mario.

"I'm sure." He kept a firm grip on Jules's hand, and kept shaking it.

"Yes! I remember now."

Mario gave Jules a puzzled look. "Are you kiddin'? He slowed down the handshake.

"The Post Office. My mug shot is all over the place."

Mario finally let go of Jules's hand, and laughed. "Boy Jules, you're a real funny guy."

"One thing is for sure, you shook my hand so hard, you probably have my fingerprints over your's!" He smiled, and tapped Mario's head.

"Yeah. My PaPa taught me that. He's so strong, he can crack walnuts with his bare hand. Someday I'll be able to do the same thing."

"Ok-ok Mario," Rocco said, "you go ina kitchen now. You ana Jules can talk perhapsa later on."

"Do I have to?" He looked disappointed.

"C'mona now, PaPa's gotta business to do. Go aheada, you help Paco, ina kitchen. Shoo, Shoo.

Rocco looked at Jules, and said, "He thinks he's the boss aroun' here."

Aww c'mon PaPa, I wanna listen, maybe I can give you a few ideas, please?"

Rocco raised his voice. "Mario!"

Mario jumped from his rugged voice. "Ok-ok, I'm outa here." He quickly left the room.

Mario was 9 years old, and good-looking. His big black olive eyes were beautiful. He had soft curly black hair and thin matching eyebrows. Warm light brown complexion, and when he smiled, his teeth glistened, and his pug nose wrinkled. He looked fragile. Thin boned.

"Nice boy you have there, Rocco. The girls are gonna chase him around in a few years."

Rocco smiled. "Mario's a gooda boy, he justa never forgets his MaMa. She was killed in a car accident two years ago. Someating happened to him. His head goes coo-coo some a da time. Somea days he no talk, he cry ana cry. The tutor, she comes over ana Mario likea dat. She say to me, Mario's a bright kid ana he just needs a frienda, at's all. Maybe you get to know Mario, no?"

"I'd enjoy that, Rocco. I have two younger brothers, so I know how they think."

"Dat'sa good." He dipped the end of his stogy in the glass of wine, and let it soak for a moment.

"Ana now, we talk about you." Rocco took his stogy out of the wine, tapped it on the rim of the glass, and put it in his mouth.

"I watch you ina restaurant when you pull-off that trick, you know what Rocco talk about. I no can say da name of da place." He laughed, and dropped his head for a moment, he was embarrassed.

Jules smiled, but understood. "Guilfoil's Restaurant."

"I no can say this name. Anyway, I watch, ana watch you do disa con, ana I wanna laugh but I no think da timing was right-- Rocco no want to give away disa scam you do. I know disa guy Mickey, da owner of da place. He's gotta lotsa money. Rocco heard he's got so much money he hides some up his assa. Dis is da most

entertaining evening Rocco's had in a long timea. What a clever
kida I say to myself, maybe ina couplea years I teach disa kid da
ropes. Rocco make Greek outa him, ana maybe--"

"Excuse me, isn't a Greek a professional cardsharp?"

"At'sa right. You street smart alaright, kid. Anyway, I say
some more to myself, maybe I can teach him how to handle da dicea
ana cards. Rocco watch da fast hands you have. I come to
conclusion. You start work ina kitchen, ana you work upa da
ladder. You understand Rocco when he say work upa da ladder?"

"I know what you mean." Jules said. He sat in the large
leather chair like a gentleman and listened to every word Rocco
said. He wished his father had talked to him like this.

Rocco give you twenty dollars a week for now. You gotta
questions? You talk to Rocco now. You wanna say someating, no?"

"I have no questions Rocco, but thank you for being so
generous." He knew down the road he would be one of the big boys.

"Dat'sa good. You gonna work out justa fine. Rocco knows what
he talk about. So, for now, you start day after tomorrow, 7 a.m.
sharp. Paco, my chef, will show you da ropes. Now you go, Rocco
gotta tings to do, cabeech?"

Jules got up and shook Rocco's hand. "Okay. Thank's again
Rocco, have a nice day." He pushed the half-closed door open and
stopped then turned and looked at Rocco as if he wanted to say
something.

Rocco took the stogy out of his mouth and stared curiously at Jules. "You gotta someating to say to Rocco? Go ahead, I no bite you, come over he so Rocco can hear you."

Jules walked to the desk, and said, "Well, I just want ya ta know I'm gonna be the best worker ya ever had, that's all."

Rocco nodded his head, and said, "You justa show Rocco kida, Rocco be da judgea deez tings. You wait one minoote, Rocco have someabody show you where to come ina da kitchen from da outaside." He smiled as he pressed a button on the desk. Within seconds three brawny men entered the office looking as if there was a problem. Their eyes studied the room and they were ready to attack anybody that should't be there. Once they were content and knew there was no danger, they looked at Rocco with serious faces.

"Whad's da problem boss?" Said the one with the patch on his eye.

"Have someabody take da kida outsidea ana show him where to come ina kitchen."

"Ya got it. Tawt ya were in trouble dare fer a secon'."

"You do good. Rocco wanna make sure you ona da ball justa ina case Rocco pusha again, cabeech?"

"Know whad yer sayin' Rocco, dats our job." He looked at Jules, "C'mon kid, we'll git ya dare." Patch eye said.

Jules followed Patch eye across the smoke filled room, and thought, Jesus! Look at this joint--card games goin on like there's no tomorrow, crap an' blackjack tables jammed an' roulette an' one-arm bandits--what a gold mine. Did I get lucky or wha'. Sheeeeit, I'm tangled with the big boys now. I don't believe it yet. I gotta let it penetrate a bit. I mean, how often does a little guy like me get spotted doin' a con by a Mafia boss? I'm gonna be rich.

CHAPTER 7

NEW YORK, DECEMBER 13, 1925

6:00 A.M.

Jules sat in Shrap's Pub and had his usual cup of coffee. After reading the newspaper, he left for the park to meet with Smiley. He better at the park, Jules thought. By the time Jules got there, Smiley was standing near the bench scratching his scrotum and crotch like a madman. The park was deserted. Jules hid behind a tree and watched him for awhile. Smiley scratched and scratched away looking around frequently to make certain no one caught him in the act. At times he'd use both hands.

Jules couldn't stand it anymore. He shouted, "What a touching moment, I wish I had a camera!"

Smiley jumped from fright. He looked as if he seen the big bad wolf ready to attack him.

"H-how long you been there?" He stopped scratching and rubbed his nose.

"Long enough ta see ya scratchin' yerself like crazy."

"Awwww sheeeeit...I'm totally embarrassed, damn." He dropped his head, and shook it slowly.

Jules walked over to the park bench, and sat down. He looked serious. "You may have a major problem in your pants there." He enjoyed bantering Smiley. "You've got the godamn crabs, moron! Why'd ya lie ta me the other day about this? When you lie, things come back at you much worse--I don't understand you sometimes, no shit. I don't like ya, can't be trusted." Jules stared at him with a angry look painted on his face.

"Awww jeez, ok, ok, ok, I lied. At the time I felt ashamed, honest Jules, ya gotta believe me. I prepared myself to tell you today, you--"

"Gotta believe me, I know-I know. I know how ya think--it's stinkin' thinkin'. I can't stand you. You deserve--"

"Jules-Jules-Jules, I'm really sorry, cross my heart an' hope to die." He crossed his heart, and looked convincing.

"Yeah sure, ya should be so lucky." Jules said under his breath.

"Aw jeez Jules, my nuts are bleedin' from scratchin' so hard, what am I gonna do? I mean, are ya gonna let me die?"

"You aren't gonna die, moron." He thought a moment, I'll fix this storyteller. I have just the remedy for this lying piece a shit. "Can you move your bowels?"

"Sure-sure. What's that got to do with it?"

"If ya want to get better, answer the questions will ya?"

"O-ok-ok."

"You evidently aren't sleepin' to good, right?"

"Who can sleep? Haven't slept in days."

"Are you gonna do what I tell ya?"

"Yeah-yeah Jules, c'mon I'm dying here."

"Say you're sorry an' ya won't lie again."

Poor Smiley scratched away. "Ohhhh Jules, from the bottom of my heart I'm sorry, I'll--"

"Sorry for what?" He was just having fun.

"Sorry for not telling you the truth."

"No more lying, right?"

"Ya have my word."

"Okay then, go right now and get some kerosene, a half a gallon should do the trick. Go home and get your ass in the bathtub or better yet a large pan. Take off your clothes and squat in the pan, then pour the kerosene slowly over your private parts, and soak your behind for at least twenty minutes to a half hour. Do this at least three times today. I promise those crabs will be long gone, and you'll be back to normal."

"You shoulda been a doctor, Jules. I'll go right away, I can't stand it."

"Wait a second. As a back-up, you may want to go to the drug store an' tell the pharmacist about your problem. I think there's an ointment that should do the job too."

"Yer a great guy Jules. I'm on my way...so long."

"Wait-wait, I almost forgot to tell ya."

"What Jules, c'mon, I'm dyin'."

"I got a job at Rocco's Restaurant. Startin' tomorrow mornin'--is that great, or wha?"

"You gotta be kiddin'! How'd ya swing that?"

"Lucky. Lady luck just happen to come my way at the right time, that's what I believe." Jules said.

"What a break, what a fabulous break! If anybody deserves it Jules, you happen to be the chosen goompa, no question about it. I'm happy for ya pal, real happy. Good luck. I gotta go, see ya later." He ran off scratching his scrotum.

Unbeknown to Jules, his position at Rocco's restaurant as a garlic and potato peeler and having other duties of the sort would eventually, after drastic events take place, lead him to be the best "seasoned mechanic" around.

CHAPTER 8

NEW YORK, DECEMBER 14, 1925

6:50 A.M.

Jules arrived at Rocco's Restaurant. He knocked on the side service door excitedly. A short, thin, handsome bald-headed man with a pleasant smile opened the door.

"Good morning, Paco? I'm Jules."

"Come ina-come ina Jules, I'ma Paco himaself for sure. C'mon, it'sa cold out. I was expecting you." He shook Jules's hand.

"You don't look anything like I thought." Jules said with a big smile.

"What you think Paco suppose to look like?"

Well, with all the big guys aroun' here, I thought for sure, you'd be one of those 200-pound people too."

Paco laughed. "No-no, nota Paco. I hope I no disappoint you." Paco laughed a little harder than before, he sounded as if he were gargling and singing at the same time; he had a high soprano voice. "I stay alla time the same, one hundred-twenty pounds." He grabbed Jules's arm, "C'mon, we go ina kitchen, we musta fuel up firsta, then we work at the best performance, you know what Paco say?"

"Exactly." Jules responded.

"Take off your coat ana boots, put 'em over here...then you sit ina yellow chair," he pointed, "over there. I go check ona breakfast--it should be ready in about five minootes."

Jules took off his coat and fedora and put them on the hook, slipped off his boots then walked in the kitchen. He studied the room. "Jeez Paco, I thought I kept a neat kitchen. This place is immaculate. Everything looks like it's in the right place."

"What you say, Jules? I no hear everyting you say."

"We have something in common already."

"What's that could be?"

"Your kitchen is so neat an' orderly."

"Oh, tank you. The ears someatimes no hear, ana my Englisha needs to be better. Please excuse how I makea da words come out."

"You speak good English Paco, don't worry about it. We'll work together and make it better, how's that sound?"

"That is good Jules, I look forward to this. Now, what did you say about having someating we have ina common?"

"Oh yeah. I keep a neat 'n clean kitchen too, I'm kinda fussy in that department, know what I mean?"

"Ma-shu, I know what you say. I justa know onea ting, when I was a little boy, tree-four years younger than you, I was taught to appreciate everyting my family owned, and we no have very much. We were poor. To make a long story short, I learned to keep everyting like new. My PaPa told me...ahhh, let me see...how I say ina good English." He tilted his head slightly, rubbed his chin and looked at the ceiling, contemplating. "Ok, I can say now. My PaPa was a carpenter in Sicily, ana his tools were so clean alla time, he could tell if somebody else monkey-roun', I mean to say, toucha them."

"How did he know that?" Jules asked.

"Well, every night after dinner, he'd go to the backa room ana take me along with him. We'd clean ana clean, ana oil, ana oil all the tools he had. Someatimes it would take two hours to make alla tools look like new. He put them back justa so. He would know if somebody monkey-roun' wid 'em, you cana bet on it. He no mind to loan some tools to somebody, but one should aska first, outa respecta. Dat's da story. I tink it rubbed off ona Paco. I'ma tink Paco is a compulsive nuta case too, no?"

"I don't think so, but let me ask you a few questions."

"Go ahead Jules, ask Paco anyting."

"Do you dream?"

"Alla time." Paco said.

"Do you dream the same dream all the time?" Jules asked.

"Ma-sure. Why do you ask disa question?"

"For now, just answer the questions. What's the dream about?"

"Alla time I dream crossing a bridge, at's all."

"Ok. Good. Well Paco, according to the dream books I've read, when you dream of a bridge--to cross or even to see a bridge means there is some danger coming to the dreamer. If I were you, I'd be careful."

"I will Jules, I'm superstitious for deez tings. Maybe I try to dream of making love, ana being a slob, no?"

Jules laughed. "You're a comedian, Paco."

"I know-I know, but I gotta tell you someating else. My PaPa say to me before he die, Paco, for a long time we kept my tools likea brand new. You see, we don't own anytinga. Goda, he made everytinga. Maybe someaday for sure, he wanna use them. Ana when he does, they gonna look justa like new."

That's beautiful, Paco. I can appreciate what your PaPa told you."

"Okay, enough of the stories. You having Paco's special dish, ana besides, Rocco tolda me, you look like stringabean, ana he wants me to take extra care for you ana put plenty of meat on your bones."

Jules laughed. He stood up, "No way Paco, no way will you or anybody else ever see me looking like a gorilla. I know exactly what I'm gonna look like when I reach the age of sixty."

Paco returned back to the table from the oven with something on a tray, covered with a white cloth napkin. With one hand he swiftly pulled the napkin off the tray, and spun it around into the air, it gracefully rested over Paco's arm. He lay the tray on the table, and bowed to Jules.

Jules was impressed. "Holy cow Paco, you sure can put on a show."

Paco smiled. "Dis is simple appetizer, Paco justa play aroun'."

"What's it called Paco? I've never seen grapefruit come out of a oven before."

"Dis isa good for you. We gonna have some juicy fresha hota grapefruit, for da appetizer. Isn't it heavenly?"

"Will ya look at that. How in the world did you make this?"

Paco sat down. "Eat 'em up, c'mon, you gonna love dis." They started eating their grapefruit. "Wella, before I do anyting, I'ma wash da grapefruit, thena cut em in half. Thena, cut aroun' inaside to spoon size pieces, thena I sprinkle onea tablespoon of sugar over da top. After dat, I shake some cinnamon ona top of sugar. I put a nicea red cherry ina da center ana put em in the oven ona tray ana cook em at three hundred-fifty degrees for fifteen minoots. When we take em out of da oven, you have Paco's ala Grapefruit Divine. Dat's all it is. What you tink, huh? Dis isa fruit for da Angles."

"Jeez, this is delicious, actually outstanding." Sugar and cinnamon stuck to his lips, while grapefruit juice rolled down his chin.

"Paco took another spoonful of grapefruit. "Mmmmmmm, dis is one of my specialties. Paco has much-much more, you gonna. see, ana

learn to make too. I like to hear compliment. Tank you, my new
frienda, Jules."

Jules never forgot his first gourmet breakfast. He ate two
grilled two-inch thick pork chops, four scrambled eggs, hash
browns with peppers and onions, three one-inch thick slices of
Italian toast smothered with olive oil and black pepper and three
glasses of chocolate milk.

For two years Jules worked hard in the kitchen. He peeled
garlic, potatoes and onions, washed pots and pans, he did all the
dirty work. In between, Paco taught him how to prepare several
special dishes. Eventually he was promoted. He waited on
customers and served drinks to the gamblers on the second floor.
Every week he gave his mother what he had earned.

Four times a week, Jules and Smiley hustled the "Mickey
Mouse" until Jules decided it was time to quit before they got
caught. They successfully pulled-off their scam for almost a year
and averaged one hundred forty dollars a week apiece. This amount
of tax free cash in the 1920's was considered to be in the high
income bracket, especially if compared to that amount in today's
economy.

Jules played the percentages, and knew when to hold, and when
to fold. Now, he needed something to supplement his income until
Rocco thought him man enough to work the crap and card tables;

this was where the big bucks were. Jules always gave his mother a
extra fifty dollars a week. He told her the tips were very good.
He had opened his first bank account, and always walked around
with a hundred dollars in his pocket. He knew that a man who kept
cash in a wallet was considered to be cheap and conservative; a
place where they hoarded the only thing that was theirs.

A week went by, and Jules tried to figure out some sort of
scam that wouldn't hurt anyone. The apple (victim of the con man)
had to have enough money to lose and be a compulsive gambler. He
thought and thought about it but nothing to his liking had grown.
Rocco started to teach Jules a few simple card tricks. Then worked
up to rolling the dice; snaking and palming. With a marked deck
of cards, Rocco taught him how to read them, shuffle, fix the
deck, cut the deck one-handed, all the moves. Jules practiced day
in and day out, he'd fall to sleep exhausted in the early morning
hours most of the time. He was determined to be the best. In the
gambling business, to be considered a "mechanic" was one thing. To
be the very best (a seasoned mechanic), was another. And Jules's
goal was nothing less than top shelf. It would be at least another
year, maybe two, before Rocco would think him man enough to work
the tables. Jules concentrated harder on inventing a sting. His
determination to invent a sting started to become a obsession with
him. Being a bright boy, he knew being obsessed can do more harm
than good. His mind made up, he stopped the heavy thinking because

it affected everything he did. He decided to concentrate on now.
Jules knew it would come to him. It all had to do with timing. And
when the time came, his brilliant mind would vitalize the sting
completely.

Two weeks later, Christmas, 1928, while looking in a pawn
shop window, he overheard a conversation between two bookies. He
knew one of them, he came in Rocco's and was a high roller. Jules
listened to them, and it gave him an idea pertaining to the sting
he had closed his mind to two weeks ago. He could see it as clear
as day. He figured out the details and invented another sting he
named "THE BROWN PAPER BAG".

How did it work? Jules searched for a bad guy, a wealthy
compulsive gambler, one who can afford to lose, with a reputation
of being a criminal. After asking questions to cops he knew,
bookies and street people, he thoroughly researched his long list
of potential apples (victims of a con man). The list was long, it
took him days to pick his first apple. He finally found what he
was looking for, a quack dentist, the perfect mark (victim of a
con man). Jules had a meeting with the quack dentist, and
convinced him to be his partner as a bookie. Jules told him he
had built-up a clientele of more than two hundred fifty factory
workers and construction crews that played the horses only. He
also had a large professional group that made large bets on the
horses. He handled the professionals personally. And every day

Jules and his runners pick-up the bets and pay-off the winners
before the day's race began. He continued to tell the dentist the
reason he needed a partner was because business had become too
large for him, he didn't want to take any chances if there were
big winners, he may not have enough money to pay them off. As far
as profit, Jules told him, on average, his earnings have been
twenty two hundred dollars daily, including expenses. He's
worked the business since he was a young boy. When his father died
he took over. His father was the biggest and most respected bookie
around. It will easily double having a partner. The profits
would be fifty-fifty; losses the same. After making the
collections, Jules and Smiley would bring a locked leather case
containing a brown paper bag with the money and betting slips
(markers) to his partner, the dentist. The dentist would unlock it
with a key Jules is responsible for. The dentist would count the
cash and briefly look in the brown paper bag at the markers and
confirm it's contents. The dentist would keep in his possession
the money and markers in the locked leather case until the next
day. Jules kept the key. They were to meet at the dentist's office
at 5:15 a.m. sharp the next morning to tally up the results.

The greedy quack dentist ate up the convincing story Jules
presented to him. The reason Jules knew the apple would like the
deal was because Jules did his homework, and he also knew greedy
wealthy compulsive gamblers with criminal minds have a tendency

to take a illegal offer they just can't refuse. But this is what actually happened:

The next day, at 3:30 a.m., Jules and Smiley were checking yesterday's--and the early edition of today's newspaper. They would find the sports section, where the race tracts were listed, and pick three of Jules's favorite tracts. The bettor (there aren't any) can wager only at the three race tracts printed on the marker. On the first line of the marker, printed in small print was: Name of horse track, there were three choices followed by a blank line. Second line: Name of horse or horses to be played, followed by a blank line. Third line: win - place - show, followed by a blank line. Forth line: race # or races numbers followed by a blank line. Fifth line: Amount of wager, followed by a blank line. And on the bottom, a code number followed by a ID number designating the location where the wager came from and the bettor's ID receipt.

One hundred markers were filled in with selections chosen from the entry column of yesterday's races. Each of the one hundred markers were filled out. Each horse a loser. When completed, the markers were folded in palm size squares. The markers were deposited in the brown paper bag. Jules counted out two hundred fifty dollars in ones, sixty fives and twenty five tens, totaling eight hundred dollars. He looked at Smiley and gave him a wink. Smiley returned a wink and gave Jules a toothy smile.

He wrapped the cash loosely with a rubber band to make it look bigger than it was, then deposited it in the leather case separate from the markers. He put the brown paper bag in the leather case and locked it with his key.

Jules and Smiley proceeded to look for the winning horses in the results column from the day before's selections morning paper and picked three winners. Jules filled in three markers with three separate winning horses. The amount wagered on one marker was ten dollars, the second, fifty dollars and the third, one hundred dollars--he calculated the official pay-off on each horse; two were first place winners, the other, to show. He added the three winning horses pay-off amounts, and calculated the total amount to be thirty two hundred dollars. Then he folded the three win markers the same as the others and put them in his pocket. After countless hours of research and figuring out the meticulous game plan, he was now prepared to con his first partner with the best "sting" he dreamed up so far.

Jules thought, I'm startin' off with this creep dentist, he's my first choice. This guy comes from bad stock. His ravenousness will always be the same, just like the others I have on the list. The pervert even has a record of putting girls and his young lady patients to sleep, then had sex with them. He's been in the can so many times, you'd think he'd wise-up. He's nothin' but a degenerate. I'm gonna enjoy screwin' his ass, you can bet on it.

Jules and Smiley walked a half mile or so, they enjoyed
keeping in good physical shape. They had to be prepared to
hightail it if the time ever occurred. It was cold. Snow and wind
couldn't stop the twosome. They were brave and aggressive and
would pull-off a con no other hustler would ever think of doing.
They were determined to be rich. They knew stinging a con man or a
thief or a criminal was a dangerous and conceivably fatal way to
make it, but that's the name of the game. Come blazes or towering
water, Jules knew he had to make it happen. They reached the
dentist's office. It was a well-kept brownstone home and office.
They went up the front outside stairs and stood on the landing
staring at the door. A white shade covered the inside window. A
motto "LET US DESIGN YOUR SMILE" was inscribed in the upper
portion of the shade with black letters. In the center, CLOSED in
bold black letters appeared. Near the center bottom in white
lettering on a black background, WOLF SCHWARTZ DMD PA, and RADU J.
PATEL DDS and telephone number appeared printed in 1 inch letters.
It looked like a legitimate dental organization.

Jules looked at Smiley, and said in a whisper, "I want you to
keep yer mouth shut. If I want ya to talk, I'll give ya the sign
by rubbing my nose, meanin' it's ok, ya got that?"

"Ok. My mouth will be so closed you'll think I had false
teeth but forgot to put them in." He closed his mouth tight and
folded his hands. He looked as if he were a priest after asking

his congregation for a donation.

Jules stared at him. " Who ya trying ta kid? Yer here to perform--act-act, like an actor playing the part of a gambler. Ya look scared ta death fer Chris' sake. Relax. Ya gotta put on a face of a tough an' rugged bookie who don't trust nobody. Yer clothes are good, now all ya have ta do is match the face with the clothes an' you'll have it coordinated--where's your cigar?"

"In my pocket, why?" He stood there trying to change the saintly look on his face.

"Put the godamn cigar in your mouth an' get that saintly look off yer face, c'mon, Jesus Christ!" He said in a heated whisper.

Jules calmed down then turned his head towards the door to make sure no one was there. He turned back to Smiley.

"Look Smiley, it's easy. We should've practiced the facial look you should have for this deal. I don't know what the fuck's wrong with you? We're here, an' it's to late for that. The apple's behind that door," He gestured with his eyes towards the entrance of the dentist's office, "he's a real bad guy. Listen to me good, before ya know it yer gonna have the tough look on yer face. Pretend yer here to break the legs of one of the mother-fuckers that screwed your mother." He thought, that should do it.

Smiley's face changed from a saintly look to a face only a thug would have just before he was ready to break the legs of his victim.

"Good. Keep that look, it's perfect. Pretend we're the two main characters in a movie. Are ya ready?"

"I like it."

"Okay. Camera's rollin'...action."

Jules turned toward the door. He was about to knock.

"Cut-cut--I forgot my make-up, Jesus Christ!" Smiley said.

Jules turned around quickly, "Sonofabitch! Yer pissin' me off! Get serious or get the fuck outa here!"

"Ok, ok, ok, I'm sorry. Thought I'd give you a last laugh before show-time--good luck."

Jules shook his head, and thought, will this moron ever grow up and stop bustin' my chops? He knocked on the door. Waited ten seconds or so and knocked again, this time a little harder. He waited a bit then knocked ten or twelve more times harder than before.

You know what I think?" Smiley said softly, "I think our friend inside is sniffin' panties."

Jules turned to Smiley, "Shhhh, shut the fuck up, the camera's rollin', just hold the pissed-off look."

Smiley did exactly what Jules told him to do.

Jules knocked six or seven times this time. He closed his eyes to remain composed and thought, that Loretta sure is somethin' else. I have to ask her out. A good movie would be perfect. I'll play it by ear. He opened his eyes and peeked inside

and thought, can't see a thing. He promised he'd be here. He
knocked twelve or fourteen times harder than before.

Smiley let out a loud burp accidently. "Sorry bout that, I
don't know where that came from." He leaned to his left around
Jules to look at the door, and in a low whisper said, "The swine's
probably playing with himself. I'd give it another two minutes,
he's had plenty of time to get his rocks off by now!" He put one
hand over his mouth and muffled his laugh.

Jules grabbed Smiley's ear, and said in a harsh whisper, "Ok
moron, yer provin' ta me yer not cut out for this job. Wise up
pal. This is the last time I'm tellin' ya."

Smiley nodded his head and kept his tough-guy look. Jules
reached in his pocket and pulled out a fresh pack of Camel
cigarettes, opened them and put the raveled wrap in his pocket. He
took two deep drags of his cigarette, then noticed that the shade
moved on the door; it was the dentist peeking through. The door
unlocked, and there he stood. Wolf. Messed gray hair. Baggy eyed.
Well trimmed yellow stained gray beard. Wrinkled thin face and
hands. At six feet tall and one hundred ninety pounds, he looked
like a likable man. But Jules knew better.

"Hey Jules." Wolf said. "I was tied up in the lab. One of my
patients wanted to get even with me. I heard you knocking but
couldn't disentangle the godamn rope." He laughed like a crazy
man. "Come in. I set up a room in the back. Come on boys, I'm not

drilling at this hour." He laughed harder than before. "Who's your friend, Jules?"

Jules and Smiley stepped inside. "Before I tell ya, look at the smile on his face. He has a perpetual smile, it never disappear's. He could be in a dentist chair or have a day of bad luck, it just stay's on the face, thought you should know. Smiley, meet Wolf."

They shook hands. Wolfy's eyes pierced into Smiley's, he had a serious look on face as if Smiley had deceived him at one time or another.

"Pleasure Wolfy, pleasure indeed, as long as you don't decide to probe around in my mouth."

Wolfy let go of Smiley's hand instantly, and said heated, "I know you from some place?"

Smiley swallowed loudly. He discreetly looked at Jules and waited for a sign. Jules gestured a sign with his lips by licking them, meaning it's ok, answer the question. Smiley looked back at Wolfy, took his cigar out of his mouth and replied skillfully.

"Me? I don't know you from a bag a beans. The only thing I know about you is you're a dentist and I'm not crazy about drill artists or false chopper specialists." He put his cigar back in his mouth and thought, holy shit, was I good or wha? I don't know where that line came from but it's the truth. Jules is gonna be proud of me, I'll hear about it later, as sure as this greedy quack's gettin' fleeced.

Jules and Wolfy laughed. Wolfy gave Smiley a light punch on his chin.

"I got me a bad habit of playin' aroun', Smiley. I always wanted to be a drama actor. I keep practicin', you understand, right?" He laughed.

"Sure, sure, I can handle it." He thought, hope you can handle it after we're through with our performance, you swindling mother fucker.

Wolfy's laugh was that of a crazy man who escaped from the insane asylum and was never caught. They followed him through the reception room passing the dentists working rooms for patients. A fragrance of cinnamon filled the air until they entered the back room; a hint of perfume lingered in the air as if a woman had just been there. The room was 8 feet by 10 feet consisting of filing cabinets, a desk, a surgical table covered with a blanket and each wall had pictures of every con man known, from Daniel Drew to Al Capone. In one corner a make-shift card table with six folding chairs await the newly formed bookies to tally up the results.

Jules and Smiley looked at the pictures on the walls, "Jesus, these photos are incredible Wolfy, where did you find these?" Jules said.

"I'm a collector. I love these guys, they inspire me. You're lookin' at forty years of searchin', stealin', drillin' heads off, you name it. Take a look, the history on each one of those master minds is under their mug shot. I'll get the case in the other room." He hurried out of the room as if someone was going to steal it.

Wolfy looked cool. He was a self-centered, vicious criminal, and one mistake made by Jules or Smiley would be fatal.

Jules thought, yeah sure, he's a collector alright. The pervert get's his rocks off lookin' at these hustlers an' con men. When he comes back just be as calm as you are, it'll be over with in no time.

He went up to Smiley, and whispered, "You all together? Got yer head screwed on tight?"

"I'm as ready as a anaconda waiting to strike it's prey--shh, I think he's coming--good luck, sweetheart."

Jules gave him a wink in addition to a convinced smile.

Wolfy easily walked in the room. He had a cynical look about his face as he said, "Okay boys, lets go." He placed the leather case on the table, then violently punched the wall with his fist.

"Shit! Need my fuckin' glasses. Be right back." He quickly sprung back and made a beeline out the door as if there were something of more importance awaiting his presence.

Jules picked up a small oval mirror and looked at one of his front teeth. As he adjusted the mirror to get a clearer look, in the reflection he noticed outside the window behind him a sixteen

or seventeen year old girl sneaking her way through the shrubs
alongside the building. Once out, she ran along the grass toward
the alley in the back. He placed the mirror back where he found it
and thought, he forgot his glasses alright--the creep had her in
the back all the while. How could he live with himself and not
know he's harmin' the girl's life. He's a sex pervert amongst
other things, his ass is mine. He took a deep breath to relax
himself from the thought and focused on bilking Wolfy, big time.

Wolfy came back in the room. "Found 'em. Need another pair--
whataya think of my collection? Love everyone of 'em."

"They're phenomenal. Now that you found yer glasses we better
start figuring up, we gotta make our pick up's as soon as we're
through here." Jules said.

"Sound's good, comrade. Go ahead, you know how to set the
table up, let's get started."

Jules set his and Wolfy's chairs side by side and one chair
to the side in view to all present. Smiley had already taken his
chair. He sat eight or nine feet away from the table pretending to
be reading the morning paper. His job was to observe Wolfy's every
move. Jules unlocked the case, took out the bundle of cash and
counted the eight hundred dollars to make sure it was all there.
When he finished counting, Jules gestured a quick nod to Wolfy to
indicate it was okay. He lay the cash in the case, at the same
time taking out the brown paper bag and put it in front of Wolfy.

He closed the case and set it on the chair for all to see. Wolfy turned the brown paper bag upside down and the markers came tumbling out and scattered over the table. In Jules's left hand were the three winning markers he filled out earlier. The moment the markers hit the table, Jules quickly and cautiously released the three winning markers in one smooth motion and mixed them in with the rest of the markers (it looked as though Jules was stopping the markers from falling off the table.)

It took approximately forty-five minutes to read off the markers and finalize the results. Jules and Wolfy had a bad day. The three winners totaled up to thirty-two hundred dollars. Wolfy had to spring for sixteen hundred dollars, his half. After all, collections had to be made that morning. More important, the winners had to get paid off.

Jules gave Smiley forty percent of the profits. They delivered the brown paper bag to Wolfy's office every day. And every day at 3:30 a.m., Jules and Smiley made up new markers for another sunshine day.

Jules made sure they had good days too. But unfortunately, in the eleven or twelve months that had gone by, the pervert dentist Wolfy, busted-out. As a small-time bookie, it was a high price in pay-off's alright. Jules and Smiley stung him for a hundred eighty two thousand dollars. When you compare dollars in the 1920's with the dollars of today's economy, it was indeed a

a considerable sum of money. Nobody ever learned where the dentist
moved his practice.

Out of the sixty percent (forty nine thousand dollars),
Jules's share of the sting, he gave his mother twenty-five
thousand and deposited the rest in his bank account. Smiley? Well,
he had other idea's. He spent his thirty-three thousand on wine,
women and song, an overflow of clothes and lastly, blew it away
gambling.

Jules had a business mind--he played the percentages. His
mind made up, it was time to pull out of the Brown Paper Bag scam
before his luck ran out. He could have gone on, after all, he
worked hard on researching his list of other rebels and con men
and compulsive gamblers. But being superstitious and knowing what
greed can eventually do to a person, he decided to dream-up
another sting. He knew when to hold and when to fold. Smiley, on
the other hand, didn't know the meaning of the word. He told Jules
he wanted to take over the Brown Paper Bag deal. He wanted to be
the big-shot bookie.

"Jesus Christ Jules!" Smiley shouted. "Why you gettin' outa
the Brown Paper Bag deal for? I mean, we made big bucks for Chris'
sake--now you want out? Yer gonna blow it away? What yer sayin'
is bye-bye to the deal--all the negative bull-shit. Don't make
sense--I mean, don't make no fuckin' sense at all! You're a fool,
I think you're a bigger fool than that pervert Wolfy, if ya wanna

know the truth!"

He stood erect directly in front of Jules's face. He had a look of a arrogant wiseguy painted across his face.

Jules heated, grabbed Smiley by his new silk tie and twisted it tight enough to make him choke. Saliva oozed out from between his lips. He slapped his face knocking the cigar out of his mouth then put his nose against Smiley's, and said, "Whadaya mean yer takin' over! Where ya gonna get the apples (suckers) from, me? Wrong. I wanna see you take over--who ya gonna be stingin'--queer guys?" He laughed. "I thought ya had yer act together? Yer never gonna straighten out! Yer nothin' more than a illiterate two-face. Not only that, yer proving ta me yer not loyal like you promised. A piece-a-shit is what yer drivin' me to swallow. If this is so, ya are a moron, I always called you a moron in a kiddin' way--must be true. Ya don't know the meaning of loyalty or devotion." He shook him. "Yer a defeatist obsessed with greed and--"

O-gay, ahhhg, ahhhg, o-gay-o-gay...c-can't breath...leg-go will ya!" Smiley's face started to turn pinkish blue.

Jules loosened his grip a bit. "I know you so well, friend, so well I've come to the close. Yer just a two-bit has been. Don't you come aroun' my way--never!"

Jules was so heated, the wings on his nostrils were enlarged. He released Smiley then pushed him back. "It's time you stood on

yer own two feet. You made a rube (victim of a con man) out of
me--never thought you'd bamboozle me. That's okay, better it
happened now--yer a sucker for small change, anyway. The Big Store
(any confidence game requiring a fake front, such as an office,
bank, gambling den, bookmaking parlor; also called "joint" "the
store," or "the big con.") is where I'm destined--see ya aroun'."
He started to walk away.

    "Wait!" Smiley's knees trembled. He stared at Jules with a
shameful look painted across his face. He couldn't look at Jules
straight in the eye because he knew everything Jules said was
right. Smiley, being emotional, realized his impulsiveness would
lead him in a heap of deep trouble with Jules. He also realized
the disrespect he had given to Jules. He thought, how am I gonna
get out of this? Oh God, please, help me, you know Jules is my
best friend, please lay it on me, you have the right words right
in your back pocket. Give me a break, I'll change my bad ways,
promise. He remembered a trick Jules taught him; he looked
directly at the bridge of Jules's nose, there was no way Jules
would know the difference. He raised his arms as if he was ready
to make a statement to the Pope.

    "Jesus H. Christ!" He roared out. "Yer not walkin' till we do
some talkin'! Yer gonna listen to me if it's the last fuckin'
thing I say to you!" His face had a scornful look about it.

    Jules had already walked halfway across the room heading

toward the door. When he heard Smiley shout, he stopped and turned facing his impulsive two-faced friend. He crossed his arms and stared in his eyes. The expression on Jules's face was that of a snarling dog waiting to attack.

With a low snappish voice, he said, "This better be good!" He thought, this is gonna be one of his great tales, I can tell. The least I can do is listen to the poor soul. What the hell, this'll be the last of the moron anyway. "Well! I'm waitin'!"

Smiley's voice was a croak. He couldn't get the words out.

"Easy now, you've been a sick boy. The cat finally got yer tongue?" Jules said, as he lit a cigarette, and looked concerned.

Smiley swallowed, and tried again. "N-no, I just want you to know I appreciate you not walkin' out on me. And I thought you'd be interested in the two apples (suckers) I found, that's all. These two apples been dyin' to do business with us--ther' loaded. One's a surgeon, the other's a chief accountant for a big corporation. They're compulsive gamblers and qualify for the undesirables we do business with. We can make a fast sixty-seventy grand. Come on, just one more time, you know, like, one for the road, so it's said--whataya say?"

"Ya just don't get it, do ya?" Jules looked at the floor and casually walked toward Smiley. He crushed his cigar with his shoe, gave Smiley a smile, and walked out.

Smiley looked sad. "Sonofabitch, those weren't the right

words. Blew it! Lost my best friend. God, what do I do now!"

On the rooftop of Jules apartment building that evening, while his Mama and two brothers were asleep, Jules gift wrapped eight beautiful towels and a pink bath robe in a box for his Mama. It was no special occasion, he did this because he loved his family. He also bought two pair of slacks, shirts and books for his brothers, Peter and JoJo. He wrapped them in gift paper and placed two twenty-dollar bills in a card, and wrote:

Dear Peter & JoJo,

You two brains are going to Collage some day.

By rights, you should save this money.

But it's okay to do what you want with it.

I'm very proud to be you're big brother.

Love you,

Jules

He brought the gifts in his mother's room, and quietly placed them near her bed, then reached in his pocket and pulled out a piece of paper addressed to his Mama:

Dear Mama,

When you brought me into this world,

I always thought how thankful I have been

to have a Mama like you.

I love you with all my heart,

Julius

He put the note under the ribbon of the gift then went to his
bedroom. JoJo's blanket half covered him, and Jules gently pulled
it up. Peter snored away curled like a pussycat. Jules had bought
them new beds and sheets and pillows and quilts, as he did for his
mother. He quietly çlosed the drape surrounding his new bed; he
didn't want to disturb his brothers from the light in his
diminutive private corner. He sat back and propped his three new
goose down pillows and lay back staring at the ceiling. He
remembered the pointless remarks Smiley had made about taking over
The Brown Paper Bag scam, and Jules thought, Yeah, sure, if he's
takin' over anythin' it's gonna be the cuckoo's nest. He has a
defeatist attitude toward life and the guy will never change. The
moron is poverty prone and it just doesn't want to set him free,
ever since he started drinkin'. He's a frustrated extrovert, a
sex maniac with no moral standards. Sheeeit, I can go on all
night. But on the other hand, he is fun to be aroun', at least
when he's reasonable. I know he's capable of making good of
himself...well, after he talk's with a shrink...that's it! A
psychologist is exactly what that ding-a-ling need's--a little
therapy, like a year or two will bring him back to reality...I'll
see, maybe I'll have a talk with him. But first I want the piece-
a-shit ta sweat it out for a stretch. He reached up to one of his
choice Sigmund Freud volumes and started to read.

The next morning, Jules was in Shrap's Pub having his coffee.

It was around 6:30, and Jules already had his third cup. Louie just made delicious three inch by two inch thick butter biscuits. He brought two to Jules's table with a side of strawberry jam and home fries.

"Mon-ja-mon-ja, eat em up-eat em up--dis-a batch is special just-a for you. I dun-know Jules, some-a time's it scare's me I make dee-za biscuits so...how you say...ahhhh, I gotta da word now, extraordinary, dats-a da word. I mean to say, deez biscuits simply are da best, you gonna see."

"Louie, yer the best."

"At-sa nice you say dis to me. O-gay, I go for now, I no wanna burn da pizza. I bring you some after." Louie hurried off, his breadbasket wobbled similar to a large bowl of ready-to-eat jell-o in the beginning of a earthquake.

While chewing on a biscuit, and reading the morning newspaper, Jules leafed through a few pages and a picture of Meyer Solowsky and "Spooky" Lieberman caught his eye. And underneath the picture, in a cartoon drawing, Meyer Solowsky is standing near a private plane with a wide closed-mouth smile dressed in a conservative suit and tie, holding a suitcase. Behind Meyer, a brutish looking henchman is looking over his shoulder with his hand inside his jacket near the breast pocket grasping on to something deadly. Near his feet one large suitcase and a small overnight case await boarding. Meyer Solowsky is

looking at two Arabs nearby and are dressed in their traditional
attire. One is talking to the other. The one listening has a frown
on his face and his arms are crossed. Underneath the cartoon, the
Arab talking is saying: "His name is Meyer Plasky and he says
he'll make us an offer we can't refuse." Jules laughed. He
thought, what characters, "Lucky" Luccano and Moey Sedsow are
probably hiding out somewhere far away--Nevada may be just the
right spot, snakes love it. Am I glad I broke away from that gang,
thank's to my "Mickey Mouse" friends. He turned a page and
started to read. Louie came back to Jules's table with a piece of
pizza.

"Hey, Jules, eat-em up my pizza, this is-a da best-a. When-a
you eat dis Sicilian pizza you no want to be a Neapolitan, never
again."

"Louie, yer not only the foremost, you're the beginning of
the end."

"I like-a dat. You very intelligent, Jules. I remember one-a
time I ask-a you some-a-ting, I no-no when, but you say to me you
hungry to read, you starve-a to read all-a da books you can get-a
you hands on. But I no ever see you wid-a books. Why, how come?"

"I don't read books in public except on rare occasions. I
demand privacy when it come's to these things, know what I mean?"

"Ma-sure. Dats-a good. You make me satisfied. I must-a go for
now. You just-a call, if-a you need me." Louie was halfway to the

kitchen as he was talking.

The front door opened, it was unusual for a customer to come in at this hour, not only that, the place didn't open until 7:00 a.m.; obviously, Louie forgot to lock the door. He always let Jules in because they were friends. Wind and snow came whirling in the place, sections of the newspaper Jules had on the table blew everywhere. Jules peeped over the top of the paper watching what the stranger's next move would be. Frozen snow had accumulated on his black knit ski mask; his head and face was covered as if he had plans to knock off the place. Then the stranger removed his ski mask and looked at Jules. Jules dropped the newspaper and stared at him, he couldn't exactly make out who it was until a certain move gave him away. He thought, I don't believe my eyes, what the hell is Smiley doin' here? Jesus, he looks like he slept in the street. His face is smeared with grease or something. He didn't shave--looks like a panhandler. He's got balls showin' up here. I can't wait to hear the great tale he concocted, the kook probably spent all night creatin' it. The only thing that look's fresh is his khaki-colored scarf. This better be good or...

Smiley took a few steps in the direction of Jules, he hesitated a moment not being sure if Jules would talk to him. His face had the look of weariness written over it. Jules stared at him for the time it took him to put a unlit cigarette between his lips.

"C'mon over big-shot, I'm not gonna bite ya." Jules said, in a welcoming voice and vague smile.

Smiley's expression changed from gloom to joy.

"Looks like you had a bad night?" Jules said, while putting the rest of the newspaper on the chair.

Smiley strutted with confidence to Jules's table, pulled out a cigar from his breast pocket and put it between his shiny white teeth assured he was welcome. He stood behind the chair, his fingers twirling the cigar in his mouth and staring at the bridge of Jules's nose. Sonofabitch, he thought. One minute I'm pal's with Jules, and the next minute I'm on the shit list. He's as close to me as a brother, and I'm gonna find a way to apologize to him. But how? I'll just be me, that's all. Looking at the bridge of his nose trick works for me good. Just remember, be honest.

"So?" Smiley said, scratching his privates. "How's it goin?"

"Not so good. I have a problem that's gonna take some time to figure out. Sit down, have some coffee."

"Maybe I can help, Jules, what's it all about?"

"You Smiley, it's all about you. I don't know why I'm talkin' to you, but I guess it doesn't matter. I just want you to grow up and learn the meaning of respect and loyalty for starters. I spend a lot of time putting together these flimflam deals. It takes a lot of planning and teamwork to perfect these things. Once a deal is put together, and your thinking is right, you have to stay in focus--you have to be serious. We never had money--we never had much of anything--the whole idea behind pulling-off these scams is to persevere. The key is--don't get greedy. Keep a low profile. No short-cuts, there are none.

If you're gonna do something, do it right or do yerself a favor an' blow town. I have a goal and I'm gonna make it happen--I'm gettin' my Mama an' brothers outa this neighborhood pretty soon, they deserve the better things in life. I don't know how long my Mama's gonna be aroun', she's gettin' treatments, no guarantees. My brothers are goin' to collage down the road, it takes big bucks ta make that happen. Nothin', I mean nothin', is gettin' in my way. My family comes first." Jules raised his voice, "Why the fuck can't you comprehend this!"

Smiley took his cigar out of his mouth and dropped his head in shame. A tear rolled down his cheek. He looked up at Jules.

"When I told you I wanted the Brown Paper Bag deal and you walked out on me, well, a dreadful feeling came over me. I realized I wanted something you formulated and I was going to steal it for my benefit. I had remorse like never before. I didn't want to cheat my best friend. I walked the streets thinking how I could make it up to you. All night I thought about it. I slept in an alley to remind me what it was like when I had nothing. I knew you were here and had to come over to apologize for making a fool out of myself."

"If you want to make up for what you did to me, you're
attitude has to change." Jules said, softly.

Smiley gave Jules a curious look, "Jesus, where do I start?"

"I want you, Smiley O'Brian to see a physiologist."

Smiley looked dumfounded. "A shrink!"

"What's wrong with talking with a shrink? People who care
about themselves want their lives to be stable. They're only
finding out why they do bizarre things, no big deal. I know once
you go and pour your heart out, you'll be the Smiley I knew back
when."

Where do I find a shrink? How do I know if he's competent?"

"Don't get paranoid over this--let me think for a minute." He
tapped on his chin and thought..."Yes. That's it. Psychology
professor Norman Bamberg. I met him four years ago, right here,
Shrap introduced me to him. At the time he was teaching at the New
York College of Education and Behavioral Sciences. Shrap told me
the professor had written five books on Psychology--read each one,
got em at the library. I gotta buy em, add em to my collection.
He's retired now, but I heard he practices at his home not to far
from here. Ask Shrap, he'll give ya the details."

"I'll do it, Jules." Smiley looked restored. "Okay pal, I
hate to tell you this but you won't be seeing me for a while--
don't say anything, please. I decided to just work, save a few
bucks and do a lot of reading. I want to be a better person.

You've encouraged me through the years, gave it your best shot. I finally realized all the things you did evidently didn't rub off.

He stood up, squeezed Jules's shoulder and walked out.

Jules stood there with a unmarked face. He thought, so long friend."

CHAPTER 9

NEW YORK, OCTOBER 24, 1929

7:45 A.M.

Four years later United States President Franklin D. Roosevelt, in his first inaugural address, made some attempt to assess the enormous damage of the Great Depression: "The withered leaves of industrial enterprise lie on every side; farmers find no markets for their produce; the savings of many years in thousands of families are gone. More important, a host of unemployed citizens face the grim problem of existence, and an equally great number toil with little return."

His words were inadequate. This economic catastrophe and it's impact defied description.

The hard times didn't alter Jules's plan's; he moved to a back room in Rocco's Restaurant; the room Rocco lived in when he first started his business twenty-one years ago. Jules's mother, Peter and JoJo moved to her sister Arlene's home in up-State New York. It was the perfect place to live. Arlene lived alone for three years ever since she lost her husband to cancer. She loved the idea of having her sister and the boys live with her in Albany. Before his family left Jules put a sealed envelope in his mothers purse. He wrote:

Dear Mama,

    Hope you and the boys have a safe trip.

Look forward to receiving a letter

and cash every month.

I sure am going to miss you guys.

Say hi to Aunt Arlene for me.

P.S. Don't worry about me, I'll be fine.

  Love you,

   Jules

Nothing meant more to Jules than his family. He would do anything for them.

The room Jules moved into consisted of a round handmade oak table with a round thick base carved with leaves and branches of an olive tree. The two matching chairs had the same carving on the inner and outer upper back rest. One with an eye for quality could tell it was made from a craftsman. The walls were dark stained vertical planking, and the teakwood floor had the likeness of the deck on a luxurious yacht. The bathroom had just enough room for the miniature four by three foot bathtub; it was adorned with painted tiles of olive leaves and impressive Greek warlords and opened footlockers showing the contents; a dwarflike fan of five cards with a bitsy spade in the left hand corner of each one and a pair of dice minus the dots and a unusual abacus with seven cards across the bottom portion and four buttons attached to a rod under

each card, and the top portion contained seven cards across with
four buttons under each card; each of the thirteen cards had blank
faces apart from a spade in each left hand corner. The artist who
painted the magnificent drawings on each six by six inch tile
indeed held the hand of an Angel. A path of dark iron stains
marked its way down and around the drain from the dripping shower
fixture. A gray on gray canvas shower curtain large enough to
surround one person dangled from a round metal rod attached to the
ceiling. On the interior in the oval wash bowl were painted olive
branches, and the unusual toilet was enclosed with a walnut frame;
the wood cover of the commode didn't open in the customary way, it
pushed into the wall to open and pulled out to cover the top. The
bathroom resembled a manly jon on an elegant sailing vessel made
exclusively for the Captain. The doorknobs were octagonal and
white ceramic, surrounded with a rectangular brass leafed door-
plate. Out of the bathroom and back to the one-open-space room, in
the far corner, a over-stuffed single goose down mattress rested
on a low wood frame seven or eight inches above the floor. It was
propped on wood blocks. Four thick pillars supported a legless
crap table above; the special bed and crap table looked similar to
a bunk bed. The pillars were hand carved with olive leaves.
Along the wall, next to Jules's special bed was a book shelf seven
feet long by six feet high; his medical books and volumes of
Sigmund Freud and other great men were neatly arranged including

his personal belongings. Four fancy multicolored octagonal glass lights hanged by their cords from the eighteen foot teakwood ceiling, and one over the crap table. Jules had a personal stand up light near his bedside. On one wall, a large painting had been taken down, a faded rectangular spot remained. A large dresser the length of the six foot wall was plain and simple. And the large walk-in closet was completely surrounded with shelves.

During the three years, Rocco taught Jules how to master reading the cards, palm the dice, all the important moves. His hands were becoming as swift as a flash of lightning. Jules made moves that were imperceptible, even to the trained eye. He shuffled the cards, cut them one handed, could pull an ace of diamonds out of the deck, place it back in the deck, shuffle the cards every which way, then would recover the ace of diamonds like magic. His passion to do good was very strong. His determination to be the best was pure. He spent hours and hours practicing in his room, hardly ever going out. And when he finished practicing, he'd read. Exhausted on many occasions, before retiring for the evening, he'd reverently look at himself in the mirror, and would say: "It won't be long now, I've got that feelin', it's gonna happen, I know it's gonna happen--the phone is gonna ring, an' Rocco's gonna tell me ta get my ass ready ta rock 'n roll! I feel it, can smell it, taste it!" Then he'd wink at himself along with a big smile. He didn't say those fifty-two words from an ego point of view, he just wanted to be successful. Rocco watched

Jules practice frequently on the crap and card tables upstairs.

Rocco knew Jules was becoming a one-of-a-kind mechanic, because he

did it from his heart. Even though Jules knew the games were

fixed, he had no choice in the matter. He would find a way to

clear his conscience someway. He had a strong conviction:

"Everything is meant to be for a reason." Knowing this, no matter

what the circumstance, his perceptiveness prevailed.

It had begun casually three months later. In the middle of a

quiet day, Jules received a message that Rocco wanted to talk with

him. They met at the bar. Rocco asked Jules to give him a hand in

the basement. Jules followed Rocco to the stockroom that had just

been made bigger. The room was stacked with boxes of wine and

liquor.

Jules asked, "What's goin' on Rock?"

A moment later, Rocco was on the second basement step pulling

the string from the light that dangled above, but it didn't turn

on.

"Some-a-bitch! How many times I gotta tell dat dummy to make

all-a da lights work in da base-a-ment--you tell dis-a clean-em-up

guy he better check each one today or else...

"I'll take care it, Rock."

They walked down the creaky stairs to the dirt floor, it was

dark. The only light was from the room upstairs, and that barely

shed any light. Once the eyes adjusted to the darkness, it wasn't
so bad. Thin rays of daylight found their way through the boarded
basement windows. At the bottom of the stairs, Rocco reached up
for a long string that turned on the light, it flickered for a
moment then burned out.

Heated, Rocco said, "I no believe it! When Rocco see dat
dummy, da rope, Im-a put aroun' his neck, for sure!"

"Relax Rocco. The light bulbs will be replaced today--yer
blood pressure is gonna go up."

Rocco reached in the darkness to a shelf and found a candle
attached to a Chianti wine bottle smothered with a thick layer of
wax. Once lit, tables and chairs came into sight leaning against
the staircase.

Better than no light at all. Jules thought.

"Ahhhh, now dis-a light we can depend on." Rocco laughed.

"Not for anything Rock, the nice thing about a candle is it
works every time, huh?

They laughed as they walked along. Enfolded with cobwebs and
dust, they passed crap tables and slot machines and wine barrels
and card tables and oil paintings and furniture.

Jules thought, not that I'm chicken-hearted or anything,
b-but this is kinda spooky. I hope we're close to where we're
goin'. I'm not to crazy about this.

Carefully they walked through another section of the damp

basement, the stench of beer and wine lingered in the air. They had to bend over slightly going through the next room. It looked as if it was a dungeon at one time. As they got closer to the wine cellar, the reek of stale wine was very strong, it made Jules choke. He covered his nose and mouth with his shirt. He would be embarrassed if he whimpered in the presence of Rocco.

Being optimistic, and feeling a little tipsy from the wine in the air, he thought, sheeit, the smell in here is pure heavenly. Everybody should be down here, especially if yer a heavy drinker. He pulled his shirt down and took a deep breath.

"Hey Rocco? The odor down here has a likeable scent, don't ya think?" He choked and vomited.

Rocco turned, "What's-a wrong, my son-a?"

"I'm okay-I'm okay...ohhhh...aghhh...I'm f-fine. Breathin' in to much of this air, I guess."

"Ma sure. Rocco know what you mean. You want some-a Rocco's wine? It will make-a you better."

"N-No-no, I'm okay now, we can go, thank's anyway."

"We all-a-most there. You gonna see where Rocco make-a-da wine. C'mon-a...oh, I forgot to tell-a you. Some-a-time when you smell dis-a stinkin' odor, especially for the first time-a, you belly she go upside-a down, but soon enough you no can smell it-- you gonna see. Rocco know's many tings, but you must-a be very, very careful--or perhaps-a you may like it too!"

They laughed. Rocco grabbed Jules around his neck, held him
tight then quickly messed his hair.

They laughed harder than before, especially, with Jules's
chic porcupine hair-do.

Jules knew Rocco was a intelligent person, despite his broken
English.

God, I'm embarrassed, Jules thought. I want to die. Did I
have to get sick in front of him?

Somehow, from some deep wellspring of will, he managed to get
over it. He put on a happy face. "Tell me Rocco, do you come down
here often?"

"Once in-a while, when Rocco make-a special wine. Rocco come
over he maybe four-five times a year. My wine maker, he make da
wine for Rocco, now. Rocco no have to do get da hands dirty no
more. Rocco gotta a lots-a bus-iness, he take care of every-ting."

"I can understand now, all these barrels an' boxes aroun'."

Jules followed Rocco closely to a steel gate with a large
chain wrapped around it. A large padlock the size of a small
frying pan secured the chain. Rocco handed Jules the candle and
reached for a three foot broom handle with a hook attached to the
end. He raised it onto a large metal ring with two metal keys
attached, and lowered them between his teeth and gripped them
firmly. Then he rested the broom handle against the wall. The
keys were rusty and larger than Rocco's hand. They had a strange

ringing sound, a slight echo could be heard that was frightening
to Jules. Rocco grabbed the keys with his one arm and chuckled.

"You like disa trick? When Rocco lost-a-da arma, Rocco come
down here an-a try an-a try to find-a secret place to put da keys.
Boy oh boy, when Rocco finally find disa place, the keys, day fall
on-a Rocco's face, but Rocco no give up, even when Rocco's nose
gotta broke, an-a da eyes turn-a special colors."

"You're extraordinary Rock, absolutely incredible."

"Rocco like it when you say dees-a words. Okay, you hold da
candle over Rocco's shoulder."

Jules put the candle close enough so Rocco could see. He
unlocked the padlock, and opened the gate. As it opened, the eerie
sound of a squeak gave Jules the chills. Deep down, he had a weak
spot for uncanny things. His fondness for ghosts or any frightful
happenings didn't quite turn him on. He'd shiver, and think of
Frankenstein, and all the other horror movies he seen when he was
a boy.

"At'sa good." Rocco put the keys between his pants and belt
buckle. "Soon enough you gonna see a big-a surprise-a."

"I can imagine." Jules said, under his breath.

"You talk to Rocco?"

"No...talkin' to myself, that's all."

"Give Rocco candle now, we just-a bout there. You feel
better now, huh?"

"I feel like I took a sip of yer home-made vino, if ya wanna know the truth!"

Rocco laughed. "I no remember you to tell lies-a to Rocco!"

Jules laughed, and gave Rocco a light punch on his arm.

"Yer just playin' aroun' with me. Can't fool me." We're in for a good day, Jules thought.

The duo walked through the opening of the wine cellar, past racks of full wine barrels resting on their sides; they were stacked on wooden racks up to the twenty foot ceiling on both sides of the room. They passed several racks of bottled wine resting on their sides, on wood racks that reached to the ceiling. The ceiling had four huge thirty foot rough cut wood beams spanning the length of the room. Beams of sunlight pierced their way through a stained glass octagonal window, guarded by steel bars. On the back wall, racks of one-gallon dark burgundy wine gleamed from the rays of sunlight as if something sacred existed in the room. Resting on shelves against the other walls, quarts of wine extended wall to wall. The width of the room was twenty-twenty-eight feet. Above the jugs of wine, and touching the ceiling, empty wood grape boxes stained with red wine and mildew and ten gallon wine barrels smothered with cobwebs occupied the rest of the rack. In the center of the wine rack which held the gallons, bundles of garlic were hanging to keep evil spirits away. Rocco was a superstitious man. Below the garlic, a painted sign read:

Domestic

Vintage 1920

The walls were made of large rectangular stone similar to the castles and temples built in the 16th century. Suddenly, Jules felt something strange come over him, the same feeling he had before, but this time much more intense. He started to feel uneasy. He trembled, beads of sweat formed on his forehead from fright. A coldness in the room felt as though evil spirits were present. The phenomenon slowly enhanced until the room felt enclosed with spirits. Jules was horrified, he thought a ghost passed him, he rubbed his eyes and studied the room. Nothing of any sort was visible. His face looked as if he seen a ghost. A few moments passed and suddenly the strange feeling vanished. Then a peacefulness filled the room. It felt holy and pure. Jules became calm. During Jules's experience, Rocco was looking at the wine bottles and straightening a few wine barrels. He reached for a long string that turned on the light; the bulb flickered a moment, and burned out.

"Ma, someabitcha! Disa bust-a too!" He looked up at the burned-out light bulb, and shouted, "I no can believe dis-a bull-shit!" He paused and scratched his head, then laughed, "Ohhhhh, I tink-a my friend-a Skiatho, he play aroun' wid-a Rocco."

"Skiatho? Who's he? First time ya ever mentioned his name."

"Skiatho is-a da ghost-a who come aroun' dis-a place when-a Rocco come aroun'. He no hurt you. By and-a by you gonna see."

Jules's eyes widened, and he shouted, "See! A ghost!" Rocco's drunk, he thought. The stench finally got to him. He's playin' with my head. I don't think it's funny.

Some-a-time deez-a ghost-a play aroun', dey no like when-a stranger come in dis-a place. You just-a relax, pretty soon dey go away."

Rocco grabbed a 2 by 4 and smashed the dangling burned-out light bulb, and shouted, "Dis-a get fixed too, for sure!"

Suddenly, the room started to vibrate, something frightening was happening, the vibration became furious, it shattered a section of glass from the window and a blast of wind howled all round, newspapers and boxes were blowing around as if they were feathers. The floors creaked and cracked and wood-dust and debris whirled around everywhere. Suddenly, it stopped. Jules had never witnessed a phenomenon such as this before. Perhaps a balmy demon had been jarred from it's quietude, and was not to thrilled with Rocco's temper.

Damn! Jules thought. I'm in no mood to be sympathetic to Rocco. I gotta get outa this creepy place. Then he felt a strong grip around the back of his neck. He became paralyzed and couldn't move. His eyes faded into darkness. Oh, God, I'm a gonner. He thought, how can this be happenin'? His eyes cleared, he could see again. What if they take me away? Who will take care of my Mama? Holy sheeeit, where's Rocco? They possessed him--holy Christ-- Rocco's gone!...Oh God, gotta find--"

The grip loosened. Suddenly, he was being shaken vigorously. He heard Rocco's voice, "Why you like statue? Maybe you afraid of-a da ghost-a?

"I-I, I'm ok-I'm ok just dreamin' Rock, tired I guess."

"No be alarmed, deez are friends of Rocco. Disa place has many ghosts. Dey like-a to come aroun' when Rocco come aroun'. I can-a see da ghosts some-a-times--some-a are little boys an-a girls, some-a are beautiful women, an-a once in-a while, Rocco can-a see a handsome Greek-a gambler, he try to give Rocco a pair of dice-a but Rocco no take em. Rocco no no why. I call-a special man one-a day, he know all about deez strange-a tings. He look up-a an-a down, he look to da four winds. By and by he say to Rocco, da wine-a an-a alcohol in-a da air make-a you drunk. He no convince me. C'mon-a, Rocco gonna show you some-a-ting very special."

Jules thought, that's it, makes sense. The air down here is full of a blend of alcohol, stale wine 'n decayed mildew. I have to read about hallucinations and apparitions. I gotta read about the whole experience. What happened a little while ago convinced me it was real, alright.

Rocco set the candle in the dirt floor facing an unusual wooden door. It was five feet high by five feet wide. He turned the white ceramic doorknob counterclockwise and pulled it open. The white ceramic doorknob was out of place here. The door was thick and squeaked as Rocco pushed it against the wall.

Jules thought, jeez, Rocco must have his life savings in there. The place is a fortress fer Chris' sake.

Rocco bent over supporting himself against the door frame and reached in the corner. His arm wandered around in the darkness in the hope he'd find what he is looking for.

He shouted, "Ma funfoo, where is-a dat locker! Rocco put em over he." He dragged his knees a step or two, "Rocco got em now, some-a-bitch!" He laughed and grunted as he pulled out a footlocker; it had cobwebs all around, a heavy coat of dust and ashes. Suddenly, the room went into darkness. The only light came from the stained glass window. Rocco accidently knocked over the candle.

"Today no Rocco's day. Dare's a light over he some-a-place." His arm wandered around and his fingers grabbed onto a kerosene lamp. He lit it and the room glowed with light. "Now dat-sa nice-a." He set it on the floor, then pointed at a soiled rag near Jules, "Hand to Rocco da rag near you hand-a."

"Got it." Jules handed it to him, "Sure is nice havin' light aroun' here."

"You gotta dat right." He wiped the top of the locker. Rocco said, "When-a my Papa die, he give to me dis locker. He say to me his great-a great-a grandpapa make dis by hand-a. Rocco try an-a try to make sense out-a dis-a game but Rocco give up, no understand. Dis-a game in-a-side is-a very-very complex-a. So Rocco put em away where no body can-a find."

Jeez Rock, what kind-a game is it?"

"You gonna see."

"Can ya at least give me a clue?"

"You ask-a Rocco what da game is? Is dat-a what you say?"

"Yes. C'mon, yer teasin' me."

"If Rocco give you clue, you gonna know. An-a if you know, dare is-a no surprise. Capeech?"

"Yer headstrong alright."

"Maybe so. And-a Rocco know you gotta overflow in-a da brain. In-a dis-a locker should-a be a piece a cake for you. Rocco tell you some-a-ting more. Dis-a locker, Rocco give to you."

"You gotta be kiddin'! Should this be for Mario? He is your only son an' everything or maybe you forgot?"

"No-no. Mario's brain-a go coo-coo some-a-times, ever since his Mama gotta killed in car accident. Dis-a not for Mario, an-a beside's, he no understand deez-a tings. We talk another time about Mario. For now, Rocco show you some-a-ting."

After Rocco cleaned the footlocker, Jules stared at the

beautiful handcrafted olive trees carved in a circular design on the top center of the locker. He stepped in closer to get a better look; it was 47 inches long by 25 inches high by 36 inches wide.

Jules thought, what unusual dimensions, this is out of the ordinary. The dark stained finish is rich. Will ya look at that!

Each corner had a hand-pounded brass plate, and thick leather grips on each side. There appeared to be no lock. Jules touched the engraved olive tree on the top.

"Ya know Rocco, these olive trees represent the sign of power and lasting life." He thought, God, whatever's in here must have something to do with a special Greek game of some kind. I should know, I've read all about those people. I'm dyin' to see what's inside.

Rocco looked at Jules with a confused face. "Rocco no know dis-a about olive tree." He looked at the olive trees on the top of the locker and touched them. "You know Jules, Rocco no ever tink about dis-a, but you right about power an-a long-a life. Da room Rocco give you, at's all you see is-a olive tree an-a da leaves all over da place. It'sa gotta mean some-a-ting more dan power an-a long-a life, no?"

"No. The olive tree or the leaves mean the same. It's the same as wearin' a St. Jude metal aroun' yer neck or a rabbit foot, know what I mean?"

"Ohhhh, Rocco remember now. You make-a Rocco's brain-a not to forget anymore."

"Awww, yer puttin' me on. You know more than you want people to think."

"Okay, you watch Rocco." He placed his right palm on one of the corner brass plates, pushed down, at the same time turning it clockwise until it clicked open. Then he reached for the other brass plate and did the same thing except this time he turned the brass plate counterclockwise until it clicked open. A moment later, the top slowly opened automatically and it click-locked in position. "You see how Rocco open? One-a side one-a way, da other side opposite way. Capeech?"

"I caught that move--clever."

"Look-a. When you want to close top-a, all you gotta do is put-a back da two brass-a plates in-a da same position they were an-a close em up."

"I understand. This is art in the wildest form."

Rocco scratched his head. He looked inquisitive. "Rocco no understand what you say."

"Oh, I'm sorry. What I mean is, well, the mechanical way it opens and everything, a genius had to put it together, it's a form of art. Now do you understand?"

Rocco shouted, "Why you no say dat in-a first place! My great-a, great-a gran-a-papa make dis, I told you before. He was-a brilliant-a man, my Papa told me dis. His brain-a no come to me.

Okay, now, you look over he an-a pay attention...I no know, maybe da ghost come out." He laughed. "Maybe we gonna see."

Jules didn't laugh. He sat on his calves and rested his palms under his chin and at the same time stretching his neck looking over Rocco's shoulder to see what was in the locker. Suddenly, Jules felt something strange in the room, something cold and eerie.

"I f-feel kinda strange, Rocco. It's s-spooky in here all of a sudden. Is it me or do you feel it too?"

"Rocco feel the same as you. All-a-time Rocco open locker, dis-a ghost come out. My Papa told Rocco dis-a ghost hang aroun' all-a time. Rocco no ever see him but can feel some-a-ting. He no hurt you. Maybe he just-a want to see who Rocco give dis-a locker too, at's all. I figure out some-a-ting, many times Rocco try an-a try to understand dis-a game but Rocco fail, dis-a ghost no help me either. Rocco come to conclusion, he no like me. So Rocco close em up da locker an-a hide in-a secret place. No more Rocco try."

Holy sheeeit, what am I gettin' into, Jules thought. Awwww, wait a minute, Rocco's tryin' to scare me, that's it. we're havin' a reoccurrence of the stench down here. B-but, the feelin' down here is there. I'll just play it by ear. Ohhh, God."

"You can-a see okay?"

"Yeah. This is excitin'--especially with that ghost aroun'.

He feels like a friendly guy, after all, he's only a ghost, right Rocco?"

Suddenly, the eerie feeling in the room vanished.

Jules whispered in Rocco's ear, "Did you feel something leave the room or am I crackin' up?"

"Dat-sa awright, dis happen some-a-time. Now shut-a you face--watch Rocco, you gonna see every-ting. Dis-a kid can-a come up-a wid some fancy words, for sure. He thought. He gonna be surprised when he see what is in locker.

Rocco raised the lantern to see better. The light frightened two large snakes that were entwined together inside on top of a folded green felt cloth.

Jules bolted back, and shouted, "Look out!"

Rocco leaned forward and reached in the locker, and in a surprised voice, he said, "Ohhhhh, dares my bambinos, Rocco look all over for youuuuuu. Papa here now."

Jules didn't hear Rocco talking to the snakes. He shouted, "Holy sheeeit, what the fuck ya doin'! Ya blowin' yer top er wha'! Those are killer snakes, get out-a there-get out-a there! He grabbed the back of Rocco's shirt and pulled him away from the snakes. The lantern dropped to the floor, extinguishing the light. The room was in total darkness. Rocco lay on his back, confused about what happened. Jules's pants were wet from urine. He looked at Rocco, feeling good about saving his life.

"Are ya ok Rock?

Rocco lay on his back, and didn't move. Jules could barely see him but could make him out enough to see Rocco was hurt.

"Rocco! Rocco!" Jules shook him lightly. Rocco! God, what the hell did I do to you!" He grabbed Rocco's chin, and in a frenzy he shook his head. Nothing. No response. He's dead, Jules thought. The snakes got him good. I better get some--"

"I'm-a da ghost. It'sa time Rocco leave an-a go to live wid da devil." Rocco said, in a low monotone voice.

Jules bolted back from fright, "Wha!"

Rocco sat up quickly, and howled as if he were a coyote.

Jules looked around the dark room, trembling, "W-what's goin' on!" He shouted.

"Rocco fool aroun' wid you. Rocco make you tink-a Rocco die forever. You all-a right?" He gave out a rugged laugh then lit the kerosene lantern.

Jules was relieved. He hugged Rocco as he did with his Papa a long time ago, "Ya had me scared there for a while. I'm sorry I knocked ya down, those snakes could-a killed ya for Chris' sake."

Rocco embraced Jules with his half arm and patted his back while talking, "You no hurt Rocco. It'sa gonna take maybe more dan one bull-a-dozer to harm-a Rocco."

"But the snakes, I don't understand!"

"Deez-a my pets-a, dey no hurt you. Now you shut-a you mouth for now, Rocco talk about my pets-a later."

"Yer a fun guy, even though my pants are all wet."

"An-a today you save Rocco's life, no?"

"B-but how did they get in the locker? An' how could they survive without food an' --"

"Shhh, Rocco gotta see some-a-ting." He examined the locker all around and found a small hole on the bottom portion of the locker in the back. "Ah-huh, some-a-bitch, my pets-a go in-a-side from hole over he. Rocco forget to fix em up. Dey like where it'sa warm. Rocco no know what dey eat, dey look-a healthy to Rocco."

Rocco picked up his pet snakes and put them in a empty wood case. He adjusted the wick in the lantern for a brighter light.

Awright. Now Rocco show you in-a-side locker."

Suddenly, the strange feeling came back in the room. The top of the locker slammed shut, even though it was locked-open. The wine bottles vibrated and the dirt floor whirled around the footlocker. Jules and Rocco covered their eyes. Then it happened...

CHAPTER 10

NEW YORK, JANUARY IO, 1930

3:15 P.M.

A soft spoken voice said, "I am here to help, you will see."
Then a calmness filled the room. Jules looked at Rocco, and
said, "Did you hear a voice or was it my imagination?"

Dis-a ghost, Rocco hear all-a time. No worry, dis-a guy is-a
okay. He try to help Rocco but my brain-a no understand. C'mon-a,
Rocco show you now."

He opened the locker and pulled out a green felt tablecloth
and lay it on the floor. Then reached back in and took out a
folded handcrafted card table and held it; he asked Jules to help
him unfold it and set it up. Once the legs were propped open,
Jules turned the table right-side up. It was large enough for a
dealer and six players.

"You put-a cloth on-a table for Rocco." He guided himself up
holding on the locker. Jules draped the felt cloth over the table;
it was forty-five inches wide by eighty-three inches long. There
were thirteen painted cards in the center forming a rectangular
sequence; looking at the cards from the front of the table from
left to right, top row: King, Queen, Jack, ten, nine and eight.
Under the eight, to the right 5 inches, the seven. Second row from

right to left: six, five, four, three, two and Ace. The King,
Queen and Jack's attire were that of 100-44 B.C. The Ace had a
large black spade in the center with a white background. Each of
the other cards had no numbers, the number of spades on each card
represented the number. Five inches above the Jack, a white
rectangle the size of two playing cards, with the words LOSE was
printed boldly. To the right of the LOSE rectangle, another
rectangle with the word WIN was printed. Above the LOSE/WIN
boxes, center, closest to the end of the table, was a solid white
rectangle, the size of a playing card. The dealer obviously
positioned himself here. Jules leaned over the locker while Rocco
opened the top of one of the three compartments. This compartment
contained multicolored chips; burgundy, lime green, oyster shell
and black neatly stacked. The compartment was seven inches wide by
twenty inches long by seven and 1/4 inches deep. Each chip had an
octagonal shape and was made of walnut. In the center of each chip
was a miniature olive tree hand carved to the exactness. Jules
lightly touched them, brushing his fingertips over the olive
trees.

Rocco took out a few and handed them to Jules, "You take,
they no bite. Deez-a most beautiful chips Rocco ever see, what-a-
you tink-a, huh?"

"Jeez Rock, there so heavy." He rolled them around in his
palm and gently felt the rich texture with his fingertips, "They

feel like silk the way they slip through the fingers an everythin'."

"Rocco knows. Many times I play aroun' wid em. Rocco put em back for know. Rocco show you some-a-ting more."

Rocco put the chips back. Abutting the chip compartment, he opened another compartment the same size. It contained several decks of cards sealed in wood containers. He took out a deck.

"Look at dis." He pulled the cards out of it's container, lay them on the table and fanned them in a straight line, then in one fast movement, flipped the cards over, "See, Rocco no get rusty."

"Fantastic! Yer the best."

Each card had an unusual design on the face; it had an assortment of colors; in the center was a tiny circle that gradually got larger and larger, it had the effect of ripples, each having it's own color. The border was gold and silver. If one stared at it long enough, one would feel light-headed. The King, Queen, Jack and Ace were the size of the card, and a small spade was in the upper left hand corner. The deuce had two large spades which represented the deuce. The number of spades on each card represented the card number.

Rocco looked at Jules, and in a firm voice, he said, "You look-a deez cards, tell Rocco if-a some-a-ting wrong. Pick em up, Rocco wait for answer."

Jules inspected the cards thoroughly, "God, these cards are

like butter, never felt them like this. There's something about them that make me feel as if I'm in complete control--it's kinda weird, if ya wanna know the truth." He handed the deck to Rocco.

"I tink-a you weird-a." Rocco pulled a card from the deck and handed it to Jules.

"You try again. Look. Feel every-ting-a. Go ahead, touch-a up-a an-a down, all-a corners."

Jules felt the cards, he slid his finger up and across and down but couldn't seem to find whatever he was suppose to find. He handed the deck back to Rocco. "I have to say Rocco, the cards are genuinely the works of an artist of the highest degree. Outside of that, they're very unusual. I'm sorry, I can't find anything uncommon or curious. Did I overlook something I should know about?"

"Maybe Rocco to tough wid you dis-a time." He pulled a card and put it in front of Jules's face, "Look, see over he? Da card in-a da corner, it-sa shaved just-a right so we know da card face up-a or face down-a. We say in-a business, "read-a," dis is-a how to "read-a" da cards."

"I should have known better--heard about it but actually never seen them. Now that I know, it's obvious."

"Rocco teach you how to do dis-a soon. You like to know how to "read-a?"

"Sounds great, can't wait. Can you show me that move again,

you know, when you had the cards on the table, spread em and
flipped em over? I'm havin' a problem with that one."

"No now, Rocco show you more in-a locker first-a. Rocco show
you in-a couple-a days--just-a practice many times, at's all."

"I'll never be as good as you."

Rocco squeezed Jules's cheek, "Rocco no ever hear you talk
negative before, what'sa wid you talk like-a dis? In-a fact, you
gonna be da best-a of da best-a, you see, Rocco tell da truth."

He grabbed the cards, cut them then cut them again, this time
cutting them three ways through his fingers and palm then quickly
flipped them together in one swift movement, in one hand. He
tapped the cards on the table to square them then slipped the
cards into there container and put them back in the compartment.
Jules was stupefied, the excitement of Rocco's moves left Jules's
mouth hang open. Rocco's reflexes were super fast, he could catch
a fly in mid air. Jules witnessed this event on many occasions.
Rocco reached to the bottom of the locker and brought out
something wrapped in leather and tied with rawhide.

"You take-a da string off an-a open em up on-a table."

Jules carefully took the package from Rocco and he gently lay
it on the table.

"Open em up careful, dis-a leather very dry, you can-a see."

Rocco got up and leaned on the table watching Jules. He had a
smile, and thought, Jules is-a gonna love-a dis. Rocco is-a happy

to give locker to my friend-a.

"Boy, this is dried out, you should put some olive oil on it, it will preserve it."

"At'sa good idea. Dis-a belong to you now, you know what-a to do."

Jules carefully unfolded the leather wrap. His eyes widened. An abacus! He thought. This is the most beautiful piece of art I ever seen! He was so excited his voice turned to a whisper.

"Oh my God, t-this is not real, it's out of a dream!" He gasped for air, then looked at Rocco, "Never seen a abacus anything like this before, never! And I studied them from way back. Jesus, Rocco, I-I'm lost for words."

The abacus was made of dark walnut; six and one-half inches wide by eleven and one-quarter inches long in it's folded position; two small metal hinges attached on the inside frame made it convenient to swing open; the total length opened was thirteen inches; embedded side by side in the bottom half, seven miniature cards, two inches by one and one-half inches appeared; from left to right, all in spades: ace, deuce, three, four, five, six and a blank box. On the upper half, seven cards embedded side by side, right to left: seven, eight, nine, ten, Jack, Queen and King of spades. On the bottom portion below each card was four one-half inch ivory buttons attached to a four sixteenth metal rod. Each button easily slipped up and down. The buttons attached to the rod

in the upper half were the same, the only difference, they were
above each card.

Jules gently pushed the ivory buttons up and down, they
functioned as smoothly as a finger touching silk, but stayed in
position if the abacus were jolted briskly or picked up upside
down.

"You like-a dis, no?" Rocco said, with a concerned smile.

Jules didn't look at Rocco, he was hypnotized by this
uncommon abacus. Why me, he thought. That's all I have to do is
figure out this game, but why me? Maybe because this is the way
I'm gonna be rich?...That's it...I'm gonna be rich with this game!

Rocco raised his voice. "Ma, what you tink about? It look to
Rocco, you brain-a some-a-place Rocco no know about, huh?" He
laughed.

Jules snapped out of it and looked at Rocco with total
appreciation for the magnificent gift Rocco had given him.

"Rocco, I can't tell you what this means to me. There is no
gift in the world that could come close to this. I'll treasure it
for the rest of my life." He went up to Rocco and gave him a big
hug. Jules thought of the beautiful moments he had with his Papa
and the most devastating, when he threw his Papa down the stairs.
He sobbed and hung on to Rocco.

"You no have to cry, my son-a. Rocco justa give you disa
locker."

"W-well, it is the most beautiful gift--"

"Rocco know-Rocco know, but-a you forget, you must-a figure dis-a game out-a, capeech?"

Jules let go of Rocco, and stepped back. "I'll figure this puzzle out, it may take a while but I'll put the pieces together."

"At's good. Now, go in-a locker, in-a da udder compart-a-ment an-a you gonna see two small-a box--bring to Rocco."

Jules wiped his eyes with his shirt sleeve, went to the locker and found the two small boxes then gave them to Rocco.

"Come-a close to Rocco." He lay the boxes on the table and opened one. There were several pairs of dice neatly stacked. They were genuine ivory. He took out a pair and handed them to Jules.

"You see deez-a dice? Deez-a very special an-a made to win-a. In-a da business we say, deez-a dice are "fixed". Go ahead, you shoot 'em on-a table." Rocco placed a two by four across the far end of the table for a back-stop.

Jules scrambled the dice around in his hand, he felt a mysterious power, a craving deep down in his stomach, an ache so strong that once he released the dice, he felt he would be invincible; in complete control. He rested his hand on the table, opened his fingers and slowly let the dice roll onto the green felt cloth. A seven appeared. A questionable look became visible upon his face as he reached to pick up the dice for another try. His hand and fingers scooped them up then he dropped them again. A

seven. He eagerly reached for the dice. His hand somehow couldn't
grab them; something prevented his hand to move forward; he could
feel a power of some kind holding his hand dead fast. Suddenly,
his hand was deliberately pushed down on the dice. He wanted to
comprehend this uncanny incident but he wasn't allowed; he was not
in control with his thoughts. He scooped up the dice and locked
them in his palm. His expression reversed from questionable to
daring, he thought, Jesus, I must be blowin' my top, I don't
believe this! Something is forcing me to roll these dice! I can't
resist! Okay-okay, just go with the flow Jules baby, just go with
the flow. He relaxed, shook the dice vigorously then rolled them
across the table into the back-stop. A seven. He felt his heart
pounding from this extraordinary incident; an aura of superiority
surrounded him. One of little faith could not comprehend this
phenomenon if present. He made ten more rolls over the table
smashing the dice against the back-stop; a seven or an eleven
appeared each time. It was spine tingling, and at the same time
he felt corrupt. Deep down, he felt aglow, but no one would have
ever suspected it. For some reason, he couldn't let his excitable
feelings show; a uncanny force seemed to take over Jules's body
when he rolled the dice; his normal excitable expression had
turned into a cold vicious one. He felt as though he had been
possessed by a demon. With the dice out of his hand he was able to
think clearly.

"What you tink-a, huh? Deez-a dice-a give you big-a head for sure, no?" He laughed, and messed Jules's hair with his fingers.

"These dice are weird too, Rocco. It seems like when I pick them up, well...something strange happens."

"Rocco know dis. It's-a da ghost. He try to help you keep a straight-a face. All-a professional dealers must-a have face-a like stone. When-a you cheat at da tables wid udder players, dey watch-a you face all-a time. Rocco know dis-a all-a time, but he no help Rocco wid da rest of game. No be afraid, you gonna be da master." He patted Jules on his hand. "Rocco go to jon-a over dare, Rocco come right-a back." He lit the candle and took it with him into a small room where the toilet was.

Jules thought, I don't believe Rocco, I mean, here's a agnostic guy, and yet he tells me about his friend the ghost; his great-great grandfather. Good ol' Rock has either lost his marbles an' takin' me along or he's already there. He picked up the dice, and suddenly felt the power and inner feeling he had before. He rolled the dice to the center of the table--a seven. He threw the dice six more times, all were sevens or elevens. Unbelievable, amazing, Jules thought, I'll have plenty of time to figure this game out. Maybe I'll even get acquainted with our friend, the ghost. Hey now, I need all the help I can get. I'll ask Rocco if he knows the first name of our invisible friend. He rubbed his temples and began trembling in his upper arms. What the hell is this? Why am I shakin'? He thought.

Rocco came back. "Ahhh, nutting like a gooda piss-a. You
gotta go?"

"I already did! My pants, remember?"

Rocco laughed. At'sa right, you go when-a you see my pets-a."

Jules didn't pay much attention to Rocco, his mind was
in deep thought thinking of what took place with the dice.

"What's-a wrong wid you?" Rocco grinned and scratched his
head. "You look-a to me like-a da ghost come aroun'."

Jules just starred at the dice on the table. "No. I-I, just
thinkin'."

"What you tink about? Tell Rocco. Rocco know about lots-a
tings, no be afraid."

Jules looked at Rocco with a confused look painted on his
face. "This is weird. When I was throwin' the dice, it felt as
though somebody else had control. Then when I left the dice on the
table, my upper arms started to tremble. Why?"

Rocco put his arm over Jules's shoulder, "You know, Rocco no
believe in-a God-a an-a deez-a tings, an-a when Rocco open em up
da locker for first-a time an-a roll-a da dice, Rocco shake too.
Dis go away when-a you understand how you must-a look in-a you
face an-a da feeling you feel in-a side you gut. No be afraid,
Rocco's greata, greata gran-a-papa will help you, Rocco promise
you dis-a. Rocco believe da ghost is-a true. You must-a believe

wid all-a you heart too--no be like-a Rocco, an-a give a hard time to him, dats-a why he no like Rocco. Dis-a ghost have lots-a patience, but Rocco no have dis-a patience, capeech?"

Jules thought, oh God, I don't believe this bullshit, but I'll go along with it. "Tell me Rock, do you remember your great-great grandfather's name?"

"Ma-sure. His-a name, they call, Skiatho. He was-a born in-a Greece, at's all Rocco know. Maybe if Rocco took-a more interest an-a investigate every-ting-a about him, Skiatho like Rocco more, I no know for sure."

"Yer a strange guy, but I love ya just the same."

Rocco took his arm off Jules's shoulder. He looked confused. His eyes became snaky, and they pierced into Jules's like he seen when he was mad about something.

"What you mean when-a you say strange?"

"Well, I meant that as a compliment. Your a curious guy is what I mean, yer extraordinary, somethin' very special, you know. I would have never believed you could even come close to believing in ghosts--don't get me wrong, I respect that. I just find it bizarre an' inconceivable, that's all, know what I mean?"

Rocco rested his hand over Jules's shoulder again. He squeezed it a little and let up a little while he spoke. "Rocco know for sure what you say. But-a you must-a understand, when you roll-a deez dice-a, in-a side you heart, you get excited, you

feel-a very-very strong-a--like-a you have much-much power--an-a
you know some-a-ting? You do! At'sa because you know you gonna
win all-a time you roll-a deez bones. Dis-a feeling never, never,
ever go away. Now, for last time-a Rocco tell you dis-a. An-a
Rocco tell-a you dis-a too, Rocco like-a compliment when you say,
Rocco strange." He laughed, and shook Jules by his shoulder.
Jules rubbed his chin with his fingers and concentrated on Rocco's
wisdom. I'm trying to understand, but have doubt. Jules thought.
I'll understand the whole thing after awhile. Rocco has never let
me down. I guess this is all to much in one day.

Rocco squeezed Jules's shoulder muscle real hard to get a
response. "You dream again? You pay attention what Rocco say?"

Jules jumped back from the excruciating pain. "Ouuuuch!
Jesus, that hurts! Why'd you do that for?"

Rocco laughed. "It look to me like-a you tink about some-
a-ting, an-a you no pay attention to Rocco--dis-a squeeze work
all-a time."

Jules laughed. "Yeah, that's for sure." He massaged his
shoulder muscle, "Beautiful Rock. I heard every word you said. I'm
a fast learner, you know that. I'll work hard on this game. I'm
impressed. Ya know, yer closer to me than my Papa, and I just want
you to know I appreciate everything yer teachin' me." He squeezed
Rocco's shoulder muscle as hard as he could--he didn't flinch or
even look like he felt pain. "Holy sheeeit, didn't you feel that!"

Rocco laughed. "Rocco no feel dis-a pain."

"God!" What a brute. Jules thought.

Rocco dropped his head. "Rocco feel-a pain when-a my wife die." He paused a moment, wiped a tear and looked at the locker. "Dats-a dat. Now-a, da last ting-a in-a da locker is-a extra table cloth. At's all we got-a left. You no have to take em out. Maybe you have some-a-ting to say for Rocco?"

"I have good feelings about this beautiful gift, Rocco."

"Dats-a good-dats-a good, go ahead-a, talk-a to Rocco."

"Don't take this the wrong way, promise?"

Rocco raised his voice, "Ma, you gonna put Rocco to sleep-a. Talk-a! Talk-a!"

"Well, I'm just being honest, but I think this game was meant for me, that's all, know what I mean?"

"Rocco know exactly what you say." Rocco was content to know Jules would keep the footlocker alive.

"I'll treasure this for the rest of my life. Thank you with all my heart."

He embraced Rocco and kissed him on his rough unshaven face.

Rocco shed a tear as he wrapped his arms around Jules, and whispered, "You good-a boy, you good-a boy. You da best-a, you gonna see."

Deep down in Rocco's heart, he had always wished his son Mario was like Jules.

"Ats-a good for now, c'mon-a, we put away every-ting-a an-a bring in-a you room. Rocco got-a business to do."

Everything was placed back into the locker. When Jules click-closed the top, something felt absent from the room. Something Jules became a part of suddenly vanished. Something that will make him....

CHAPTER 11

NEW YORK, FEBRUARY 13, 1932

2:45 A.M.

Three years later, on a damp night, a black sedan slowly moved along past several parked cars. It stopped in front of Rocco's Restaurant. The visibility was fifty or fifty-five percent. The low clouds almost caressed the sidewalk, then would abruptly flow away finding a new place. On this occasion, the mist covering the black sedan drifted away making it plain to see. A chauffeur dressed in a black uniform got out of the car and opened the rear door. A big bulky man got out puffing on a long cigar. When he exhaled, the smoke dawdled around his face; it was difficult to distinguish the person. The black fedora he was wearing had its brim bent down all around and had a one-inch leopard skin band around the rim. His ankle length black cashmere coat had a quarter inch border of leopard skin along the collar and down the border of the buttonholes. Before he buttoned his coat, his hand adjusted a bulge in his pants pocket then he buttoned his coat. He nervously studied the area for a moment with a cocky smile, and checked the time from his pocket watch. Two men came out of the restaurant looking happy. They stared at him for a moment and walked away as if he was never there. When all appeared clear, he walked to the entrance, turned to the chauffeur, nodded his head, and the black sedan quietly departed. He turned his head facing the street light, his face was clear, Tony Cheese is his name. Heavy loser. He got his name when he first opened his business many years ago. He stood on the sidewalk in front of his Italian Deli and gave free samples of cheese to people passing by; a front, to promote his thriving business. He had a specialty--luring young girls in his store for job interviews; excellent pay, including a guaranteed lay-down bonus. He was a perverted pimp. He bribed the girls to the back room for sexual favors then eventually hooked them on alcohol and other entertainment. In time, they would be working for him as streetwalkers. He had accumulated six houses of prostitution, and controlled more than one hundred-twenty prostitutes, keeping the lonely and unfaithful and politicians and police department and many other influential people discretely content. He also had a sophisticated escort service equal to none.

Tony Cheese was a big beefy individual with greasy blue-black hair combed straight back. His matching eyebrows were thick, bushy and grew together leaving no space in the center. The bridge of his nose had been broken at one time leaving a medium sized lump; his nostrils were large and hairy. Deadly black eyes, close together. Absent of eyelashes, he darkened his lower eyes with pencil. Thick lips. Yellowish brown stained teeth with a separation between the two central incisors. A thin rat-tail mustache darkened mostly with pencil. Oily, shiny dark complexion. Several pock marks inlaid on his fat cheeks. He had an odor about him that smelled like burned garlic. He knew what he smelled like,

and didn't care about offending anybody. He was Tony Cheese. His
wardrobe consisted of the same clothing. He always wore a black
fedora with a fine three-sixteenth of an inch leopard skin band
around the brim, and a his black cashmere coat had leopard skin
trim surrounding the collar. He was five feet seven inches tall,
his long coat made him look even shorter than he was. A neatly
pressed black suit, dark burgundy shirt, black tie and ankle high
Italian black shoes. He never has been seen dressed in anything
else or smelled any different.

He pushed on the buzzer next to the door, and nodded a
greeting to the doorman.

"Evenin' Mis-fer C." Trip, the doorman said. He wasn't the
brightest doorman around, just a big brawny brute.

It had been customary to use last initials only in Rocco's.
Cheese ignored the doorman as if he were beneath him. Trip
escorted Cheese through the crowded bar and up the rickety stairs
to the second floor where another doorman, standing flat footed
recognized Cheese and nodded approval for him to enter. Without
an escort, Cheese walked slowly looking around the room of
chattering clamoring gamblers hoping to find someone. He
continued walking slowly past the crap, blackjack and roulette
tables to the back of the room where cashiers were counting stacks
of money and paying off gamblers, under the watchful eye of a six
foot, two-hundred fifty pound guard with cold snaky eyes dressed

in a black tuxedo. The guard gave Cheese a insincere smile as he
reached his hand in his jacket to a slight bulge; obviously it
wasn't a baseball bat.

The guard stared at Cheese, nodded his head and admitted him
in the room with the red door. Cheese deliberately bumped into the
guard giving him a dirty look. He murmured loud enough so the
guard could hear him.

"Fuckin' stupid-own, wid-out-a da bullets, you nut-ing."

Once inside the room, Cheese's eyes were instantly fixed on
Rocco talking with Jules in the back. Rocco felt Cheese's stare
somehow and pretended not to see him.

Rocco softly said to Jules, "Ma, what-a Cheese here for? He
lost-a over seven thousand dollars last-a week. Dat should-a
cleaned em out-a. He's up to no good-a, Rocco know."

Jules looked in the direction where Cheese lingered.

Rocco kicked Jules's foot, "No let Cheese-a see you look at
him. Dis-a man gotta black-a death on-a da face. He want some-a-
ting from Rocco--he come over he."

Mario came over to ask his father something, "Papa, Papa, I'm
starving, we gonna eat something pretty soon?"

"No now. Papa gotta unexpected business to take care of. You
an-a Jules have some-a-ting my tough-a guy." He messed Mario's
hair with his fingers, "Papa no be long."

"We'll wait for you, Papa. We'll hang around here."

Mario grabbed Jules's hand, "C'mon, lets play cards."

As soon as Jules and Mario left Rocco, Cheese walked casually toward Rocco. Cheese came within an arms length and stopped. He stared at Rocco while blowing smoke in his face then moved closer to him. Rocco could smell him the instant he was beside him, he stepped back. He would have shoved Cheese away but Rocco didn't want to create a scene--for the time being, that is.

"Mister Cheese-a, what-a bring you over he?" Rocco said, mannerly, then blew his cigar smoke in Cheese's face.

Cheese's cold snaky eyes pierced into Rocco's, then he smiled and stood there thinking, I'm gonna fix dis-a snake once an' for all. He tink's I'm one of his suckers aroun' here. We'll see about dat.

Rocco knew Cheese's smile was insincere. He knew the pig better than anyone else. And Rocco was on guard for just about anything.

Cheese leaned forward into Rocco's ear, "Important business. Gotta talk Rocco my friend-a, private."

Rocco turned to Mario. He gestured with his hand for him to come over. Mario came instantly and waited for his father to speak.

"Mario my son-a, you come-a quick like rabbit when-a Papa call." He messed Mario's hair, "At's-a good boy. Bring-a some vino to office for Mr. Cheese-a an-a Papa."

Mario ran off, and Cheese followed Rocco into his office. The door half closed. Rocco sat behind his desk, and Cheese's eyes studied the room.

"Sit down-a Mr. Cheese-a, you look-a up-a tight. What'sa trouble wid you? One-a you hooker girl-a-friends run away wid-a you cash?" He laughed.

Cheese laughed. Dat's a good one." He sat in the large leather chair, "Ahhhh, dis-a chair is comfortable."

Cheese sat back in the chair puffing on his cigar looking like a arrogant fanatic. Rocco just stared at him and didn't say a word. Dis-a man looks-a like some-a-tings up his sleeve. He thought. Rocco wait for him to talk-a first, he no fool me.

Rocco puffed on his cigar, rocked in his chair and stared at Cheese. Cheese looked around the room as if he was casing the place, but with the expression of approval painted across his face.

Cheese slowly leaned forward, "You have a unusually nice-a office, Rocco my friends-a. And-a somethin' else I wanna say, many people I know that come here, they like the entertainment, you know? But-a they never win. Maybe you should-a change some rules aroun' here--no disrespect to you my friend-a, my people are gonna go elsewhere, you understand? I know how to satisfy my customers, how come you no do the same?" He sat back and grinned, blowing smoke in Rocco's direction.

Rocco smiled and puffed on his cigar looking interested as he
nodded approval. "What you tink Mister Cheese-a, maybe you help
Rocco change-a da name? Maybe like-a--Rocco's an-a Cheese-a Pimp-a
House an-a Bistro?"

"No-no-no, my friend-a, the right-a name should-a be, Rocco's
Clip-a Joint!"

Rocco laughed. "You know Mister Cheese-a, Rocco like dis-a
name but Rocco no run a barber shop-a over he." His eyes bored
holes into Cheese's, a look Cheese didn't like.

Cheese turned his head the other way and blew his cigar smoke
out avoiding the look Rocco gave him. Cheese leaned forward and
looked around contemplating for the right words to come back with.
He clinched his fists, and raised his voice.

"I no understand, all I know is I got-a cheated. You robbed
seven grand from me, you took me good, whadaya gonna do about it!"

He wrinkled his brow and gave Rocco a dirty look, at the same
time boldly cracking his knuckles.

Rocco knew Cheese would panic if he grabbed him by his tie
and lifted him off the floor then shook him around a little, but
that would end the conversation. Instead, he leaned forward,
resting his arm on the desk and put-on a serious face. He
intentionally whispered in a mellow tone so Cheese would have to
lean forward to be close enough for Rocco to grab hold of him
should Rocco change his mind.

"Rocco no can hear so good today, you come-a close."

Cheese knew Rocco was playing games with him but he leaned forward anyway resting his arms on the desk and patting Rocco's hand.

"What are you gonna do, my friend-a?"

Rocco had the opportunity to grab hold of the snake, but he didn't. The time wasn't right; Mario would be coming in soon with the wine.

Rocco backed off, "You wait till-a now? You accuse-a Rocco of-a do some-a-ting dishonest? No-no, Mister Cheese-a. When-a everybody win-a, dey joyful an-a feel like big-a-shot. When-a dey lose, at's all dey do is-a cry like baby. But-a for sure, Rocco tink when-a you lose, you take it like a man-a!" He grabbed a telephone book, placed it under his chin and ripped it in half as if it was a piece of paper.

Cheese ignored Rocco's display of strength. His sneaky eyeballs turned as far to the right as they could possibly go in their sockets observing the half-closed door. He knew Mario would be coming in the room soon. He held himself back from doing what he came for. He couldn't make a minor detail destroy his game plan. Cheese looked back at Rocco then lay his cigar in a ashtray nearby.

In a forgiving voice, Cheese said, "Okay-okay my friend-a, I know you a strong Sicilian, but take it easy, Jesu Christ-a,

just-a because I'm-a born from Naples, why you make-a me feel
like peasant? Ma, I said some-ting to offend you? I don't mean
to have any dis-a-respect, you know Tony Cheese talk to you
straight-a. My only request-a is for you to listen to what I ask.
You can do this for a good customer like Tony Cheese-a, no?"

Rocco smiled and anticipated Cheese's sneaky way of trying
to talk and make things sound as if he was sincere, but Rocco had
his number. Cheese had a particular look in his eyes Rocco had
seen before, they were detrimental and cold, it was just a matter
of time before something would break out. Rocco just sat back
rocking in his chair remaining silent and studied Cheese.

"You no have nothin' to say, my friend-a?" He stared at Rocco
for a moment, there was complete silence until he started to moan,
"Ohhhhh, aghhh, somabitch-a, my back-a--I must-a sit more
comfortable, excuse me." Da fuckin' kid, where is he? Cheese
thought. Dis-a dumb asshole, he's-a makin' me lose my patience. He
cheated me, now he sits there like a big-a shot--ma-fungoo. Now
it's-a my turn to sit behind desk. Dat bastard shit-face kid
better get his ass in here or...

Cheese moaned as he adjusted his body in the chair.

"You wanna some-a-ting? Da pain she go away for sure." Rocco
said.

"No-no." Cheese adjusted himself to another position, "Ahhhh,
at'sa better...my back-a give me trouble once in a blue moon-a. I

gotta move aroun' once in a while, forgive me."

He stood up facing Rocco and pulled the chair forward until
he thought the chair was close enough to the desk then he sat
down. Easily, he raised his legs in a bent position, his feet
resting against the desk until he felt comfortable enough to know
the position was complete. He slowly dropped his legs to the
floor, all the while not looking suspicious. His plan to do what
he came for had been successful so far.

"Jesu Christ-a Rocco, I no come here to make-a you upset--I
want to ask you for a favor--I tell you straight. Ahh, shit, just-
a minoot-a, my pants-a, dey go in-a my ass-a--I can not talk-a
when I'm-a not comfortable." He stood up groaning and pulled his
pants down a bit then sat down. "Ahhhh, much-a better, maybe I
eat to much." He made this move for insurance, just in case Rocco
might have suspected him. He thought, now I'm ready. I wait five
minoots. Disa kid no gonna fuck em up my day.

Rocco's eyes watched every move Cheese made. He had a faint
smile as though he enjoyed Cheese and his garlic breath being
present. He looked content as he puffed on his cigar and made
smoke circles in the air. He remained silent.

Cheese leaned forward looking at Rocco as if his pants went
back in his butt.

"I give it to you straight. My home-a I'm-a losin', da wife,
she leavin' me wid-a my bambino in-a-side her--Jesu Christ-a,

Rocco, just-a grand, at's all I need, it will save much grief an-a sorrow--at's all I ask." He remained in a forward position staring at Rocco, waiting for him to reply.

"A loan-a? Rocco make-a you loan-a, dis-a no problem."

Rocco turned his chair, stood up to the large oil painting behind him, flung it back, and dialed the combination on the safe behind it. Mario came in. Rocco turned his head at him and motioned to put the wine on the desk. The door behind didn't half-close like usual, it stayed three-quarters of the way open because Jules stood behind the door holding it with his foot listening to the conversation in the office. As Mario left the room, he noticed Jules standing behind the door with his finger over his lips so Mario wouldn't give his presence away. Mario stepped aside, across from Jules, out of view of his father and Cheese and decided to stay and listen too. Jules gestured to the boy to leave, but Mario defied Jules's hint and gave him a dirty look accompanied with a short sticking out of his tongue, at the same time pressing his ear against the wall to hear what his father and Cheese were up to, too. Jules gave him a dirty look and raised his fist, shaking it, meaning, get out of here. But Mario moved a little closer to the door with a wrinkled brow and held his post.

Heated, Jules slapped his forehead with the palm of his hand and looked up at the ceiling, and thought, that stubborn little prick, I'm gonna break his ass. I can't blow my cover now. He's gonna have to stay right where he is, goddam it!

Rocco reached in the safe, turned and lay the loose ten one-hundred dollar bills on the desk. Cheese raised his head slightly eyeing the cash then his sneaky eyes rolled up to the open safe. He slowly sat back in his chair with a blank face until Rocco turned his back to the safe. As Rocco rearranged some cash he had toppled over, Cheese's face suddenly turned into a savage beast; his eyes widened as he reached at his waist pulling out a knife. The switch-blade clicked open in mid air as Rocco stacked the overturned cash. Rocco heard the click from the knife and turned, too late, Cheese looked like a madman. Suddenly, his powerful legs shoved the desk into Rocco, slamming him against the wall, knocking him off-balance and aside. Wide eyed, and raging mad, Cheese shoved the desk again so he could get to the safe. He leaped forward, reached in the safe, and scooped as much cash as would fill his pockets, then backed towards the back door. Rocco snatched up the desk as though it were a toy, and shoved it at Cheese. Cheese fell on his rear, but managed to keep the knife. In one fast movement, he kicked the desk back, knocking Rocco off-balance and falling over a heavy chair. As he got up, Cheese lunged at Rocco, and plunged the knife into his side. At the same time, Rocco swirled around, the knife sticking from his side, and grabbed his baseball bat. Mario heard the commotion, ran into the office and screamed, "Papa! Papa!" His son's entry threw Rocco's concentration off, just long enough for Cheese to grab the knife from Rocco's side, and pull it out. Rocco dropped the baseball bat from the excruciating pain and swiftly grabbed the knife out of Cheese's bloody hand, and instantly slashed Cheese's face from his forehead, down his left cheek, ending at his lower left ear. He bolted back, at the same time, instantly covering the gash with his hands, compressing it. Blood streamed out through his fingers and hands spattering everyplace. His hands trembled as he dropped them palms up, to arms-length looking at the blood. Enraged, he looked at Rocco, slammed his fist through the wall then leaped at him, grabbing the knife from his hand and plunged it once again-- this time in the stomach, twisting the blade up into his heart. As he jerked out the knife, he gave out a triumphant snarl. Rocco fell to the floor. Cheese spit on him then bent down wiping his hands on his ripped shirt.

"You no get me dis-a time, my friend-a. So, I have a scare on-a my face-a now, like you--big-a deal. It will be a reminder." He laughed wildly, "Now you die on-a floor. Tony Cheese-a even da score wid da big-a man, Rocco D'Lucca." He laughed insanely.

Mario screamed, "No! No! What did you do to my Papa! What did you do! He leaped onto Cheese, biting a piece of flesh off his nose, scratching his ears and neck wildly. "I'll kill you! I'll kill you!"

Cheese snapped the boy off of him and through him against the wall as if he was a rag doll. Mario landed on his rear, but somehow felt no pain.

Cheese yelled out, at the same time pointing at the boy with his blood stained finger. "Fuckin' kid! Stay away or you gonna be hurt real-a good!"

Mario screamed back. "Fuck you creep! Yer gonna die, the slow way too, you'll see! Yer so dumb, half the money you stole is on the floor!" He just said that to throw Cheese off then he laughed.

Concerned, Cheese looked down. Mario's scheme worked. He got up from the floor and gave Cheese a smashing blow between his legs, then another.

Hysterically, Mario came back with a smart remark, "How's that for starters! Yer more stupid than I thought." He laughed insanely.

Cheese let out a painful groan and gradually melted to his knees. Mario continued laughing forgetting how close he was to Cheese. Suddenly, Cheese leaped forward grabbing Mario, he wrapped his arm around the boy like a anaconda, bringing him to his chest. He squeezed him and laughed at the same time. Mario could hardly breath. Out of pure desperation, Mario slammed the back of his head into Cheese's bloody face, causing him to drop the knife. He lowered the boy away from his face then flipped him around; facing his chest to Cheese's face. He squeezed him harder than before until Mario passed out.

In a brutal voice, Cheese said to Mario, "You tink I fool aroun' when I say you gonna get hurt good, huh? You just-a fuckin' wise-a guy. You play wid da big-a boys now!" He shook the boy like a madman. "Awwww, you no wanna talk now? At'sa good boy, you know who da boss is-a now." He laughed wildly.

By now, Jules was halfway across the floor, Cheese's eyes widened more than what they were.

Cheese yelled out, "Stop-a! You stop-a right where you are or da kid's back--I break!"

Jules slid to a stop, pointed at Cheese, and said in a firm voice, "Put the boy down Cheese, c'mon, he ain't got nothin' to do with you--put him down!" He trembled as he stood there, he wanted to kill Cheese, if only he could get his hands on him.

Cheese's eyes closed to a horrifying slight crack. Blood oozed from the gash on his face. He ripped off part of Mario's shirt and swirled it around his hand then held it on his bloody gash, then squeezed the boy harder. Mario let out a painful wheeze.

"Dis no nice you talk to me like-a dat, you should have more respect. An-a, you give threat to me?" Cheese said softly to Jules.

"No-no. I don't make threats, just promises--now, put the boy down." Jules said in a heated voice.

His eyes scanned the floor, looking for the baseball bat.

With a deadly smirk, Cheese growled and threw Mario's blood drench shirt from his face at Jules. He squeezed Mario until his back made an awful crunching sound; Cheese broke Mario's back. Mario screamed in agony. Blood streamed down Cheese's face as he threw the boy at Jules trying to block his path; poor Mario bounced and rolled two or three times and settled face up near his father. Suddenly, Jules tackled the heavy man, and ripped the pockets from his pants. With tears streaming from Jules's eyes, they both scrambled across the floor for the knife. Cheese snatched it up first, staggered to his feet, and aimed the knife at Jules. He looked at Jules, his eyes enraged, his face, hands, and clothing spattered and smudged with blood. He started laughing like a crazy man as he moved slowly back to the rear door, then he stopped. He acted as though nothing had happened. He reached for the bottom of his coat and brought it up to the jagged gash Rocco gave him and compressed it with one hand. With the other hand, he put the bloody blade of the knife into his mouth and sucked it, bringing it out slowly, leaving the blade clean. He spit it at Rocco then waved the knife at Jules with a deadly smirk.

"Mr. Cheese-a finished wid my visit over he. I got-a what I came for plus-a interest. Nobody beat Tony Cheese-a--nobody. Some-a-ting on your mind-a? Go ahead, talk-a." He patted his gash with his coat and laughed, "It feels to me Im-a have scare like-a Rocco. You gonna say some-a-ting? Maybe da cat got you tongue."

Jules felt helpless. For a moment, he wanted to leap at
Cheese, not caring about the knife. He wanted to kill him, push
him down the stairs, anything to end his life. But something held
him back; a force he had felt before, when he was in the basement
with Rocco, rolling the dice. Not only that, the odds were against
Jules, all the way, he couldn't possibly survive, not with a
deranged animal standing six feet away from him.

Jules's eyes penetrated into Cheese's. He had enough time to
compose himself, he said, softly, "Don't you think you should
leave? There's plenty of time, Cheese--plenty of time to catch up
with yer act. You may have never realized, but butchers like you
lose it after awhile, they have a tendency to get even with
themselves--you can only go downhill from here. Too bad, but
then, I don't make the rules."

Cheese grinned. His eyes widened. Suddenly, he snapped his
arm out and took a short step towards Jules, pointing the knife,
shaking it wildly.

"You like-a make promises to Tony Cheese-a, huh?"

Jules didn't flinch. He remained cool and forthright.

"Where did ya ever get that idea?"

Cheese broke-out with a erratic laugh, then it stopped
abruptly. He raised the knife over his head as if he was ready to
throw it into Jules's body.

Enraged, Cheese said, "Kid-a, you got big-a balls. I no

wanna see you on-a street, in-a jon-a--anyplace! You gonna look over you shoulder, for sure. I no know why, bad-a luck some-a da time come by, bing-a-banga-boom-a, it'sa all over--when-a you least expect." He laughed wildly and opened the door keeping the knife aimed at Jules. He turned to the stairs and swiftly made it to the first floor. The door exited to the rear parking lot was locked. In a frenzy, his powerful body smashed the private door open. He walked easy to his idling limousine nearby and got in. His elderly English chauffeur drove out of the lot cautiously. When the car reached the street, it leisurely drove off.

"Where too, Sir?" The chauffeur asked, looking at his master in the rear view mirror.

"Home-a, Antney...Home-a."

"Excellent sir. Your evening sir, it must have been quite a bloody success?"

"Lady luck-a come to me. Dis-a Rocco's place is good to me, Tony Cheese-a make a killin'." He laughed wildly.

Mario moaned in pain, Jules rushed over to Rocco, crouched down, and tried to stop the flow of blood with his handkerchief, his shirt, anything he could find. He shook his body.

"Rocco! Rocco! Say somethin'! Open yer eyes! Move! Do somethin'. He shook him again. Nothing.

"Jesus Christ! Rocco, get up! Sonofabitch, get up! Goddam!"

Jules looked at Mario with tear filled eyes, then back to

Rocco. He was confused but he did what he thought was right.

Jimmy, the dealer, and a few gamblers cautiously entered the office to check out the excitement. Jules lay his head on Rocco's stained chest, crying out, "Goddam Rocco, will ya get up! How am I gonna do this without you? How? How? Jules realized Rocco would never get up again.

Mario moaned, and uttered painfully, "J-Jules...h-help..."

Jules turned to him, and quickly, on his hands and knees, franticly went to his side. He wiped the boy's blood stained face and mouth with his T-shirt, tears rolling down his face.

The boy mumbled, "I-I...can't feel my l-legs."

Jules wiped his tears and dripping nose with the sleeve of his shirt, "It's okay kid, take it easy, we're gonna take you to the hospital right away. Don't move, just pray, try real hard, okay?"

"I w-will...can't move...s-scared." Mario whispered. His eyes slowly closed.

Jules looked up at the ceiling, and screamed, "Noooooo! God!"

The eight or ten curious gamblers, including, Jimmy "the Dealer", stood in their tracks, as if they had been frozen. Their faces had disbelief painted on them; they looked as if they were shot, but didn't know where.

Jules cried out desperately at them, "Call a ambulance! Call a ambulance! Anybody! Jesus Christ, the kid's dyin'!"

Mario's body trembled, it started to recoil. Jules grabbed the boy's hand, and held it firmly.

"Yer gonna be okay, I know you can hear me...just keep prayin'. You tell the boss upstairs to keep you aroun', we have things to do, places to go, people to see, just talk to him."

The small crowd didn't flinch; they were motionless, and remained bonded in their spot, obscure, and continued gawking at the tragedy.

Jules looked up at the crowd with deep concern, and shouted, "Somebody call a ambulance, for Chris' sake!"

He looked at everyone. He couldn't believe his eyes, or ears; not a word was spoken, they just stood their, frozen. His mind scrambled around insanely. He instantly got up, and grabbed the first person he could get his hands on. He slapped him four or five times across his face and shook him until his hairpiece fell off his head then shouted in his face.

"Get yer goddam ass out-a here, call a fuckin' ambulance, can ya hear me! Are ya in a coma!" Jules shoved the man against the wall, "What in God's name is wrong with you!" He squeezed the man's face and bounced his head against the wall. The man became alive. His eyes widened, and he ran out of the room, shouting wildly, "I'll make the call! I'll call-I'll call!"

Jules looked at the rest of the dumfounded gamblers, and shouted, "Can't you morons see the kid's dyin'? How would you feel if the fuckin' curtain was comin' down on you, instead of the kid!"

Suddenly, as if magic words were spoken, the crowd became active. Without delay, they stampeded out of the office like a herd of wild horses. The room had cleared, with the exception of two or three; they were still in mild shock, and glued in their tracks. Jules stepped back in disbelief, and yelled out, "The cops are raidin' the joint!" The two or three frozen in their tracks instantaneously came to their senses and charged out of the room, wordless.

Jules dropped to his knees next to Mario. The boy lay there breathing lightly, he recoiled from time to time.

"Mario! Mario!" Jules shouted, "Mario! Mario! Can you hear me!" He slapped Mario's face lightly trying to revive him but it didn't work. He took his pulse immediately; it was low, he checked again, it gradually got lower. Jules dropped Mario's arm, and screamed, "Oh God! Pleeease, pleeease, don't take him away too! I can take care..." He looked at Mario, the boy stopped breathing.

Jules screamed, "Nooooo! Nooooo! Whyyyyyyy!"

CHAPTER 12

NEW YORK, FEBRUARY 16, 1932

10:00 A.M.

Jules had a way about him that made people respect, love and never forget what he stood for; he refused to be cheap; he took pride in doing things the right way. At the cemetery, Father Faffaro, a friend of Jules was performing mass. A light steady rain came down. You could hear the pitter-patter of rain bouncing off nearly two hundred umbrellas. As Jules looked around, he thought, I should be so lucky to have this many people show for my last rites, huh, Rocco? I never realized there were so many people that liked you. Hey, now, don't get me wrong, didn't mean anything by that remark, givin' ya the business, that's all. Occasionally, a gust of wind would come about. The sky gradually darkened, and would progressively become brighter from time to time. Suddenly, a gust of wind whirled about and ripped the roof off a makeshift shanty nearby. People looked around everywhere; they didn't know where the noise was coming from. The sound of snapping wood and tin and rusty nails picked up the roof as if it were a piece of paper. The sound was terrible. It was worse than if the nasty teacher had scolded a hundred children, and they resented it by screaming, stomping on the floor and hissing, then scraping their fingernails along a big long blackboard with

their fingernails; amplified seventy or eighty times, it was
frightening. People screamed, some ran off, others watched as the
roof blew away, until it slammed into a large oak tree, then
crashed to the ground. The wind diminished to a pleasant breeze,
everyone was relieved. Chattering and clamoring echoed all
around. Jules studied the shanty, the entire front section had
collapsed to the ground, creating it to slant; it looked as if it
was touched, it would fall over. Jules took a few steps forward
and stared inside the shanty. There were shovels and wheel-barrows
and bags of cement and wood planks, raincoats and rain hats and
rubber boots and six or seven round rippled trash cans upside down
on top of a pile of top soil; each trash can was shoved into the
top soil and submerged at a different depth.

Jules thought, of all the goddam places in this boneyard,
they had to put that broken-down hole-in-the-wall, right there--
Jesus Christ!

Father Fafaro looked at the crowd, and he gestured with his
arms to calm down--this didn't work. He had no choice but to shout
to get their attention.

"Brothers!...Sisters!" Everyone turned to him with saintly
faces, leaves could be heard falling to the ground, it was so
quiet. He gestured again, waving his arms and hands about, and he
lowered his voice, "Relax. Relax now--the Lord works in
mysterious ways, you know he does. Now, each and everyone present

here today can thank Rocco in our prayers--through Jesus Christ, our faithful departed confidant," He turned and pointed to where the roof rested, "and forced, that's right, forced that roof in another direction so as not to harm anyone present here today. Rocco was blessed with the strength of a lion. We have been blessed with mercy through the grace of God. Be not afraid, those who run have no faith." He made the sign of the cross to everyone, "God have mercy on your soul. Let us pray in silence."

After the prayer, Father Fafaro continued with the service.

Holy Christ, Father Fafaro must-a had more than his share of wine this morning. Jules thought. Rocco must-a tightened his fists when he heard Father give those lines. He chuckled to himself. Rocco has donated wine to the church for years. The other priests love that wine...no wonder they walk aroun' kinda slow an' are tight lipped most of the time. He looked up at the sky and prayed in silence, forgive me God, I was just kiddin' aroun', you now.

Jules couldn't get into listening to the priest giving the last rights for Rocco, he had been staring at the shanty and listening to the rain. Slowly, his hearing became acute to the beat of the rain rapping against the metal shovels and rippled trash cans in the shanty; the pitter-patter sound of the rain were in cadence, and sounded as if a tune was being played; like an old lullaby Rocco always hummed and sang in Italian; the one his Mama sang to him when he was a little boy.

Boy oh boy, I'm really blowin' my top, first I hear Father tellin' everybody Rocco deflected the roof, now, I'm hearin' a lullaby created by the rain Rocco used to hum. Hey Rocco, if yer playin' games, yer doin' one hell of a job. Jules thought.

A soft voice from behind said, "You okay Jules?"

Jules didn't hear the voice, he had Rocco on his mind and the pitter-patter of the rain had him slightly in a trance. His mind drifted off and he imagined Rocco sitting at his desk, humming the lullaby.

A voice from behind again said, softly, "Jules," then a nudge followed.

Jules snapped his head to clear his thought, and turned slightly, he found himself facing Smiley O'Brian, his deserted best friend.

Smiley looked at Jules with his enduring smile, and whispered, "Sorry Jules, I know how much Rocco meant to you."

Jules reached behind and grabbed Smiley's coat, forcing him forward, to be beside him, "Excuse me," he said to one of the dealers, "move down a little will ya, thanks." He looked at Smiley, and whispered, "Nice to see you here, Now ya have the best view. Talk later." What a surprise seein' Smiley here, haven't seen him in three or four years. Jules thought. That's when he decided to find himself.

Suddenly, six female mourners dressed in black, and with

their faces covered by veils, mourned in sorrow over Rocco. The
fragrance of flowers surrounded the area.

Jules looked at the casket, and thought, Christ Rocco, I'm
gonna miss ya. I'll take care of Mario, so don't worry about him.

Before the casket was lowered, Jules placed a rose on the
top, and all others did the same.

Meanwhile, Tony Cheese was hurriedly packing his belongings
in three big footlockers and several large suitcases. He was
nervous and anxious to leave the City. He packed sloppily, and
when his luggage couldn't hold anymore, he threw everything he
owned in boxes. His clumsiness caused him to bump into, and break
antique cups and dishes that were of no interest to him.
Outside of Cheese's brownstone, three black sedans parked by the
curb idled with their trunks open, and Cheese's thugs waited
patiently to load his luggage. They were enjoying themselves,
eating hot peppers and sharp provolone cheese on hot Italian bread
smothered with olive oil and black pepper. Tony Cheese took good
care of his boys, he made sure they ate a good lunch. They also
had two bottles of Chianti in each car. The steady rain continued
coming down, there were large puddles of water in the streets and
sidewalks; the drainage gutters were cluttered with trash and
debris; the street would be flooded soon if Cheese didn't hurry.
Finally, Cheese came out waving his arms frantically to the boys;
he was in a hurry to leave in fear of getting killed.

"Awright, awright, lets go! Come on! Move-move!" He shouted, "Get my luggage n shit! What da fuck ya eatin' for!"

His boys jumped out of the cars wildly, dropping their food at their feet, in the road, all around, they were scared of Cheese. They ran up the stairs into Cheese's place and got the luggage. As the cars were being loaded, they slipped and fell on the oily bread they carelessly dropped everywhere.

Cheese couldn't believe his eyes, and shouted, "You stupid-a fools, don't break-a any-ting!" He hit two or three of the boys with his cane, shouting, "Stupid-a-stupid-a!"

When the cars were loaded, they screeched off, plowing through the high water. By the time they reached the end of the second block, all three cars stalled and came to a stop; splashing water caused the engines to cease running.

Heated, Cheese punched the dashboard with his fist, and shouted, "What da fuck! Push-a da cars out-a da water!" He pointed at a vacant lot down the road, it was above the water line. The other two cars did the same.

Push-a! Push-a! Son-a-bitch, we never get out-a dis town!" He slammed the dashboard again, "Ma Jesu Christ-a!"

On their way to Rocco's Restaurant, from the cemetery, Jules, Jimmy the dealer and Trip (the 300 pound doorman) sat inside the limousine contemplating. The limousine stopped at an intersection,

Trip started to talk out-loud to himself. Most of his teeth were
gold capped, except for his two upper central incisors and four
upper lateral incisors adjacent to his canines, he didn't have
any. His lower jaw protruded, which made him look like an ape
man. Two days ago, his upper bridge fell out of his mouth into the
meat grinder while he was grinding meat patties in the kitchen at
Rocco's restaurant. He couldn't talk to well since then. He had
a gentle way about himself; a pussycat would best describe him but
as the doorman at Rocco's, everybody knew best to avoid him,
especially when he became irritated. He's thrown out many
troublemakers bigger than himself, and being a manic depressant,
which he never knew, he had the strength of a bull. He had
dilutions of grandeur occasionally, and Jules knew how to keep him
under control when an episode occurred. Jules listened to him
talking to himself and interpreted Trip saying in a low monotone
voice: That fuckin' pervert! He's nothin' but a wap bastard.
Cheese killed my friend, Rocco--almost killed my pal Mario, too--I
want him, want him real bad. Trip looked at Jules, and stared at
him with a angry look. Jules and Jimmy the dealer sat side by
side across from Trip, they knew not to upset Trip during one of
his episodes. Jimmy the dealer looked away from Trip to avoid
laughing, while Jules stared into Trip's bulging eyes. Jules knew
he could out-stare Trip, and he patiently did. At the right
moment, Jules faintly kicked Trip's foot. Jimmy the dealer,

trembled as he watched, he stiffened like a ice block. Jules
continued staring into Trip's eyes with a blank face. Suddenly,
with a full-breath growl, Trip raised his butt and released a
deafening blast of gas that continued blaring for at least four
seconds. The smell was blinding. Jules quickly opened the
window and shouted at Jimmy the dealer.

"Open the goddam window! C'mon-c'mon, move-move!"

Jimmy the dealer didn't move, he didn't flinch, he maintained
a frozen position and didn't look as if he'd ever thaw out.

Jules shook him wildly, "Snap out of it! Snap out of it!"

Jimmy the dealer came to his senses and looked at Jules wide
eyed, "I-I, whadaya crazy shakin' me like that? Awwwwg, what's
that smell?"

Jules shouted in his face, "Open the goddam window before the
car blows up--Trip's lettin' loose! Open the fuckin' window!"

Jimmy the dealer instantly rolled the window down and gasped
for air, "That bloody stench can kill a horse." He put his head
out the window and took in several breaths of fresh air.

Trip groaned and let loose of another long blast, his face
looked as if it was ready to fracture. His eyes blinked then he
rubbed them several times.

"Jesus Christ!" Jules shouted, "What the fuck's wrong with
you, Trip!"

Trip didn't answer. He sat there looking as if nothing had

happened. He let loose another loud burst, lasting three or four seconds and smiled in content.

Jules shouted to the chauffeur, while his head was halfway out the window, "Stop the goddam car! Pull off anyplace, fer Chris' sake, hurry!"

Trip didn't say a word, but his face started to turn red and the veins in his forehead began bulging as if he was ready to let loose again. Jimmy the dealer held his breath, his eyes rolled to the extreme left, maintaining his stiff head forward, and straining his eyes to see what Jules's next move would be.

The chauffeur pulled off the road onto the wet shoulder. He slammed on the brakes and skidded ten or fifteen feet. Jules and Jimmy sailed across the floor and smashed into Trip. On their knees they stared at each other for a moment, then jumped out of the car for fresh air.

Scilly, the chauffeur, leaped out of the car and ran down the road shouting, "I'm through! I had it!"

"Scilly, wait! Where ya goin'?" Jules bellowed out.

Scilly slowed down and turned to Jules, while running backward, and cried out, "Can't take the bloody job any more, you'll be okay without me, cheerio." He waved good-bye, went a few feet, stopped, and turned to Jules again, yelling, "It's been a gas!"

And off Scilly went. For a 60 year old, he ran down the

highway pretty fast.

"I don't believe it!" Jimmy said, heated. "We're out of a
bloody chauffeur! What-a we do now?"

"Whataya gettin' so uptight about, he's headin' for the
restaurant, he's not quittin', he just lost it when Trip let
loose, that's all." Jules said laughing.

Jimmy had a cynical temperament, and could make a gorilla out
of a chimpanzee.

"I'm drivin', get in the car an' weep."

Trip was sitting up and snoring, making full-mouthed gurgle
sounds.

Jules looked at Jimmy, gave him the "office" (a quick rub on
the nose which means OK amongst con people) then waved to Jimmy to
get in the car, at the same time, putting his finger over his
lips, meaning; be quiet.

They drove a mile or so and Jules turned to Jimmy with a
smirk painted on his face and whispered, "We won the battle pal,
but didn't win the war yet."

Jimmy nodded his head, looking worried.

Jimmy rolled up the privacy window real easy, closing it
tight. He moved in close to Jules, and whispered in a cocky tone,

"We don't have to worry about Trip, the guy's in a coma back
there. I heard the crackpot escaped from a insane asylum years
ago. He probably realized another world existed, and broke out of

the bloody joint." He laughed with a soft mischievous wheeze and nudged Jules. "Look at him--he looks like a bloody ding-a-ling."

Jules didn't flinch. He didn't like Jimmy making bad remarks about Trip.

Jimmy nudged Jules again, harder than before. "Look at the scatterbrain, you're gonna laugh yer ass off, I promise."

"Jesus!" Jules said in a heated whisper, "Ya don't have ta break my goddam ribs!" He turned, looked at Trip, then took a double take as if something odd happened. He turned back to the road with a confused look.

Jimmy studied Jules. "What's wrong? You didn't find Trip amusing with his tongue halfway on his chin an' droolin' from the mouth?"

"Yeah, real funny, Jimmy." Jules faked a laugh, and thought, holy sheeeit! Am I blowin' my top or did I see Trip give me a wink? Naaa. Hey, he put a finger over his lips. That didn't come from my imagination. Holy sheeeit, Trip heard what Jimmy said about him! I'm gonna have some fun with this one. Jimmy's gonna eat those words he said about Trip--I'm gonna fix his ass real good.

A apprehensive look appeared on Jules's face. He gave Jimmy a light tap on his leg, and in a shaking whisper, he began to play-act. He talked from the side of his mouth.

"Tr--." His voice was a croak. He acted as though he

couldn't get the words out.

"W-what's wrong?" Jimmy said.

Jules swallowed and tried again. "Trip, he's not sleepin', he's f-fakin' it! Jesus, don't look back there! He want's you for lunch--you're in deep shit, he heard every word you said about him. You better come up with a convincing story, something to make him know you were just jokin' aroun' or..." Jules looked at Jimmy with heated eyes. "I can't believe you made those defiled remarks about Trip--he saved your ass many times from getting yer head smashed in. Ya better come up with a convincing story, kid."

Jimmy laughed. He covered his mouth with his hand to muffle the sound. Are you bloody serious? You're good Jules, but I wasn't born yesterday, for Chris' sake!."

"Yeah, right Mr. Know it all, so, why don't you tell Trip to his face, everything you said about him?

"I-I, I mean--"

Fagedabout it, there's only one solution to becoming a better person, and rid yourself of being a two-face-chicken-hearted-piece-a-shit."

"Thank's Jules, I needed that."

"It's the truth so don't be offended. Yer gonna learn to say it the way it is."

"Now, wait a minute Jules--"

"No--you wait a minute! If ya pay attention to what I'm gonna save yer ass, if ya listen!"

"I'm listenin', I'm listenin', go ahead."

"Okay, just have an open mind."

Jimmy's eyes widened with anticipation, "Jesus, it's open, it's open, c'mon will ya, Trip is gonna have me half swallowed before you get started!"

"Awright, calm down. The whole idea here is to clear your conscience of bad thoughts, when you don't release them, they bottle-up in your subconscious, making you feel inhibited; you'll talk to yourself thinking of what a coward you really are, and worst. The more you continue doin' this, keepin' your emotions within, the more baffled you become. And as the years go by, you psychologically become frustrated, pessimistic, your attitude toward life becomes that of a defeatist to name just a few traits you will inherit. All in all, you made yourself a two-face slandering fool, and a lonely soul. The sad part is the person generally don't know why or how this happened. The half-way intelligent ones who care will see a good shrink. The ones who could care less continue living in a glass jar. I'll give you the perfect example: Lets say one night your introduced to a guy at a party. He does lots-a talkin, doesn't say to much of anythin' on the positive side. He let's you talk, but knock's just about everything you said. He's a complete asshole. You want to tell him off, but you're afraid, lets face it, yer a coward. You can think of a million excuses why you shouldn't tell the jerk off, but you don't, how could you, you haven't let go with others in the past, why would you change now? Well, this is now--this is what you do: you look in the guys eyes and follow thru with a hardy laugh while grabbing his arm, then you say: Ya know Duke, if you were my brother, I'd call you a asshole! At the same time, yer still laughin' an' holdin' on his arm, squeezing it a bit. What did you do? You released your anger--you really meant what you said to him, and you had a good laugh at the same time--your gonna feel absolutely terrific, why? ya told the truth. It's simple, just like when you were a kid, remember?"

Jimmy snapped his head toward Jules, his eyes bulging, he stared at Jules for a moment then in a voice of panic, he said,

"Sounds good. Leave me alone for a minute, I think I have a great story."

Jimmy looked at Trip from the side of his eye, Trip turned and rolled into the corner, he looked as though he was sleeping like a baby. Jimmy wiped the cold sweat from his forehead and started to think. Two or three minutes later, he looked at Jules.

"Jesus Christ, how do you expect me to do the 'if you were my brother, I'd call you an asshole' story?...I can get bloody killed."

"Trust me. If you want to respect yourself, as others will, just do it. Fear begets fear. It's not a big deal. Every time you clear your conscience and say it the way it is, you'll be another step closer to freedom. It gets easier an' easier until you're dues are paid." Jules said patting Jimmy's leg.

"Okay Jules, I'm an easy mark, I'll do it."

"When?" Jules said, at once.

"T-today. But I want you around, you know, as a bystander."

"I wouldn't have it any other way. I'm proud of you, Jimmy, ya got what it takes."

"Thank's Jules, you're a sweetheart." Jimmy said in a soft whisper.

"Do ya have the story altogether?" Jules said, looking serious.

Jimmy rolled down the privacy window. "I have a great story."

"You got balls openin' that window, too."

"Yeah, I do. Only because Trip's been sleepin' all this time."

Suddenly, Trip jumped up and grabbed Jimmy by the coat. He lifted him off the seat, his legs pounding on the dash and eyes bulging. He couldn't say much because his shirt was choking him.

"Aghhh! Ughh!" Jimmy gasped for air, his hands trying to open his shirt collar.

Jules shouted, "I told ya, I told ya Trip was faking it." He made a sharp turn of the steering wheel to the left and back again causing Trip to go off balance and fall on the floor. Jimmy slammed into the passenger door and settled on the seat, minus a shirt collar.

"Are you crazy!" Jimmy cried out at Trip. "You tryin' ta kill me! Ya ruined my new shirt! Yer a bloody animal!"

Trip sat up and leaned in the privacy window. He looked at Jules and gave him a wink to assure him he was just playing around with Jimmy.

Jules grabbed Trip's arm, gave him a wink to make Trip know he was playing the game also, and pushed him back.

"What the fuck you doin'? This is Jimmy, not one of the ball-busters that come in the joint!" Jules said heated. "Settle down fer Chris' sake, Jimmy want's to tell you something." He looked at Jimmy, and said in a whisper, "Trip's okay, he's just a little sensitive. He can't understand why you said all those bad things about him. Okay Jimmy, tell Trip why you called him all those brotherly things, you couldn't have a better time than right now."

Jimmy's eyes widened, his face had panic painted on it. He froze in a half-turned position and stared at Jules.

Jules slapped Jimmy's face to make him come alive. "Sorry bout that Jimmy, c'mon, you know what to say to your ol' pal Trip, talk to him--yer chances of getting killed are slim. Go ahead, he has to know what you really meant, go ahead, you'll feel good about it."

Jimmy snapped out of it. "Wha, ya slapped me--y-you're bloody crazy. What's got into you anyway"? "Straighten out Jimmy, yer makin' a big deal outa

this. Say what ya gotta say, and it's over...go ahead, go ahead."

Jimmy's face turned pinkish red as a cold sweat beaded on his forehead. It was an

effort to talk, but the words came out, and he said, "Ok Jules, you win...here I go." He

turned to Trip, and said, "Ta tell you the truth Trip, if you were my own brother I would

have told you the same thing. You're an asshole from the word go. What I'm really

saying is I love you like my own brother. Now, if you're going to take that literally, then

I'm not going to be a brother to you or even a pal. Now , what's it gonna be?" Jimmy

looked straight in Trip's eyes and sat there cocked, not knowing what was going to

happen.

Trip dropped his head in shame, and quietly said, "Awwww, I wath jokin' aroun',

Jimmy...yup, juth a joke. I'm thorry. Alwayth wanthed da be yer brodder." Trip sat back

in the seat and fell asleep.

Jimmy looked at Jules, his face perplexed, and said, "I-I don't believe it! I don't

believe what I just o-observed, Jules. There is magic to those words. You're a genius.

Thanks Jules, thank you indeed." Jules patted Jimmy on his face, and said, "Would I

guide you off the right path, Jimmy?"

CHAPTER 13

NEW YORK, AUGUST 3, 1932

7:40 P.M.

After Rocco's burial, Jules had a gathering at Rocco's Restaurant. Later on, when everyone left, Jules got dressed, and sat in silence at a table. He heard a knock on the door.

"Who's there!" He said.

"It's me, Smiley."

Jules opened the temporary door. When Jules, Jimmy, The Dealer and Trip arrived at the restaurant earlier, an unidentified car fired several shots with Thompson sub machine guns trying to kill Jules. Paco was killed, and the front of the restaurant was riddled with bullets. Jules was lucky, and he knew Tony Cheese was behind the whole thing. A contractor friend of Jules temporarily boarded the place up.

"I heard what happened Jules. The place looks like it was on the front lines. Jesus, you sure got close to getin' yerself wiped out, huh?" "Wasn't my time, that's all. I don't mean to rush you Smiley, but I'm on my way to see Mario, and gotta talk to the doctor." "OK, OK, I won't hold ya up." Smiley said. "Stop by tomorrow mornin', aroun' 10, the construction crew will be here." "Sorry Jules. You look great, an' dapper as ever. Are ya sure yer OK? you look beat, you'd tell me wouldn't ya Jules?"

"I'm alright. Lucky. Sorry Smiley, gotta run." Jules said
tightening his tie.

"Ok, ok, I'll let you go. Hope Mario will be alright. If
there's anything I can do, just ask. See ya tomorrow...oh, I meant
to ask ya, how do ya like the new suit?"

"I meant to give you a compliment on that, dark pin stripe
suit, white shirt, gorgeous silk tie, not bad Smiley, not bad. I
like those black Italian shoes too. You look prosperous. You talk
better, you act better. We'll talk tomorrow. Can I go now?"

Smiley laughed. "Same ol' sense of humor. Okay Jules, I'll
let you go, didn't mean to be so selfish. See ya later." He
walked away looking proud.

Jules hurried to his room, and slipped into his beige sport
jacket. He dressed sharp with his black slacks, white shirt, dark
brown silk tie, black socks and black Italian loafers. He took his
raincoat out of the closet, and threw it on the bed, then grabbed
his black fedora, looked in the mirror and put it on, lowering one
side of the rim halfway down. He winked at himself, and thought,
today isn't over yet, but pulled through somehow. I better get
outa here, got a nine 'o clock appointment with Mario's doctor. I
want to see Mario first. I sure hope the kid's gonna make it.
Bellevue Hospital is a good twenty minutes from here. He went out
the back door to the parking lot. He forgot his raincoat, but
decided not to get it and ran to his late model Cadillac

convertible, Rocco had left him. He lit a cigarette and screeched away.

When he arrived at the hospital, he walked through the lobby like any normal visitor would do, passed the register desk where a elderly nurse was intensely reading a romantic novel, and continued walking like most visitors would not do. He headed for the stairs to the third floor. He knew visiting hours were over, nothing stopped him from following through once his mind had been made up to get the job done. Besides, he had a appointment with Doctor Cohn in forty-five minutes, this made everything right. He made it to the third floor, and on the entire door in bold red lettering on a white background read: Intensive Care Unit. He opened the door and came out to the hallway. Their were six or seven patient rooms on one side, and five or six on the other. The smell of ether and disinfectant lingered in the air. The place looked like a morgue with the light gray walls with black trim and dark gray floors; depressing would best describe the atmosphere; it looked like a prison. Jules removed his fedora, and thought, Jesus, you'd think they'd have cheerful colors in this joint. The whole idea is to get better in here. Maybe they do it on purpose just to get the "maybe" patients ready for boot hill. I know-I know, that's not a nice thing to say -- just don't make sense. Mario's room is aroun' here somewhere, I'll find it. I hope the kid's gonna make it --fuckin' Tony Cheese....

Jules walked down the hallway, he didn't see a soul around. As he curiously walked along looking for room 302, he noticed a door three-quarters of the way closed; in the room there were four nurses talking and relaxing, enjoying a smoke, and sipping coffee. He nonchalantly continued on, past the nurses desk to room 302. A dim light came through the slightly open door. He took a few steps into the room and stopped. He looked at poor Mario, there were tubes and needles and apparatus attached to him. A white cast enclosed his entire body; his eyes and nose and mouth and hands were the only things not covered. Jules looked around in the private room, and thought, God, this room is worse than the hallway. Christ, you'd think they'd be bright 'n gay. Okay Jules, knock off the negative bullshit. He took a few steps to Mario's bed and held his hand.

In a soft voice, he said, "Mario...it's me, Jules...are ya awake...? If you can hear me, twitch your eyes, once for yes, twice for no..." Jules patiently waited, nothing happened. He dropped his head; his heart ached for the boy, he didn't know if Mario would live or die. He raised his head, and looked at him.

"I know you can hear me Mario, you gotta hang in there, don't give up on me now, yer a brave boy. This is just a temporary set-back. It's like the time you wanted that hot fudge sundae, remember? Your father told you, you could have the ice cream, but not the hot fudge until you finish cleanin' the kitchen, remember?

Boy, did you cry. I talked with you, and asked if that hot fudge
was worth waiting for, I mean, you only had a few pots 'n pans to
wash. You said, yes. It only took fifteen-twenty minutes. You got
yer hot fudge, you were happy, yer father was happy, we all were
happy, all for a few minutes out of yer life, you got what you
wanted. The point I'm trying to make here is, this is no
different, you laying there is just a matter of time. You gotta
want to get better. I need you Mario, we all do. Now you have the
time to put things together, rearrange your future, an' look
forward to all the good times we're gonna have, know what I mean?
I know, I know, yer Papa's not aroun', I loved him very much too,
he was closer to me than my ol' man, I bet you didn't know that? I
gotta tell ya this Mario, I gotta let it out, deep down in my
heart, I want to run, run far away an' hide, just die, but that's
the easy way out, we have to fight all that bullshit an' face
reality, be brave, that's what's it's all about, know what I'm
sayin'? Think about that for awhile. Look, I gotta leave ya for
now, I'm havin' a talk with your doctor in a few minutes, at least
I'll know what the situation is with you. I'll see ya before I
leave, so just remember what I told you." He gave Mario's hand a
light squeeze, and stared at the cast.

Nurse Lynne Marie, the head nurse of I.C.U., entered the
room. Jules didn't hear her come in, he was still staring at
Mario's cast, feeling sad. Nurse Lynne Marie looked annoyed.

"Excuse me!" She exploded with authority. "Who are you?
What are you doing here? What gives you the right to be in this
intensive care area after hours?" She stood there hands on hips,
tight lipped and waited for an explanation.

Jules didn't flinch from his position, he didn't even show
the slightest hint he heard her. He slowly turned around and
looked at her, gave her the up and down, and thought, outside of
her big mouth, she's gotta be at least five feet, nine, her
shoulder length hair could be shorter, an' her blond hair needs a
touch-up. Pretty face for 27-28. She carries those large head-
lights pretty good. Nice hour-glass figure, long thin legs. She
must be aroun' a hundred ten-twelve pounds. Boy oh boy, she looks
pissed, I'm in trouble. He rubbed his chin, and said softly,
"Well, to tell you the truth--"

"Never mind! Remove yourself from here, immediately, before I
call a guard!" She snapped her fingers ordering him to leave,
"Let's go-let's go, come on, move it."

Jules raised his voice, "Aren't you talkin' rather loud?
This is a hospital or did you forget? I'd appreciate it if you
spoke in a civilized manner -- now calm down, you don't crash in
just any room like a wild mare. Okay-okay, so ya had a bad day,
you're entitled, but don't take it out on me, nurse. Not only
that, ya have lotsa nerve comin' in here an' scarin' the livin'
daylights outa me, good thing I have a good ticker. I know, I'm a

bad boy, but I'm waiting for Doctor Cohn -- Mario is my

responsibility -- I thought the doc and I were meeting at 9, right

here, is there a problem?"

Nurse Lynne Marie looked shocked. She thought, now there's a

man, I like his aggressiveness, they don't make a stud like that

anymore. I shouldn't have been so rude. I'd love to catch me a guy

like this -- ohh, he's so handsome. She walked up to him, and said,

sweetly, "I'm terribly sorry, Mr...."

"Jules Salarno, Jules, is what everybody calls me. I didn't

mean to be so hard on you, please forgive me. I'm very concerned

with Mario an' all, I lost it there, you understand, right?" He

reached out and shook her hand.

She swirled her shoulder-length hair to one side, and in a

apologetic tone said, "I have to admit, Mr., I mean Jules, this is

the first introduction I've ever had to such a bold gentleman,

Lynne Marie is my name.

Jules looked into her light green eyes.

"It's a pleasure, Lynne Marie, but no more scaring me half to

death. He smiled, then they laughed.

"You're funny, I had it coming. This floor is my

responsibility, and I'll have to admit, there are times we get a

little too serious. Nurse Carmen and I are assigned to Mario,

excuse me, I have to check a few things on the boy."

"How's he doing?" Jules asked softly.

"Mario's condition hasn't changed. Hopefully he'll come out of this dreadful coma. Doctor Cohn will explain to you in detail the boy's prognosis."

When yer through, maybe you can get me a aspirin or something?"

"I'll have nurse Carmen bring them in. I think you should get off your feet for the time being." She checked Mario. "We're doing all we can for the boy. There isn't much we can do while he's in a coma." She walked up to Jules. "I'll bring coffee."

Jules sat down looking sad. "Thank's nurse."

"Are you alright, Mr. Salarno?"

I'm fine, just a little tired, hectic day, that's all."

Nurse Lynne Marie felt his forehead to see if he had a fever. "You're a little warm, you need rest Mr. Salarno. Relax, I'll be back shortly."

Jules got up from the chair and went to the window. He looked into the darkness, as he gazed at the stars, he had a backflash of Rocco, when he ripped the telephone book in half, and the expression Tony Cheese had on his face, then a flash in the basement, when Rocco gave him the mysterious footlocker, then when Rocco lay helplessly on the floor bleeding profusely and died in his arms, then Mario being crushed, and Paco getting shot, a cold sweat covered his face. Suddenly, Jules felt a hand on his shoulder shaking him lightly, and a voice, he jumped from fright.

"Mr.Salarno, Mr. Salarno, are you alright? Nurse Lynne Marie
asked softly.

Jules shook his head, and rubbed his eyes. "Huh! Wha! Oh,
just daydreamin'...coffee'll straight'n me out."

"Come on now," she grabbed his arm, "Your coffee's on the
table. Let's sit down and relax."

A hint of rose perfume cast off her body. The smell reminded
Jules of Loretta.

"You're very kind." Jules said.

In her low voice, she said, "Doctor Cohn is in a meeting
going over Mario's x-rays. I told him you're here. It'll be twenty
minutes or so. If you need something, I'll be at the nurses
station right down the hall."

"Thank you, nurse."

As she went out the door, Smiley accidently bumped into her.
She almost fell, but Smiley grabbed her just in time.

"Oooooops! Sorry! Let me help you." Smiley said. "Are you
okay? I'm so sorry." He held on to her so close, you couldn't slip
a feather between them. His unlit cigar broke in half, it dangled
from his mouth.

"Who are you? There are no visiting hours after 8 p.m. -- are
you going to let me go, or kiss me?"

Smiley took the broken cigar out of his mouth, and kissed her
on the lips. She didn't move, nor struggle, she couldn't, he held

her too tight; the kiss lasted three or four seconds at the least.

"Lynne Marie Polinski!" Smiley said, not letting go.

"Smiley! Is that really you?" She gave him a wet kiss, and wrapped her arms around him.

They hugged and rocked as if they knew each other for years.

Jules watched all the while looking confused. "What's Smiley doin' here, I told him we'd get together tomorrow, he thought. He's always been a ladies man alright -- the horny bastard. He got up, and went to the doorway.

"What's goin' on? Smiley, what are you doin' here? I thought we were gettin' together tomorrow? I never remember you being on time for anythin', yer way to early fer tomorrow aren't you?"

Smiley laughed. "Jules, Lynne Marie's an ol' flame of mine, can you beat that? Of all the places. It was meant for me to be here Jules, I had to see how Mario's doin', an' give you support, hope yer not mad at me."

Embarrassed, Lynne Marie pushed herself away from Smiley, and swirled her shoulder-length hair to one side.

"You still have that killer kiss Smiley. I have paper work to take care of, we'll talk later. Get in the room, both of you, and be quiet." She walked away.

Smiley looked at Jules, "Has she got a pair er what?"

"No question about it, you never told me about her."

"I didn't? Smiley said looking surprised.

"Don't worry about it, you've had so many I wouldn't expect you to remember them all. Lynne Marie is a good nurse, don't let her get mad, she can be like a wounded tiger. C'mon, have some coffee."

"She's a wild cat, ohhhh, I love it." Smiley said with a big smile, "She killed me many times -- what a way to go."

"I can't imagine."

"How's Mario? I've never seen anybody wrapped up in a cast like that before, poor kid."

"He's in a coma -- fuckin' Cheese."

"He'll get his, you'll see to that, right Jules?"

"I'm in no hurry. I know I'll catch up with him -- gut feelin', and when I do...he's gonna pay, big time."

"What's that suppose to mean?" Smiley said puzzled.

"I'm not sayin' right now. There's options I'm workin' on. When I'm ready, you'll know about it."

"I know you Jules, you've always been professional in layin' things out right, he's gonna be a real sweet kill, huh?"

Jules knew Smiley was trying to worm his plan out of him, he changed the subject.

"As far as Mario's concerned, I don't know much, they can't do a thing until he comes out of the coma. The doctor will be here soon, he'll tell me the whole story."

"Maybe I should leave, Jules?"

"Yer okay, stay right where you are. I'm curious, what have

you been doin' for the past four years? Christ, seems like
yesterday."

"I know, amazing. It's been a adventure, that's for sure." He
laughed. "A few days after I told you I needed to go away for
awhile because I wanted to straighten my life out, and so on, I
asked Shrap if he knew a psychologist or somebody who could help
me with my problem. He recommended his friend, a retired
professor of psychology. Shrap did me a favor, and set-up an
appointment for me at his home in Queens."

"What's his name?" Jules asked curiously.

"Professor Korsakov." Smiley said.

I've read some of his works, he's a brilliant man, and has
contributed his genius in solving emotional problems and the
disturbed minds of individuals for many years. Who would think
Shrap would know a person like that?" Jules said.

Smiley jumped in without hesitating. "Maybe Shrap was his
best patient?"

They thought about that statement for a moment, then laughed.

"It just goes to show you what a small world it really is."
Jules said. How quick 'n sharp Smiley responded, he thought.
That's the Smiley I once knew. His grammar improved as well, what
a relief.

"You have him pegged Jules, that's right, you keep up with
all that psychological stuff. He's a regular guy -- likes his

vodka, wine too, he can put it away...prrretty good."

"You must owe him yer life."

"That's one of the best parts of the deal. I don't know what Shrap told him about me, but the prof told me he didn't want money, he asked me to bring him a gallon of Shrap's homemade wine instead, each time I visited him. Now c'mon, is this guy a sweetheart or what?"

"Very generous of the prof. You deserve it Smiley. And the professor, he sounds like a dedicated individual -- he's probably a great drinkin' partner too."

"He is...the greatest. I never seen him drunk or fluctuate from his normal behavior, the guy has a wooden leg, no question about it, he's unbelievable."

They laughed, then covered there mouth to mute the sound, they didn't want Nurse Lynne Marie to come in the room and give them the third degree.

"I have to tell you Jules, I really miss all the laughs, the jobs we pulled-off. Goddam, there were times I felt so lonely and apart from the world I wanted to forget about making myself a better person. But the prof an' I talked about my inferiority complex, and he verily helped me. I've seen him twice, sometimes three times a week for four years. Can you imagine that? Smiley O'Brian, pulling-off a big deal like that? And I owe it all to you, my best friend."

Jules looked at Smiley square in the eyes for a moment, then grabbed his arm, "I'm proud of you. I can see a definite change in you. You're the one that made it happen, you wanted it -- sure, I gave you the business some of the time to make you aware what a great asshole you were, but again, you did it for you, and that, my friend, takes a lot of courage."

What a modest guy. Jules give's out more than he take's in, he's always been like that, Smiley thought. He'll never take credit or talk about anything he did good. What a great guy. I can't afford to fuck-up anymore. Jules needs me. He is truly my best friend.

Lynne Marie and another nurse came in the room.

"This is nurse Carmen," Nurse Lynne Marie said to Jules. "And this is Smiley, an old friend of mine."

Jules stood up and hesitated as he looked at nurse Carmen. They stood there in a spell, staring at each other, and fell in love at first sight. Jules gently shook her hand.

"Hi nurse Carmen, please, call me Jules."

"Nice to meet you, Jules." She said shaking his hand. Her beautiful blue eyes penetrated into his.

As Smiley got up, he spilled hot coffee on his lap, then accidently dropped the cup on the floor, breaking into pieces.

"Oh Jesus! I mean, jeez, how clumsy of me!" He jumped around holding his hands between his legs. "Oh boy-oh boy, this is h-hot!

How s-stupid...oooooo, I'm embarassed...ooo, ooo."

Both nurses rushed to him, grabbed his arms and sat him down.
Jules stood there shaking his head. What a fuckin' moron, he
thought. He'll do anything for attention.

Smiley tried to take his mind off the hurt. "How ya doin'
nurse Carmen, sorry we have to meet under these circumstances --
coffee's great, you make it?"

"Hi Smiley." She poured cold water over a towel and placed it
on Smiley's lap. "No, I didn't make the coffee, but we better get
some ice towels right away. Are you alright?"

"Ohhh, well...I'm f-fine, just fine, thank you nurse, I'll be
o-okay, you can bet on it--"

"Shhhhh, be still, you may be burnt seriously, we--"

"But I'm--"

"Shh for now, don't say a word, sit still."

Nurse Lynne Marie quickly left the room to get a few ice
towels.

Jules stood there and watched. Oh God, he's hurtin' so bad,
I can taste it, he thought. The poor guy's tryin' not to show the
pain. Mr. ego, that's what I should call him. He smiled.

"Awww, you don't have to fuss over me nurse, I'm okay,
honest."

"I know, just have a little patience or would you like a shot
for the pain?" Nurse Carmen said smiling.

"No-no. I'll sit still." Smiley looked alarmed. He glanced at Jules, gave him a smile as if to say, there's nothing I can do.

Nurse Lynne Marie came with the ice and towels, and placed one on Smiley's lap. She held it in position.

"Everything is going to be fine." Nurse Lynne Marie said patting his thigh.

Nurse Carmen gave him two aspirin then placed a cold towel over his head and eyes.

"I love to be pampered. You nurses are wonderful." Smiley said.

Jules thought, I wonder if nurse Carmen has a boyfriend. She's a knockout. God, I never had such a strong feelin' over a woman before, not that I've had many, but there's something about her I really like. I love her short strawberry-blond hair. She's attractive, and can't weigh more than a hundred-three pounds. Georgeous figure. Perfect legs an' thin ankles, just the way I like 'em. She's just right at five-five, everything fits perfectly with her height. A cute little ass, and her breasts look well proportioned. Oh God, those hazel blue eyes got me the first time. I'd love to talk with her -- I will, later.

"What do you think, nurses? "Is our boy Smiley gonna make it?" Jules said smiling.

Nurse Carmen looked at Jules with a sweet smile, then a wink. "We may have to remove his trousers to check the degree of burn."

Lynne Marie's eyes rolled up at Carmen's. Carmen winked at
her. Lynne Marie got the message.

These nurses are amusing, I can't wait to see this move,
Jules thought.

Smiley pulled the cold towel off his head, dropped his hands
to his belt, and at the same time looked at Lynne Marie, wide
eyed.

"Awwww, ya don't have ta do that, h-honest!"

"Smiley! Don't fight me." Lynne Marie grabbed his belt, and
started to unbuckle it.

Smiley struggled. "Aw, come on Lynne Marie, will ya, I'm--"

"Smiley! There's nothing to be embarrassed about, those burns
need attention right away."

Smiley's face reddened, beads of sweat started to appear on
his forehead.

"Wait-wait, hold on a m-minute, will ya please! I mean, it's
not that I'm gonna d-die, believe me, I'm alright, jeez, I
appreciate everything you nurses are doin', b-but to be honest,
I'm embarrassed. Look, I'll just go home and relax in the bathtub,
lots a ice, long time, okay?"

"You don't think much of yourself do you? Do you want to get
a infection? Lynne Marie gave Carmen a distinct look with a
immediate nod, then looked at Smiley. "Are you sure that's what
you want, Smiley?"

Aww, c'mon Lynne Marie, you know me...wha...heeeey!"

Carmen grabbed Smiley's shoulders from behind, and held him
back while Lynne Marie pulled down his pants; she left them over
his thighs. His silk black striped on green boxer shorts remained
intact. Carmen looked at Jules, they smiled then looked at Lynne
Marie, the three looked at Smiley sitting there foolishly, and
broke out in laughter. Smiley gawked at Jules with a silly face,
he didn't realize a gag had been pulled off on him. Suddenly, he
understood he had been had. He jiggled his pants up, and smirked.

"Okay, ok, ok, you renegade nurses got me good, boy, ya had
me worried there for awhile. Whadaya think Jules, did they
get me or what?"

Jules smiled. "Yer easy. You should put something on that
burn or you're gonna be walkin' funny."

"Nahhh, I'm okay now. There's one thing I can use though?"

"I can't imagine." Jules said.

"A cup of black coffee would be perfect!"

They laughed. Carmen picked up the broken coffee cup, and
Lynne Marie wiped the coffee from the floor.

"Oh!" Carmen said looking at Jules, "I forgot your aspirin!"

"No you didn't, I took them while you were holdin' Smiley."

"How silly of me."

A nurse glanced in the room, "The doctor's on his way."

CHAPTER 14

NEW YORK, AUGUST 3

9:35 P.M.

A tall thin doctor -- with neatly combed soft white hair and a matching groomed beard entered Mario's room holding a manila folder. He took off his gold-rimmed glasses.

"Good evening gentlemen. It appears on the report that Julius Salarno is the person responsible for Mario. Which of you is Mr. Salarno?"

Jules stepped forward and shook hands with the doctor.

"Pleased to meet you doctor Cohn, Jules Salarno."

"Nice to meet you, Mr. Salarno."

"Doctor, I'd like you to meet a friend of mine, Smiley O'Brian."

"Good evening, Mr. O'Brian." They shook hands. Smiley nodded his head, remaining quiet.

"Mr. Salarno, I'll get right to the point. Mario's back is broken. Nerve pathways make up the spinal cord, and this Mr. Salarno, allows us to control our movements and detect sensation, such as touch or heat. Mario's spinal cord is damaged. Part or parts of the body below the point of injury may be affected. Now, the damage may only be temporary, but it usually leads to some degree of permanent disability since these nerve pathways help control many actions and functions--"

"Excuse me doctor, I know you're going to give Mario the best possible care. He's gonna be nine years old in two more months, what are his chances of pullin' through?"

"Mr. Salarno, Mario's injury is serious. He may be paralyzed from the waist down. I can give the boy the best of care, this is my specialty. To answer your question, only God knows if Mario will pull through. Right now, while he's in a coma, we're unable to do anything. I promise you, he's in good hands. Please excuse me."

Doctor Cohn walked to the end of Mario's bed, and picked up the clip board hanging there. He studied the reports page by page, then looked at both nurses.

"Let's give it another twenty-four hours. I have a gut feeling Mario's going to pull out of this. Watch him close. I'll see you nurses later."

The doctor walked up to Jules. "Mr. Salarno, you'll be informed should there be any changes in Mario's condition. He's stable, and I feel the best thing for you is rest, relax your mind, let God do what he think's is best. I'm pleased Mario has a concerned guardian such as you that will guide him through life."

He shook Jules's hand, and smiled.

"Thank you doctor, have a pleasant evening."

The doctor shook Smiley's hand. "Pleasure, Mr. O'Brian."

"You're a gentleman, doctor. Thank you sir, thank you very much for being so informative to my friend Jules." Smiley said bowing, and carrying on like a diplomat.

Jules watched the doctor leave the room, and thought, he's a good doctor, more personal than I thought. And Smiley, he sounded like a chip-man at a crap table sayin' good-bye to the doc -- what a character. He laughed to himself.

Leaving Mario's bedside, nurse Lynne Marie walked up to Jules.

"Doctor Cohn is so sweet, we simply adore him. Everything will come out for the best." She patted his arm, and smiled.

"Thank you Lynne Marie, yer a sweetheart." Jules said.

Lynne Marie went up to Smiley, and grabbed his hand.

"It's so nice to see you again, you big lug." She slipped a piece of paper in his pocket. "Call me, love. We have a lot talk about." She kissed his cheek.

Smiley held her face with both hands for a moment, then he kissed her lightly on the side of her lips then her cheek.

"Promise." He whispered.

As she walked sensually out the door, Smiley eyed her up and down, and thought, ohhhh God, did we have some good times. They just don't make 'em like her anymore, no way, no how. She's always been a friend, and a great lover. I'm not losing her -- not this trip around.

"You still got it Smiley, always have."

"Awww come on, your just saying that."

"No, honest. I wouldn't bullshit you."

"You're leading me into one of your psychological maneuvers,
I know you to well, come on now, this is the new Smiley you're
dealing with -- not the old gullable one."

"I gotta hand it to ya, you've become pretty sharp."

"Why don't you say what's on your mind, come on Jules, I'm
mature enough -- great imagination too."

"Yes, you're all these things -- okay, when you see a woman
for the first time, what is it that catches your eye? Her
breasts, rear-end or her legs?"

"I like it Jules, you've never asked me this one before."

"And I haven't seen you in four years either. You're a big
boy now, just answer the simple question without getting
technical, c'mon, your judgement has become exceptional."

"Thank you. I'm a tit-man. That's the first thing I look at.
They tell me everything I want to know about a woman. What's the
story behind that one?"

"Just curious." Jules said sipping his coffee.

"Oh no you don't, you can pull that psychological bullshit on
somebody else pal, but not me. I know you to well to fall for that
line. Come on, this is me, Smiley, your goompa."

"You're a womanizer, that's all."

Smiley looked puzzled. He tapped his finger on his lip, and stared at Jules.

"Is something wrong? Did I hurt your feelings? Ohhh, I know, you want to know what I look at first, right?"

Smiley's expression changed from the deep thought look to a surprised one. "Jesus, that's exactly what I was going to ask you, how'd you do that?"

"You get to know how a person thinks when you hang around them long enough. And that's what you have to learn, listen more 'n talk less, you'd be surprised what you'll learn."

"You're right, I'll work on that." Smiley said in a serious tone. "Okay, let's get back to you."

"I look at everything; her face first, how she dresses, her walk, the legs, the ankles, I love thin ankles, then the butt. The last thing I look at are the breasts. I can prejudge a woman pretty good by this observation."

"You're definitely not a womanizer, that's for sure. What would you be classified as being?"

"I never gave it much thought, but now that you mentioned it, patient and particular would best describe me."

Nurse Carmen was still working on Mario, and couldn't help not listening to the conversation.

"Yes sir Jules, that's you alright, totally. Ya know, one of

the things I like about you is, you're a class act. I know that
won't go to your head 'cause you already now who you are. And, I
gotta say, that's a great evaluation, sounds like one of Freud's
brilliant experiment's to me, did I guess right?"

"You did. Boy, your brighter than I thought. I love reading
his material. He contributed much to humanity. And I also know
you've had more girls than the average guy. You'd rather jump in
the sack with any babe, get your rocks off, and go on yer merry
way. You'll find it more rewarding to ask the girl lots of
questions first -- find out all you can about her, ya gotta take
a serious interest instead of thinking with your penis."

"It's strange you said that. Professor Korsakov told me the
same thing. He told me I think more with my penis than my brains."

"Excuse me," nurse Carmen said to Jules softly, "I'm leaving
now. You can stay another ten minutes or so. Nice meeting you
both."

Jules adjusted his tie, and smiled. "Very nice meeting you
nurse Carmen. We're leaving. I didn't realize the time."

Her warm blue eyes penetrated into Jules's. "Mario is
fortunate to have someone like you to look over him. Now you
better get some rest."

What a beautiful thing to say. I'm grateful to have you and
Lynne Marie watching over Mario." He touched her hand.
"Goodnight."

Smiley stood up, he bowed his head up and down while talking.
"I repeat the same, Carmen. Most of all, I have to thank you for
assisting in pulling down my pants, my day wouldn't have been
complete without your first aid."

They laughed. Nurse Carmen left the room shaking her head.

"We'll continue this conversation another time. I want to say
goodnight to Mario." Jules and Smiley walked over to Mario's bed.
Jules held his hand. "Mario? It's me, Jules. I talked with the
doctor, and he told me your back is broken. Everything is gonna be
fine, but you have to come out of this coma first, then he'll be
able to fix you. So, will ya hurry up, how much sleep ya need?
Okay kid, I'm leavin', talk to ya tomorrow, goodnight for now." He
kissed his hand.

Smiley had a sad face as he looked at Mario. "Poor kid. I
feel so damn bad. The kid's gonna pull through Jules, you'll see.
Come on now, you look beat out." Smiley put his arm over Jules's
shoulder, and they left the room.

They walked down the stairs, through the lobby, and outside.
A heavy mist covered the few cars that were in the parking lot.

"You look like you can use a drink." Smiley said.

"I'm not sure yet."

"Awwww, come on Jules, just one for Chris' sake, name the
place."

"Alright-alright, Rocco's. I'll meet ya there -- hey, wait a

first thing I thought of when looking at this fog, and I musta
been daydreaming, I'm walking in Rocco's place looking for a crap
table or a blackjack table, but couldn't find one -- I couldn't
see with all that goddam smoke." He laughed. "I must be
overtired."

"Maybe somebody's tryin' to tell you somethin'." Jules said.

"What's that suppose to mean." Smiley said looking puzzled.

"Maybe you shouldn't gamble. Don't you figure out your
daydreams and dreams?"

Smiley hesitated a moment. "Never, but that's a good idea, I
will. You should be a psychologist, you'd be the finest."

"If I became a psychologist, I'd have a full time job looking
after you -- no thanks, I know where I'm goin'."

"Yer a comedian. It looks like this rain isn't gonna stop,
and my umbrella is still in the store. I been meaning to buy it,
but never get around to it."

"Relax, it's just water." Jules said. "Sonofabitch, I just
remembered, you can't swim, right?"

Smiley looked at Jules dumfounded for a moment, then broke
out in laughter. Where do you come up with these lines...? Lets
stop for a drink, whadaya say, partner?"

"I'm not sure yet, give me a minute."

"Awwww, come on Jules, just one for Chris' sake, name the
place."

"Alright-alright, Rocco's. I'll meet ya there -- hey, wait a
minute, how'd you get here?"

"I didn't tell you?" Smiley said surprised.

"Tell me what? Do I look like a mind reader or wha'?"

"Well I'll be. Look over there, the yellow Ford convertible.
No, not there," He pointed, "Right there, in the spot where your
not suppose to park. It has a rumble seat, spoke wheels, pink 'n
blue 'n black panties in the glove compartment, she's loaded. Is
she a beaut 'er what, Jules?"

"Class, real class. I proud of you Smiley. If I were you, I'd
get rid of the panties. Lynne Marie won't tolerate with that, you
know what I'm sayin'?"

"Holy shit, I'll take care of that right now." Smiley opened
the door, and pulled out twelve or fourteen multicolored silk
panties from the glove compartment. "Hey Jules, give me a hand,
here, hang on to these for a minute, I'll be right out, I'm
looking for a bag...I should have one around here."

Jules grabbed the panties, he looked around feeling
uncomfortable. "C'mon-c'mon, get yer ass outa there, I feel like a
degenerate holding these things -- hurry up will ya, Jesus
Christ!"

Smiley called out from inside the car, "Be right there. They
smell real good, don't they?"

"In ten seconds, yer gonna be eatin' silk 'n lace!"

"Ya know Jules, this car is only two years old, you'd never know it would you? I love it...I got it, the only bag I ever had -- I knew I had it around here some place." He stuffed the panties in the bag, and put it in the glove compartment.

"Why the hell did you put the bag in there?"

"I won't forget to take 'em out. I like a clean neat car."

Jules shook his head, lit a cigarette, and thought, he's such a moron. "You still workin' at Shrap's?"

Smiley slipped out of the car, and fell on his butt. "Wha, what the hell...slippery--"

"Whadya do, smell those panties before you put 'em away?"

Smiley got up laughing. "You better believe it -- they get me every time. Oh yeah, Christ, I put in twelve to fourteen hours a day. Shrap's helped me more than I ever thought. He's the one who fixed me up with the party who had this car for sale. You'll never guess who I bought it from. Two bucks say's you'll never guess, and I'll give you three guess's."

"Okay, yer on." Jules rubbed his chin while scanning over a few minor details on the car. "My first guess would be -- let me see -- I'd say you bought it from professor Korsakov."

"Wha'-- how'd you know that!" Goddam Jules, you scare the shit outa me some times."

"For Chris' sake, a idiot would know that! Look, look on the windshield, the sticker, if you could read, it tells you the name

of the university, and the professor's name, and don't ever say
"never", Mother Nature hear's you say that word, and she'll make
the opposite happen, trust me."

"You may have a good point there." He laughed. "Where do you
come up with these things? Yer a piece of art. I'll consider it,
here's the two bucks."

"Put it away, ya weren't thinkin' when ya made the bet."

"Awww, come on, you won it fare 'n square."

"You can buy me a drink if it'll make you feel better."

"Yer on." Smiley said. "Oh, I forgot to tell ya -- that
sticker? I can park in all the no parking zones. I mean, when the
cops spot the car, and see who it belongs too, they don't ticket
the car. I take advantage of it. Never had a ticket yet."

"Yer gettin' one soon." Jules said boldly.

"Whadaya mean?" Smiley said in a serious tone.

"You love that word, "never", I told ya, 'never say never'--
you'll learn."

"Awww shit, will ya stop with the superstitious bullshit, fer
Chris' sake, you think I'm still gullable? Well, yer way off
base. This is the new Smiley Patrick O'Brian you're conversing
with. But wait, wait, considering your I.Q is far more superior
than mine, I'll try to eliminate that word from my vocabulary,
how's that?" He pinched Jules's cheek, and laughed.

"Do what you want, it's yer life. You should do it, not try,

you have to do it for you. I'm just tryin' to help you, that's
all. And another thing, it's too late, once you say "never",
there's no way you can take it back, that's how Mother Nature
operates, so expect something to happen you aren't gonna like."

"Do you really expect me to believe--"

"We gonna stand here 'n bullshit all night or wha? Do what
you want. When it happens, you'll hear it from me till the end of
time -- see ya at Rocco's." He walked away.

"Wait!" Smiley shouted. "I have a question I--"

"Save it. See ya at Rocco's."

Smiley screeched off. He was out of sight before Jules got
to his car.

By the time Jules reached Rocco's, he spotted Smiley's car
parked in a illegal space directly in front of the restaurant.
Jules pulled in the parking lot and noticed nine or ten cars. He
thought, what's goin' on? These cars belong to the dealers.
Somethin's up. He walked to the front of the restaurant, and
Smiley lay on the sidewalk next to his car, face down in a puddle
of blood.

CHAPTER 15

NEW YORK, AUGUST 3

11:10 P.M.

Jules ran to Smiley shouting, "Smiley! Smiley!" He dropped to
his knees beside him and touched his shoulder. "Smiley! Smiley!
Get up, goddam it, get up!" He didn't move. He grabbed Smiley's
wrist and checked his pulse. "It's normal, he's alive!" Then he
checked to find wounds -- nothing visible. He rolled Smiley on his
back looking for bullet holes, knife wounds, anything -- nothing.
Jules slapped his face lightly a few times trying to revive him,
but there was no response. "C'mon-c'mon, open yer eyes goddam it,
yer not dead yet! The Irish die havin' sex -- c'mon-c'mon!" He
strained himself as he pulled Smiley's foot out of the gutter.
Jules lost his balance and almost fell on top of Smiley, but he
quickly braced himself with his arm; the palm of his hand and
fingers fastened on to Smiley's genitals.

Suddenly, Smiley jumped up to a sitting position and shouted,
"Wha! Heyyyy! Whadaya think yer doin'!"

Jules looked dumbfounded, and roared, "What! You shouldn't
be sittin' up like that! He grabbed Smiley's coat, and gently
pushed him down. "Jesus! Ya wanna die? What the fuck happened? I
didn't see any wounds or anythin'. Are ya in pain? I'll call a

ambulance -- whatever ya do, don't move!" He started getting up to
call the ambulance.

Smiley grabbed Jules's coat sleeve to stop him. He abruptly
started to choke badly, and gasp for air, as he did, a stream of
blood flowed from his mouth onto his chin. He sounded as if the
end was near.

Jules touched Smiley's face easy. "Goddam Smiley, hang on
will ya, yer the only guy I give the business to, an' get away
with it. Yer gonna make it, c'mon ya Irish bastard, hold on."

Smiley suddenly burst out in laughter. He sat up and laughed
some more, shouting, "Don't bother calling anybody, I pulled a
fast one on you, sucker." Still laughing, and talking, he
continued saying, "Were even sweetheart -- I mean, the five
million times you got me through the years, I never got even, I
figured the time couldn't be any better than tonight to get you --
big time. I had to make it good, real good. Are you mad at me? I
wish you could see your face."

Jules didn't move from the kneeling position he was in -- he
didn't move a muscle. His eyes pierced into Smiley's. A deadly
serious expression was painted on his face. He grabbed Smiley's
coat with both hands, and jerked him forward.

In a threateningly soft voice, he said, "You're a very sick
person doin' something that low. You did good -- better than me --
we're even, pal." He broke out in laughter. "Great performance

Smiley, excellent acting."

Smiley laughed, and hugged Jules. "Ya know Jules, yer the
first guy that ever had me by the balls."

Jules bolted back to arms length, and said softly, "Did ya
like it?"

Smiley dropped his head looking bashful. He hesitated for two
or three seconds, then looked at Jules.

"N-no! But if you will, would you do it again, 'cause only
then I'll know for sure."

They laughed until tears filled their eyes.

Jules accidently rested his hand in the pool of blood. He
smelled it then tasted it with the tip of his tongue.

"This is tomato sauce, fer Chris' sake -- it's seasoned with
garlic, basil, the whole nine yards -- you don't use this crap, it
smells, wrong color too. All ya need to do is strain some plain
ol' ketchup, water it down to the consistency of blood, then add a
few drops of vanilla extract to kill the tomato smell. Now yer
cookin'. Get some capsules, five or ten is all you need, empty
them, an' fill them with the new mix. Seal the capsules an' yer on
yer way. Store them in the refrigerator just like ya would with
ketchup. When yer ready to make a score, place it in yer mouth
with one finger, maybe two, slip it between the back molars and
the jaw bone. When it's show-time, just bite down on the capsule
an' let the liquid ooze out the lower corner of the mouth. That's

the deal. There's one more thing, the most important. If ya don't do it right, don't waste yer time -- it takes practice, practice an' more practice in order to perfect this little stunt. It has to look real, that's what it's all about."

Smiley looked astonished. "Where the fuck! I mean, where the fuck do you get this information? Goddam, that's genius -- absolutely incredible!" He had a surprised expression painted on his face. His finger slowly tapped his chin as he gazed in Jules's eyes.

"Read." Jules thought, he's acting like he just got laid fer the first time fer Chris'sake. Look at him, what a character. He shook his head, and laughed.

"I know-I know," Smiley said, "you're thinking about this fake blood, tastes familiar doesn't it? Louie made it. Great sauce-great sauce."

"I thought it tasted familiar." Jules said smacking his lips.

Smiley got up, opened the door to his car, pulled off his stained coat, and slipped on a sport jacket.

"I came prepared."

"So I see. Yer becoming efficient for a moron. C'mon, lets go inside before it start's rainin' again."

Smiley laughed. "You're a ball-buster. I'm going to move the car in a little while, it should be alright -- whadaya think?"

"I already told ya the deal with the cops, they don't mess

aroun' on this street -- do what you want."

"I'll take a chance and move it later."

They started walking to the front door, and Jules stopped.
He lit a cigarette, and gave Smiley a serious look.

"I don't mean to tell you yer business, but maybe, just
maybe, you didn't think about the fact that the professor's name
is on that sticker. Why would you want to park yer car in a
conspicuous place, especially in front of this joint -- not only
that, but why would you want the cops to think the professor is in
the place? Christ, once they spot that car, the sticker, yellow
convertible an' all the bullshit, their gonna get ideas, 'n word
get's aroun' fast with these guys. Sure, Rocco always paid them
off to look the other way, they have not ever busted us. But they
get a hard-on ticketing cars on this street. Do yourself a favor,
get rid of the sticker, be a diehard. It's better to be keep a
low profile than being a show-off. You can be a show-off only
when you have to, you know, when we do our thing, know what I
mean?"

"Yer right-yer right, I never, I mean, I didn't think about
it like that. But Jules, my meatball friend, me? Lookin' and
dressing like a F.B.I. agent? I'd find it rather difficult being
square." He took a few steps until his nose touched Jules's ear,
then pulled back slightly. He looked around, then put his nose
back on Jules's ear again, and whispered, "I'll work on it pal,

but please, this is between you 'n me." He stepped back, and with
a closed-mouth smile, he looked around, then turned back to Jules.

Jules stared at him and thought, what's this guy on? "You
takin' pills? Did the prof recommend some sort of drug fer yer
insaneness? What's the deal?"

"Y-you think you know it all, don't you?" Smiley said looking
around again.

"Well Jesus Christ boy, yer actin' strange. Yer lookin'
aroun' like a couple a thugs are on yer tail."

Smiley's eyes widened, "Wha! Whadaya mean? Ohhhh, that. You
aren't going to believe this, but I've been practicing."

"Practicin'! Practicin' what!"

"You know."

"Know what!"

"You know -- F.B.I.? Agent? I already started practicing,
something wrong with me starting now? Early? My new image? I'm a
slow learner, you know that -- I have to work twice as hard to get
thinks down pat." He stood there with his endless smile puffing on
his unlit cigar.

"You know I'm a patient man, right?" Jules said calmly.

"No question about it, the best." Smiley replied.

"Can't you simply answer the question?"

"I did!"

"Alright! Alright!" Jules said loosing his patience a bit. He lit a cigarette, and thought, Smiley's taken pills, the guy's not right, he's in trouble. I'll get it out of him. Jules raised his head, looked at the sky, and thought some more, God, you been good to me, and I'd appreciate it if you would give me a little more strength, you know. This piece of work ya molded together is wearing me out. He's a character alright, don't get me wrong, I like the poor soul, after all, he is my best friend. Thank you.

Jules calmed down. He took another drag from his cigarette, a long deep one this time, and left it between his lips, then looked at Smiley. "Jesus, I feel bad. I been too hard on ya." His hands reached out to Smiley's face, and he lightly patted his cheeks. "Are ya taken antidepressants or something?"

"What!" Smiley shouted. "Do I look like I do!"

"Don't get mad." Jules said softly. "Why do I always have to pull things outa ya?"

Jules knew when a dimple appeared on the lower left cheek of Smiley's face, he was lying.

"Okay, yeah, ya hit it on the head, yer right again -- right-right-right-right." Smiley said calmly. A tear rolled down his cheek.

Jules grabbed Smiley's shoulders, and shook him. "Talk ta me-talk ta me, whatever yer taken ain't workin'." He said heated.

"I don't know why I lie, I'm having one hell of a time kicking the dirty habit." Smiley said sadly.

Jules shouted, "Never mind about that, what the fuck you poppin' in yer mouth!" He held Smiley's shoulders firmly.

"I'll tell you -- only because I love you like a brother." He wiped his tears, and took a deep breath. "You hit it, your right on the money, I'm taking antidepressants. You know me, I've always been a up guy. I really can't tell if these pills elevate me more or bring me down. I've been fucked up ever since I been takin' 'em."

"How long is that?"

"Three years."

"Who gave you the prescription?"

"Professor Korsakov recommended a shrink friend of his, Dr. Cornelio, he's a good psychiatrist, nothing like I imagined, he's been treating me too, he gives me the prescription."

Jules let go of Smiley, and lit another cigarette. "I thought I knew you. What do you do when you sit with the shrink, analyze him? Yer suppose to talk to the guy, tell him how you feel with the medication yer takin', ya gotta tell him everything, everything fer Chris' sake."

"Your right. I analyze him for fifteen-twenty minutes."

"Does he ask you questions?"

"Sure."

"What questions?"

"He ask's me how do I feel, and gives me my prescription."

Jules raised his hands, and waved them about, he looked angry. "I knew it! I knew it! What's wrong with you!? I want you to call that shrink first thing tomorrow, make a appointment, an' tell him exactly how ya feel, ya got that? He'll fix you up with another drug that should work. Ya probably got toxins in yer blood. Ya wanna die?"

"Jesus, no."

"Well, ya better make that appointment then." Jules pinched Smiley's cheek. "C'mon, I need a drink."

"By the way," Smiley said, "I like that Caddy yer driving, she's a beaut."

"Rocco gave it to me. He was a generous man. C'mon, I'm curious about what's goin' on inside."

They walked up to the temporary doors, and Jules knocked.

"Jesus," Smiley said, "look at the fucking bullet holes all over the place. I bet there's a hundred pounds a lead jammed in those walls, son-of-a-bitch. This looks professional Jules, you know, the pervert? Tony Cheese? The queer who screw's anybody in the ass as long as it's a guy?"

"He's a intelligent individual, and very dangerous. He'll pay for his wrongdoing when he least expect's it." He knocked on the door harder than before, and yelled, "What's goin' on in there!"

"Looks like somebody's fixing up the place." Smiley said looking at the temporary front doors.

"Yeah, I talked with MoMo earlier, he didn't waste time comin' over. He had his crew with him. They cleaned the mess, and put these temporary doors up. They'll be finished in a couple days. Jesus Christ! What the fuck they doin' in there!" He reached in his pocket for the key, at the same time kicking the door several times. He straightened the circular wreath hanging on the door in respect for Rocco. "Why we standin' here like dummies?" He nearly put the key in the lock, and the door opened.

Trip stood there unable to talk because he had a mouthful of meat; half of it protruded from his mouth; his cheeks bulged, and gravy and saliva dripped off his bearded chin.

"Juth!...Mmmm mm mm!" Trip said wide eyed and surprised. He looked like a chipmunk chewing rapidly.

Jules said to Smiley, from the side of his mouth, "He said, Jules!...Mmmm mm mm. No. He said, Jules! Come in. That's what it sounded like anyway. I don't know how this palooka eats without teeth...strange."

Smiley laughed. "He can't eat 'n talk at the same time, that's for sure. And it may be a good idea to wipe yer face, coat too, I wouldn't want you to get malaria or rabies, if ya know what I mean."

Jules gave Smiley a dirty look. "Grow up," he said heated. He reached in his pocket and pulled out a handkerchief then wiped his face and coat quickly, and thought, the goddam bonehead spattered

half a mouthful on me, Jesus, I hope this gravy don't leave a
stain -- what a half-wit.

Trip stood there chewing away like a starving dog. He made
chomping sounds and acted as if he would never eat again. He was
holding a big oval glass dish on his shoulder containing what
appeared to be roast beef or a large leg of lamb. It must have
been at least twenty-five or thirty pounds. It looked and smelled
outrageously delicious saturated with glazed brown sugar and
covered with pineapple chunks, onions and cherries. Surrounding
the base of the meat were neatly cut sweet and boiled potatoes.
And in a decorative style, wedged apples and peaches and oranges
and grapefruit circled the rim of the dish. The roast rested on a
thick layer of chopped coconut and black olives. Trip had a
gourmet touch alright.

Jules gave Trip a dirty look, and said laughing, "If you were
my brother, I'd call you a fuckin' slob!" He laughed harder than
before, at the same time he pinched Trip's bulging cheeks.

Trip didn't move a muscle. He stopped chewing, gravy and
saliva oozed down his bearded chin. He was embarrassed, and
totally ashamed.

Jules thought, Oh God, I didn't mean to hurt his feelings, I
feel bad for the poor guy now. He grabbed a potato and took a
bite. "Just kiddin' Trip, somebody's gotta give ya the heat
aroun' here. Mmmmm, whatever ya made there is makin' my mouth

water...what is it?"

Before Trip could answer, Jules turned his head to the dining
room where he heard laughter. He turned back to Trip. "Who's
here? What's goin' on? Heyyyy...what the hell you doin' here at
this hour? Cookin'? Now? I smell a rat."

"It's not that leg of lamb, that's for sure." Smiley said.

Trip wanted his roasted bear leg to be a surprise. Later,
after everyone had their fill, he would tell them.

Jules and Smiley walked into the dining room. The twelve
dealers that worked with Jules were sitting around a large round
table talking and drinking. Two flickering white candles attached
to Chianti bottles were on each end of the table, and there were
four one gallon jugs of homemade wine in the center. The boys were
having a good time. Sol, looked up and noticed Jules and his
guest.

He shouted, "Heyyy, here he is everybody! Heyyy Jules, glad
ya made it! Come in-come in, yer always welcome in yer house!" He
laughed with a rugged wheeze that didn't stop.

Everyone stood up and laughed at Sol, then applauded and
whistled and carried on for Jules. They didn't stop applauding.
His presence seemed as though he just had been appointed the new
Godfather. Each one of the boys came up to Jules, they embraced
him, and kissed him on both cheeks. They loyally worked for
Rocco, long before Jules came into the picture. They were shills,

flimflammers and dukemen (card cheat's) and were the best
professionals in the country. The boys loved Jules, and respected
his new position as their new boss, and owner of Rocco's
restaurant. He introduced Smiley to everyone, then he and Smiley
walked to the table. The boys applauded again.

Sol, the loud mouth said, "Sid down-sid down, dis is yer
table, Jules. I'll pour you'z guys some a dis wine, it'll relax ya
good, yaaa, maybe too good." He laughed with a rugged wheeze.

The boys laughed, and pounded on the table.

Smiley sat down, and Jules stood there. He rested both palms
on the table, and didn't say a word. The two glasses of wine Sol
filled were passed along by the boys, and given to Jules and
Smiley. Jules looked at each and everyone of the boys with a
straight face, and waited for them to calm down. When they did, a
complete silence filled the room. He pulled out a cigarette, lit
it from one of the candles, and took a deep drag. He looked
aggravated.

In a heated voice, he said, "Who's responsible for this!"
He looked at each of the boys, then stopped at Sol. He stared in
his eyes, and waited for a explanation. Jules knew Sol arranged
the celebration. Sol flinched, dropped his head slightly, then
swallowed. He cleared his throat, and looked at Jules, with great
concern.

In a low grizzly voice, he said, "Me!" He raised his glass.

"And for da honor, I give you a toast." Everybody raised their glasses. "We want you ta know Jules, as you ascend up dat hill of prosperity, may your friends tag along with a firm grip! Salute."

Everyone laughed as they touched glasses and tasted their wine.

"Thank you, but that's not gonna get you off the hook, Sol. "Don't you think? Did you forget we buried Rocco today? Is this the way you show respect?" Jules said heated. "It had to be you -- yer the only big mouth aroun' here that could convince the rest of the boys that this would be the perfect time to pull-off this get-together. Well, I'm gonna tell ya somethin' -- ya screwed up good this time, I got a bad taste in my mouth. I'm disappointed in ya. There's two reasons why I'm pissed-off, Mr. organizer, but before I tell ya, tell me why you arranged the gang to be here tonight? Are ya capable? Maybe yer too drunk."

Sol had confusion painted on his face. "Y-yeah, sure, I made a mistake, wasn't thinkin', sorry, Jules. I feel bad about dis."

Jules raised his voice, and slammed his fist on the table.

"You should, goddam it. I wanna know what the fuck is goin' on aroun' here, and why did the goddam boys stop applauding me so soon!" He stood there with a straight face.

Jules's convincing story was just a joke. Sol had never been fooled before, he knew if someone was playing games with his head, not this time.

The room became silent. Everyone had a blank look on their face for a moment. Suddenly, the room filled with blaring wild laughter. They realized Jules pulled-off a joke on Sol for the first time.

Sol stood there looking embarrassed, he tried to hide it, but couldn't so he pounded on the table with one of the wine jugs to get attention, it broke in half spilling on the table. The bottom half contained a quarter of wine. He picked it up with two hands and held it to his chest.

He shouted, "Okay, okay, calm down-calm down. S-so he got me -- big deal, you'z guys been had lotsa times, don't forget it. So watch who yer pointin' yer finger at...now shud up!"

One of the boys shouted, "Yeah, sure Sol. This may be yer first, but guess what? It ain't yer last -- yer a marked man now!"

The room filled with laughter.

Sol shouted louder than before. "Awww, shud up, it ain't da end a da world ya know." He drank a mouthful of wine from the broken jug; most of it flowed down his chin onto his shirt.

Everyone laughed harder than before, they whistled, stomped their feet and pounded on the table.

Sol took another swig, the remaining wine from the jug spilled all over him. He looked like a clown.

Another voice from the crowd shouted, "Hey Sol, maybe somebody's tryin' to tell ya somethin', ya get it!"

Everyone laughed. One of the other boys cried out, "Sit down! Sit down, ya bum!" Then everyone joined in shouting, "Sit down! Sit down! Sit down!" They laughed harder than before.

Sol put the empty wine jug on the table. He waved his arms about trying to say something. "C'mon will ya, gimmie a break fer Chris' sake." He didn't have a chance. A few of the boys assisted him off the table. "Awwww shit, you win-you win." He directly went to the rest room, wobbling a bit. Everbody applauded his finale.

Jimmy "The Dealer" stood up, and raised his glass high. "Jules, seein' that bloody bloke Sol couldn't finish, I will. Everyone laughed, and raised their glasses. "This toast is to celebrate yer new position as our boss. We want to wish you the best of health, happiness, lotsa love an' success. We're all behind you, just as we were with Rocco. Here's to ya Jules...Rocco too. Salute."

"Salute," Everyone said. They all touched glasses, and tasted their wine.

"Okay gentlemen," Jimmy "The Dealer" said, "I'm the senior dealer around here, Smiley. I'm supposed to be in charge of these renegade boys aroun' here --you'd never know it with that bloody blabbermouth Sol. "He smiled, and raised his glass to Smiley, then sat down.

Everyone laughed.

Sparrow stood up. His hair was brown, short and it looked

like each hair were standing at attention. Thin long brown and
dark brown eyebrows. No eyelashes. Large brown eyes close
together. Long pointed nose with small nostrils. Small lips. No
chin. Pale complexion. He stood around 5 feet 5 inches, and looked
like a sparrow, that's how he got his name. He spoke very fast,
and moved quickly. Sharp dresser.

"Hey Smiley, we met earlier. I deal cards, I'm good, fast,
an' know the score. If there's anything ya need, talk ta me
later." He sat down, looked at one of the boys, and said in a low
whisper, "I don't why I told him my life history!"

"Why don't we break it up guys." Jules said. "You can talk to
Smiley later. Drink up, have some fun. I'd like to tell ya
something about Smiley, first." He put his arm around Smiley's
shoulders. "We been pals a long time, we went to school together.
We've done a few crazy things to survive along the way, but Smiley
is not the trouble-maker he used to be -- he became a master."

Laughter filled the room.

"I just wanted to warn you in advance. One more thing about
this guy as you have probably noticed, he has a year roun' smile
molded on his face, and the only change you'll ever see, is a
bigger one."

Everybody laughed and applauded.

Smiley got up and walked around the table shaking hands with
Jimmy "The Dealer, Sparrow, Joey "Tat", Teddy "The Boost", Fat's,

Jimmy "Blue Eyes", Angel, "The Rig", Eyes, "The Hawk and Sol. The
boys wandered around the room eating cheese and crackers and
chewed the fat. Smiley walked around making conversation. Later,
Smiley came back to the table and joined Jules, Jimmy "The Dealer
and Jimmy "Blue Eyes". After a half hour or so "The Dealer" and
"Blue Eyes" excused themselves.

Smiley nodded his head a few times as he looked around at the
boys, took his unlit cigar out of his mouth, and looked at Jules.

"You have a nice bunch of guys here." He laughed. "That Sol
is a character. He told me about the time he got shot in the head.
Did he ever show you the two slugs he saved from that deal?"

Jules laughed. "The world seen those slugs. His head is as
hard as a rock. He had a small card room an' motel in Reno. One
night two robbers broke in his place when he was cashin' out, an'
one of 'em took two shots at him and left him for dead. They ran
off with fifteen hundred bucks. To make a long story short, the
two slugs ricocheted off a stone wall, bounced off Sol's head, an'
settled in a wood beam. He kept the two .22 caliber slugs, an' had
them gold plated. He has them in glass container. How old ya think
he is?"

"Fourty-five-fifty." Smiley said.

"How's thirty-one. If he took off that penciled-in rat-tail
mustache, he'd look much younger. For a short guy, he moves that
hundred minty pounds aroun' pretty good." Jules said.

Smiley said, "He don't seem to have any class."

"Class? Sol don't have any. But the guy will go out of his way for just about anybody. He's a sweetheart."

Sol yelled across the room at Jules, his white shirt and beige pants were stained red from the wine. "Ya need more wine? Ya look like ya kin use another drink, huh?"

Jules raised his glass, it was half full, he made sure Sol seen it.

Sol gestured with his hand, okay, and gave him a wink.

"He's feelin' pretty good." Jules said laughing. He finished off his wine. "Pour me a little more of that wine, I don't feel a thing, how bout you?"

"This is my first and last. I may have an occasional drink, but outside of that, I quit."

"Good for you. There's cider on the table behind you, want some?" Jules said.

"Later, I need a nipple for what I have now."

Jimmy "The Dealer" stopped at the table where the cider was and poured himself a glass.

Jules called out to him, "Jimmy "The Dealer"! He turned to Jules. Jules said, "C'mon over, bring that jug of cider with ya while yer at it."

Jimmy "The Dealer" gave a nod and stopped at Jules's table. "This is what I'm drinkin', this is the best cider aroun'

Jules, if you know what I'm tryin' to say. Yes sir ree, baby, yes sir ree. Two glasses

of this dynamite will sure as hell blow you away." He pulled the cork from

thecider jug and reached for a glass. "Looks like your holdin' up pretty good

Jules, my man. I'm drinkin' this apple juice, much safer, know what I'm sayin',

sweetheart?"

"Good boy, Jimmy, good boy", Jules said, as he held his glass up to Jimmy.

Jimmy filled his glass, raised it over his head and made a toast rather loudly.

"Awright, you bums, listen to what I got to say!" He filled a few glasses

around the table. "Try that, guys, you may want to kiss me after you sip this

stuff."

Joey "Tat" jumped in and said, "You're such a sweet guy, Jimmy. I can see

why Jules made you the dude in charge of all the dealers."

"Sure, sure, Tatsy fatsy, don't forget it. Now take a sip outa the glass an' let's

forget the kiss."

Everybody laughed.

Sol opened his big mouth, and said, "Youz guys are a bunch a losers. I mean

a bunch a pedigree, moocher-like losers, if ya know what I'm sayin'!"

Everyone at the table yelled out, "Sit down you bum! Yer drunker than all of

us. Sit down, sit down....go put yer head in the crapper!

They laughed and laughed, slammed their hands on the table and chairs.

They were having a great time. Somebody yelled out, "Sol's a great guy!"

"Take Joey Tat, talkin' with Jimmy The Dealer now. He got the name Tat, which means--"

Jimmy The Dealer came back to the table, "Sorry Jules, but the Tat had a minor problem with a lady friend, we got the bloke straight now. I musta been a bloody marriage counselor in my other life -- wish they'd lay off me tonight, Jesus Christ!"

Jules and Smiley laughed.

The Dealer turned and grabbed Joey Tat by the back of the his neck, and said, "Come here Tat my boy, don't be shy -- did you meet Smiley yet?"

"Yeah, sure. How ya doin' Smiles, we met--"

"His name is Smiley," the Dealer said, not Smiles."

Tat looked at The Dealer with a wrinkled face, and said softly, "I know Jimbo sweetheart, I know -- I call the dude Smiles." He looked at Smiley. "No disrespect Smiles." Then he turned to The Dealer, "You got somethin' against that?"

Jimmy The Dealer grabbed Tat's lower lip, and held on to it firmly. "I thought you had manners! You can call him anything you want Tatty baby, but don't embarrass me!" The Dealer pulled Tats lower lip out a bit farther, and stared at him with a closed-mouth smile.

"Ahhhh, Ooooo, awright-awright, lego ill ya!" Tat cried out in pain.

Tat hated his lip pulled, but Jimmy The Dealer knew how to

handle him. He let go of Tat's lip. Jimmy The Dealer had an expression on his face as if he concurred the world.

Tat adjusted his red swollen lower lip, and moaned.

"What da fuck, Jimmy!" He said heated, "Ya know I can't stand dat pullin' on da lip routine ya do! Goddam man, dat hurts!"

"I know," The Dealer said, "but when you get smart, that lip of your's stick's right out waitin' for me to straighten it out. You had it comin', so I apologize for the hundredth time -- I'll do it again when I think yer not so nice, don't forget it."

Tat smiled and gave The Dealer a hug. "Ya know I love ya Jimmy. Yer one of da few guys dat really cares fer me...Jules too that is."

"I know pal." The Dealer looked at Jules and Smiley, "See ya later Jules, you too Smiles."

The four laughed, and Tat waved his arms.

"I don't don't have to go to a circus comin' here, right Jules?" Smiley said.

"This is the greatest show aroun'. Whadaya think of Tat?"

"Unusual name. I've heard it before. I think Tat means con, don't it?" Smiley said uncertain.

"That's right. He's called Tat because he was a hot-shot pro in the short con game. He worked in nightclubs all over the country with crooked dice. He got caught an' spent five years in prison. He works with us now. He's fast, cool and very serious when rollin' the dice in this joint."

"He wears his pants so high on his waist." Smiley said.

Jules laughed. "Look at him, you could see his ankles fer Chris' sake. He's a tough dude, a hundred-eighty pounds of pure granite. The Dealer's been workin' on him, he'll be alright. That cider's good, fill me up. Try some."

Smiley poured Jules's glass, then his. Teddy The Boost stopped to say hello to Jules. He was a duplicate copy of Boris Karloff, the actor who played the character Frankenstein. The word Boost amongst con men means; shill (one who lures a victim to a con game). Teddy The Boost was the best. He stood six feet, three inches. Two hundred-thirty-five pounds. Fourty-three. Red hair greased back. Thick red bushy eyebrows. Dark green eyes. Large square nose. Neatly trimmed red and blond full mustache. Light red complexion. Sharp dresser. And a low smooth voice.

"Hey Jules, Smiley, nice party," The Boost said. "I have to hand it to Rocco's wine, it's pure magic. I'll lay odds 10 to 1, part of the ingredients in this wine is joy, an' joy is greater than sorrow, an' others say, sorrow is the greater. But I say, after the fourth glass, who cares!"

They laughed.

"Sit down Boost," Jules said, "Rocco knew how alright. I have the recipe, an' it will be made exactly the same way. I'm gonna order more nitro, we're runnin' low." They laughed. "Two glasses of this stuff takes ya down without warning."

They laughed harder than before.

"There's a secret to drinkin' this wine, Rocco always told me that, but he never told me the secret. I'll lay 5 to 1, you know, Jules. Ya gotta tell me." The Boost said.

"The secret is, ya gotta swallow it fast. This wine is a special batch made in 1924, it'll knock yer socks off."

"You joken with me? That's the secret?" The Boost said.

"That's the secret, no bullshit. If ya feel yer nipples gettin' hard, watch out! That's the beginin' of the ultimate erection."

They laughed.

"Jesus, this is my fourth glass," The Boost said, "Yer right about certain thing's gettin' hard. I hope it last's till I get home."

They laughed.

"Whatever you do, don't spill any of that wine on those expensive shoes yer wearin' it'll stain them for sure, trust me."

The Boost smiled. His upper left canine tooth and premolar tooth next to it was gold capped. They glittered. "Ya know Smiley, this guy think's of everything, he don't miss a trick. Can I bother you for some of that cider? Here, you can pour it in my glass, it'll dilute the goodness left in this wine, thank's pal."

Smiley filled The Boost's glass. "There ya go Boost, I'm the best when it comes to mixing drinks."

"Thank's Smiley." The Boost said. "Jules, is Mario...you know, is he going to make it? I don't mean to sound so brusque, he's such a sweet kid. What's the deal?"

"He's in a coma right now. Broken back. Hopefully he'll come out of it soon. We have to wait it out."

"My prayers go out for the boy, Jules. If there's anything I can do, don't hesitate to ask me, we got a deal?" Boost said.

"Yer on Boost, thank's."

"Excuse me gentlemen," Boost said, "we'll talk later." Off he went. His feminine walk gave him away.

"When I met him earlier, we talked for a few minutes, interesting guy. I love his short-step walk." Smiley said.

"The Boost has a boy friend in this room, I'll bet you a glass of cider you can't pick him out."

"You're on." Smiley raised his glass to Jules, and said, "May we treat our friends with kindness -- finish the toast, Jules..."

"And our enemies with generosity."

They touched glasses, and tasted their cider.

"This must be a special time in the evening, here comes Fats, all three hundred-sixty pounds of 'em." Jules said smiling.

Fats was five feet five inches tall. Thirty-two. Dark greasy complexion. Shaved head. Light brown eyebrows connected in the center. Small nose with large nostrils. Well groomed light brown and blond beard trimmed to a two month growth. Sloppy dresser. A Greek (professional cardsharp).

"How could I forget Fats, If you couldn't see, you'd think you were talking to a woman." Smiley said.

"He's got a women's voice alright. It's a high pitched one like my grandma's." Jules laughed. He act's kinda delicate. He had to take hormones of some kind when he was a kid to help take off the fat. It don't look like they worked. He's a gem."

Fats reached the table. "Jules, Jules, Jules." Fats rested his hand on Jules's shoulder. "I been waitin' an' waitin' to come over. Gosh, I thought if another guy comes over again, I'm gonna come over anyway. Oh-oh, I've been very-very rude. Hi Smiley, sorry bout that, please forgive me." He giggled, and looked at Jules. "Ohh, he so handsome."

"He's with me Fats, don't get any idea's."

They laughed. Fats sat down. His belly was so large, it drooped over the table slightly.

Jules said, "Why didn't you come to see me anyway? Ohhhh, now I get it, you thought I'd talk to you guys according to weights an' measures, that's it."

They laughed. Fats large belly wobbled every which way; it shook the table, and moved it at least a foot. Jules and Smiley held it down so it wouldn't move any farther.

Jules rubbed his hand across Fats's bulged-out paunch, and

looked at Smiley. "Fats here is not only a comedian, but he has hands of gold, and a nice big pillow here ta rest yer head."

They laughed harder than before. Fats's giggle made it funnier. Fats stayed in his original sitting position so as not to disturb the table again.

"Shit, Jules, I wish I came over to this table earlier, I ain't had laugh's like this in a long time. I love ya Jules, you're the best. Oh-oh, I hope Mario's gonna be okay, I love--"

"You gonna hog dis table all night or wha', fat boy?" Jimmy Blue Eyes said from behind as he wrapped his strong arms around Fats's upper flabby chest.

"You can't fool me. I'd know that cologne if you were six feet under. Are ya gonna let go 'er tell me ya love me?"

"Who am I, fatso?"

"Who else -- Jimmy Blue Eyes, ya dumb fuck!"

"I love ya Fats," Blue Eyes said, "but I refuse lettin' go unless ya promise ta loose at least two hundred pounds within the next twelve months -- then we'll get married, an' go to Niagara Falls, whadaya say?"

"Can I stay on the Canadian side, and you on the U.S. side?"

"Sure, but there can be complications." Blue Eyes said.

"I don't get it, what are you sayin'?"

"By the time you lose all that weight, you won't like me anymore."

"Aw, Blue Eyes, I'll always like you, squeeze me harder."

"This is the longest you allowed me to hold you like this --
my mind is made up. You're to easy, you scare me -- fuck the
Falls -- I give up." Blue Eyes grabbed Fats fat face with one
hand, squeezed it, and kissed his head. They all laughed.

Fats and Blue Eyes frequently teased each other. It was a
game they played; whoever held out the longest had the most
patience. Apparently, Blue Eyes lost this one.

"I got ya this time, Blue Eyes." Fats said giggling.

"So, big deal, you lose most of the time," Jimmy Blue Eyes
said. "I gave it to ya this time, now, shad up n drink yer wine."

They laughed. Jules excused himself from the table, and went
to the rest room. Smiley, Fats and Blue Eyes talked and laughed
while waiting for Jules. Angle, one of the dealers stopped by to
see what the laughter was all about.

Blue Eyes seen him coming, and grabbed him by his upper arms,
and said, "Angle!" Blue Eyes looked on the floor where Angle was
standing, he shook his head in disbelief. "I-Impossible! Those
yer's?!" He continued looking on the floor.

Angle looked down and around, "Whataya talkin' aboud? Dare's
nothin' there!"

Everybody was concerned, they looked on the floor also.

Blue Eyes released Angle, bent over slightly, and pointed at the floor nearest to Angles foot. He looked dumbfounded, and raised his voice, "You blind!"

Angle looked again. "What da fuck! Whadaya talkin' aboud? Dat vino's gone to yer head."

Blue Eyes reached in his jacket pocket, nobody seen him, he bent down near Angles shoe and dropped a small handful of goosedown feathers.

"Here! Right here! Am I crackin' up, 'er what! Maybe ther' invisible to yer eyes -- look, he's sheddin'! Look!"

Everybody looked. They couldn't believe their eyes. They were feeling pretty good, but not that good yet. The foursome broke out in laughter. These were the silly things the boys would do to pass the time away.

Angle looked at Blue Eyes, then at Fats, then at Smiley. "Caught again. Am I a lay down 'er wha'?" He had disappointment painted across his face, then he smiled.

Jules came back to the table. He looked at Angle knowing Blue Eyes just caught him.

"How ya doin' Angle? I been meanin' to give you somethin'.

CHAPTER 15

NEW YORK, AUGUST 3

11:10 P.M.

Jules ran to Smiley shouting, "Smiley! Smiley!" He dropped to
his knees beside him and touched his shoulder. "Smiley! Smiley!
Get up, goddam it, get up!" He didn't move. He grabbed Smiley's
wrist and checked his pulse. "It's normal, he's alive!" Then he
checked to find wounds -- nothing visible. He rolled Smiley on his
back looking for bullet holes, knife wounds, anything -- nothing.
Jules slapped his face lightly a few times trying to revive him,
but there was no response. "C'mon-c'mon, open yer eyes goddam it,
yer not dead yet! The Irish die havin' sex -- c'mon-c'mon!" He
strained himself as he pulled Smiley's foot out of the gutter.
Jules lost his balance and almost fell on top of Smiley, but he
quickly braced himself with his arm; the palm of his hand and
fingers fastened on to Smiley's genitals.

Suddenly, Smiley jumped up to a sitting position and shouted,
"Wha! Heyyyy! Whadaya think yer doin'!"

Jules looked dumbfounded, and roared, "What! You shouldn't
be sittin' up like that! He grabbed Smiley's coat, and gently
pushed him down. "Jesus! Ya wanna die? What the fuck happened? I
didn't see any wounds or anythin'. Are ya in pain? I'll call a

Blue Eyes and Jules helped Angle up from the floor. They had tears in there eyes from laughing so hard.

Blue Eyes said to Jules, "My nuts are gonna crack any second now, this is too much."

"Angle's a piece of cake, especially when he's drinkin'."

Fats said, "Hey guys, here comes The Rig and his goompa, The Hawk. They know where the action is."

"Hey guys, listen up," Jules said. The boys looked at Jules with intrigued expressions. "Before they get here, Smiley, Fats, an' Blue Eyes, drop yer heads on the table, pretend yer passed-out. Angle an' me will slump to the side of our chair a little an' fake we're plastered. Okay...now."

Walking towards Jules's table, The Rig and The Hawk were talking with each other. They stopped, it looked as though The Hawk was trying to make a point to The Rig, the way he was waving his hands about. They were only fifteen-twenty feet from the table. Jules watched their moves.

The Rig used to be an organizer of big con and fake gambling dens around the country. He rigged the games, set the crooked games up before the arrival of the victim(s).

The Rig was six feet, two inches tall. Two hundred twenty-five pounds. Forty-two. A Greek (professional cardsharp). Black hair slicked-back. Thick eyebrows to match. Black bold eyes. Large crooked nose. Black rat-tail mustache. Hands completely scared. Dark greasy olive complexion. Sharp dresser. Gentleman.

The Hawk. Noted for selling a victim on the idea of participating in a confidence game. A pro with crooked dice. Five feet, eleven inches. One hundred-seventy pounds. Thirty four. Light brown collar length groomed hair. Dark brown eyebrows. Light brown eyes. Very handsome. Year round tan. Sharp dresser. Wise-guy.

The Hawk made his point, and they proceeded to Jules's table.

"Here they come." Jules said.

"What da...I don't believe it!" The Rig said looking shocked. "I told ya dat wine catches up wid ya...look at deez guys!"

The Hawk slapped his forehead in disbelief. "Holy shit! An' we ain't eatin' yet!"

The Rig went over to Jules slumping over the chair slightly, and shouted, "Jules, you awright!" He straightened him out. "Jules baby, you awright!"

Jules opened his eyes slightly, and looked at The Rig, and said, "Ya better not drink too much a dis swine, it got me pretty goood...heyyy, who'er you?"

The Hawk was standing next to The Rig, he said, "Never seen Jules smashed before, you?"

"Never. Look at deez guys -- sonofabitch, we missed da best part a da party." The Rig said.

Smiley jumped up a bit, and said, "Heyyyy, I h-heard those

fluckin' remarks. Are yooz cops? Well, we're closed. Go arrest yer
mother, if ya know what's good yer ya. Gaaaaaaaaa." He fell on the
floor.

The Rig jumped over to help Smiley off the floor, and sat him
against the wall. He went back to Jules, and shook him.

"Jules, Jules, c'mon will ya! Snap outa dis!" He looked at
The Hawk, and shouted, "You gonna stand dare wid yer finger up yer
ass! Do somethin' yer Chris' sake!"

The Hawk rushed over to Smiley. He was gradually slipping
sideways heading for the floor, too late, Smiley sank to the
floor. The Hawk patted him on the shoulder.

"Stay right there pal, you look comfortable for now."

Fats raised his head and arms, and shouted, "The dames! They
shoulda been here! Where the fuck, what the...I want my mother...
He tried to stand up, got halfway, and slammed back down on the
chair. The chair broke, and down to the floor Fats went. He lay
there looking like a big blob of fat.

That did it. Smiley couldn't hold it any longer, he broke out
in laughter, then Angle, then Jules, then Blue Eyes, and Fats,
they laughed so hard, tears rolled down their faces. The Rig and
The Hawk stood there for a moment looking puzzled until they
realized the joke was on them. They laughed. Fats tried to get up,
but fell back down from laughing so hard.

Jimmy The Dealer came over and laughed at everybody laughing.

"What's so funny? Fats, why you on the floor? I'm missin'
somethin' good aroun' here, can someone explain?"

"Yeah, sure," The Rig said laughing, "give us a hand with
fatso."

The Dealer looked at The Rig. "What! You need a bloody tow
truck to get him off the floor."

They laughed harder than before.

Fats yanked on The Dealer's pants. "Never mind the tow truck
crap, help me up or you ain't eatin'."

It took five of the boys to get Fats back on his feet. They
picked up the broken chair, and replaced it with a sturdy one.
Trip brought the roast out and placed it on the table. Everybody
was starving, and feeling no pain. They sat at the table.

Sol yelled out, "Doe's dis look good 'er wha'!"

They applauded, howled and whistled.

Jimmy The Dealer stood up and waved his arms about trying to
calm the boys down. "Okay-okay, relax." The boys wouldn't stop.

Angle yelled out, "Shut the fuck up! Can't ya see the bloak's
got somethin' important he's gotta say 'bout himself!" They
carried on. "Hurry up, we wanna eat!"

They shouted and cheered. The Dealer hit the table a few
times with his glass, and the boys settled down.

"Thank you gentlemen, thank you very much. We're hungry, but
I just wanna say thanks to each and every one of you for helping

out on this special occasion. Jules, you have something you'd like
to say?"

Jules stood up. He looked at the boys, and said, "Ata boy
Trip, that's one hell of a leg of lamb ya put together. Whatdaya
say boys, lets give him a hand."

Everybody cheered and applauded.

"And I want to thank you gentlemen, this is quite the
surprise. I'm gonna make this sweet 'n simple. Everything will
remain the same here at Rocco's, yer jobs are secure. In three
days, we'll be opening for business, so let's eat."

The boys applauded and cheered, then became animals as they
devoured the food.

Later, after everyone had eaten, they sat content around the
table talking and laughing. The roast and potatoes and coconut --
everything had been eaten up. The only thing left was the bone,
and it had been picked so clean it glared. Trip cleaned off the
table, and brought out a large container of coffee on a rolling
cart, then reached below, and pulled out a magnificent assortment
of peaches and bananas and oranges and tangerines and pears and
strawberries and a variety of mixed nuts. He placed it in the
center of the table. Everyone applauded and whistled.

One of the boys yelled out, "Hey Trip, ya ol' fart, ya did a
hell of a job on dat leg o' lamb!"

Another one of the boys yelled out, "Best we ever had, Trip

ol' buddy!"

"Hey Trip," Sol shouted, "if ya don't gimmie dat recipe, I'm gonna keep on callin' ya fuzz nuts!"

"Yup." Trip said, smiling.

Everyone laughed. They cut peach wedges, and soaked them in their wine and cider. They were having a good time.

Later, around 2:40 a.m., Sol yelled out in his grizzly voice, "Hey Jules, before deez guys breakdown, da boys 'n me wanna give ya a little somethin -- okay boys!"

They stood up and applauded and howled and whistled.

Trip whispered something in Jules's ear. Jules gave him a surprised look, and laughed, then patted him on the shoulder.

Jules stood up, reached in his pocket, and pulled out a hundred dollar bill, and said, "Trip just informed me what we ate tonight, I'm referring to that delicious roast -- here's the deal. Whoever guesses what the roast was, get's the hundred...now wait a minute -- did we eat, pork? Beef? Lamb? Wild bore? Whatever, I'm gonna write it down on this piece of paper, and have Trip hold it. Okay, we'll start with Jimmy Blue Eyes."

After ten-fifteen minutes, no one had the right answer. A few thought it was beef, some said leg of lamb, and Sparrow swore it was aged pork mixed with veal and venison.

"Okay, I keep the hundred -- tell 'em Trip, tell the boys what you made special...go ahead."

Trip whispered in Jules's ear again.

"Don't worry about it Trip. Give the piece of paper to whoever you wish." Jules said.

Trip looked around. He handed it to Jimmy The Dealer.

"Trip can't talk to well without his teeth, don't give him the business either. Okay Dealer, tell us what that delicious roast was." Jules said.

The Dealer unfolded the paper. He stared at the answer. His face turned white as he swallowed. He looked at everyone trying to keep his composer, then cleared his throat. "Bear! We ate bear!"

Everybody but Jules, Smiley and Sol, jumped up gagging, coughing and swearing, and ran off to the rest rooms. They were all pale, and acted as if they ate bear meat.

"I wonder what that was all about?" Jules said.

"Connoisseurs? I don't think so." Smiley said sucking on his unlit cigar.

Sol looked at Smiley, and with a serious expression said, "Yer right, yer absolutely correct, what da fuck do deez guys know 'bout da gourmet scene." Then he looked at Jules. "Hey, don't get me wrong, I've eaten all kinds a wild stuff, even rattlesnake. But dis bear is da best I ever had." He coughed a few times, and swallowed several times. Suddenly he jumped up, and gagged. He ran across the room, and out the front door, and vomited on the Smiley's car.

The boys gradually returned to the table. They still looked a little pale, and didn't say a word. Sol was the last to come to the table, he looked as if nothing had happened.

Sol said loudly, "Well gentlemen, dis is a night ta remember. Hey Jules, how 'bout a final toast, ya know, one for da road."

Jules stood up, and raised his glass, and all followed suit.

"Here's to you and here's to me, and may we never disagree, but just in case we ever do, here's to me, ta hell with you." They laughed. The ringing of glasses echoed through the room. It was a great night.

CHAPTER 17

NEW YORK, AUGUST 5

10:15 A.M.

The next day, Jules went to Bellviue Hospital to see how
Mario was progressing. He stopped at the front desk.

"Mornin' nurse, how are you on this sunshine day?"

The petit elderly nurse was sharpening a pencil. She had
beautiful short silver hair. She raised her head, and looked at
Jules. She stared at him for a moment, then smiled. Her wrinkled
hands were so small they could be put into small mouth jars.

"Well, good morning to you young man. What a delight it would
be if everyone was as pleasant as you. How can I help you?"

Her voice shivered as she spoke. She stared at Jules, her
head quivered as she patiently waited for a response.

"I'd like to find out how Mario De Lucca is doing, if ya
don't mind." He noticed her name on her ID tag; it was Previna.
And being a charmer, he poured it on.

"What a beautiful name -- Previna sounds French, did I do
good?"

She looked astonished. "You know young man, I've worked here
for twenty-four years, and you're the first person that has ever

taken interest in my name. How wonderfully right you are -- do you speak French?"

He smiled. "No-no madame. I can barely speak English for God's sake. But I talk with my hands in all languages."

She giggled, and lightly slapped Jules's hand resting on the desk top.

"You must be Italian, I know my men, and I know I'm right, how'd I do on that one sweetie?"

"With a name Julius Salarno, they don't make 'em any more Italian than that, know what I mean, Previna baby?

They laughed. Previna stood up, and kissed Jules on his cheek.

"I haven't had fun like this in a long-long time, Julius."

"If ya call me Jules, like everybody else, I'll take you out to dinner, and you could bring anybody else along too, how's that sound?"

"Aren't you a sweetheart. I'd love to, but tomorrow I'm leaving for Paris. My son lives there, and I'm spending the rest of my life with him. I'll be eighty-five years old in another week. He needs me. I've lived a full life. And you, my dear Jules, have made my days complete."

"You're so sweet." He patted her fragile tiny hand."

"Oh gosh, I better look in this registration book, they'll think we're lovers carrying on like this." She giggled." His name is Mario DeLucca -- let me see know." She turned several pages, talking out loud to herself. "DeLucca...DeLucca...hmmmm."

After a minute or so, she looked up at Jules. "I don't see the name DeLucca registered here."

Jules had a look of dimay on his face. "How can that be? I was here last night, seen him, talked with doctor Cohn. Nurse Lynne Marie, an' nurse Carmen are assigned to Mario. The poor kid is in a coma. There must be a mistake. Check again would you please, Previna, I don't get it."

"What floor were you on?" Previna said.

"Third -- intensive care. Room 302. Maybe ya overlooked it."

Previna re-checked each page throughly, no Mario DeLucca.

"I'm terribly sorry Jules, we have no patient in this hospital with the name, Mario DeLucca...wait, let me make a phone call."

Previna talked with the head nurse on duty on the third floor. After a minute or two, Previna jotted something down, then hung up.

"We found something. There's a Mario DeLorenzo in room 302, can this be the person you're looking for, Jules?"

Jules thought, I remember the day when Rocco was killed, an' Mario laid helplessly on the floor. The ambulance took them both away. I followed them in my car. The hospital had ID for Rocco, but not for Mario. I came back to the office, and searched in the safe. There were two birth certificates in Mario's name; Mario DeLucca an' Mario DeLorenzo. I remember being confused, and picked up one of 'em, I think it was the one with the name, Mario DeLorenzo, now that I think of it...Jesus, that's the one I turned into the hospital, stupid...I made a mistake! I should have given them the other one, Mario DeLucca. What a moron. God, how do I get outa this one? He looked up at the ceiling thinking, okay, no big deal, it was meant to be for a reason. I'll work it out.

He looked at Previna, and smiled. "Ya know Previna, you must have made me fall in love with you or something. I don't know what I was thinking. You made me fall head over heals for you. After thinking about it, I realize I made a very embarrassing mistake, please forgive me. Now whatever you do, don't fall outa love with me, promise?" He clasped his hands together, and stood there with a apologetic expression painted on his face.

They stared at each other for a moment, then laughed softly, looking around to make sure no one was watching.

"Don't be silly, wait till you get to my age." She giggled. "You can go up to the room now, but there is on one condition."

"I'll give it my best, what is it?" Jules said.

"Make sure when you visit the hospital again, you'll think of me in London." She smiled, and threw him a kiss.

"Promise. A guy rarely gets a chance to talk to an angle anymore." He threw her a kiss, and headed for the stairs.

While walking up the stairs, Jules thought, I hope the kid
comes out of the coma. I can take care of him. I can't figure out
why Rocco had two birth certificates for Mario. I'll look into it
later, I'll be able to think clearer. It sure would nice if nurse
Carmen were here. With my luck, she's probably off. I'd like to
get to know her better. She's my type of lady.

He reached the third floor, stopped for a breather, and
thought, Whoo! These cigarettes are killin' me. I should quit. I'm
a procrastinator. I'm not ready yet, just when I walk up these
goddam stairs I get that urge to quit. He walked towards Mario's
room, and passed two nurses taking care of their patients. He
reached Mario's room, and walked in. To his surprise, nurse Carmen
was making out a report at Mario's bedside. She didn't see Jules.
Her short strawberry-blond hair glittered from the sunlight
coming through a small opening of the drawn curtain. He couldn't
help not to notice her beautiful legs, delicate thin ankles, and
her petit hour-glass figure. That's for me. What a package. She's
got it. Hey! What's she doin' here? Talk about dedication. I
better say somethin'. Jesus, don't scare her. What should I say?
Oh fer Chris' sake, go ahead, just be you. He removed his fedora,
and wiped the perspiration from his brow with his thumb.

"Excuse me," he softly said, "nurse Carmen?" He stood there
with a half smile, and thought, why did I question if it was her?
Loosen up Jules, come on now.

She turned quickly, and looked at him seriously, not knowing who
it was. Then with a big smile, she said, "Hi Jules? I was just
finishing up. How are you?"

"I'm fine. I didn't expect to see you here today. You look
absolutely beautiful...I mean..." He thought, awww Jesus, why did
I say that? C'mon Jules, relax-relax, yer actin' stupid.

"Thanks. I needed that. Sit down, I was just going for a cup
of coffee. Now I have someone I can talk with. You like your
coffee black, no sugar, right?"

"Thank you." Jules said softly.

She was full of enthusiasm. "Stay right there, I'll be right
back, I have to turn in this report. Mario...I'll tell you when I
come back, you just sit there, it's good news." She hurried out
the door.

Jules sat there for a moment, looked at Mario, and thought,
good news? How can she leave me hangin' in the air like this? It
must be about Mario, Jesus, I hope so. Look at him, poor kid,
he's gonna pull outa this, I just know he will. He got up and went
to his bedside. He wanted to see his eyes move, his hand,
anything. Nothing. He lay there in peace with himself, helpless,
not knowing what's going on around him.

Jules held his hand. "Mario? It's me Jules. Yer gonna be
alright, you keep on prayin' an' somethin' good is gonna happen. I
sure miss those big black olive eyes of your's. The boys had a

surprise party for me last night, we had a great time. They all
said hello and miss you. They told me to tell you to hurry up and
get yer butt home so they can tease you, an' answer all those
questions you ask them. I have a good feelin' you're gonna be
comin' back real soon. When you do, they can operate on yer back,
so hurry up will ya? You may have to hot-rod aroun' in a
wheelchair for awhile, but that's okay." He gently touched Mario's
eyes. "Yer gonna be fine kid, you'll do it, I'm bankin' on it."

Jules walked to the window, pulled the curtain open just
enough to look out. It was a overcast day, and the sun hid behind
the clouds for awhile then suddenly would appear. He could see
children playing in the park. A boy that resembled Mario hit a
baseball, and he ran to first base. Jules rubbed his eyes in
disbelief, thinking the boy was Mario. His eyes squinted from the
bright sun that eased out from a cloud. He closed the curtain, and
wiped a tear from his eye. On his way back to the chair, he
thought, I wonder where that Cheese bastard is hiding-out. He put
Rocco in his grave, an' had the balls to take an innocent kid an'
leave him for dead. What kind of person can do this? A sick,
greedy, fuckin' maniac, that's who. I'll catch up with him, and
when I do...

"I'm back." Nurse Carmen said cheerfully. She had a pot of
coffee and two mugs on a tray. "It's nice n strong, made it
myself." She poured his coffee, then hers, and handed Jules his

mug. "Be careful, it's hot."

"Mmmmm, smells good," Jules said, "just what I need."

"Me too. They called at five-thirty this morning asking if I would come in. I said no!"

Jules smiled. He loved her sense of humor. "You're not only beautiful, you're loyal and a dedicated person. You must have a wonderful mother and father."

Her head dropped slightly, and her eyes saddened as she looked at the floor for a moment. Then she looked back up at Jules.

"Yes, the best." She said.

Jules thought, she don't want to talk about her parents for some reason. She looked and sounded uncertain. I better change the subject. "This coffee is perfect, it's exactly the way I like it."

"Thank you." Nurse Carmen said.

"You must be tired."

"A little. I'll be fine. I'm suppose to be relieved at one this afternoon. They gave me the rest of the day off for being a good girl."

"That sounds great. But first, you better tell me the good news about Mario, then we can have lunch, whadaya say?"

"I'd love to Jules, but..." She turned to Mario for a moment, then back to Jules. "I was checking Mario's pulse this morning, as I looked at him, his eyes quivered for a moment. It happened so

quickly. I checked the time, it happened at 7:03, isn't that
wonderful?"

"That's the best news I've heard in awhile. I know he's gonna
make it, I just know."

Nurse Carmen patted Jules's arm. "It's just a matter of time.
And if you haven't changed your mind, I'd love to have lunch with
you." She smiled, and squeezed his arm.

"You know, I thought there for a moment you had a boyfriend,
I never asked you."

"I do. You know him very well. I'm looking at him."

They laughed. Suddenly, a roly-poly nurse Millie came
wobbling in the room. She looked like a wrestler. She briskly
walked up to nurse Carmen.

"Excuse me Carm, our sweetheart Mario has flowers downstairs,
is it okay to send 'em up?"

"Sure." Carmen said.

"I wanted to make sure, that's all. You know me, jumpin'
here, jumpin' there, unscrewin' things, nothin' is ever right in
that delivery department. Boy, can they screw things up." She
looked at Jules. "Hi there." Then looked at Carmen. "See ya Carm,
have ta give a class to those incompetent screwballs down there.
Oh, I heard Mario had movement this mornin', how wonderful,
indeed...see ya."

In less than a minute, another nurse walked in the room. She was tall and wiry. She carried two floral wreathes, and walked

directly to the base of the window, and set them down.

"How's this sweetie, this is the spot, don't you think?

"Hi Tammy. That's ideal. They're beautiful flowers." Nurse

Carmen said.

Georgeous, simply adorable." She turned, and walked by nurse

Carmen, then stopped quickly, and looked at her. "I heard the

good news about Mario, my prayers go out for him, Carmen. It's a

miracle, thank God...sorry, but I have to run...have a nice day,

sweetie." She quickly left the room waving good-bye.

Nurse Millie's head peeked through the doorway.

"Excuse me Carm, I forgot to tell you, you can leave anytime,

your back-up is here. Outside of...oh my, what lovely flowers...I

gotta go-go-go, see ya." As she turned, she nearly walked into the

janitor wheeling in more flowers. "Oh my!" She shouted. Her echo

carried through the hallway. Nurses, patients and a few doctors

peeked through doors to see what the commotion was. Heated, she

waved her arms about, and said, "Everything is fine-fine-fine, go

about your business, go ahead, go ahead now. And you Jonesy --

watch where yer goin' next time!" She looked like a locomotive as

she wobbled quickly down the hall.

Jonesy pushed his cart full of flowers through the door, and

stopped. He looked at nurse Carmen with a look of dread painted on

his face.

"Jonesy! More flowers?" Carmen said.

Jules was astounded. "This must be the day the flowers bloom." He leaned forward to get a closer look. "They're beautiful. I wonder who--" .

"You look terrible Jonesy, what's wrong?" Carmen said.

"I'm not meanin' ta complain 'er nothin' Miss Carmen, but jumpin' grasshoppers, that big nurse lady, Miss Millie, can sure make a guy feel awry, da ya know what I'm sayin', Miss Carmen? You should awta call her, freight train Millie. If she didn't stop real quick like, I wouldn't be wheelin' in these here flowers. Twas a close call, yes sir-ee. Is it okay ta bring in these here flowers, nurse Carmen?"

Jonesy. 5'9" tall. Southern gentleman. 60 years old. 110 pounds. Large floppy ears. Black shiny hair parted down the center. Thin black eyebrows. Big black eyes. Long nose. Small lips. Wrinkled face. Boney face and frame. Dark complexion.

"Sure Jonesy, put them with the others. You know how to arrange them. And I'll have a talk with nurse Millie, how's that?" Carmen said.

"Why thank-ee nurse Carmen, I wish the rest of the nurses aroun' here took a likin' ta me as you. You make me feel like a somebody, that is fer sure, thank-ee again Miss Carmen, thank-ee."

Jonesy arranged the flowers on the floor making sure they were well balanced.

"That Jonesy's a meticulous type of guy," Jules said to
Carmen, "look at him, he cares about what he's doin'. He's a okay
guy. And liking you doesn't hurt." He smiled.

"He's so sweet. We get along fine. He goes out of his way for
the nurses." Carmen said watching Jonesy rearranging the flowers.

There were yellow roses and red roses, lilies and carnations
and gardenias and a pot of daises. The two wreaths had an
assortment of beautiful flowers and fern and red and yellow ribbon
on one and blue and gold on the other. They were beautiful.

Jonesy said, "Never seen so many flowers delivered at one
time, by golly. That Braunstein florist seems ta get all our
business, ther' the best aroun' this neck a the woods, yup, the
best." He stepped back, and looked at what he had accomplished.
"Yes sir-ee, that should do the trick. What cha think Miss Carmen,
is that to yer likin'?"

"Jonesy, you should be a florist, you did a wonderful job,
didn't he Jules?"

Jules got up and went up to Jonesy. He shook his hand, and at
the same time slipped a ten dollar bill in his hand. "Yer a good
man Jonesy--"

Jonesy looked at the ten dollar bill, and said, "jumpin'
grasshoppers mister, I can't take this, this is almost what I make
in a week!"

"Is yer mother alive?" Jules asked.

"Y-yes sir-ee." Jonesy said looking confused.

"You send yer mother a rose with that money, then call her --
tell her you love her, and thank her for bringing you into this
world. You can do that, right Jonesy?"

"Ya know mister, that's the nicest thing I ever heard. I'll
do that, promise. Thank-ee, an' may the Lord bless you." He shook
Jules's hand, and didn't say another word. He grabbed his push-
cart, and walked out the room looking overwhelmed.

"See ya Jonesy." Carmen said.

Jonesy didn't hear her. He was simply touched by what Jules
had told him.

Carmen went up to Jules. "That was very kind of you, Jules.
You're a nice guy. Knowing Jonesy, he'll always remember you."

"I meant it. He takes pride in what he does. I respect people
like that." Jules said. He went to Mario's bedside, and held his
hand. "How ya doin' kid? I heard the good news, that's just
great. It won't be long now, that's all you have to do is climb
another mountain, maybe two, an' you'll be back. I know you have
the faith and strength. Keep yer head up, an' don't look back. A
step at a time, that's what you take, you'll be back sooner than
you think. Okay, I'm gonna check out these beautiful flowers that
were just sent to you, I dyin' to find out who sent them. We'll
talk later."

He walked over to the flowers, pulled out a red rose, smelled it and handed it to Carmen.

"I want you to have this Carmen, I know your heart is here, and I know if Mario could see everything you've done for him, he'd do the same. Shhhh, don't say a word." He kissed her on the cheek, then turned and looked at one of the flower arrangements.

A tear rolled down Carmen's face. She clutched the rose to her bosom.

Jules talked out loud to himself as he looked at the carnations. "Beautiful, where's the card?" He looked inside, and around. "Here it is, hell of place to bury it...let's see:

Dear Mario,

Thinking of you

Get well real soon

Sincerely,

Smiley

Very nice, Jules thought. He read the card on the gardenias:

Dear Mario,

We're all here behind you.

The nurses on the third floor.

How thoughtful.

The rest of the flowers were from "The boys", Mario's tutor, Peter, JoJo and Izzy, and Jules.

Jules turned, and looked at Carmen, "The flowers are beautiful, thank the nurses for me would you? I can thank you

right now." He noticed a tear on her face. "Hey now, I see a tear
here waiting to be wiped away." He wiped the tear with his finger.
"I'll save this tear," he put it in his pocket, "just in case I
need an extra one."

Carmen laughed. "You're funny Jules, that's cute."

"It's difficult for me to see tears, I don't know why, but it
is. Why are your eyes filled with tears Carmen, did I say
something wrong?" Jules said, looking sad.

"Oh no Jules, your just a nice guy...that's all."

He wrapped his arms around her, and rocked for a moment.

"Okay, okay now, yer just over-tired, maybe you should skip
lunch, and go right home, I think that's a good idea." Jules said
softly.

"But I'm starving!"

Jules laughed, released her and backed-off a bit. "You're
priceless, talk about comical...yer beautiful, no question about
it. He gave her a light kiss on her lips. I'm starvin' too."

"I'll meet you in the lobby in fifteen minutes. Do you have a
place in mind?"

"I know the perfect spot for lunch."

As Carmen left the room, she walked out looking excited. It
was a big deal having the rest of the day off. Jules needed
someone special in his life, and Carmen seemed to fit the picture
just right. She had a certain something about her that Jules

couldn't figure out yet. They both felt they had known each other, in another time, and in another place.

Before leaving, Jules went over to Mario.

"See ya later, kid. I'm goin out to lunch with one of your nurses, nurse Carmen. I like this girl, Mario. There's something about her that intrigue's me. Yer gonna love her. Well, that's the deal, talk ta ya later." He stared at him for a moment, and thought, Jesus, I hope to God you come outa this, we have lot's a things to do. Then he patted his hand, and left.

Jules walked down the stairway to the second floor. He stopped and lit a cigarette, and thought, I have to find out a few things about Carmen that are drivin' me up a wall. I'll be easy on her. She didn't want to talk about her Mother or Father...why? I'll get it out of her. I have to do it in a gentle way. She'll open up, I know she will.

CHAPTER 18

NEW YORK, AUGUST 5

12:20 P.M.

Jules sat in the lobby reading a newspaper while waiting for
Carmen. A few minutes later, a pair of hands with soft leather
gloves wrapped around his eyes from behind.

"Guess who?" The strange voice said.

"The voice sound's familiar...the scent of your perfume is a
dead give-away -- it's nurse Lynne Marie."

She took her hands away, and stepped in front of him.

"You're good. Carmen asked me to tell you she'll be five more
minutes. I have to change, running late. Have a nice lunch. See
you, handsome." She hurried away.

"What a..." Jules sat there with his mouth open, he thought,
Christ, I'm just about ready to say something, and she's off like
a mare, dames. He shook his head, and smiled.

Fifteen-twenty minutes later, Carmen walked to where Jules
was sitting. He had the newspaper above his eyes engrossed in the
sport page. Carmen stood there with a simple black hat turned up
in front, a silk leopard scarf wrapped loosely around her neck, a
light gold silk blouse, a thin black leather and gold belt, black
skirt, black high heel shoes and a black three-quarter length

coat. She was a knock-out. Her make-up had a light touch; she looked natural and beautiful.

"Hi Jules?"

Jules dropped the newspaper on his lap, and looked at her up and down, and said, "Excuse me, are you talkin' to me, madam?"

She hesitated, and thought, he's playing a game with me. I'll just go along with him. "Oh! Excuse me, I thought you were someone else, please forgive me." She had a astonished look painted on her face. Then she looked around acting as if she were looking for someone.

"I'm waiting for someone, Jules said. We're suppose to have lunch, I think she forgot. Or maybe it was dinner. She really get's to me, send's me, if ya know what I mean. Would you care to join me for lunch?"

Their eyes met, and they stared at each other for a moment. Jules sat their waiting for an answer. Suddenly, they burst out laughing.

Jules got up and raised both hands, and said, "Nurse Carmen? Is that you? I thought you were a dream." He touched her face. "You are a dream, but I can still feel you. You look georgeous."

"Thank you. I could have gone on much longer, but your expressions were to much for me...you're so funny."

"You probably could have played that game all through lunch, you played the part very well."

"I don't know about that," Carmen said laughing, "but it's fun."

"I'll get the car."

"No-no. Come on," she grabbed his arm, "We'll walk together.

As they walked to the car, Jules asked her, "What are you in the mood for? Steak? Italian? Chinese?"

"I'm in the mood for turkey."

"With chewy mashed potatoes, gravy an' cranberry sauce?"

"Oh! Sounds delicious." Carmen smacked her lips. "I can taste it now."

They reached the car and drove off.

"Jules, I have a confession to make."

"A confession? I don't understand."

Remember you asked me about my mother and father?"

"Sure. I was under the impression you didn't want to talk about them at that time."

"It's not just that, this is the first date I've had since my mother past away."

"I'm sorry Carmen. When did this happen?"

"A year and a half ago. She died of leukemia. She was only fifty-four years old."

"God, that's a shame, so young. How did your father take it? I mean, he must have been very strong and had courage and hope and hung in there all the way -- you as well."

"My father--" .

Jules screeched to a stop for a red light. "Sorry, I wasn't payin' attention to my drivin', you okay?"

"It would take more than that to shake me up."

A car pulled alongside of Jules and blasted it's horn, then a voice yelled out, "Jules! Jules!" It was Jimmy The Dealer. "Gotta talk -- important."

"Meet me at the Hotel Restaurant -- our table." Jules shouted back.

The Dealer confirmed with a nod.

"I'm sorry Carmen, you were about to say something about your father."

That man in the car looked familiar, do you know him well?"

"That's Jimmy The Dealer, he's a friend of mine. Do you gamble? Ever been in Rocco's Italian restaurant?"

Carmen thought for a moment. "Isn't that a private club?"

"That's right. The place caters to people who like to gamble. And the northern Italian food is considered to be one of the best in town. The members are mostly gamblers, they enjoy being with their own kind. Were you ever in the place?"

"I remember now...Lynne Marie arranged a blind date for me, I really didn't want to go, my mother being sick and all. I had no interest with the rest of the world at the time. Lynne Marie convinced me and before I knew it, I'm in the back seat with her boyfriend's friend. I didn't like him from the start. They both

looked like they were connected. He had such a ego. I couldn't
wait to strangle Lynne Marie. He moved right in and tried to touch
me. I set him straight in a hurry. He acted like a gentleman after
that. We went to dinner, and later ended up at Rocco's for a
drink. Lynne Marie's boyfriend was a member. We went to the
second floor and there's this beautiful casino, I couldn't believe
my eyes. I've been impressed before, but not like this, Lynne
Marie too. We had fun, it took my mind off my mother. We all were
at the crap table and my date lost eight or nine hundred dollars,
he started a commotion, he was cheated. He hit one of the players
and they started to fight. A well dressed gentleman with a red
carnation in his lapel, and two large men broke it up and took him
to the side. The man with the carnation asked him some questions,
he was very polite. He gave him back his money with the condition
that he left the property. We were escorted to the bar for a
complimentary drink, but we didn't stay. The gentleman who
returned the money to my date was your friend, Jimmy. Life is just
full of surprises, isn't it?"

Jules laughed. "That's a classic story. Do you remember your
dates name?"

"Stone. Hands would be more appropriate. He bragged all
night about certain big people he knew in the Mafia. And I know
when one is connected, they certainly don't talk about it."

Jules laughed. "Jeez Carmen, you talk like you're familiar

with the organized crime scene -- that's it -- I just figured it out, you're the daughter of the Godfather!"

Carmen gave Jules a light punch on his arm, and laughed.

"You're so funny. I read the paper, pick up that lingo right on the front page."

Jules laughed. "Just kiddin', but who were the names that fellow Stone mentioned?"

"Ohhh, ummmm, Lucky...Bugsy...and Meyer, he brought his name up every twenty minutes it seemed."

"Lynne Marie must like this type of guy, huh?"

"I really didn't know her that well at the time, we worked together and after awhile became good friends. One day, her boyfriend disappeared. No one knows what happened to him. She hasn't gone out with anybody ever since then."

"I'm sorry to hear that, she's such an attractive girl." I don't know who Lynne Marie's boyfriend was, I have an idea being with that trigger-man Stone though, Jules thought. Two thugs who are on Tony Cheese's payroll. I gotta keep this under my hat.

Carmen looked at him. "Maybe your friend Smiley will ask her out. Their close friends from what she told me. I haven't seen her so lively in a long time. A good man is what she needs."

"We should've been there by now. This traffic is too much. Ya know, I wouldn't be surprised if Smiley get's together with her. He's been a friend of mine for years. If I know Smiley, he won't

waste much time, mark my words." I'm gonna try to get Carmen to
talk about her father, Jules thought. "You said earlier you like
to gamble sometimes, is that right?"

"Once in a while. I find it exciting. It must be in my blood
or something. Ever since my mother died I've had the urge to
become adventurous."

"On the average, you're probably a winner, right?"

"What gave you that impression?" Carmen said looking
surprised.

"Have you ever heard of Lady Luck?"

She laughed. "Sure, why?"

"I know you're Lady Luck, I can tell, I feel it." Jules
looked serious.

Carmen stared at him with a grin.

Jules felt her stare. He looked at her. "Why are you giving
me that look? Wait, don't say a thing. That's the look of an
angle, and angles aren't greedy, they play for the fun of it,
that's why they win most of the time. I'm completely convinced."

"You know angles pretty good, don't you?" Carmen said. I'll
play along with his little game, this is fun, she thought.

"I believe what I say." Jules said smiling.

"I'm sure then, when angles are assigned to a specific person
they're informed in detail all there is to know about the
subservient being, is that true?"

Jules put on a serious face. "Oh God, that never occurred to me -- but when I think about it -- absolutely, no questions about it. That was a good question, why did you ask me that one in particular?"

"Who do you think you're dealing with here, chopped liver?"

"Oh Jeez, I'm gonna have to clean-up on my thinking, it's been contaminated with evil thoughts. I'll be doomed if I don't."

They laughed. They finally reached the Hotel Restaurant. He parked the car.

"I can taste those mashed potatoes n gravy now, how bout it?" Jules said smacking his lips.

"My stomach is growling, mmmmm," Carmen replied. "I can eat a whole turkey."

They walked across the street to the entrance of the restaurant. As soon as they entered, one of the waiters came up to Jules and made him aware that Jimmy The Dealer was waiting at their usual table. The place was crowded with business men dressed in conservative dark suits, and sophisticated woman with sharply dressed men. Each table had a white orchid in the center. A soft pink table cloth with matching cloth chairs and black stripes made the room subtle. Hanging from the eggshell colored metal ceiling, ornate French lamps softly illuminated the area. The walls were colored eggshell with a fine black and grey pinstripe. Large oil paintings adorned the walls with scenes of landscape, ships and

alike throughout the room. An occasional bust of Ceasar, Herod
and others added the finishing touch. In the back corner, a table,
private from the rest, Jimmy The Dealer sat tasting his coffee. He
seen Jules, stood up and shook his hand.

"Sorry to bother you, Jules. I was on my way to the hospital,
I figured you'd be there, just by luck, I spotted you on the road.
I made a quick u-turn, and here we are." Jimmy The Dealer said.

"No big deal, we were on our way for lunch. This is Carmen,
Jimmy. Carmen is one of the nurses taking care of Mario."

Jimmy kissed her hand. "A pleasure Carmen. A pleasure indeed.
I've heard many good things about your hospital. And how dedicated
you nurses are."

"Thank you, Jimmy. It's so nice to hear those things. Nice to
meet you."

"Join us for lunch, Jimmy." Julie said.

"Thank's Jules, my wife and I have plans." He looked at his
watch. "I promised her I'd pick her up in a few minutes. I'll get
the bloody business if I'm too late. I'll take a rain check, how's
that?"

"Good enough. Sit down, talk to me."

A waiter came by and seated Carmen and Jules. "Nice to see
you Mr. Jules. Madam."

"Thank's Anthony. Give us five minutes." Jules said.

"What's so important, Jimmy?"

Jimmy gave Jules a look as if the conversation should be private.

Carmen understood. "Excuse me, I want to powder my nose. I'll look at some of these paintings on my way, their georgeous." She smiled, and walked away.

"Boy Jules, she's a knock-out." He checked the time on his watch. "I gotta move along, I don't mean to be rude, but here's the deal. I got a call from MoMo. He couldn't reach you so he gave me the message. He told me Tony Cheese was spotted in South Carolina with ten or twelve of his henchmen. He thought you'd like to know."

"That MoMo's got the contacts. I know Cheese better than he knows himself. He's headin' for Vegas, exactly as I predicted, you can bet on it. He's gonna set-up his hookers, put a few cat houses together, the whole nine yards. That's good, he'll make a ton of money. He's gonna need it when he begs to play in my game, the greedy bastard. But I'm not ready for him yet. I have a few things to take care of first. When it's all together, I'll go in for the kill. I have revenge for the creep, but I refuse to let it take over my total thoughts. Do you understand what I'm sayin', Jimmy?"

"I understand very well Jules, anybody else would--"

"I don't care about anybody else." Jules said heated.

"Jules, Jules, what I mean is I respect you highly for your way of thinking. I know you plan things out in detail. Knowing

you, you're working on something right now. You're gonna nail that
bloody butcher to the cross, I know you will. And when that day
comes, I'll be there, you know I will." He grabbed Jules's arm,
and smiled."

"I know Jimmy, I can count on you." He patted Jimmy's face,
then squeezed his cheek. "We'll be open for business day after
tomorrow, are ya gonna be ready?"

"I can't wait to be honest with you. I love my wife and
everything, but she's got a thing with shopping, shopping,
shopping, you know what I mean, I'm ready right now." He laughed
and shook his head. "You know Jules, it's gonna seem strange
without Rocco and good ol' Paco not being around, outside of that,
we're gonna break records."

Carmen came back to the table. Jules and Jimmy stood up.
Anthony, the waiter seated her.

"Thank you, Anthony." She said. "Jules, this is a very nice
restaurant. I didn't expect this, especially for a turkey
sandwich."

They laughed. Anthony brought hot garlic bread and rolls and
water to the table. He placed a large plate of hearts of celery,
black olives, stuffed red peppers, Italian cheeses and olive oil.

Jimmy stood up and shook Carmen's hand. "I have to run, very
nice meeting you. We'll get together at a more convenient time."

"Sounds good. Pleasure meeting you, Jimmy."

Jimmy shook Jules's hand. "Have a good day, my friend."

Jules nodded his head and smiled. "Okay Jimmy, you too."

After lunch, Jules insisted on having desert. "The custard pie is out of this world Carmen, you have to try it, you'll think you died and went to heaven."

"Jules, I'm stuffed, I'll try some of your's."

Jules gave Anthony a certain look and hand gesture that meant, don't listen to her, Anthony knew exactly what to do.

"The turkey is the best in the world here, don't ya think? And the mashed potatoes," He brought his fingers up to his lips and kissed the tips, "just the way I like 'em, chunky n chewy. Did you enjoy everything?"

"This is the best lunch I've had in a long time. I have to bring Lynne Marie in here, she'll love it. As many times as I've passed this place, I always thought to stop in, but never did. It was meant to be for you to bring me here. And now you want to kill me with custard pie?"

"Awww, what's a little piece gonna do?"

Anthony brought two plates of custard pie. Carmen looked at the pies with a surprised look, then at Jules. He stared at her with a grin on his face. Suddenly, they broke out in laughter for no apparent reason. As she laughed, her hand came down and accidently smashed the custard pie instead of hitting the table. Bits and pieces of custard pie scattered across the table onto

Jules's face and shirt. People nearby looked at Jules as if he were a clown; they chattered under their breath, some laughed, others smiled. Jules just sat there as if nothing had happened and ate the pie from his face with his fingers.

"This custard pie is the best, no matter how ya eat it."

"Oh my God, Jules! I'm so sorry." She looked at him, her hands covering her mouth, she was completely embarrassed. She immediately got up and went over to him and wiped the custard from his face and shirt with a napkin and water. Their eyes met and they laughed quietly as the crowd looked on.

"Oh Jules, I'm terribly sorry. Look at you. I couldn't do this again in a lifetime."

"Why not? This is the best custard pie I've ever tasted. Must be the olive oil on my skin." They laughed. "You don't have to clean me up Carmen, I can do it."

"Shhh, I did it, I clean it."

"But it's not right, you don't understand." Jules said softly.

Carmen stopped cleaning his face, and stared at him. "What is it I don't understand?"

"You're wiping off that delicious custard pie faster than I can eat it, know what I mean?"

She smiled. "Shush yer face. Let me have a taste." She licked some custard off his cheek and moved her tongue to the edge of his lips. "You're right," She whispered, "it tastes heavenly."

Oh God, she's torturing me. She's telling me something. Her tongue is so warm an moist, he thought. Keep calm Jules baby, control yourself. But it's so hard. Never mind, patients is the name of the game. He wanted to kiss her, but hesitated. He changed his mind and was about to kiss her, but Anthony, the waiter rushed over to the table with great concern.

"Mr. Jules, you alaright? I call doctor right away."

Jules raised his arms and motioned to him. "No-no Anthony, no big deal. When I eat your custard pie, I sometimes become a animal, know what I mean?"

"At'sa good news. I bring some hot towels right away, you stay right he."

Jules continued eating the custard pie with his fingers while Carmen wiped his face. Anthony was back in a flash with hot towels in a dish. He started to clean the table and another waiter came over with a fresh dish of custard pie, and handed it to Anthony. He placed the pie where Carmen sat.

"I know disa pie is Mr. Jules's favorite, madam. You enjoy, please. Buta I insist you put ina mouth, not ona face." They laughed.

After Carmen had finished cleaning up Jules, she sat down and tasted some of her pie. She looked at Jules intensely while taking small sensual bites.

Jules thought, I want to climb over this table an' make mad love to her. Hey now, keep cool Jules, let it happen when it happens. Oh God, help me out here, pleeese?

"What's wrong," Carmen said, "you're in deep thought."

"Who me? I was. I was? Don't mind me, must be the pie, I love custard. Guess what?"

Her blue eyes penetrated into Jules's. "You want to finish my custard pie?"

He reached over the table and held Carmen's hand. "You finish it funny girl. I had a great time, and hope you enjoyed lunch as much as me. Thank you for making my day. And thank you for watching over Mario too. I can't thank you enough for that."

Carmen wrapped her other hand around his. "I enjoyed your company, you're so sweet, especially with custard on your face. I've been on dates before, but you're different. You make me laugh, and you're a nice person."

"Boy, you know how to make a guy feel special. I have a question for you: Have you ever been to Antone's for dinner?"

"No, but I heard they have the finest Italian food around."

"The best. And being the best, I want you to join me, tonight, whadaya say?"

"No custard pie?" Carmen said softly.

"No custard pie."

"Tonight?"

"Tonight." Jules replied. "I'll pick you up at 8:00."

"Sounds wonderful, Jules."

"We'll have a nice dinner an' enjoy the evening. You have to loosen up, smell the roses, after all, we only go around once. So let's make it a good one. I'll have you home by 1:00, promise."

Carmen thought for a moment. "Holy cow, guess what?"

"Ahhhh, you may want desert after dinner? No. You're most likely to give in an' have some of mine? No. Their cheesecake is the living end, and that being the case, you'll definitely want your own." They laughed.

"You're funny, not even close. It dawned on me just a second ago, I'm off tomorrow."

"That's perfect -- oh Jesus, I just remembered -- almost forgot." He gave Carmen a discouraged look. "My apologies Carmen, I-I, well, I just wanted to remind you that it will be okay when it comes time for desert to try that hand trick again." They laughed.

"You're a convincing guy, Jules. You had me there for a minute. I thought you had other plans that you forgot about."

"Aww Jeez, I'm sorry, Carmen. I have a bad habit doin' that."

"Don't be silly, you do it with conviction. I love it. You have a talent very few men have. So you had horns when you were a kid. Most boys shed their horns before they reach the age of twenty. Your's are permanently attached, and are there for good intentions."

Jules looked deeply in Carmen's eyes for a moment. "You are an angel." He stared deeper in her eyes, and felt a calmness about himself that he never perceived before. His hand touched her's, and his body tingled. I'm falling in love with this girl, heavy, he thought. There's just something about her I know, it has to come to me sooner or later, but it will come. Goddamn it, she makes me want her. I ache with fire.

"Your eyes are so beautiful, they give me butterflies." Carmen whispered.

"Thank you. No one has ever told me. Would you like something else?"

"Oh gosh, no. When I reach my eighties, I have always envisioned myself weighing one hundred-five pounds. I've maintained that weight since I was eighteen. I refuse to look like the typical Italian grandma. You understand, right?"

"Absolutely. So you're prognosticating already about having desert tonight, right?"

Carmen laughed. How did you know what I was thinking?"

"You. You give me the power." He smiled.

"You're out of the cartoons." She said laughing.

"Would you like me to drop you off at home or the hospital?"

"I always drive to work, but today for some reason I decided to take a cab. Isn't that strange?"

"Not at all. Remember when we were kids, the wild impulsive things we used to do? We didn't contemplate on doin' what we wanted to do or worry about the repercussions. We just did it because nothing in the world meant that much to us. Then we grow up and worry and think about all the reasons why we shouldn't do this or that. We become ol' fashion, not knowing what's goin' on. Everything becomes negative most of the time. We stay at home and become a part of the wallpaper. Well that lifestyle is not for me or you. So you did something out of the ordinary, that's only because of habit, and we're all creatures of habit. And that my pretty lady is the story for the day."

"You made a good point. In fact you opened my eyes to something I lost."

Anthony, the waiter came by and placed the bill on the table.

"Is there something else I can get you, Mr. Jules?"

Jules handed Anthony the bill and cash. "Thank you my friend."

"Thank-a-you, thank-a you, Mr. Jules."

He looked at Carmen with a smile, and handed her the white orchard that was in the center of the table. "For you, madam."

Carmen was touched. She looked as though she wanted to cry.

"Thank you Anthony, this is absolutely beautiful."

With a sincere smile, he bowed his head at her and quietly walked away.

"What a nice thing to do." She brought the orchard to Jules's nose. "Isn't it precious?"

He sniffed the orchard. "As precious as you."

Carmen got up and kissed Jules on his soft cheek. "Thank you for the beautiful lunch."

On the way taking Carmen home, Jules thought, I'd like to ask her about her father. So far she was interrupted twice, just when she started saying something about him. I'll gradually work my way towards asking her. "I feel a little foolish asking you this question, but I don't recall asking you if you like Italian food?"

"I love Italian food. My parents were born in Naples." She looked at Jules, and smiled, then gave him a gentle punch on his upper arm. "You knew I was Italian didn't you?"

"To tell the truth, I would have never known until now. And I was born in Naples."

"No kidding!"

"That's right. My father, mother n me came to the U.S. when I was eleven years old."

"When is your birthday?"

"December."

"December what?" Carmen said.

"December 11th. Are you thinking of sending me a card or something?" He laughed, at the same time giving her a light punch on her arm.

"What a coincidence. That's my birthday too!"

"How bout that. Amazing. You're the first person I've ever met that had the same birthday as me. Incredible. Hey, maybe we're even related, you know how the Italian men are -- not all of 'em, just the majority." He laughed. "Joke, just a joke."

"You're funny. You better slow down, I live on the next block. You can see it from here." She pointed. "It's on the corner, the two-story brownstone with the beige trim, on the right."

"I see it. Nice neighborhood." Jules said looking around.

"It's quiet too. I love it here."

Jules pulled in next to the curb. "Here ya are kid, pick ya up at 8?"

"I can hardly wait. Would you like to come in for coffee?"

"I'd love to, but I have a few things to take care of. I'll take a rain-check."

"You're on. Thank you again for the fun lunch, I'll see you at 8." She got out of the car and started walking towards the house.

Jules shouted out to her. "Carmen!" She turned and walked back to the car. "Give me your phone number. I think I know where I am, but just in case, ya know what I mean?"

Carmen reached in her purse for a pen and paper and wrote her

telephone number down and handed it to him. She smiled. "See ya
later, Jules."

Jules left. After taking care of business, he went home to
Rocco's restaurant, and practiced rolling, snaking and scooping
the dice. When he had enough of the dice, he switched to the
cards and practiced his routine Rocco taught him so well. When
done, he took a shower and got dressed for a fun night with
Carmen. He looked sharp in his dark blue suit, white shirt, solid
burgundy tie and black Italian loafers. A final look in the
mirror, and placing his black fedora on a slight angle with the
brim half down, he gave himself a wink and a big smile. He went
to his car, started it, put the top down, and lit a cigarette with
the car lighter. Jules was so excited as he screeched off, he
inadvertently tossed the lighter out the window. As he drove
along, he thought, I don't know if I want Rocco's place, I've
been thinkin' about it lately -- Jimmy "The Dealer" could run the
joint while I'm gone, I'm beginning to think somebody's tryin' to
tell me somethin'-- it's cloudin' my thoughts. Revenge can do
that, that's for sure; when you want to even the score with
somebody so bad you can taste it, an' nothin' else matters, that's
one sure way of makin' big mistakes, it can make a person become
impulsive an' get thrown to the wolves. Well I'm not fuckin'-up
with Cheese, or any deal as far as I'm concerned -- I gotta game
plan half worked out for that rat -- an' I like it so far. All I

gotta do now is figure out the game Rocco gave me. He gave me one hell of a mystery to piece together. I'll figure it out. I'll be able to concentrate an' work out the rest of the game plan. Yeah, that's exactly the right move.

He turned on the radio, it had been tuned in to his favorite jazz station. He tapped on the steering wheel with enthusiasm, and stayed in rhythm with the beat of the music. He hummed and rocked.

"Now that's music." He looked in the rear view mirror, and said, "Got me a woman crazy for me, plenty of cash, what more can a guy want for?" He palmed his glossy hair in place then winked. "You're in for a great night, kid." Suddenly, a car pulled up alongside Jules's car; the black sedan and the two men inside looked suspicious. His heart pounded as if it were about to explode. He spotted a gun in the hand of the passenger in the back seat. He instantly slammed on the brakes. As the black sedan passed, Jules heard two shots from a shotgun. Due to Jules's fast thinking, the two shots fired missed their target completely. Jules pulled over and watched the black sedan disappear into the night. He checked the exterior of the car; a total miss. He knew Tony Cheese had a contract out for him.

That was to close for comfort. I'm changing my strategy for that fuck. He may be winning the battle, but I'll win the war.

CHAPTER 19

NEW YORK, AUGUST 5

8:00 P.M.

Jules reached Carmen's home at 8 sharp. Two ornate lights were brightly shining on each side of the door on the front porch. As he walked up the slight incline of the sidewalk, he noticed the well manicured lawn and pretty flowers bordering along the base of the porch. The exterior of the home was well kept. He walked up 6 or 7 wooden stairs to the door, and knocked. The door opened and Carmen stood there looking beautiful.

Jules looked at her up and down. "You look absolutely georgeous. You have to turn around for me, I want to see you everywhere."

She turned slowly like a ballerina. She was wearing a black curvy knit dress with a fairly low neckline, and when she turned, her short red hair bounced in the air. The back of her dress had a sexy lattice design from her lower neck shaped into a v one quarter down her back. A thin leopard skin belt. Tiny black pierced ear-rings and black high heeled shoes.

"Thank you. Come in Jules. You look so handsome. Sit down, I'm on the phone with Lynne Marie. I'll be with you in a couple of minutes." She walked in the other room. Carmen's home was decorated in a contemporary and Japanese motif. The colors were

black and white. A large white polar bear rug lay on the floor
with two large leopard cloth pillows in front of the fireplace.
There were several photographs in silver and gold and black and
silver mesh frames scattered across the mantel.
The double couch and chairs were off white and contemporary.
Japanese lamps and appointments and three large oil paintings of
Japanese and Italian portraits beautified the room. The wall to
wall off white carpet and black marble foyer made the room
complete. Everything looked and smelled new.

Carmen came back in the living room, and picked up her black
furry stole. "Am I going to need this, Jules?"

"Let's see, put it on. I put the top down, I'd bring it."

She put it on. "I will. I'll bring it, just in case."

"I love it. You look terrific. Your home is beautiful. And
the fireplace, now that's where I'd be relaxing every chance I had
if lived here."

"My mother and I did all the decorating. Would you like a
drink?"

"Not right now. I'm starvin', how bout you?" He opened the
front door.

"Yes, I'm so hungry." She grabbed his arm, and they walked to
the car. "What a pretty car."

"Thank you." He opened the door for Carmen, then hurried to
the other side, and jumped in. "She's a beaut. Someone very dear

to me gave it to me."

"What a beautiful gift."

They took off. "You look just perfect in it." He put a
cigarette between his lips, and reached to push in the lighter, it
wasn't there. He thought, it was there earlier -- oh Jesus, I just
remembered, I musta misplaced it -- no, I don't usually misplace
anything. I think I tossed it out the window, thought it was a
match, that's it, what a stupid thing to do. I must have been in
deep thought for me to pull that off. He laughed to himself.

Carmen pulled a lighter out of her purse, lit it, and put the
flame in front of his cigarette. "Is this what you're looking
for?"

"Thank's. What a beautiful lighter, I didn't know you
smoked."

"I do once in a while. My mother left it to me, it's solid
gold and weigh's a ton. My mother's boyfriend gave it to
her...oh, look, there's Antone's, you know the short-cuts pretty
good, we got here fast."

I'll be damned, Jules thought, there's been interruptions
all day. She started talkin' about her father earlier, we're
interrupted. Now she bring's up her mother's boyfriend? I don't
get it. Well, it's not goin' away, an' I don't want to sound to
pushy, damn, I shoulda took the long way. I'll find out the whole
story before I take her home later. I'll feel better about it.

I'll sleep better too. Her mothers boyfriend?

He pulled into Antone's, he had been here several times with Rocco and the boys. Two valets quickly opened the doors, and greeted them. A doorman opened the entrance door, "Good evening Mr. Jules, madam, welcome to Antone's."

"Evinin' Gustavo." Jules said.

They were greeted by a maitre d' dressed in a tuxedo, "Good evening Mr. Jules, madam, your table is ready. Right this way, please."

Jules nodded his head, grabbed Carmen's hand, and followed the maitre d'. They were escorted through the intimate formal dining room to a special table in a corner away from the crowd. A dozen of red roses and a bottle of wine was on the table next to long flickering candle. On the stage nearby, a pretty sexy woman began singing, "The man I Love" accompanied by a pianist, guitar, saxophone and drummer.

The maitre d' seated them, and said, "Is everything satisfactory, Mr. Jules?"

"Thank you, Benvenuto."

Benvenuto nodded his head at Jules, then Carmen, and walked away.

Carmen lightly touched one of the roses and smelled it, "The roses are beautiful, Jules." She touched his hand. "Thank you."

"They're as beautiful as you."

"You're so romantic." She pulled out the small envelope attached to one of the roses. "Can I read this to you?"

"Please. But whatever you do, read it tenderly." He smiled.

"You're something else." She shook her head and smiled as she pulled the card out of the envelope, and read:

Dear Carmen,

Thank you for being you.

May every day be happier than the last.

My Love, Jules.

"How sweet." She smiled and pressed the card to her heart, then leaned over to Jules, "You're making me fall for you, you know that don't you?" She gently kissed him on his lips, it was soft, wet and simply wonderful.

"You know something, Carmen? your lips--"

A waiter came to the table. "Good-a evening sir, madam, my name is Roberto, may I pour your wine?" He handed two menus to them, and stood there erect with a serious look painted on his face.

Jules nodded his head. The waiter, like magic, waved a napkin in the air and quickly enveloped the bottle of wine, popped the cork and poured a small amount in Jules's glass; it was quite impressive. Jules tasted it.

"Excellent, Roberto. You sure know how to open a bottle of wine alright."

Roberto filled their wine glasses, and said softly, "I learn this-a trick from my father. When I was little boy, ana I do someating bad, my Papa, he give to me ona my you know what. So, I do this alla time to remind me to be a gooda boy." He grinned for a instant then his face turned back to the serious arrogant character he had to portray; Antone's image was not only northern Italian gourmet food, it had the reputation of being aristocratic, and those that worked for Antone were competent and zealous people. While Roberto poured the wine, he said, "You have a finea taste for wine, sir. I will return for your order. The Northern Italian antipasto is superb." He brought his fingers to his lips, and kissed them. "I be back a little bit, gratzi."

"Make it ten minutes, Roberto."

Roberto bowed his head to Jules, then to Carmen. "My pleasure." He proudly walked off erect and with a earnest look wrapped around his face.

"Did you mean what you said on this card?" Carmen still had the card clutching to her heart.

"Every word."

Jules picked up his wine glass, and made a toast. "To now. May the time pass slowly. For there's no tomorrow."

They smiled as their glasses touched. Simultaneously they said, "Salute."

Fifteen minutes or so later, Roberto, the waiter came back to

the table, and they ordered dinner. Not long after that, another
waiter brought the Northern Italian antipasto that came with their
dinner. After enjoying the light antipasto of stuffed red and
green peppers in olive oil and Romano and Parmesan and Provolone
cheese, and black olives and oysters and shrimp, they sipped their
wine, while Jules enjoyed a cigarette. Their main dish of shrimp
scampi was brought to the table with a side order of clams casino
and veal scallopini. Roberto made sure there was plenty of hot
garlic bread on the table, and kept their wine and water glasses
full at all times. Jules, as well as Carmen loved to dip the hot
bread into the light gravy; it was like they died and went to
heaven.

When they finished with their dinner, Roberto came to the
table and handed them a desert menu. "Excuse please," he said,
"the hot wined melba is superb." He brought his fingers to his
lips and kissed them, bowed, then left.

"That sounds like the perfect ending of a great meal." Jules
said.

"I love raspberries and peaches with vanilla ice cream. My
mother made melba when I was a little girl. She added just the
right amount of wine and lemon juice. It settles the stomach after
a meal."

"I think I'll wait a few minutes, how about you?" Jules said
as he took in a deep breath.

"I feel just right. The chef know's how to prepare the right
ingredients so as not to make you fell bloated. This is how we
should feel after every meal. Maybe I'll have some later."

"Maybe you'd like a cigarette, there's plenty of time to make
your mind up."

"Okay. I have a craving right about now."

Jules lit two cigarettes at once, then gave her one. "I love
to watch you smoke."

"Your such a romantic guy." She took a drag and blew out the
smoke perfectly and sensually. "You're the first guy that ever lit
a cigarette that way for me."

"I've never thought of myself as bein' romantic. I have to
work on that a little harder. I have to tell you, can't hold it
in, you have such a sexy way about you when you smoke."

"Really? Does it turn you on?" She touched his hand and
rubbed it gently.

They stared at each other for a moment, then Jules turned his
hand over and squeezed Carmen's hand lightly.

Jules said, "The only desert I'm havin' is you...c'mon, let's
dance."

The female vocalist was singing "My Funny Valentine". They
danced and danced and became increasingly fond of each other.
They danced until only another couple were on the dance floor.

Out of nowhere, Carmen looked at Jules, and said, "Jules, I

love dancing with you and everything, and I know we just got through with dinner two hours ago, but I'm starving, let's go some place and get something to eat. I'm in the mood for ham n eggs n rye toast, how about you?"

Jules laughed. I was just thinking the same thing. Let's go, I know the perfect spot." He left cash on the table, and they left.

Between 10 P.M. and 10 A.M., Poodles Diner was the place to go. They catered to the late night crowd, serving hot Italian bread smothered with steak, peppers and onions with home fries or sausage, peppers and onions or a variety of large sandwiches or any type of omelet desired. Poodles would make just about anything to please the customer. No one ever left hungry. Jules knew exactly what he wanted without looking at the menu that already had been placed on the table. Carmen looked over the menu as if it were a legal contract. She couldn't make up her mind what she wanted after sitting in the booth for five or six minutes.

"How's the onion omelet? How's the liver and onions? How's this? How's that?" Carmen asked Jules. There was nothing on the menu Jules told her that was negative. He patiently answered her and occasionally looked around for a waitress. A waitress came to their table and Jules ordered two cups of coffee. He told her to come back in a few minutes. The waitress brought the coffee right away, but Carmen still hadn't made up her mind what she wanted.

"Come back in a few minutes, sweetheart, we haven't made our minds up yet." Jules said to the waitress with a sincere smile.

"Sure honey, take all the time you need, be back shortly."

Jules patiently waited while Carmen looked over the menu. Four-five minutes later, Carmen still couldn't make up her mind.

"I'm sorry Jules, I thought I wanted ham and eggs. Gosh, they have so many good things here."

"Don't worry, take your time, nobody's in a rush in here."

Five more minutes later, the waitress came back to the table and filled their coffee mugs. She was a pleasant and patient waitress, and asked, "Did you find something to please yer fancy yet, sweetheart? I'll be the first to admit, it's kinda hard to decide what you want with a hundred n sixty-two choices to choose from."

Carmen looked at Jules, and asked, "What are you having?"

"The steak, peppers n onions. I thought you were in the mood for ham n eggs n rye toast?"

She looked at the waitress, and asked, "How's the onion omelet?"

"Outstanding, you'll love it."

"How about the spinach omelet?" Carmen asked, looking at the menu.

"If you like spinach, it's delicious." The waitress said patiently.

Jules interrupted, smiled at the waitress, and said, "Maybe you'd like to sit down and join us?" He smiled.

They laughed. After Carmen asked the waitress five million more questions about how's this and how's that, within the twenty minutes of dissecting the menu, she asked the waitress, "What do you recommend?"

"I've had everything on the menu except the spinach omelet. The ham n eggs are my favorite, to be honest with you, everything on the menu is freshly cooked an' simply delicious, sweetheart."

"Okay, I'll have the ham and eggs with rye toast, medium well with the ham."

The waitress retained the order in her head. She looked at Jules, to make sure the order was correct: "Steak, peppers n onions -- homefries come with that sir, or maybe you'd like french fries, applesauce or cottage cheese instead?"

"Homefries are fine. Make the steak medium rare, thanks."

"You got it -- medium rare on the steak n homefries." She looked at Carmen, "Ham n eggs with rye toast for the lady -- medium well on the ham, how would you like your eggs, sweetheart?"

"Straight up, spattered with lots of hot butter."

"You like 'em like I like 'em, pliable but bubbly and oozy -- we call it, "burned in the sun", clever, huh?"

"You couldn't call it any better than that." Carmen said.

The waitress yelled out to Poodles, who was cooking over the

grill, "One "moo-moo" with white tears n green bells, medium rare
with home-made's, and one "burned in the sun" with rye, and a poor
porky, medium well."

Poodles confirmed her order, and yelled back, "You got it my
loyal princess, done deal in five." Then he rang a cow bell to get
attention. Every soul in the place watched Poodles, it was so
quiet, one could hear the grill sizzling. "Okay my children," he
politely said, in one graceful motion, he flipped a omelet with
one hand, and simultaneously flipped a large pancake with the
other, both making a perfect landing on the grill. He looked at
the customers, and politely yelled, "Pass the hat princess, we
gotta buy dat new Caddy!"

The room broke apart with laughter and praise.

"Is this place a riot or what?" Carmen said laughing.

"The later it gets, the funnier Poodles carries on. He's one
of the most lovable guys around. He love's people -- he make's you
laugh. He may get into his routine, it's funny. He always has
something new an' original. He's beautiful."

"I like this place. Look at the table where our waitress is
at, I never seen so many earrings on guys before."

"The one talkin' an' wavin' his hands about is Truman Capote,
he's a up an' coming author. The fella next to him is his agent. I
never seen the other two. This is a celebrity hangout -- you never
know who's gonna land in here next -- look who just walked in!"

She leaned over in Jules's direction and whispered, "He looks just like James Cagney, the actor, a-and the person with him, resembles H-Humphrey Bogart!" Carmen said excitedly.

"That's them in the flesh sweetheart. Okay now, put yer dukes up or kiss the ground (Jules imitated a line from one of Bogey's movies) Jules sounded exactly like him. It's hard to recognize these people in person, but they're for real alright".

"God, Jules, my heart is going to pound it's way to daylight! This is exciting!"

"I can get you an autograph if you like -- of me of course."

Oh, Jules, you had me going there for a minute. I don't know who's the funniest, you or Poodles."

After a good laugh, their food came. Carmen looked at Jules's steak, peppers and onions.

"That looks delicious." She looked at her plate, "Jules, will you look at this ham steak, it's enormous." She took a bite of her ham steak, and said, "Mmmmm, you have to try some." She cut a small piece and put it in Jules's mouth.

Now that's a "poor porky"! Out of this world." He cut a piece of his sandwich, and put it on Carmen's plate. "Try this, it's still oinkin'."

She tasted it. "Oh Jules, that's what I call a tender "moo-moo"! Poodles is a clever guy for naming all his dishes after something that was, and is now, there cute, don't you think?"

He choked a bit, then swallowed. "Did I hear you say,
'Something that was, and is now?'"

"Yes, why?" Carmen replied.

"No -- I mean, that phrase is like poetry in motion -- no-no,
that's not exactly what I'm tryin' to say." He tasted some coffee
then wiped his lips with a napkin; he was stalling for time; he
was contemplating on the right way to clarify his meaning. "Let's
see, where was I?...oh, yes -- that phrase is a mind twister --
it's like the tale, "Jack in the Beanstalk", you know, anybody may
think they know the meaning, but they should be given pause by the
fact that for Bruno Bettelheim, whom most people would consider a
competent psychologist (or at least not stupid), the tale is
really about penis envy -- surely a minority opinion. Some might
say that the tale is about the victory of childish innocence; some
might say other things. The point is that what makes us take
pleasure in "Jack in the Beanstalk" is not necessarily our sense,
as we read or listen, that some basic philosophical question is
being dramatized and illuminated, though in other fictions theme
may indeed be what chiefly moves us. I believe that was the
closest example I could give you to your phrase, 'something that
was, and is now' -- I like it."

"I have to say professor Jules, you have a way with words. Do
you do short stories too?"

He laughed. "Sorry. Didn't mean to carry on. But to answer

your question, I'm a long story teller, a "big-breath story
teller" kinda guy, so it's said, and in effect I do what is most
natural. "Big-breath story tellers" have, unlike the impatient or
short story teller, the endurance and pace of a cheetah. And
there's a kind of ambition peculiar to the "big-breath breed" -- a
taste for the monumental. I read that somewhere, it stuck in my
mind for some reason." Jules enjoyed his sandwich while talking.
"It's a true story. In fact, that's the shortest story I ever
told!"

They laughed.

The waitress came to the table, picked up Carmen's empty
plate, and put a steak, pepper and onion sandwich in front of her.
She filled their coffee mugs again, and said to Carmen, "Looks to
me sweetheart, you enjoyed your ham n eggs. I have no idea where
yer gonna put the steak sandwich, you must be starvin'." She
looked at Jules, "Great sandwich, huh? I love to see a man eat
slow. You must be patient, I'd bet on it, I know men like the back
of my thighs. I don't mean to get personal, an' I'm not, I just
love people." She looked at Carmen, "You sure are a lucky woman,
sweetheart. I've been looking for Mr. Right for a thousand years.
I'd be in heaven to find a guy like the one sittin' across from
you." She wiped a tear rolling down her cheek and forced a smile.

Carmen smiled, and touched her arm, "You know, if you stop
looking in places where you think you'll find the Prince of your

dreams, and go to places where you would least expect to find that
certain guy, you may just find what your looking for. You're to
nice of a girl to be single."

The waitress stared at Carmen as if she said magic words.
She stared at Carmen for at least five or six seconds then lay the
coffee pot and Carmen's empty plate on the table. She looked
around to make sure her customers were content then turned and
faced Carmen with a perplexed look painted on her face. She
crossed her arms over her chest and lowered one side of her hip.

"You know, I never thought of that! You're so sweet to think
of me. I like it! An' bein' so kind, your bill is taken care of."

Jules grabbed the waitress's arm, "I don't want you to do
that. There's a lot of good advise for you around, and it's free.
Now forget takin' care of my bill, thank you, that's very generous
of you. Now on the other hand, if I took the cash from you for
whatever the bill is, and leave you a twenty dollar tip, how would
that be?"

The waitress looked at Carmen with a confused face, then
turned her head to Jules. "I think I can relate to that..." After
a few seconds, her eyes widened, and she broke out in laughter. "I
get it now! Never heard that one, you're a funny guy, that's a
humdinger line." She laughed again and shook her head. Okay,
okay, I don't wanna embarrass you but thank you very much for your
advice, yer good people." She picked up the coffee pot and

Carmen's wiped clean with rye toast empty plate from the table.

"Excuse me," Carmen said to the waitress, "I didn't order this sandwich." She looked confused.

"You better talk to your sweetheart on that one." She left the table dancing and twirling.

"She sure is a happy girl now, wouldn't you say, Jules?"

"You gave her hope. She's what all waitress's should be."

Jules, did you have something to do with ordering this steak, peppers n onion sandwich?"

He raised his hands, palms towards Carmen, "I'm the guilty peasant alright. When you were eating and not payin' attention to me, I motioned to the waitress to bring you one of these great sandwiches. Her timing was perfect."

She smiled. "You must think I eat this way all the time." She took a bite. "Mmmmm, I wanted this when I tasted your's."

Jules and Carmen shared the large sandwich. When they finished the sandwich, they were stuffed. Jules left cash on the table for the bill plus a eight dollar tip. He liked real people, people that knew what hard times were and didn't complain about it, and said it the way it is. They got in the car, took in some fresh air, and had a cigarette. A light drop of rain hit the windshield occasionally but not enough to put the convertible top up. It was a beautiful morning watching the sun rise.

"Well, I better get you home," Jules said. "I'm not gonna eat for a week."

"Me too. I just remembered something, Jules."

"What's that?"

"We didn't have the Melba at Antone's!" Her face had the look
of a serious woman being consecrated for her sacred life as a nun.

Jules's mouth opened as he snapped his head in the direction
of Carmen. His face looked as if he was just shot. Then he
pointed at her, shaking his finger about. With a closed-mouth
smile he slowly turned his head back and forth three or four
times, as to say; no, no, I don't believe what you just said!
Suddenly, they broke apart laughing.

Jules started the car. Still laughing, he put the gear handle
in drive, pulled out two or three feet then screeched to a halt.

"What's wrong!" Carmen said.

He shoved the gear handle back up into park, and leaned over
the steering, holding with both hands, then gave Carmen a puzzled
look, and said in a disappointed voice, "I don't believe it! I
just don't believe it! I can't believe my mind! I have a pretty
memory, usually don't forget things -- don't believe this! For
some stupid reason, I forgot to remember to tell you something --
it's very meaningful too!"

Carmen looked at him gravely, and said, "Oh Jules, think! For
heaven's sake, if it's important it'll come to you -- wait-wait,
don't think -- get your mind completely away from it -- and like

magic, it will pop in your head, just like that -- I don't know
when -- but as sure as you forgot, as sure you'll get it back.
I've never seen you so concerned. I'll be quiet now."

Jules thought for a moment, then reached in his pocket and
pulled out a roll of cash. He slipped out a fifty dollar bill and
felt it, stretched it, made it pop a few times, then he studied it
very carefully. Suddenly, he looked up and shouted, "That's it, it
came to me, you were right, Carmen!"

Carmen smiled. "Well, you going to tell me or maybe a Western
Union telegram would be more convenient?"

Jules laughed as he looked at her. "Good line, Carmen."

"Well!" She said while shaking his arm.

"Okay. You mentioned the melba we forgot to eat at Antone's.
We were so hungry, we left and didn't even think about it. So I
thought I'd go over there tomorrow and pick some up, enough for a
week -- we can eat melba till we turn blue."

Carmen laughed. "Is that what you forgot to remember?"

"Actually, I didn't forget anything, I was just pulling yer
leg, I couldn't resist."

They laughed harder than before. Tears rolled down their
faces. They were having a great time. They screeched off and
watched the sun rise along the way.

Jules stopped for a red light. "Carmen, can you do me a
favor?"

"What is it charmer?" She said softly.

"I have some business to take care of, it may take one, two days at the most. Could you call me if Mario has any change?"

"Are you trying to tell me in a nice way you don't want to see me anymore?"

Jules pulled the car over to the curb and stopped. He turned to Carmen. "I want to see you again Carmen, real soon. I want you in my life." With both hands he lightly held Carmen's face and kissed her. "Your lips are like bubble gum." He kissed her again. "On second thought, they're more like foam from a champagne bottle right after the cork was popped."

"How romantic. I never heard expressions so beautiful, and funny at the same time. Thank you."

"It's true." Jules said as he lightly moved his finger across her lips.

"I'm sorry Jules, I didn't mean to be so selfish...I mean... what I'm trying to say is...oh Jules, I feel so g-guilty...w-what I'm trying to--"

"Say it Carmen, let it out, don't be afraid."

Tears rolled down her cheeks. "You're such a nice person Jules, I-I didn't tell you the whole story."

Jules wiped Carmen's tears with his fingers. "Jesus, don't go cryin' on me now...yer makin' me feel bad -- whadaya -- awww jeez Carmen, why ya cryin' like this?"

She sniffled slightly then wiped her nose and tears. "Do you
remember when you asked me about my father?"

"I remember alright, you were interrupted a couplea times.
When you didn't bring it up, I thought you didn't want to talk
about it. Ya know, sometime's it's better to keep the mouth shut."

"I've held this in for years." Carmen said with teared filled
eyes.

"I'm sure you'll feel much better if you talk about it." He
embraced her.

Carmen backed-off, she trembled and looked sad.

"I'll try to tell you...it's very difficult, I don't know
why, but it is."

CHAPTER 20

NEW YORK, AUGUST 6

7:45 A.M.

Jules gently touched Carmen's hand, and said softly, "Relax, blue eyes--detach yourself of all thoughts, and concentrate on your father. Once you start talkin' about it, it's gonna wanna keep rollin' out like you were on a roll at a crap table."

Carmen laughed." Boy, you sure know how to make comparisons, don't you?"

"Not really. Bad choice of words. Think about this one--once you start talkin' about it, it'll be like two yentas carryin' on arguing over which one found the right find for Mrs. Goldstein's daughter!"

Carmen laughed harder than before. "Oh Jules, you're crazy, I haven't stopped laughing since we met." She kissed him gently, and whispered in his ear, "Thank you."

Jules backed-off a bit and smiled. "Here's lookin' at you, kid. He gave her a light tap on the chin with his fist.

Carmen stared at him with a contented smile.

"Do ya feel a little better now?

"You're magic."

"Nothin' like a few laughs before spillin' the beans, huh?"

With a closed-mouthed smirk, she shook her head a few times
then moved close to him. "You have a certain something, it's a
beautiful characteristic."

"What's that?"

You can rid sadness and bring joy. Did you know that?"

"I--I didn't know that." He looked up at the sky speechless,
and scratched his head. He looked as if he was in deep thought.
After a few seconds, he looked back at her. "What's most important
to me is you're feelin' better."

"You know Jules, en masse, you make me feel brand new--and
that's one hell of a accomplishment for a broad like me."

He laughed, and thought, she's loosenin' up, alright." He
raised his voice a bit, and said, "Broad? Did I hear you say
broad?"

"Yes, why? I was being a little hard-hearted just to hear
your diverting come-back lines." She smirked, and gave him a
light punch on his upper arm.

"Ohh, you speak French as well. Gettin' pretty sharp kid, you
musta ate yer razor blades somewhere between Antone's an'
Poodles--that's funny--real funny. When you said "broad", it
reminded me of somethin'--I gotta tell ya, you'll appreciate it.
The street word--"broad", came out in the early twenties ya know,
an' tenacious women held on to their sugar daddys with a firm
grip. The sugar daddys spent big bucks on these "broads"--that's

how the big spendin' women got the name "broad." He looked at
Carmen, waiting for a response--nothing.

She stared at him with a wrinkled brow in complete silence
for at least 4 or 5 seconds. She exhaled loudly, and said in a
vague voice, "I don't get it."

Jules's eyes widened, and his voice raised an octave. He
said, "I thought--I mean--you know--"broad"! As in large--big--?"

Carmen crooked her head a bit, stared in Jules's eyes while
tapping on her chin. She had a dubious look about her face. Jules
had to turn away, he nearly lost control and broke out in laughter
but he faked it and coughed instead. After all, Jules was a
gentleman.

Jules looked back at Carmen, "Awww come on. Think about women
spendin' gross amounts of cush!"

"Ohhhhhh, I get--what's cush?"

Jules held back from laughing, but held back like a
aristocrat.

"You are definitely a comedian. Money--it's a cons man word."

"Ohhhh, I get it. Hot digity dog, now I'm gettin' street-
smart an' learnin' the con lingo ta boot!"

"Yer gettin' sillier as the sun goes up. Think of how you'll
be like at high noon!"

They laughed, tears rolled down their faces. Their
foolishness and curiosity made everything just wonderful.

Carmen wiped her tears, "Oh Jules, my stomach hurt's from

laughing so hard. I have to tell you, occasionally after I cry, I
get this uncontrollable urge to laugh. I become like a zany drunk
broad thinking everything is hilarious, isn't that kinda silly?"

He paused, his eyes were on a traffic light ahead.

"I love it, you make me laugh, but next time after you cry,
without delay, think deep down about the eeriest event you ever
had, an' after you cried you're gonna feel as normal as a flower
blooms." He stared at her with a warm smile, and thought, how
lucky can a guy get, she's precious--not only that but she's like
one of the boys--I like that.

"I'll try that, Jules. You're in deep thought, what are you
thinking about?"

"How lucky I am to have met a broad like you." He chuckled.

"How sweet. You are my sugar daddy, aren't you?"

"I never had a broad before--why not--we only go aroun'
once--know what I mean?" He was joking using the word broad.

They laughed and kissed and laughed some more, they were like
two kids discovering each other. Jules knew exactly what he was
doing--because he cared. How can he know more about Carmen when
the question he asked about her father was never answered. One
thing for cocksure, Jules is the artificer of patience. Carmen
sat back and looked out the front window staring at nothing, she
was in deep thought. She swallowed, took a deep breath then
brushed her tears with her fingers from laughing so hard.

"Jules?" Carmen whispered.

"I'm right here."

"I'm still tense--I don't know what's wrong with me. I want to tell you about my father but...

"Listen to me," Jules said softly, "Visualize a lazy river calmly movin' along and yer sittin' against a tree just relaxing. The warm sunshine makes you feel lazy--and every once in awhile, a fish jump's out of the water--just to see if you're enjoying the day as much as she is--this makes you feel free--then calmly a mermaid comes halfway out of the water--you're not afraid because it's your mother, she's coming to visit you. She's radiant and beautiful--you've been waiting for her. She nonchalantly rest's her elbows on the waters edge and places both palms under her chin, and tell's you: Carmen, I miss you, everything is so wonderful where I live. I want you to tell me for the last time what happened on the day I told my husband about you not being his child. You see, I have to release this from my conscience--as well as your's--then, and only then, you and I will be free again-- completely. My love for you is unending--as your's is for me. Have no fear my darling.

A haze slowly descended upon the car; a strange stillness filled the air; it was so unmoving and eerie, it felt as if Carmen's mother was truly present.

Carmen paused a few moments, she breathed lightly and looked completely content; Jules had hypnotized her to a degree. Her eyes closed. After a few minutes she was motionless. She whispered faintly, "Mother? Oh God, you're so beautiful--I miss you so so much. I remember it all to well mother--it's been a terrible nightmare for me. You were pregnant with me before you married, remember telling me? I cried. You never told your husband-to-be-- him--that's what I've always called him. He always treated me like I was a nothing. How could anyone love somebody without caring or be recognized or returning love. But I remember well, on my sixteenth birthday you finally decided to tell him. When you did, he turned into a enraged animal. I heard him arguing and screaming at you from my bedroom--he slapped and punched and shouted ungodly words at you. I couldn't stand his screaming--I had to cover my ears--I pretended it was all just make believe; like a bad dream. I could hear him beating on you and yelling at the top of his lungs--I wanted to scream b-but couldn't--I couldn't scream, I-I couldn't t-talk--I gasped for--my breath--I couldn't breathe. My mind, I don't know how--I somehow remembered reading something in the medical book you gave me about anxiety, nervousness, short of breathe. I recognized this was happening to me. I inhaled ten long deep breathes and exhaled slowly then prayed desperately for guidance. Eventually I composed myself--I could breathe again. My hatred for him gave me enough courage to tip-toe to the end of the hallway--I watched as he beat on you--you were helpless--oh God--a

force inside of me made me want to kill him. I sobbed, tears were
streaming down my face, my nose was stuffed an' drippy--oh God--my
nighty--I-I covered my mouth--didn't want him to hear me. I
trembled with fright. I was never so scared in all my life. I
watched as he punched your face and stomach--then he pushed you--
oh God, it was horrible--you-you lost your balance and f-fell--hit
your head on the fireplace--b-blood from your head--trickled on
the base of the fireplace, onto the rug--mother, you didn't move!
Oh dear God, I can't tell you how much I wanted to come to you. I
thought you were dead. I screamed and clawed my fingernails
through the wallpaper--I--some--something happened to me, I
couldn't run, couldn't walk--I was paralyzed--and he seen me in
the darkness. Oh God, he charged at me a-and ripped my nighty off.
He slapped me and called me dirty names. Then h-he picked me up,
I couldn't breathe, he held me so tight. Before I knew it he had
me on the bed. He stripped me naked--he raped me--he hurt me real
bad--oh God--I'll never forget that day as long as I live. He'll
pay for this, mother. He's a nothing for what he did to us--I'll
never forgive him--never." Carmen almost started to cry, she
sobbed and sniffled a bit but composed herself at once. "He left
you and never came back. A few years later you told me you heard
through the grapevine that he, the good for nothing tracked down
my real father--they had a horrible fight--my real father had part
of his arm c-chopped off--by him." She started to sob, and

uttered sorrowfully, "with, with an ax--the snake."

Carmen lost it. She came back to reality. She sobbed then
took a deep breath straining to hold her calmness.

Carmen turned to Jules, and said, "I don't know if I can go
on, Jules. I--don't--"

"Shhhhh." Jules softly brushed his finger across her lips,
"Okay, okay, you're doin' fine, just relax, relax. I'd like to ask
you something."

"Are you my sugar daddy?"

"As sure as a sunshine day."

She laughed and shook her head a few times, "You're so funny,
ask me anything you want, I won't bite you. I do feel better
already."

"You should. But I want you to feel marvelous. What I mean
is, well, it doesn't make sense withholding this anguish and
letting it destroy you--you've come a long way Carmen, let the
rest of the poison out, go ahead, let The prince of darkness take
it all in, after all, he thrives on evil doin's." He kissed her
forehead lightly, "You do want to feel marvelous don't you?"

"I want to. When I reach to that plateau, will you care for
me as much as you do now?"

"No question about it--even more. Remember, where there's a
beginning, there's the end. Now you just relax, and conclude this
nightmare. Do you have the vaguest idea why?"

Jules wanted Carmen totally relaxed so she would release her anguish completely.

Carmen gave him a smirk, "So I'll feel better."

"You're close." Jules said.

She sat back against the seat and stared out the front window as if she was preparing herself to finish the story. "What are you trying to tell me, Jules?"

"I--umm--well, when I asked you, 'do you know why?' I wanted to say something stupid like marvelous, I thought you'd say, so I could feel marvelous--you said, better--not important--sometimes I can say the stupidest things, now let's fagedaboudit (forget about it). I want you to just relax now, bring yourself back to where you were. You were at the point where 'your real father had part of his arm chopped off in a fight with--with that crazed--"him". Close your eyes--concentrate--bring yourself back--you can do it...you will do it...I'm right here beside you." He brushed her forehead lightly and whispered, "That's it...that's it...rest, yer slowly...slowly goin' away...back to that beautiful place beside the river's edge...your mother's waiting...

She closed her eyes, and whispered, "I'll try, Jules...I will...hold my hand."

Almost at once Carmen was reposed. She drifted off to where her mother had waited. In her mind she envisioned her mother in the water, elbows resting on the ridge, with both palms under her chin.

Carmen's arms raised slightly, she said, "Hi mother, I'm sorry I left you in such a hurry--I lost it. I mean--" Carmen became silent.

Her mother said, "That's alright darling, in heaven, time is of no importance unless we're summoned for a assignment. No need explaining to me. I know your every thought, your every wish and what the future has in store for you. You are embraced with love more than you can conceive. Knowing this, you must get on with your life. You must have faith in what I say." She hesitated, looked at her reflection, and noticed a cardinal in the tree above. She turned in Carmen's direction, and said confused, Oh dear God, I-I had something very weighty to tell you...oh my." She looked up for a moment at the beautiful cardinal on a branch; it was brilliant red with a black face and pointed crest, and it's eyes stared at her, they looked like burning warbles of charcoal. They stared at each other for at least ten or twelve seconds as if they were having a silent conversation. Then she looked back at Carmen. "Yes--I recollect now, how silly of me. Darling, while you were away for those brief moments, one of our Angels of Dispatch delivered a assignment to me. I must leave soon. The creature I married has finally arrived." She looked up to the heavens, "Please forgive me." Then she looked back at Carmen. "He committed suicide. The Big Man isn't to thrilled with his

behavior, especially children who are chicken-hearted, you know.
The Angels of Felo-de-se incarcerated him this morning. He's on
the most formidable elevation in the heavens--purgatory. He will
be judged soon, and I must be present. They don't fool around up
there--it's slap bam see ya sram or B-B-Baba-Boo-boo, the latter
being negotiable--they waste much to much time down here. Anyway
darling, I am very pleased, you have told me everything I needed
to know--I am well satisfied. But I must warn you, when a feather
descends from the wing of the cardinal, I must go...come, kiss
your mother good-bye, it will be soon."

They kissed. Carmen caught a glimpse from the side of her eye
a beautiful cardinal. It flew past her, and as it did, a feather
dropped; it descended and rotated extremely slow; she watched it
as it lightly kissed the water and lay still on the surface.

"Mother!" Carmen pointed at the feather, her eyes dropped to
her mother. "Mother! Where are you!"

She had disappeared. The only sign was a large circle of
ripples nearby to where she and Carmen were talking. Carmen
remained silent. In her mind she thought her mother was talking to
her, but all the while Carmen's conscience had accepted this
information that had been chained in her subconscious, and, at
last she was free from the dreadful thoughts and nightmares of the
past. Suddenly, she instantly covered her eyes and part of her
forehead with her palms and fingers. She squeezed tightly as if

she was in pain--as if something terrible had happened, and she couldn't do a thing about it.

She screamed, "Mother! Mother! Don't leave me...please don't leave me...when will I--wha--whe...oh God...Jules? Jules?" She snapped out of it.

"I'm right here, Carmen." Jules gently wiped the perspiration from her forehead, then brushed her face and hair with his fingers, "You pulled it off, kid. You got what it take's."

She turned a bit, looked at him, released a breath of air, and smiled."

"Here's lookin' at you, kid." He kissed part of her lips and part of her cheek.

Carmen wrapped her arms around Jules's body, "I feel brand new Jules, thank's to you. At least now I know where "he" is."

Jules bolted back a bit, and said gravely, "Well, I've said it before, an' I'll say it again--what goes aroun', comes aroun', don't matter where your at." He rested one arm and rested it on Carmen's shoulder, the other, halfway in the air, "Don't misunderstand me Carmen, I have compassion for the poor soul, and I heard you sayin' somethin' to yer mother, '"he's" bein' judged soon', within the hour or so--that's how I interpreted it anyway. They don't play games up there. My notion is, "he's" gonna get either the place or condition of utmost happiness or be dodgin' flames and bein' miserable with a blistering ass for a long-long ime, you can bet on that, Carmen".

She lowered her hands and said, "Jules, you're a remarkable person. You know so many things."

"Well, I'm just a street-smart guy."

he stared at him and said nothing. Her hand gently touched his lips.

ules just looked in her eyes and smiled. "You're something else, Carmen; I mean you're imply beautiful".

She didn't say a word, just rolled her finger over his face and eye's.

Jules rested his head on the back of the seat and closed his eyes.

"Jules, try not to go to sleep, just relax...relax...relax."

"Carmen?"

"What is it Jules?"

"Would you put your hand...I mean..."

I think I have a fever -- check it out would you please."

'What are you trying to say?"

he laughed and gave Jules a tender kiss.

Jules, I don't mean to repeat myself, but you are a very intelligent person. You know all the aswers .....I'll bet on it."

Jules backed away a bit, he looked in her eyes and said, "To answer your question Carmen, read voraciously, the majority of the time. Not for anything, but, I can't tell you the olumes of knowledge I have read. There sure is a lot of wisdom to comprehend ."

"I think that's wonderful, Jules."

"My favorites are Freud, Alexander the Great, Caesar, Darwin and Shakespeare."

Once I got the hang of it I was able to read between the lines. I perceived how human and real and humorous they really were. As a result, here I am, a peasant in disguise. I'll show you my humble library sometime, okay? What else would you like to know?"

"That's really interesting, Jules. I'd love to see your library. Between being street smart and reading the heavy stuff, you must be a genius."

"Not by a long-shot. You may consider me as a duke-man, a card cheat. Here's another one--Tat-man. A Tat-man is a con game worked in nightclubs using crooked dice. Other than that, I'm just a ace, that is, having the ace in the hole to be assured that legal authorities will not interfere with a confidence game after they have been suitably bribed. Here's another street smart expression. Have you ever heard of the fix?"

"You have to be kidding Jules. The only fix I know is, I'll fix it myself or you can fix it yourself or better yet—I'll fix your ass!'

"How clever. Ace mystify's me. I have an idea what it means."

"Go ahead, you have it altogether, tell me."

"Ace to me is something Admirable or Excellent."

"True. Ace in street talk is the same as "a fix" you know, when somebody pays somebody to fix this or that and did it with class and dignity."

Jules had always been humble, and indeed his mind was genius. As far as he was concerned, applying common sense had always been the name of the game. He wasn't totally truthful telling Carmen what a Dukeman, Tat man and Ace was, a half truth would be more like it; he wasn't a liar, never ever; if anything, depending on the circumstances, he knew how to bend the truth a bit. He didn't think this was the right time to tell her he inherited Rocco's Italian Restaurant and all. Jules was a show-off; possessions, leaving a generous tip to whoever serviced him; he knew how difficult people had to work to persevere. He firmly believed in giving when you have it, and giving when you don't.

Carmen said thrilled, "So jeez Jules, that makes you a notable street smart sugar daddy, right?"

"To tell you the truth, I never thought about it--sounds pretty good though, there's truth in those words alright, but yer gettin' silly on me again." He tapped her lightly on the chin with his fist, and shook his head smiling.

They laughed. A few funny lines made things more good. Carmen

tried joking with Jules. She wanted to get even. Jules went along
with her like a good sport. They were just having a little fun
like most crazy lovers do.

Jules continued laughing. He tried to get serious, he
progressively did. "Ya know Carmen, your real father wasn't
mentioned at all--what ever happened to him?"

"I don't know, I never met him but...he always sent my mother
more than enough money for years."

"Does he still send it?"

"It stopped when my mother died. I tried to find out who he
was and everything but always came up with a big blank. My mother
left me everything she owned. What good is it when you can't share
it with someone you love. Oh Jules...this is depressing, I don't
want to talk about it right now." She took a deep breath, and
rested her head on Jules's chest.

"That's okay kid, you did good, relax, yer sugar daddy's
right here, he know's how emotional a broad can get, yet I'm
doubtful about something."

She left her head on his chest, and laughed softly, "This
better be good Jules. I'll take the bait, what are you uncertain
about?"

"I--well--I've never been a sugar daddy before, I already
told you that, and I also told you I've never been out with a
broad, so I'm havin' a problem thinkin'--would a choice dame react

the same way? You know, emotional? Sensitive? High strung?"

Carmen sat up, "Jules! What are you on about?"

"What!" He laughed, "What kinda talk is that suppose ta be?"

"What do you mean?"

"You know, 'What are you on about!'"

"Ohhh, I'm sorry, I picked that cute little phrase up from Elizabeth, one of the nurses where I work, she's from London."

"That's all well in good Carmen, but what's it mean?"

"It means, what are you doing. What else could it possibly mean?" She looked at him strangely as if everybody knew.

"I--err--to be bloody honest about it, like Jimmy the dealer would say, sound's to me like yer askin' somebody what kinda drugs they're taken an' about how much."

Carmen laughed until tears rolled down her face. Jules sat calm, and thought, she sure get's a bang outa what I say once in awhile. That's what it sounded like to me...I like it. How'd she say it? Oh yeah, 'What are ya on about'. Cute.

"Oh Jules, you're much to much." She snuggled into Jules and put her head on his chest for twenty or thirty seconds, then whispered, "I remember, my mother's best girlfriend and her were talking. I heard them from my bedroom. My mother said my real father had a business--a front or something, it had to do with gambling I believe. She said he treated her like a princess, and he was married with a son. His wife died in a horrible car accident. Strange how things just come to mind out of nowhere."

"You're free of those miserable nightmares and thoughts,
Carmen. You have to let it all out. Once you do, everything will
be clear, believe me. Tell me, did your mother ever mention his
name?"

"I accidently found a letter under my mother's hope chest one
day when rearranging the furniture in her room after she died.
There was a hundred dollar bill inside the letter, and at the end
it read: I'll always love you, Rocco. That's the only letter I
ever found."

Jesus! I can't believe what she's sayin', he thought. "Do you
still have the letter?" He looked at her and thought, oh God, I
hope she has it, I'd know Rocco's writing on a dim night.

"I misplaced it, looked everywhere, couldn't find it."

Jules slowly pulled away from Carmen and rested his head on
the steering wheel in disbelief. A few drops of rain absorbed into
his sport jacket. The convertible top had been down but Jules was
deep in thought, this is a nightmare, how can all this break loose
outa nowhere like this? I can't believe Carmen--she's the daughter
of Rocco! Of all things--never knew he had a daughter--Jesus
Christ! Talk about coincidences--I think I'm in mild shock!
Tears filled his eyes, he thought, what am I gonna tell her? How
am I gonna tell her? He couldn't seem to compose himself all the
way, and thought, okay, okay Jules baby, everything is meant to be

for a reason, but-but...awww, come on-come on...I guess I should just lay it on her straight, an', an' j-just be me, now knock off with the bullshit, you know you can do it.

"Jules, what's wrong?" Carmen leaned over and touched his shoulder.

His eyes filled with tears, and embarrassed to have Carmen see him like this, he instantly got out of the car, and thought, awww Christ, gimmie a hand here will ya? He leaned against the car thinking of nothing aside from hoping he'd think of something.

Carmen got out of the car, and ran over to him, "Jules, what's wrong! You look like you've seen a ghost!" She embraced him tightly. A light shower started, they were so emotionally involved the rain didn't seem to bother them; they didn't realize.

"She backed off, "Jules!" She shook him, "Jules!" She shouted, "What's wrong? Did I say something to offend you? Talk to me!" She grabbed his jacket and shook him again shouting, "Tell me what's wrong for God's sake!"

Jules snapped out of it and looked at Carmen then wrapped his arms around her for a moment. He pushed her back easily and looked in her eyes. Rain dripped from their faces without knowing as if it were a sunshine day without their knowing.

Carmen, I have to tell you something important. I should have told you earlier but I wasn't sure. Not only that, you never asked me what kind of work I do. What I'm trying to say is--I'm a

gambler, a rogue to keep it simple--a thief--that would lock it in
a nutshell. Deep down I don't like to cheat people who can't
afford to lose, it's against my morals. My mama 'n brothers have
to eat. My mentor, Rocco DeLucca was killed recently, I'm sure you
read about it, they plastered it all over the front pages of the
newspapers. He was your real father, Carmen. He taught me
everything I know. And Mario, the boy you've been looking after in
the hospital is your half brother." A tear rolled down his face,
he tried to hide it, he didn't want Carmen to see him this way.
"I'm sorry Carmen, I feel terrible telling you this way. I-I
didn't want--"

Carmen put her hand over his mouth, "You know something?" She
took her hand away and brushed his cheek.

"What?"

In a loud whisper, she said, "It's raining! We're getting
wet!"

Julie turned in the direction of the car, and shouted, "Holy
Christ! The top! The goddamn tops down!" He quickly jumped in the
car and desperately raised the convertible top then the windows.
Carmen got in the car and started to laugh. Jules reached under
the seat, pulled out a terry cloth towel, wiped his face a bit
then gave it to Carmen. After drying herself, she wiped the front
seat and everything else around.

"Why is it you guys have towels under the seat? Some guy I

went out with once used to have a towel under the seat, in the
trunk too but they weren't clean and didn't smell of bay rum like
your's--I don't need a explanation on that one Jules, it's better
to ask some of the questions than to know all the answers."

Jules looked at her with a blank face, then broke out
laughing.

Carmen looked puzzled for a moment then realized she said
something stupid. She took the towel and messed Jules's hair. They
laughed. He shook his head, put the car in gear, and screeched
off.

"I don't know where you picked up that line but it was a humdinger. I've done a few foolish things before but nothin' like
this." He glanced at Carmen, and thought, she's awfully quiet, did
she hear me telling her about her father? If she did, she's actin'
pretty cool about it.

She heard every word Jules told her. She felt as if the old
world went away and a new one was beginning.

"Oh Jules, I feel sad in one way and happy in another but
it's over and I'm thankful. I have a peace within I haven't had in
a long time. There's so many questions I have concerning my
father. And Mario, so many questions, I'm touched. I'm lost for--"

"Okay now, relax, think about how wet you are, an' how bad
you'd love a cup of coffee, we can warm-up a little too."

She snuggled up to him and squeezed him tight, "Okay."

A few miutes later, Jules thought, there's a greasy-spoon joint five minutes from here. Haven't been there in years. The coffee's the worst in town--big deal, as long as it's hot an' we don't get diarrhea, it don't matter. This girl's got me in a whirlwind. I can't figure out why she's taken this in such a calm way. Maybe she's in mild shock--no-no, it's not that. Maybe she's suddenly gonna cry on me? Oh God, I hope not. Jules baby, why don't you just shut up an' play it by ear for Chris' sake.

He spotted the diner ahead, "There it is kid, you ever stop in this place before?"

"I've driven by several times but never went in."

The rain came down in buckets. Jules pulled in the front parking lot. There were three cars taking up five spaces but he managed to wheel into a safe spot. The diners windows were fogged, and you could barely see the sign in the window but if you tried hard enough, it read:

> **Best coffee in town**
>
> **or don't pay.**
>
> **The food is the worst**
>
> **If yer hungry, you'll love it.**

Carmen laughed. "Did you read funny sign on the window, Jules?"

"Clever gimmick. Maybe they have a new owner that don't cook everything in bacon grease, an' he promised his wife he'd make the place a success--c'mon, lets make a run for it."

They ran to the entrance, and went in. A waitress was bending over with her arm over a taxi driver's shoulder at the counter. Everything she owned was very clear. She turned while chewing gum as if it were going out of style, and said, "Mornin', thought you'd never make it. Yer suppose ta take the clothes off when taken a shower ya know. Coffee?" She blew a bubble the size of a softball then sucked it in. She was a professional bubble gum blower alright.

Jules smiled at her, and said, "Nice bubble. Make it two coffees--and while yer at it, bring over some of that bubble gum too." He gave her a wink and smiled.

The waitress giggled, and took her arm off the taxi driver's shoulder, and said to him, "Ya know Lenny, now that's a nice guy. I gotta get their coffee, don't move, be right back."

"You're so funny Jules, I don't think she had panties on, do you?"

"I didn't notice." He said innocently, "But she can chew up a storm with that bubble gum can't she?" Jules thought, Boy oh boy, that Carmen is sharp. She tried to catch me to see if I eyed the bush country of that waitress. I could have told her the truth-- yeah, like I'm gonna admit it. I've read a book or two on how women know exactly what to ask the guy to catch him off guard. Hey Jules baby, you could be a little paranoid too ya know.

Carmen found the right spot in a booth next to a window. The
waitress was right behind them with the coffee and put it on the
table as Jules slid across the seat across from Carmen. The
waitress looked at Jules then at Carmen and back to Jules chewing
and snapping her gum wildly, and lay two towels on the table.

"Better take these towels 'n dry off before ya both catch a
cold." She reached in her pocket and pulled out two wrapped pieces
of bubble bum and put them on top of the towels. "On the house,"
she said, "My boyfriend Lenny over there buys me tons of this
bubble gum, it blows colossal bubbles. I've tried 'em all but
"Blow Yer Bubble" bubble gum really, really's the best. Would you
like a menu or something?"

"No thank's, coffee is what we need. Thank's for the gum,
towels too." Jules said.

The waitress looked at Carmen, chewing and snapping away,
"Are you okay, honey?"

"I'm just a little chilly, that's all. Very sweet of you to
bring these towels over. I'd love to dry off, where's the rest
room?"

The waitress pointed, "See the jukebox over there? Walk thata
way, pass it, and aaaaa, oh ya, hang a right an' yer there. It's
the cleanest jon in town, honey."

"You're sweet. Thank you." Carmen picked up a towel, and got
up.

"Give me a shout if ya need anything." The waitress said to Jules. She walked away sensually.

"Be right back." Carmen said, as she touched Jules's face.

Jules grabbed the towel and wiped his face, then some moisture off the window. He stared at his reflection, and thought, how in God's name can this be happening? The girl I fall head over heels for turns out to be Rocco's daughter. This is scary--a rare coincidence I might add. And I do believe all things are meant to be. I'm gonna do my very best to make Carmen happy. I hope she's okay. Awright, awright, knock off with the--"

"Excuse me, I brought a pot a coffee, this way ya don't have ta call me." She placed it on the table. She smelled like a French hooker. "I'd love to blow you..." She sneezed.

"Bless you." Jules thought, is she for real 'er what!"

"Thank's." She replied. "Like I was sayin', I want to blow you a bubble, okay? You'll see what I mean about this bubble gum." She blew a bubble as large as a honeydew, then sucked it back. "Whadya think of that?"

"Outstanding!" Jules tapped his spoon on the table a few times.

"Look's like youz guys are gonna be here awhile, take yer time, nobody comes aroun' here when it rains. Call me if ya need somethin."

Jules nodded his head and smiled, "Thank's, ya give one hell of a blow there girl."

As she walked away, she shook her butt at Jules, as to say, thanks honey, anytime.

He shook his head, and tasted his coffee, and thought, what a wild broad. Besides blowin' bubbles, she make's good coffee. He looked out the window, and thought, look at that rain, what's with all the rain? At least the car will get cleaned. I--

Carmen slid in the booth, "I'm back. Isn't this rain awful?"

"Yeah. Looks like it's gonna rain all mornin'. Did you dry yourself good?"

"Yes. I feel better. How's the coffee?"

"Yer gonna love it." He poured her coffee, and said, "Ya know Carmen, a best friend is hard to come by in life, don't you agree?"

"We're lucky if we have just one, why are you asking?"

"Well for the short time we've been together, I feel as though I've known you all my life, an' if we're gonna be best friends, that means we have to be totally straight with each other, right?"

"That's what it's all about--why are your hands trembling, are you okay?"

"Aww, I'm alright, I'm just worried about you, you know, out of nowhere I threw a hardball at ya an' , told ya about me, yer real father, Mario--you excepted it so innocently an' kindly--I thought it might have been to much for you. Are you sure you're

okay?"

She reached for his hand and held it firmly, "I'm a big girl,

Jules. When you told me, something burst inside of me, I suddenly

felt completely free--I wanted to cry and scream in happiness but

something wouldn't allow it to happen. Maybe because you told me.

You have given me strength I never had before."

Jules leaned over the table and kissed her, "You're like your

father in many ways."

"Tell me about him Jules, what was he like?"

The waitress came by, and said, "Is everythin' okay here?"

Jules looked at her, "This is great coffee, can you sell me a

pound or two?"

"We don't normally sell it but I'll fix up a bag for ya. I

think youz guys make a beautiful couple 'n everythin'. Okay, I'll

leave ya's alone." As she walked away, she hummed a tune, made a

few circles, and danced her way behind the counter.

"She's so cute," Carmen said, "I think she has a crush on

you."

"I think she knows how to get a good tip too."

They laughed. Carmen filled Jules's coffee cup then her's.

She looked at Jules, shook her head, as if to say, what a

comedian.

"You're father used to give me that same peculiar smile and

shake his head exactly the same way when I said something stupid.
I'd like to call yer father, Rocco from now on, do you mind?"

"That is his name, let's not change it now, Jules." Carmen
said lively, then her face turned serious.

Jules looked at her dismayed, he didn't know what to say.

"Eat a hot pepper, Jules? She pinched his cheek, "gotcha,
gotcha good didn't I." She laughed.

She fooled him alright. He shook his head and laughed along,
"Carmen, ya got me good this time--yer one fine girl. Rocco used
to get me everytime--now you?...I'm in big trouble." He tasted
some coffee, and thought, tell her Jules baby, tell her about her
father for Chris' sake, nobody's comin' in here ta hit ya with a
baseball bat, moron. Okay-okay I'm loose, I'll tell her-I'll tell
her. "Yer father--I mean Rocco, he hired me and taught me
everything I know. He was closer to me than my father."

He told Carmen how Mario's mother was killed, and how Mario
slipped away from reality over it and what a warm and giving
person Rocco was and how strong and generous and proud he was and
about Rocco's tragic death, in detail.

"I never liked the way he cheated the players but he told me
that the main reason they came in his joint was because they were
compulsive gamblers--they always want to get even--and if they
didn't play at his place, they'd go out of there way to his
competitors joint cross town--outside of that Carmen, Rocco was a

good man, a extraordinary father, and loved by many. I should be
so lucky to have one-tenth of the people show at my burial as he
did his. There is something else--He left me his business
including the black Caddy convertible we've been drivin' around
in."

"You could have been killed." Carmen said.

"It was the most horrible thing I've ever witnessed in my
life. You know now all there is about yer father Rocco and Mario.
Maybe we should change the subject Carmen, I get a little
emotional, know what mean? You don't need to hear anymore of this
gruesome story."

She wrapped her hand around his tightly, "I can handle it,
Jules. I remember reading about it, now that you gave me the
details. You did the best you could under the circumstances at the
time. Thank God, you walked out of there alive. Strange, when
Mario was checked in the hospital I recall his last name
distinctly, a beautiful last name--DeLorenzo--if Rocco's last name
was DeLucca, why isn't Mario's?...I'm confused."

Jules explained how confused he had been on the night he
admitted Mario in the hospital, and the admittance office needed
identification, and Jules went back to Rocco's restaurant
searching for it. He found two birth certificates in the safe, one
bared the name Mario DeLucca, the other, Mario DeLorenzo. Being
overwhelmed, Jules went back to the hospital and turned in the

wrong one; Mario DeLorenzo, not the certificate baring the name, Mario DeLucca, the one he intended to register his name under.

"I found two shoe boxes in the safe; there was a hidden safe within the safe; one had the name Mario in black ink, the other, Carmella. I looked in the safe again, this time lighting a match; I found bundles of cash--I counted it, there was fifty-eight thousand dollars; this cash had to be a reserve bank. Rocco always had plenty of cash for the big pay-offs. As far as the birth certificates, I haven't the slightest clue why they exist. I'll eventually find out." He leaned over and gently kissed her teared cheek.

"Thank you for telling me, Jules. It is difficult going back, I know. I've always wanted a brother. My feelings are good for Mario, he's going to recover soon. He may not walk but he'll be alive. He will be given lots of love, I'll see to that."

"The kid has lotsa livin' to do. And you have everything goin' your way, in more ways than one. If you need anything, I mean anything, I want you to ask me Carmen, okay?"

"I only have one."

"Anything, kid."

"Would you take me to my room?"...

CHAPTER 21

NEW YORK, AUGUST 7

7:45 A.M.

A stack of cherry wood lay neatly near the fireplace and in a open cabinet a pile of newspapers. Carmen went to her room to get something. Jules shivered in his wet clothes and decided to start a nice warm fire in the fireplace. He crumpled paper and placed logs neatly on top then more paper and a couple more logs in place. He lit the paper and within a minute smoke started coming out of the fireplace into the room and the logs were ablaze. The dry logs ignited quickly. The heat felt good but the smoke smelled bad. The flames were so intense he had to back-off. Holy sheeeit, he thought, never made a fire in a indoor fireplace before. Can't understand why the room is gettin' smoked up like this. I wonder where Carmen is."

Carmen came in the room and noticed the smoke, "Did you open the damper?" She laughed.

He didn't hear her, he was to busy waving his arms wildly and blowing at the smoke as if it would go away. He shouted, "C-Carmen, I don't know what to do!"

"Did you open the damper?" Carmen cried out.

Jules was getting nervous, "Tamper? What's a tamper?" He

looked a bit confused.

She hurried to the fireplace, "Look, under here...wait-wait, you can't now, you'll get burned, here, this handle will open it up." She pulled down on the handle and everything was fine. "The damper has to be open when you start a fire, ya crazy lug." She gave Jules a light punch on his arm, and messed his hair with her fingers.

Jules was embarrassed. "I thought there was a minor detail I left out. I've made fires in a fifty gallon drum outside but never in a fireplace inside like this--never realized, I'm sorry."

"It's clearing up, don't worry about it, it's just a little smoke." Carmen handed him a forest green silk robe, "I found this in my mother's hope chest, it's the only thing I ever saved that belonged to my father Rocco. Look here, his initials, R.A.D. are on the sleeve. I could never put together what the initials represented until now. Take your wet clothes off and put on the robe. It must have been meant for you all these years."

Carmen left the room. Jules removed his wet clothes and slipped into the robe. It was a xx large, Jules wore a medium. He rolled the sleeves up to his wrists, and thought, oh boy, this is warm and comfy. The smoke in the room was gradually disappearing. He looked at the pictures on the mantle and noticed an unusual elegant gold frame with a picture of Rocco in his middle forties. He was handsome, and dressed in a white suite, black shirt and tie

and a white fedora. Next to Rocco's picture, Rocco and a
beautiful woman in a pink large hat with a long green silk and
white dress posed together in a outside scene with waterfalls in
the background. This had to be Carmen's mother; Carmen looked just
like her, red hair and all. Carmen came in the room, Jules turned
to her. She looked beautiful wearing a ankle length black satin
negligee. The low cut front showed a part of her breasts but left
enough covered to make ones imagination run off on a wild trip.

"How do you like it, Jules?" She turned around gracefully
raising her arms like a ballerina. She smiled as her negligee
raised above her thighs slightly, then she turned around again.

Jules thought, oh Jesus, she's beautiful, absolutely
georgeous. I'm gonna have to calm down. How am I gonna do that?
I'm getting excited. She's lightin' my fire. Okay-okay, calm down-
come down Jules baby, you can do it, did you forget, you're a
romantic type of guy, remember? Right, that's true, no question
about it." He put one hand on his chin, and said, "You look
stunning Carmen, I love the negligee, can you turn around like
that again? You look sexy doin' that."

"You mean like this? She whirled around again, this time
revealing her naked body. "Have you had enough?"

"That was perfect, Carmen."

Carmen grabbed Jules's hand, "The robe looks good on you.
C'mon, let's sit on the bear rug near the fire, it's nice 'n cozy

there."

The wood crackled and sparked like a miniature fireworks for a few moments then calmed down to a steady yellow, red and blue flame. The sweet smell of cherry wood had the fragrance of rose and lily and hyacinth potpourri.

"You make a beautiful fire, Jules. I wish I could make one that good."

"With the smoke too, right?"

They laughed. Carmen reached for a bottle of wine in the wine rack nearby and two glasses. Jules opened it and poured the wine.

"Here's to happy days," Carmen toasted.

Their glasses touched and they tasted the wine. They kissed and discovered each other, then made love throughout the morning. The afternoon sun gleamed through the upper stained glass window down upon Jules and Carmen snuggled in each others arms. Awakened by the brightness, Jules got up and placed a log in the smoldering fire to cut the chill. He lit a cigarette, looked at Rocco's photo, and thought, Christ Rock, this is happening too fast. Don't misunderstand me, I can handle it but I'm crazy about your daughter. I told her what I found in the safe, you know, the shoe box with the name Carmella, but I don't think she heard me. I'll tell her later. She's beautiful Rock, just beautiful. Thank's my friend, I'll take good care of her." He burned his finger from his cigarette, and gave out a yelp.

Carmen jumped up frightened, "What's wrong! Oh Jules, w-what happened?"

"Oh nothin' burned my finger with a cigarette. Sorry I scared you." He looked around for his cigarette but couldn't find it. "I can't find--"

Carmen pointed at Jules's robe pocket, "Smoke! smoke from your pocket!"

"Holy sheeeit!" He pounded on the pocket several times with his hand, a flame ignited. He slapped at it desperately, no use, his pocket was on fire.

He ran to the bathroom and jumped in the shower, turned on the water, and shouted, "Holy sheeeit, water's ice! Jesus Christ!"

Carmen hurried into the bathroom, took off her negligee, and jumped in the shower. She adjusted the water then embraced him, and they laughed. As the steam from the hot water covered the glass doors, they made love.

Late afternoon, Jules brought Carmen to Rocco's Restaurant. They went upstairs to the office and sat down.

I remember this place, Jules. It looks so much bigger. This office is beautiful."

"This is my new office. I'm undecided what to do right now. Maybe I'll have Jimmy the dealer run the place, I haven't made my mind up yet. I'm contemplating on more serious plans."

"What did you do here before Rocco died?"

"Some times I'd deal at the poker table, mostly the crap table."

"Why would you want to give all this up?"

"Because it's against my morals to cheat people that can't afford to lose. I want to feel good about what I do and know I didn't take food off the table of some fool that needs it for his family. This is a thriving business Rocco put together but I know there are better ways, so for the time being, I want to show you what your father left for you. I'll get it, it's in the safe."

Jules walked to the large oil painting and swung it open, works the combination, opened the safe door, and pulled out two worn shoe boxes. One was marked Mario, the other, Carmella. He brought Carmella's box to the desk and opened it.

"There's a letter in here for you. I read it once before. I couldn't put it all together until yesterday--then everything made sense. Would you like me to read it for you?"

"That's okay Jules, you've never read to me before." She looked at Jules with a forced smile.

Jules read it: To my daughter Carmella,
I think about you all the time. This picture of you is all I ever had. You are beautiful and look like your mother. She gave to me this picture on your third birthday. Every kid needs a mama

and papa. Forgive me for not being a papa for you. I hope
someday we will meet. I leave you something anyway just in case I
no see you.
I love you,
Papa, Rocco.

Jules handed the letter and picture to Carmen. She read it
and looked at the photo of herself. She smiled as tears rolled
down her cheeks. Jules reached in the box and took out five ten
thousand dollar bundles of cash, in one hundred dollar bills, and
placed them on the desk in front of her.

"This is for you Carmen. There's fifty thousand dollars here.
Rocco left the same for Mario. Your father was a generous man, a
very generous man."

Carmen stared at the cash as if she didn't want it. Tears
rolled down her cheeks, she was speechless. Jules put the money
in a brown paper bag and held on to it, then he brought Carmen to
his room downstairs to show her his library.

"Well this is it, kid. Got just enough room to eat, shower,
practice rollin' the dice, 'n read. I call this room "The Turn".

"What a strange name for a room. I know it means something--
what does it mean, Jules? I'd have to guess it means something in
street talk, am I getting sharp or what?"

"You ate your razor blades alright, very good. It means when
one changes from one thing to another; like switching from a card

game to a crap table is a good example or being ordinary and
becoming extraordinary--get it?"

"Makes sense--you make it happen, true?"

"All the way."

"I like it. And your collection of books--I'm impressed.
This room is so quaint. You need a painting, maybe two, it will
add to the uniqueness of this room."

"I agree, there's several in the basement, I haven't had a
chance to look them over. This room is only temporary--things
change."

They had some wine and cheese, and talked until early
evening, then went out for dinner. Jules brought Carmen home, and
he went back to his room at Rocco's Restaurant. He had a urge to
explore the contents of the foot locker Rocco gave him. He studied
the exterior for five or six minutes, and thought, most unusual, I
hope that ghost don't come out, Jesus Christ, gives me the spooks.
Aww sheeeit, I gotta figure this game out, I'll be damned if I'm
gonna let some legendary ghost scare the shit outa me. Rocco said
it would be a piece of cake for me--hey, maybe it will be. I can
only try. So we get acquainted, big deal, maybe he'll help me like
Rocco said he would--I did promise Rock I'd give it my best shot.
I could do it--I will do it. He kneeled in front of the locker,
and said, "Okay, I'm about to open you now. If you're in there,
I'm ready to meet you. I want you to help me figure out this

ancient cabalistic game. And I want you to realize when we have it altogether, my intentions are to get Tony Cheese. I know it won't even the score or bring Rocco back, but I'll be able to bust Cheese out once and for all...here goes."

He pressed down on one brass corner plate and turned it clockwise, then the other, counterclockwise. The top gradually opened. He looked at the green table cloth, and turned his head quickly to a creaky sound he thought was a footstep. Suddenly the top of the footlocker slammed shut. Jules sprung back in terror and smashed into the kitchen table and chairs. The toaster and bowl of fruit crashed to floor; bananas and grapefruit and apples and grapes bounced off his head and rolled everywhere. He sat there, and thought, what the hell was that! Hey, wait a minute, I didn't hear a click when the top went up, that's right, when it clicks, it locks open. It probably stuck from not being open enough--that's it! I coulda swore I heard the floor creak, sounded like somebody came in the room. I'll open it again. He opened the top and pushed it back until it clicked. He took the green felt table cloth and lay it on the floor, then removed the folded table, and unfolded it. He covered the table with the green felt cloth, then reached in the locker for the folded wooden frame that slip's over the table and pushed it down in position to tighten the cloth. He studied the painted cards in the center for a while then got the two kitchen chairs and put one in the dealer's

"Well, I can see so far the dealer sit's behind the two white
boxes marked Win/Lose. And the white box behind those two squares
must be where the deck of cards are placed. That's it, dealer
sits directly in the outside center of the table, makes sense."

He took notes on every detail. He reached in the locker and
pulled out the abacus, and carefully unwraped the aged leather
wrapping and set it to the side. He measured the abacus in it's
folded position, it was, 11 1/4 inches long by 6 1/2 inches wide.
He opened it and it measured, 11 1/4 inches long by 13 inches
wide. He lay the abacus at the end of the table where the
supposed two players would be; a power of knowing immediately and
without conscious reasoning made him put the abacus there. A eerie
feeling of something seemed to be overlooking Jules's every move.
A slight chill and a faint stench of stale wine lingered in the
air. Jules thought, I'm hearin' an' smellin' things, Jesus, if I
don't get some rest I'll be seein' things. That's all I need right
now is to have that imaginary ghost, Skiatho come aroun'. Yeah,
sure, I can use some company alright, especially if I can get a
little guidance on this game. Am I blowin' my top 'er wha' talkin'
like this? Aww sheeeit, what's the big deal, he don't scare me,
an' beside's, I'm too goddamn tired to be bothered. I want to
finish up a few more things. All night long to the early morning
Jules worked at it taking notes, page, after page, after page.
Then around 3:25 or 3:30 a.m., Jules started to become irrational

and somnolent, he lay his head on the table exhausted, and fell
off into a deep sleep.

A low unnatural voice said, "Jules...Jules...you have done
well. My name is Skiatho, remember me? We have met...in a
peculiar sort of way...when Rocco opened the locker for the very
first time in years...remember? It's not to oftentimes when one
has the befalling to hold a conversation with a banshee such as I.
You and that closed-minded pisano friend of yours Rocco, thought
you were drunk and were having delusions, and all the while I was
there listening and watching. I thought it was rather comical. You
can consider me a ghost but I'm really the mind and soul of this
game. My deepest compassion for Rocco, but he's in good hands. We
talk, and he's in the hinterland right now having a grand time
with his wife and old friends, he give's you his love and is
waiting for you to put the pieces together of this game he passed
on to you. Rocco wasn't the brightest character around, he would
never listen to me. I tried and tried to show him how my game is
played but he would not listen or believe in me. I invented this
game with a purpose, more than two hundred years ago. You and I
have much in common, enthusiasm, you are true, have nerve and
indeed a perfectionist--you are whole. You are the one I have
been waiting for. Thou shall carry my sword, for I am here
forever. You will remember these clues I accommodate you with.
And as long as there are self-seeking gamblers in your world, this

game will be alive until the heavens are no more. The first thing
to be done is find a close friend, a lugger (an outside man;
convinces and sets up the victim; apple for the big game). The
lugger will search for a compulsive gambler but never ever in the
home town where he lives. Once the compulsive gambler has been
found, the lugger becomes the best of friends with him; gets to
know him like a brother; ordinarily it would take eight months to
a year to make a best friend. All information the lugger receives
from his friend (apple), is passed on to you. It's up to you to
thoroughly check out this information to make sure the compulsive
gambler (apple) is truthful. When the lugger feels the time is
right, with your approval, the lugger and apple may be out
gambling one night, the lugger playacts as if he had one to many
drinks. He has the apple drive him home. The apple helps the
lugger to his living room and pretends he's feeling a little
better. He tell's the apple this story: I have a friend, he's as
close to me as a father. Every other year he calls and invites me
to a card game at a millionaires club. My friend is the manager
and dealer. The owner goes away on business in Europe for two
months and leaves him in charge. The stakes are high, minimum
twenty five hundred dollars to nine hundred thousand limit. We
cheat the wealthy players and split six hundred thousand dollars.
I can't make it this year, my money's tied up in Switzerland. I
only have one hundred-fifty thousand dollars. The apple will ask,

"How much do you need?"

"I'm short one hundred-fifty thousand, I need three hundred thousand." The lugger say's.

At this point, "The Take Away" begins. The apple want's in on the action. But the lugger "takes it away" from the apple by saying, "I've never had a partner before, no way will my friend allow a outsider in the game."

The apple being greedy and compulsive will eventually beg his friend, the lugger to get in this high stakes game. A day or two will go by, and the apple will be persistent and call his friend, the lugger but the lugger does not answer the phone, he avoids the apple, and continues to "take it away". The lugger will not give in or contact the apple; it is said, the first one that talks, loses. When the lugger has done his job well, the apple will go out of his way to talk with the lugger; he'll find you anyway he can. When the time is right, and the lugger knows, he may accidently see the apple in one of his favorite places. The whole intent is to purposely avoid him. He'll see the lugger, the lugger will make certain of that. When at last both get together, the lugger simply tells the truth to the apple. He tells him jokingly, he's been avoiding him because he's been waiting for a phone call from his friend, the dealer (which is true). The next day when the apple calls, the lugger tells him it's a go; the apple has been approved by the dealer. Flight plans are made to

wherever the "play" (game) will be and the apple will be
interviewed by the dealer. At the interview, in your prestigious
penthouse, you must appear to be affluent. When you first meet the
apple, you should ask him, why he want's to get in this game, and,
how long has he known your partner (lugger). He will be honest
with you. If you have done your investigating well, you will know
all the answers before asking the questions. If he's untrue, the
lugger is responsible. Part of the lugger's position is making
certain the apple is completely honest with him as well as you.
First and last names are forbidden. Mr., accompanied with the
first initial of the last name is befitting. Even though you know
all the details about the apple, you have to make him think there
is no guarantee he's going to play in this prestiges game. You
must perform as if you are the king of the hill, which you are,
and behest complete control. You should leave the room looking
angry, but before you do, you say "I don't know, I'm taking a big
chance bringing a stranger to the club." This is just another
"take away". The more you "take it away", the more he will want to
be in the game. The dealer will show the apple how the game is
played, what to do to win, and tell him how much he will win; this
could range from one hundred-fifty to three hundred thousand
dollars--no more--no less, for this era anyway. And naturally,
the dealer and lugger would win the same amount--the three of you
are partners, and are out to bilk

multimillionaire gamblers at the private club in which you are in
charge of. The compulsive gambler (apple) will double the ante to
get in this game if he has to, purely out of desperation. You
want the apple to think all the while you're uncertain allowing
him to partake in the game. You'll want to leave the room to have
time to think this matter over, this is what you want the apple to
think. When you leave the room, you're giving the lugger a chance
to "take it away" even more from the apple. The lugger naturally
is going to make sure the apple knows there is nothing he can do
and he's going to act sympathetic, luckless and heavyhearted about
the whole thing. "Take away", "take away", "take it away", this is
the key, and good acting is vital. When you come back in the
room, tell the apple and the lugger to come in the other room with
you. In this room you have the original card table set up; cloth,
cards, chips, abacus, the whole set-up. The lugger and apple sit
on the end, lugger sitting nearest the chipman and the abacus
directly in front of him, and the apple to the left of the lugger.
The six, seven, and eight of spades are directly in front of them.
You will say to the apple, "Mr. A., I decided to take a chance.
I'll make things right. I want you to understand clearly--you will
not ever tell a soul about this game, do you understand?" He will
promise you his lips will be sealed. You come back, and say, "I
need a day or two to fix things so you can get in the game without
any problems. I will inform Mr. L. when the game will be. In the

meantime, you both can enjoy the sun and have some fun." You had
made reservations for them to stay in a class hotel nearby for
three days; you know the manager well enough to give you more time
if needed. The apple will be indebted to you for allowing him to
play in the game, and the lugger plays along by thanking you for
inviting his best friend (apple) to have a part of the action.
Being a good actor is a vital part in this game. You will find it
amusing once you get your feet wet.

Now I will explain how the game is played. At a small table
near your leg are four decks of cards, they are marked of course,
and you will learn how to fix them the way you want the cards to
fall. Before the game begins you look at the lugger and ask, "Are
you ready to cash in for chips, Mr. L.?" The lugger hands the
chipman a large manila envelope with their initials Mr. A. and Mr.
L., containing, let's say, one hundred thousand dollars. The cash
is in fifties and one hundred dollar bills. The enthusiastic
chipman says, "Thank you sir", and hands the envelope to you, the
dealer. You in turn would give the envelope to a security guard
(shill) who brings it to another room. The dealer looks at the
lugger and say's, "Mr. L., your in charge of the abacus for the
first game." The lugger say's, "Thank you sir." The chipman looks
at the lugger, and say's, "How would like your chips sir?" The
lugger say's, "Fifty thousand my way, and fifty for Mr. A." The
chipman quickly and smartly places the chips in front of the

lugger, and say's, "Thank you sir." Then slides the same amount in
front of the apple, and say's, "Thank you sir." Then makes a call
at the gamblers, "Place your bets gentlemen." The apple bets
twenty-five hundred on the six of spades. The lugger bets twenty-
five hundred on the seven of spades throughout the first game. The
dealer pulls the first card, lets say it is a three. Dealer holds
card up in view of the betters and looks at the lugger, and say's,
"Did you record the three Mr. L.?" The lugger pulls down one
button under the three on the abacus, and say's, "Three recorded
sir." The first card drawn, the three is a key card but means
nothing in the first game. The card is placed back in the deck,
the cards are shuffled, and the dealer has one of the betters cut
the deck. The dealer places the cards in a shu, looks around to
make sure all bets are down, and say's, "Ready gentlemen." And
draws the second card. Let's say the second is a eight, the dealer
will say, "Eight win's", lays it face up in the win square, draws
another card, let's say it is a ten, the dealer calls, "Ten
lose's," and lays it face up in the lose square. In sequence the
dealer would sound like this, "Eight wins, ten loses." The chipman
pays off the winners even money and pick's up the chips from the
losers, and say's , "Thank you gentlemen, place your bets." The
dealer takes the win/lose cards, puts them together, and lays them
face down on the table opposite the shu, then looks at the table
to make sure all bets are down, and pulls the next card, "Jack

wins," next card, "Nine loses." The chipman picks up and pays off.
The dealer picks up the win and lose card and lays them on top of
the last two. You win or lose, it is a simple game. Before the
fourteenth card is drawn, one of the players will bet will bet
fifty thousand dollars on the ace directly in front of him, he
will lose. He may grumble quietly and look a little upset but it
is all part of the show. On the forty-fifth or forty-sixth card
our gambling friend will bet one hundred thousand on the Ace, and
wins. This creates a little excitement around the table. The
last four cards in the deck, the dealer say's, "Place your bets on
the bonus gentlemen." In front of each player is a small pad and
pencil. The object at this point in time is to guess what the
right combination of the four cards or numbers will be in perfect
sequence. The betters write down their choice, fold the paper,
and bet any amount of their choice. When all bets are down, the
dealer pulls the forty-ninth card, let's say it is a King, dealer
calls out "King." Dealer pulls fiftieth card, "Ten." Dealer calls
out, "Ten." Next card, deuce, dealer calls out, "Deuce." Next
card, four, dealer calls out, "Four". The four cards are face up
on the table. The dealer say's, "King, ten, deuce and four is the
winning combination gentlemen, do we have any winners?" If no
winners, the chipman picks up, if winners, they get paid off. If
you decide to have a winner, this should be handled a day before
the game. This ends the first game.

The second game is what I call, "the sting." Showing the apple what he must do is one thing, in the actual game he will do exactly what you taught him to do, the only difference is he makes a mistake. We'll get into that later. The dealer looks at the apple, and say's, "Mr.A., you're in charge of the abacus for this game." The apple says, "Thank you sir." The chipman calls out, "Place your bets gentlemen." The dealer shuffles the cards, places them in front of one of the betters, and they're cut. The dealer places the cards in the shu, and draws the first card, let's call this key card a Jack. The dealer looks at the apple, and asks, "Did you record the Jack, Mr.A.?" Mr.A. confirms by saying, "Jack recorded sir." He pulls one button down under the Jack, and knows there are three Jacks left in the deck to be played. In this second game the first card pulled, the Jack, happens to be the key card that the apple and lugger will bet the one hundred thousand dollars or whatever the amount is when the third Jack has been drawn and has been recorded. The next card drawn will be the win card, the Jack, and it will happen sometime in the second game. The dealer is in control of this. Let's say your midway through the deck, and three Jacks have been drawn. The next win card is the Jack. The lugger and apple can see on the abacus the forth Jack is coming up next. They tell the chipman they're betting one hundred thousand dollars on the Jack which is on the far end of the table. The chipman places their chips on the

Jack, and calls, "Place your bets gentlemen." Any wager on the
Jack with a minimum bet of one hundred thousand dollars or over
pays triple. The dealer looks around the table to double check
all bets are down, and say's, "All bets down, ready gentlemen,"
and draws a Jack, and say's, "Jack wins," pulls next card, "Ten
loses." The chipman pays the apple and lugger four hundred
thousand dollars, and say's, "Thank you gentlemen," Pays off and
picks up the losers chips, and say's "Place your bets gentlemen."
The apple and lugger stay in the game and bet the minimum twenty-
five hundred on their usual cards until the end of the second
game. Before the third game is begun, the lugger whispers in the
apples ear, "Lets get out of here, we did it." The apple agrees by
a nod of his head. The lugger makes a gesture to the chipman they
are leaving. The chipman gesture's with his hand to the security
guard to escort the apple and lugger to the cashier. They meet at
the dealer's penthouse later and split the cash. This is what the
apple and lugger's job is. Once the apple see's how the game is
played and participates in practicing, he knows there can be no
slip ups. The dealer leaves the apple and lugger in the room to
practice so they could do their job perfectly. After two or two an
a half hours of practice, the apple has his job down pat, the
lugger also. Before they leave Jules's penthouse, you say to your
friend, the lugger, "I'll call and fill you in tomorrow."

I have given you the details on how this game is played. You

know what you must do. The apple and lugger know what they have
to do. In the actual game, a few things are changed. The first
game remains the same. The second game I call, "The Turn",
meaning, "the switch", as you know well. Five Jacks are in the
first deck. The first card you draw is the key card, the Jack. If
you have drawn twenty cards, for example, and three Jacks have
been drawn and recorded on the abacus, at the right time you
switch the cards you have already drawn to the fixed twenty cards
that are on the table nearest you. They must be in the same
sequence as they were recorded. The only difference is a ten will
replace the winning Jack. When you draw the ten instead of the
winning Jack, the apple will bolt back in his chair and go into
mild shock. The lugger will look dumfounded and alarmed and will
look at the abacus and the apple not believing what just happened.
The dealer pierces his eyes into the apple's eyes, and say's,
"There must be a mistake." The dealer looks around the table, then
look's back at the apple and lugger, and say's to the apple, " I'm
going to read off the cards that were drawn, Mr.A. When I read
them off, starting from the first card, answer me back if you
recorded the same card." The apple will be in a mild shock and may
try but he will not be able too. The lugger say's, "I'll follow
you sir, go right ahead." The dealer picks up the deck and reads
off the cards as they were drawn. By the time you read off the
twentieth card, it is suppose to be the Jack but it is the ten

instead. The lugger realizes his partner, his friend, the apple
made a mistake. The cards are reread, and it is for certain, the
apple made a serious mistake. The dealer calls out, "Misdeal
gentlemen." The lugger helps the apple up and holds his arm out
the door to the waiting limousine. The chauffeur opens the door
and the lugger gets in first then the apple. The lugger is so
upset, he opens his door and fakes vomiting on the driveway;
sometimes putting the finger down the throat and making it real is
better, it all depends on the lugger's capabilities--the more
real, the better the job. In a matter of two to three minutes, the
dealer will turn the game over to the chipman and excuse himself.
You look heated and walk out to the limousine. After all, the
apple made a big mistake, supposedly, and you should be furious,
he just lost a large amount of money you went out of your way for.
You look at the apple and shout, "What the fuck happened!" Then
look at the lugger, and shout, "You were suppose to watch all of
Mr. A's moves, you're both .fucking morons." You kick the door and
walk off pissed. Then you turn and shout, "I'll take this up with
you later, my place, ten sharp! Do ya have that straight,
dummies!" You have to make the apple feel even worse than he
feels. The lugger say's meekly, "We'll be there." The chauffeur
takes off and brings them to their hotel. When you go back in the
room, everything is broken down, The game is in the footlocker,
the liquor is packed in suitcases, the chairs and tables are

rearranged, and the room look's completely different from the way
it was. Pay off the shills, and put the money the apple lost in a
attache case. The footlocker is placed in one of the shills car
trunk, and will deliver it at your place. Nobodies in a hurry,
they drive at the normal speed limit and meet you at your place.
I have given you enough details for now for the first play. There
is a second play in which the apple of the first play, Mr. A.,
begs you to get even. For now, perfect what I have given you.
When you are ready and know the first play like you know the back
of your hand, I'll be here waiting to tell you how the second play
is achieved. The apple made a mistake, this is what he thinks.
He feels obligated to his friend and partner, as well as you. He
has to get even--like all compulsive gamblers do. Until then,
farewell Jules. Suddenly, Jules jumped up from the alarm going
off. It was 5:30 a.m. He said loudly, "Wha'!" He shook his head
and looked around the room looking for the voice, the person,
something that wasn't there, "What the...musta been a dream...what
a fuckin' dream." He got up and smashed the alarm clock off; the
sound of the ringing made his head spin. "Ohhh Christ, my head,
where the hell did I go in that weird dream? Musta been in
Spookville somewhere where a voice know's more about this game
than I do." He laughed. "Oooh, I feel like a over-ripe tomato
with too much garlic." He went to the ice box, and pulled out a
small block of ice, then put it in the bathroom sink, chopped it

with a ice pick, filled the sink with water, and submerged his
head two or three times.

"Ahhh, just what I needed."

He grabbed a towel, wiped his hair and face a bit, and stared
at the card table for a few moments then at his notebook. Ice
water trickled from his face and hair. He wrapped the towel over
his head and shoulders, and sat down at the card table.

He read his notes, when finished, he thought, that dream was
so goddamn vivid I could taste it--should write it down. Wait...
was it all in my head? Or maybe I thought I heard--smelled--ahhh,
whatever, big deal, it was meant to be for a reason. It sounded
sensible...maybe that Greek dude Skiatho gave me the details. He
smiled, stood up, looked in the mirror and shook his head talking
to his reflection an octave higher than his everyday voice,
"Yeeaah, sure Jules baby, he's gonna feed me my breakfast too,
right? Jesus, I better go soak my head again, maybe I'm not with
it yet. I'm really blowin' my top this time. Listen to me, listen
to me for Chris' sake! What in God's name am I sayin'. Sheeeit,
I'm worn down, feel like a piecea shit. I'll write it down for
the record, I remember every word. I'll check it out later--need
all the backin' I can get." He wrote every detail. For the
heading he wrote, Apotheosis.

Jules worked on the game all morning. He figured out most of
the details until his concentration started to taper off. For the

rest of the day he drove around thinking about making a move,
going on the road hustling at different resorts throughout the
country. He has been seriously thinking about it over the past
week or so. For some reason he was not certain. But if he did he
would have plenty of time to figure out the game, and he'd be
happy doing what he does best. Deep down he didn't want to operate
the restaurant and casino, it wasn't Jules's style. He needed
freedom, he had a system when playing cards, with wealthy gamblers
in which was part of his strategy to bilk them with class, and
they would not ever know they were cheated. Tony Cheese past
through Jules's mind frequently but he wasn't possessed with
vengeance. He wouldn't allow this to take over his thoughts. He
believed in three absolute things: Finding Tony Cheese. Believing
in himself. And maintaining the right attitude toward life. He
knew what he had to be and what to do to persevere. His qualities
such as, imagination, judgement, taste and poise had to be at
their optimum at all times. At the end of the day he decided the
timing was not just right so he chose to stick it out for a year
or two and make the best of it.

CHAPTER 22

NEW YORK, AUGUST 9

6:00 A.M.

He couldn't believe it. He looked at the bundles of cash on his desk thinking what a lucky person he is setting up the bank and covering the details for the opening day. When Rocco was alive, he had a thriving business even though he cheated the gamblers at a high percentage rate. Jules being the king of the hill now, changed things. He wanted the gamblers to have a fair chance. He set things up so they'd have a forty percent chance of winning. The house had a adequate percentage of profit built in. Jules had set up a meeting with the dealers at 12:45 P.M. Jimmy the dealer had been in charge of the dealers and held his position as well as being Jules's right arm. Jimmy the dealer had hired a chef to take the place of Paco. Enzo had the name of being one of the finest chefs in the country. Jimmy the dealer bought him off (stole) him from Antone's Italian Restaurant. Enzo and his assistants were in the kitchen preparing food for the dinner crowd. At 12:45 P.M. sharp, Jules held a meeting with the dealers and advised them on the new way the gamblers are to be treated fairly. After the meeting, the dealers set their tables up and made sure everything was in ship-shape. Rocco's Restaurant

had been a private club for twenty-one years. The dues alone paid
the expenses. The restaurant opened at 5:00 P.M., and closed at
1:00 A.M. The casino opened at 5:00 P.M. on opening day and
remained open twenty-four hours, seven days a week. Opening night
had a full house, and had to turn down reservations for dinner.
The casino had a record breaking crowd. The gamblers were making
money, and the cashiers couldn't count the profits fast enough.
Everybody had happy faces. The night turned out to be the largest
and most profitable the place ever had. Night after night the
casino made big profits. Jules found little time to figure out
the mysterious game Rocco gave him. Things weren't turning out the
way Jules wanted them too. He wanted Tony Cheese.

Two years had passed and Mario was released from the
hospital. He couldn't walk but managed to get around in a
wheelchair. Jules tried to teach him how to deal the cards and
roll the dice, it was no use, Mario didn't have it. He just loved
being in the casino watching the gamblers play and would
occasionally bring a few drinks at the tables. He lived with
Carmen, she loved talking care of him. When she worked, a tutor
educated him, and on weekends, he hung around the restaurant with
Jules rather than play with kids who were also handicapped.
Financially Jules did very well. He always sent his mother more
than enough money for her and his two brothers. He gave large
donations to the church, and the needy. He always was a show-off,

and enjoyed over-tipping. Jules put Smiley to work at the card and crap tables, he did his job very well. He and Lynne Marie were still going together, and Carmen and Jules were crazy for each other.

Twelve years had gone by, it was 1941, and the United States was at war with Germany. Jules and Smiley were drafted into the Army. Jules didn't waste time, he and Smiley were stationed in the Philippines and set up card and crap games. They served their last year in Italy and managed to continue with discrete card and crap games. The area was bombed heavily during a raid, many men were killed and wounded. Jules and Smiley were two of the many lucky ones, they were hit with shrapnel in the legs, back and arms. After treatment and rest, they recuperated all in one piece. Jules received the silver medal of honor for deflecting the enemy. He was given a honorable discharge as well as Smiley three months before the war ended.

Jules and Smiley were fortunate to be alive. They had a few scars here and there, and limped away with a little more than forty thousand dollars apiece in winnings. Jules made sure every wounded soldier on his floor in the hospital received two roses apiece and a small card saying: Smell the roses, soldier.

After a two week vacation, Jules was right back operating his business. Jimmy the dealer had been in charge of place during Jules's absence. Smiley decided to take it easy for a while.

Four years later, August 2, 1945, Jules made a decision that would change his life around to his most wildest dreams. He made a phone call. "Hello, Jimmy...Jules. Meet me at the Hotel Restaurant in a hour, important business."

"Sure Jules, I'll be there." Jimmy the Dealer replied.

Sitting at his special table at the Hotel Restaurant, Jules sipped his coffee and puffed on a cigarette while waiting for Jimmy the Dealer. As usual, Jimmy was on time. The maitre d' seated him at the table.

"Hey Jules." He shook his hand. "I'm glad you called, wanted some fresh air. Not only that, ya got me off the hook to go shoppin' with the Miss's. What's goin' on?"

"Did you see the sun come up this mornin'?

"Wha'! Oh, caught me off guard there for a second. Ahhh, I left my place at 6:15 or so, and no sun shined on me. It's gonna be one of those bloody overcast days again.

A waiter came to table and placed a cup of tea in front of Jimmy. "There you are Mr. James, your usual."

"Thank's Max."

"Is there something else I can get you gentlemen?" Max said.

Jimmy looked at Max, and said, "Max, Max, bring the sun out, that's all I want."

"I'll do my best, Mr. James." He walked away with a serious look painted across his face.

Jimmy laughed. "I'd give a hundred bucks to see that Max crack a smile."

Jules smiled, "I'm not biting on that one, pal."

Jimmy looked puzzled at Jules. "Something big is cookin', whadaya got goin' Jules? I know you better than the Miss's."

"You should get to appreciate her more, she's a fine woman." He slid a small ring of keys toward Jimmy. "These are the master keys to the joint. You've been with Rocco the longest. An' bein' loyal an' senior dealer, these keys are your's."

Jimmy looked as if he went into mild shock. "Wha', whadaya sayin' Jules? I don't get it--I mean, you goin' away er somethin'?"

"I'm goin' on the road. I'm goin' after the creep that murdered Rocco, and put Mario in a wheelchair for life, Tony Cheese. I had it with the joint, the tables, the whole bullshit. I decided to hustle resorts throughout the country while trackin' the creep down--I'll find him, and when I do...the sun will shine in my heart again. I'll have time to figure out a con I've been workin' on, an' when I get it together, you'll be the first to know about it. I want you to promise me when I call, you'll be ready with everything I need."

"Jesus Christ Jules, you got my word, you know that, b-but I--"

"Listen, consider the joint your's, run the place as usual.

The profits are your's--I don't want anything to do with it--
that's the deal, Jimmy."

"I-I'm lost for words, Jules." He dropped his head slightly
as a tear rolled down his face. He composed himself and looked
back at Jules. "This is indeed a generous deed yer handin' me
Jules, I--"

"Don't say another word. Yer doin' me a favor. I'll keep in
touch, you'll know the score."

"I'm gonna miss ya Jules, wish ya all the luck in the world."

Jules stood up and rested his hand on Jimmy's shoulder.

"Don't look so glum Jimmy, You can handle the place, ya
always have, just carry on like you did when I wasn't there."

Jimmy stood up, grabbed Jules's shoulders and kissed both
sides of his face. "Okay Jules...okay-okay."

Jules returned the loyalty kiss back to Jimmy, and he walked
away. He looked as if a great burden had lifted off his
shoulders.

The time had finally come to do what he had to do--getting
Tony Cheese.

CHAPTER 23

NEW YORK, AUGUST 3, 1945

8:10 P.M.

Jules and Carmen were sitting on the polar bear rug in front of the fireplace enjoying the cozy fire and sipping wine.

"Carmen, Jimmy the Dealer is gonna take care of the business, an' I'm goin' on the road for a while--I want you to come with me."

"Where?" Carmen said.

"All over the country. Have to take care of business. I'll have time to figure out a game Rocco gave me, an' we'll have a lot of fun, whadaya say, Carmen?"

One week later, Jules and Carmen were on the road heading south through the Adirondack mountains. Saratoga Springs, New York was their first stop. The high rollers flocked to the hotels and lake houses to gamble at the stylish Arrowhead Inn and play the horse races this time of year. Most of the trees had shed their leaves and covered the ground with brilliant colors of gold, yellow, red, orange, brown and dark green, they were georgeous. Jules looked in the rear view mirror, and a tan Ford appeared to be following him, it was steadily catching up to him. Jules stepped on it and he gradually lost him. Two deer crossed the road

sixty or seventy yards ahead. He slowed down to avoid hitting
them. Suddenly, the Ford appeared and started to pass Jules but
didn't, it stayed parallel as if he was playing a game. The
driver yelled out, "Get that piece a junk off the road!"

It was Smiley, and Lynne Marie, they sat there waving their
hands and laughing and having a good time. Smiley floored it and
pulled out front leaving a blue-black cloud of smoke behind, then
he disappeared over a hill.

Jules laughed. "That Smiley will never change."

Carmen gave Jules a punch on his arm. "You held out on me,
Jules! Lynne Marie too! What a surprise! What a pleasant
surprise!" She gave him a hug, and buried her face in his jacket.

"Don't ya love surprises?" Jules said, laughing.

"Oh youuuu." She snuggled closer, kissed his neck, and slowly
worked her hand down to his zipper, and opened his pants. Jules
slowed down and enjoyed the wind blowing in his face.

A road sign appeared: SARATOGA SPRINGS 30 MILES, and a
billboard advertising PAPA JOE'S gas station 2 miles ahead.

As Jules approached the gas station, he noticed Smiley's car,
an old man was putting in gas. He pulled in the station along
side of Smiley's car, looked at him, and said nothing.

Carmen jumped out of the car to talk to Lynne Marie.

Smiley looked at Jules, and said, "Where ya been? This little
Ford's got some power, don't ya think?"

Jules laughed. "Some car--when ya passed me back there, ya blew out enough smoke ta choke a herd of horses. While yer at it, better check the oil, yer probably down to nothin'. Nice car."

"This baby don't burn oil, but I'll check it out, appreciate it, Jules."

The old man checked under the hood, and looked up at Smiley, "Yup, yer down alla four quarts, sonny. The awl stick isa showin' nothin'. Everathin else looks pretty downright good. Want the medium er high performance in this baby, sonny?"

"I don't belie...you sure, Pop?"

"Sonny, the only leg I pull is ma wife's, n she don't kick back with any smart remarks." He hobbled to Smiley to show him the dip stick. "Looky here sonny, there ain't no awl showin'--ya gotta have awl or she's gonna freeze up on ya."

"Okay, okay Pop, put the best in, nothing's too good for my baby here." He patted on the dash, and smiled.

"Now yer talkin', she deserves the best. Yer gonna see, this awl's the best, gonna improve on yer gas mileage too. As long as this--"

"Thank you Pop, thank you, thank you, thank you, I don't need the sales pitch, appreciate you just putting the oil in, thank you sir, thank you very much."

"Awright sonny, I'll have it done in two shakes of a lambs tail."

Jules said to Smiley, "When you check in at the Arrowhead, your reservations are under Mr. and Mrs. S. O'Brian. We'll meet later at the Casino Bar aroun' 9-9:15--"

"Thar ya go sonny, she's gonna purr like a kitten, now." He looked at Jules, and dusted off the door handle of his Caddy. "Yes siree, this is a fine automobile ya have here son."

"Thank you, beats walkin'"

The old man laughed. "Yup, it sure does."

Smiley gave the old man a ten dollar bill, and said, "Okay Pop, is this enough for the good job you did?"

"Good lord sonny, thars more than enough here, I'll git yer change."

"Keep the change partner, they don't make em like you anymore."

"W-why thankee, mighty thoughtful of ya. God bless you, God bless all you nice folks." He hobbled to the garage, and waved to Smiley and Jules.

Carmen and Lynne Marie came out of the tiny store carrying popcorn and soda.

Lynne Marie waved at Jules. "Hi Jules, we're going to have a blast, don't you agree?"

"Yeah, especially when you an' Carmen start playin' those one arm bandits."

"I can't wait, can't wait," She jumped up and down, "See you later."

"C'mon," Smiley yelled out to Lynne Marie, "Those slots will be outa cash by the time we get there, c'mon-c'mon!"

"Be nice sport or no popcorn, soda or you know what later."

"Sorry 'bout that love, I love you--can I have some popcorn?" Lynne Marie waved good-bye to Jules and Carmen, and Smiley took off leaving a cloud of blue-black smoke behind. It was so thick, Jules decided to wait until it cleared. He and Carmen enjoyed their popcorn and soda for awhile.

"Okay kid," Jules said to Carmen, "The popcorn's gone, the smoke's gone, whadaya say, shall we head for the Arrowhead?"

"Let's go sweetheart, the slots are waiting for me, whoopee!"

Later on, they passed a road sign: Welcome to Saratoga.

"Here we are Carmen, we're gonna have some fun, we should be at the Arrowhead in a few minutes--you must be all worked up, huh?"

"Now that we're here, not really." She grabbed Jules's hand, raised it over her head, shook it wildly, and cried out, "Ecstatic would best describe how I feel! I'm ecstatic, Jules!"

They laughed, and sang, You Are My Sunshine.

Jules pulled into the Arrowhead Inn, and stopped at the entrance where two valets were waiting. The valets opened the doors, and a bag boy came down from the lobby rolling a shiny brass dolly.

"Do you have luggage, sir?" The bag boy said to Jules.

"Yeah. It's in the trunk, take good care of it." Jules
replied.

Jules tipped the valets $5 each.

"Thank you sir, thank you very much." The valets said.

"Take special care of this car, boys. Keep it clean, an' park
it in a convenient spot, I may have to leave in a hurry, know what
I mean?"

"It'll be taken of sir. Your car will be right here in front.
No cars will be in front of you either, sir." The red haired
valet said.

"I'll bring your luggage to the front desk, sir." The bag
boy said.

As Jules and Carmen walked through the lobby, they stopped
and looked at a large poster surrounded with lights and colored
balloons. It read:

Arrowhead Presents

SOPHIE TUCKER with Ted Shapiro.

GOMEZ & MINOR - Society's Favorite Dance Team.

TED STRAETER and His Orchestra.

NORO MORALES Rhumba Band.

Cuisine under the direction of Marcel La Maze.

"They have a nice variety of entertainment. We'll have to

make reservations. I heard Sophie Tucker has a great show." Jules said.

"I heard. It would be nice to see her in person."

"Get four tickets for the day after tomorrow--last show."

"You're a doll, Jules," She kissed him on the cheek. "I'll pick them up later." She held on to Jules's arm tight with excitment as they walked to the front desk.

"Good evening sir, madam, can I help you?" The desk clerk said with a sincere smile.

"I have reservations for Mr. and Mrs. Julius Salarno."

The clerk scanned the reservation book. "Here we are, Mr. and Mrs. Salarno. Are you planning on staying three nights, Mr. Salarno?"

"At the least."

"Very well sir." The clerk handed the room keys to Jules. "Enjoy your stay." He tapped once on a bell. "One of our bellboys will take your luggage, Mr. Salarno. He will escort you to your room."

"Thank you." Jules had a ten dollar bill folded in the palm of his hand. He shook the clerk's hand, and said, "What is your name?"

"Elton St. John, sir."

"Is your mother alive, Mr. St. John?"

"Oh, yes sir. I take care of her. She's eighty-three years

old, we walk a mile every morning."

"I want you to take this small token and get her a rose or two, please. And thank her for bringing you into the world. We only have one mother."

The clerk looked at the ten dollar bill and quickly closed his hand. His eyes looked around as if he was being watched by Big Brother, he looked dumbfounded. He leaned cautiously toward Jules, and whispered, "Oh my, Mr. Salarno, You're so very kind but if they find out, I'll get fired."

"Mr. St. John, that's from me for your mother, you're just pickin' up a few flowers for me--she'll love them, don't you agree?"

"W-well--"

"Of course she will."

"You're very kind, Mr. Salarno." The clerk looked around, and rang the bell four times. "Where--"

A bellboy quickly came to the front desk.

"Thank you Mr. Salarno. Zak here will take your luggage." The clerk looked at the bellboy, and said, "Zak, Mr. and Mrs. Salarno are staying in the Presidential Suite, give them whatever they desire."

"Yes sir, Mr. St. John. He looked at Jules, "Good evening sir, Mrs., follow me please." Zak said enthusiastically.

They took the elevator to the top floor. Zak unlocked the

door, prepped the room and walked Jules and Carmen through the spacious three bedroom suite. It was as elegant as Jules expected it, and then some.

Jules palmed Zak a ten dollar bill, and said, "How long you been workin' here, Zak?"

"Eight years, sir. I'm the senior bellboy here. If you need anything, anything at all, I'm your key man, sir."

"I'm new to the area, what's goin' on, ya know, exciting?"

"Well, this time of year we have an abundance of high rollers all over the place. Horse racing is a big event. The casino is packed every night, and the payoffs are very good. Entertainment is spectacular, and the food is excellent. If the Mrs. likes to shop, I never heard of one who doesn't, there are first class stores just about everywhere."

"Sounds good. I'd like you to do me a favor."

"Just ask Mr. Salarno, an' I'll get it for you. Let me warn you--I'm good."

"Good, I like a honest man. I'm expecting guests tomorrow aroun' 10:00 a.m., I need a large round table an' seven foldin' chairs. Can you take care of that?"

"Piece a cake, sir. If you're going out this evening, everything will be here by the time you get back--if it's okay with you, sir."

"That's fine. Do what ya gotta do, Zak. Okay, I gotta few

things to take of, talk to ya later."

"My pleasure, Mr. Salarno. Whatever else you may need, just pick up the phone and ask for me. Have a fun evening. And thank you very much for the generous tip."

Jules went into the master bedroom. Carmen was sitting on the bed reading brochures.

"C'mon Jules, lets take a shower."

"If ya scrub my back."

"You're on. The suite is georgeous, Jules. Wait till you see the bathroom, it's bigger than my kitchen."

After their shower, they got dressed to meet Smiley and Lynne Marie at the Casino Bar downstairs.

In Smiley's and Lynne Marie's room, Lynne Marie was on top of Smiley on a chair in the living room enjoying sex.

"Ohhhhhhh Smiley, push-push, don't stop-don't stop...ohhhhhh, good-good-good-good...we better hurry, oh-oh-oh-ohhhhh...don't want to be late...harder-harder...mmmmmmmmm.

How can you enjoy this moment when thinking about something else?" He picked her up and lay her on the floor.

"J-just want to be on t-time...ohhhh...ohh...you're hitting my head, Smiley." She raised her voice, "Smiley! You're hitting my head against the chair, ouch!"

"Awwww shit! What a mouth! I can't work myself up with you makin' conversation about world events, Jesus!"

"I'm sorry honey." She grabbed his love handles and pulled and pushed him in rhythm against her. "Don't stop love, I didn't mean to...to...yes, yes, yes...

Suddenly, the phone rang. Lynne Marie flipped Smiley on his back, she reached up and picked up the phone.

"Don't..." Smiley whispered. Too late.

She couldn't put the receiver to her ear because Smiley was pounding away at her like a wild stallion. She looked as if she was riding on a bucking bronco but managed to hold the receiver of the phone with a firm grip. "Ohhh...you're turned on now...feels good...ok, ok, ok...harder, harder, that's it, that's it."

For some reason she put the phone to her ear.

"H-h-hell-o-o?"

It was Jules calling from the Casino Bar. He heard what was said and put the receiver in front of his face, and looked at it with a questionable stupid look. He built up enough courage to say, "Hello--hello, is this room 510?"

Keeping her position on top of Smiley, and riding high, she said, "Jules?" She's been embarrassed before but never like this.

Smiley stopped instantly. His eyes widened, and his face turned to the color of a red rose as he looked at Lynne Marie. He sat up leaning on his elbows for a moment, moaned, then fell back on the floor covering his face with the palms of his hands.

"Yeah. We're waiting at the Casino Bar. Are ya comin'?" Jules said skeptically.

"Y-yes. I'm sorry were late Jules. We'll be there in twenty minutes. The room is beautiful. We can see the swimming pool and everything."

"Good, good, I'm glad ya like it. Are you alright? Sounds to me like I interrupted on something heavy--Smiley teachin' ya how to play craps?"

She laughed. "Oh Jules you're so funny."

"Smiley's funnier. Take yer time, I made reservations for dinner at ten. Are ya hungry?"

"I'm starving."

"Good, good. Okay, I'll let ya go."

"Jules?"

"Yeah, I'm still here."

"I just want you to know I love you."

"I love you too, honey."

"See you guys shortly, bye, bye." She hung up. "Come on lover, I'll make it up to you later, I'm sorry."

"Don't worry about it, doll. What did he say?"

"He's a sweetheart. He said to make sure you don't come to late. And it will be okay if I pacify you later. Other than that, take your time but hurry up, we have reservations for dinner in a half hour, come on."

"Sounds good to me. We better get movin', lets go."

The happy twosome walked in the Casino Bar twenty minutes
later. Lynne Marie looked beautiful in her low cut red satin
dress. Smiley's black pin stripe suit, white shirt and burgundy
tie gave him the look of a sharp professional gambler.

The Casino Bar was crowded. Jules and Carmen sipped on their
drinks. When Smiley and Lynne Marie found them, they went out to
the pool side restaurant and had dinner. They had a bottle of wine
and antipasto and hot home-made garlic bread and calamari and
jumbo lobster stuffed with brown rice, scallops and herbs and
backed potatoes on a casserole of crushed peaches and broccoli
with olive oil and garlic. For desert they had strawberries and
cream. After dinner, they enjoyed a cup of cappuccino, and
relaxed.

"This resort is set up pretty nice, huh, Jules?" Smiley
said, sucking on his unlit cigar.

"No question about it. There's plenty of money walkin' aroun'
too. They play cards," He gestured with his head toward several
tables on the other side of the pool. "over there every morning--
high stakes."

"You don't waste time researching do you Jules?" Smiley said,
laughing.

Carmen and Lynne Marie had there own conversation. They were
talking about playing the slot machines, and where they will be
shopping tomorrow.

"Gotta do the homework, that's the name of the game, know what I mean?"

"Read you loud n clear, Jules. I have good feelings about everything here, how 'bout you?"

"We're walkin' away winners, my friend--big winners."

"Jules, lets walk around and see what's going on, okay?" Carmen said.

"I thought you'd never ask. C'mon, lets take a look." Jules said, giving her a kiss.

Smiley was in deep thought looking at the card tables across the pool, he didn't hear a word spoken, and thought, we're on the threshold of makin' some big bucks here, and I get fifty percent of the action. I love it-I love it.

"Smiley!" Lynne Marie shook him. "Are you with us?"

"Wha! Oh, where is everybody?"

"Come on, were going to walk around."

"Good idea. A little walk can't hurt anybody."

An hour later, Smiley asked Jules, "Whats on the agenda for tomorrow?"

"Be at my place at 6:00 P.M. sharp, room 704, can I depend on you?"

"I'll be there, promise."

"First thing we have to do is set up the card table and everything else, you know. We want to be at pool-side by 8:00 A.M.

Carmen and Lynne Marie were browsing at the fine apparel
shops a little ahead of Jules and Smiley.

"Carmen, Lynne Marie," Jules called out."

The girls turned and looked at Jules. He walked up to Carmen,
and put his arm around her.

"I forgot to tell you girls something." Jules said
heavyhearted.

They looked at him with blank faces, and waited patiently for
a response.

"I don't mean to spoil yer fun girls but there's nothing here
you're gonna buy, that's final." His face had a serious look
painted across it.

Carmen gave him a dispirited look. She couldn't believe Jules
made a remark like that. She said, "I don't understand Jules, did
we do something wrong?"

"You sure did." He said softly.

"What is it? I-I--" She almost began to cry.

"The stores are closed, that's why--we shoulda got here
earlier!"

They all laughed. Carmen hugged Jules, and Lynne Marie gave
him a light punch on his arm.

"If it were someone else that made a remark like that, I'd be
offended, but knowing you're a ball-buster, I'll forgive you."
Carmen said.

"I'm sorry. I'll make sure not to be so easy next time. Lets sit for a minute, I have to tell you something."

They walked to the pool, and sat on lounge chairs. Several people were doing the same. The smell of Autumn leaves and flowers was all around, and the full moon made it romantic.

"Tomorrow, you girls go shopping, hang out at the pool, do whatever you want. You may get lucky in the casino. If you see Smiley or me playing cards out here, pretend you don't see us, got it?"

Carmen wrapped her arm around Jules's shoulder and gave him a kiss on his cheek. "We can handle that honey, what do you think Lynne Marie?"

"I don't know, those are strict orders."

Everyone laughed. They relaxed for forty-five minutes then decided to go to their rooms for a good nights rest.

In the morning, Jules and Smiley set up the round card table. A solid green felt table cloth was cut to fit over the top, and secured by thumbtacks under the table for a tight smooth surface. Jules opened one of the suitcases and took out a bottle of Vodka, Scotch and Gin, then placed them on the bar near the table. Smiley arranged glasses, paper napkins, ladles and olives in a jar. He cut lemon wedges, and put them in the refrigerator covering them with a damp cloth. The sterling silver ice bucket looked perfect in the position it was in. He observed his arrangement, adjusted a glass here, a glass there, and said, "How's it look, Jules?"

Jules turned, he looked at Smiley, and said, "Whadya say?"

"I said, how's it look? The bar? Does it look alright?"

Jules looked at the bar, then at Smiley standing there looking at the bar as if he made a conspicuous accomplishment.

"Now that looks like the bar of bars. If ya move the ice bucket one-eighth of a inch to your right, it'll be perfect."

Smiley looked at the ice bucket. He almost moved it when he realized Jules was given him the business. He turned in the direction of Jules, and laughed.

"You'd make a great critic pal, but givin' me the business at this hour is like, ahhh, tryin' to out-bat Babe Ruth. I'm to much on the ball, meatball." He laughed harder than before.

"Yeah, yer right, yer on the ball. I can smell the lemons alright--ya got the bat in yer hands but yer missin' the ball-- how 'bout the lime wedges, I don't smell the lime, did you cut them under a blanket or have The Babe hit them outa sight?"

"Oh Jesus, that's right-that's right, lost my head Jules, thank's for reminding me, I'll get on it right away."

Ten minutes later, Smiley finished his feat cutting lime wedges. He neatly placed the lemon and lime wedges in a crystal bowl, and set it on the bar. Everything looked superb.

"That's it Jules, we have a done deal here, take a look--you don't have to give me a compliment or anything--a kiss would get

me excited enough to get me through the day. Take a look, c'mon--
I'm exhausted from this strenuous activity." He was joking of
course. He danced around, and thought, I'm gonna have some big
bucks fillin' da 'ol pouch tonight, hot doggie-do!

Jules was on his knees opening the footlocker Rocco gave him.
He thought, what a moron he is this mornin', I'd like to throw
somethin' at him. He turned around and looked at the bar." He
couldn't see the top of the bar to well but he noticed Smiley
dancing about like a male ostrich in heat.

"Jesus Christ!" Jules blared out, "Did ya have ta blow yer
top now!" He broke out in laughter.

"I just feel good Jules, real good. Better keep the voice
down though, you'll wake everybody up in Saratoga."

"Oh sheeeeit! Wasn't thinkin'". Jules whispered. "Looks ta me
like ya gotta go ta the can--go ahead, it's right behind ya fer
Chris' sake."

"I don't have to go--I'm celebrating my first bar set-up,
that's all. How's it look? Your approval will make my day." His
smile ran from ear to ear.

"Looks great-great. Maybe we should move the bar closer to
the card table, whadaya think?"

"Wait a minute." He put ice over the lemons and lime, covered
them with a damp towel, and put them in the bar refrigerator. "Ok,
that's done. As far as movin' the bar...I think it's in the

perfect spot--look." Smiley went to the front door.   "They come in
the door here," He paced off sixteen feet from the front door to
the bar.   "Sixteen feet from the door to the bar looks to me like
the center of the room. Not only that but it's convenient for me
being chipman and bartender, everything is at my fingertips. I end
my case your honor. Am I good or what?"

"Good point. I think you were a casino consultant in your
other life." They laughed. "Set the chairs aroun' the table."   He
looked at his wrist watch.   "We're running ahead of schedule, take
a break if you want. After the chairs are placed, set the chips
up--yer doin' a good job, keep up the good work."

"Naaaa, I don't need a break, I was born to do this heavy
labor shit, Jules my boy." He placed the chairs in their proper
places while enjoying sucking on his unlit cigar.

Jules opened the footlocker and took out five decks of his
marked cards and sixty thousand dollars in chips then put them on
the card table.   Smiley sorted the chips and stacked them neatly
at the end of the table.   Meanwhile, Jules fixed the cards in each
deck to his advantage, put them back in their boxes and lay them
on a small table near his right leg where they were easy to reach.
Next to the small table, a bathroom waste paper basket was placed
for discarding certain cards.

"That should do it," Jules said to Smiley. "It's 7:32, lets
get movin'. When ya get to the patio, walk aroun' an' look for

a few apples (suckers). When you find what you're looking for, you'll know what to do. Make sure you cover your ass before you start playin', you know. Don't forget the dinner engagement you have at 6 P.M, that's your excuse for getting out of the game, you know the bullshit. Later in the game, when you know these guys good enough, casually invite them to our private game at 9 sharp, and make sure you get their room numbers--write them down, got it?"

Smiley nodded his head assuredly.

Jules grabbed Smiley's neck muscle with a firm grip and squeezed.

"Ooouch! Jesus, whadya do that for!"

Jules cracked a smile as if to say, don't fuck up. "Don't forget, Irish." Jules gave him a wry face. "See ya 6-6:30, my place."

Smiley gave him an irritable look and walked off rubbing his sore neck muscle. He thought, *why does he have to do that shit! He knows fucking-a well that pisses me off! Sonofabitch! How am I gonna deal the cards now! How the hell am I gonna shuffle an' look good! I'm gonna be sitting there with a bent neck fer Chris' sake! I love the guy regardless. OK, OK, OK, knock off with the bullshit. Concentrate-concentrate, focus-focus...just point where the rays come together...hey, I like that line! Where'd that come from?*

By the time Smiley was through thinking to himself, Jules had walked away. He was on his way looking for his prey. Ten or fifteen minutes later he had circled the pool for the second time. He studied the area well, and found what he was looking for five minutes ago. As he got nearer to his prey, the three apples were playing cards.

Jules lit a cigarette, and thought, *There they are...they look better than I thought. I'm walkin' aroun' the pool one more time, just to make sure. What a beautiful morning to do my thing. They look like they can use another laugh.*

CHAPTER 24

SARATOGA, NEW YORK AUGUST 9, 1945

9:15 A.M.

Jules wore a black boxer bathing suit, a white terry cloth top and an expensive pair of Italian loafers. He walked nonchalantly around the pool area again passing fifteen or sixteen card tables where two to four men were playing cards at each of the tables. His eyes studied the one he had picked. They where laughing and having a good time. He passed the ten or eleven people relaxing on lounge chairs, some eating breakfast, and a couple swimming. Three feet away from his three apples table, he stopped, looked around, and scratched his head as if he was upset. He turned toward the table, and thought, *okay Jules baby, it's* show *time*...and purposely bumped into their table.

"Huh! Wha! Excuse me gentlemen. I-I'm lookin' for some friends...suppose to have a game this morning, don't see them anywhere." He rubbed his bruised leg. "Jesus, I'm sorry boys!"

He started to walk away and one of the players called out to him with his arm extended, and said, "Wolfgang's my name."

He shakes Jules hand aggressively, and with an indefatigable laugh, he blared out, "Join us partner!" He continued laughing and talking at the same time. "C'mon, yer here, yer friends aren't, c'mon! Let me warn ya though, we play fer high stakes!" Wolfgang grabbed Jules' arm, and pointed at one of his friends, and said, "That bald headed guy right there is Sam... now let me tell ya somethin', if I had a scalp like him, I'd have it circumcised!" Wolfgang laughed so hard he started coughing his brains out. He picked up his lit cigar from the ashtray, took a drag, inhaled the smoke and stopped coughing. "Yes sa ree, this is my cough medicine, all right. He pointed to his other friend sitting next to Sam, and said loudly, "That character with the smile on his face is Sol. He's the guy who's gonna round out Sam!"

Everybody laughed harder than before. Wolfgang slammed his hand on the table, then got up next to Jules.

"Boy oh boy partner, yer one hell of a good sport."

Jules thought, *I hope you're as good as me when I'm through with you, sweetheart.* Jules looked at Wolfgang, and with a smile, replied, "Takes one to know one, right, Wolfgang?"

"Yeah, yeah partner." Wolfgang said. "C'mon now, set down here, we're gonna have some fun."

They sat down. Jules thought, *this game is going to be like taking candy away from a baby.*

Wolfgang turned to Jules. "Excuse my ignorance, with all the asinine laughter, I didn't get yer name?"

Jules shook hands with the threesome. "Jules, Jules Salarno is my name. Look gentlemen, I'm sorry to have interrupted your game. I appreciate the invitation, but I feel a little awkward, if ya know what I mean." Jules thought, *that line works every time. He's gonna beg me to stay.*

Wolfgang smiled at Jules, and said, "Aww shucks Jules, I didn't mean to embarrass you ... Sam here an' Sol are accustomed to getting the raspberries from me. By golly, they get me pretty good, too. Jeepers creepers, maybe I gave you the shakes when I said 'the stakes are high at this table.'"

Jules looked at Wolfgang. "The only time I get the shakes my good friend is when the IRS get to close for comfort."

As they laughed, Jules shook hands with Sam and Sol. "Your friend Wolfgang sure is a persuasive man."

Sol looked at Jules. "Ya know Jules, if ignorance is bliss, I don't understand why there aren't more happy people!"

They laughed, and Sam said, "Jules, please don't ask me what I'm doing tonight; first tell me what you have in mind."

They laughed harder than before.

Jules thought, *Jesus, these guys are as corny as they come.* He pulled out a wad of hundred dollar bills, and lay twenty of them on the table.

"What's the game?" Wolfgang replied. "Straight poker if it's okay with you, Jules."

Jules lay another ten one hundred dollar bills on the table, and thought, this game is gonna be over faster than I thought.

From the beginning of the game at 8:30 AM, till 4:45 PM, Jules has most of the chips. Wolfgang and the other two players have been drinking heavily. Jules had a few, and pretends he's feeling good and slurs occasionally. He and Wolfgang are the only ones left in this hand.

Wolfgang said, throwing chips in, "Raise 500."

Jules threw 500 in the pot and replied, "See ya and raise three."

Wolfgang throws more chips in the pot, and said, "See ya again and raise five."

"Five and call," Jules said casually.

Wolfgang lays down his hand, two deuces and a pair of sevens. Jules turns over three jacks. Wolfgang is beat.

Zak walked up to the table, and said, "Excuse me Mr. Salarno, you're expected at a dinner engagement by 6:30, shall I confirm that?"

Jules replied, "Thanks Zak, I'll be there." Jules looked at Wolfgang, and said, "I'm having a game in my room at 9:00 this evening, you and your two friends are welcome to join us."

"Sounds like a great idea, Jules. Maybe I'll have a chance ta get even!" He laughed, then said, "My two pals here will just about make it to their rooms. Hell, I won't see them till tomorrow."

They both laughed, and Jules whispered his room number in Wolfgang's ear and walked off after cashing in his chips.

Jules walked by the pool bar and he spotted Smiley. He intentionally bumped into his barstool, and said, "Excuse me," then rubbed his knee as if he had hurt it. This is known among con men as the "office" (follow me). Con men rarely acknowledge each other openly, in public.

Fifteen minutes later, Smiley is making two drinks in Jules' suite. Smiley

"How'd ya make out, Jules?"

He laughed, "I bumped into these three guys, and they lost eighteen grand. I felt guilty winning it. They drank and played like money was no object. This guy Wolfgang hung in there. Last game he kept raisin' me. I call, he lays down a solid two pair, and I show him three jacks. He couldn't believe his eyes. He lost ten grand. Easiest game I ever had."

Smiley sipped his drink, and said, "Did ya find out what they do for a living, Jules?"

"Raise thoroughbred horses. They're running tomorrow. Wolfgang gave me a few tips. Listen to this bullshit." Jules reached in his shirt pocket, and pulled out a folded piece of paper, opened it, and said, "Tomorrow's first race, Worldly Guy to win. Seventh race, All My Tricks to win, and a long shot in the tenth, Black chips to show." Jules shook his head, and laughed.

"Sounds good to me," Smiley said, with a broad grin. "We goin?"

"Why not—can't take it with us, right?"

Smiley jumped to his feet, danced in a circle a few times, and sang the tune, *Because of You*, one of Tony Benett's favorites. Smiley had his own lyrics: Because of youuu there's a horse that will winnnnnn. It's paradise to be betting with Lynnnnn. Because of you, my is life now worthwhile, an' it's because, because, because ooooof youuuu. I'm so happy Jules, I can't tell ya!"

"Good, I'm glad you're not a singer—you'd never have an audience!"

Silence filled the room. Their eyes met, and suddenly, they broke apart in laughter.

"Boy oh boy Irish, I don't know how Lynne Marie lives with you, no shit."

"How can you say that? I mean, you do! I'm a nice guy...too nice. Not only that—but a unselfish lover and..."

"Crackbrain!"

They laughed so hard, tears rolled down their cheeks.

"Besides, the girls are gonna love those ponies, don't cha think, lover boy?" Jules said.

"I wonder where the girls are—they're suppose to be back by seven. Should be here pretty soon." Jules looked at Smiley with a satisfied look, and said, "How'd you make out today?"

Smiley took his long cigar out of his mouth, and replied, "Ended up playin' with four guys. I found them under the patio. Three of them are contractors out-a Colorado. The other guy is a big time distributor of produce outa Syracuse, New York. I ended up with seventy two hundred—and yes, yes, I didn't forget to tell them about the game tonight at nine. These guys are greedy degenerates, an' they can afford to lose. Did I do good?"

Jules lit a cigarette, exhaled, and said, "Did you get their room numbers?"

Smiley slapped his forehead as his mouth opened in disappointment, and said,

"Holy shit Jules, you aren't gonna believe this, but, but...I did exactly what you told me to do." He got up from the chair, and walked toward the door.

"Where you goin?" Jules asked. "You screwed up, right? Either that or you're givin' me the tease. C'mon, talk to me, you're a dead give-away. You're good, but not that good."

Thought I'd fool ya. You know me pretty good, Jules. I'd never let you down, you know that, meatball. Ya know, I meant to ask, what's with the room numbers, anyway?"

Jules gave him a look as if he wanted to punch him. "Can't you just say it the way it is, moron? Don't answer, because at 8:30 you're gonna call each of your players and tell them the game has been postponed till tomorrow night. Tell 'em you'll see them at the pool in the morning. Call from the lobby, I'll do the same with my guys. The only person showin' up is Wolfgang, we'll take him on one on one..."

The phone rang, Jules picked up. "Hello"?

"Hi Jules, Carmen. We're in the restaurant downstairs, coming down?"

"We'll be down in a few minutes. Whadya do all day besides buying all the stores out?"

"Bought a few things. You're like them. Mmmm, lets see...a bathing suit, and a hat and a pair of shoes. And guess what?"

"What?"

"Jules, come on, guess what I bought for you?"

"What'd you get me?" Jules said, surprised.

"Oh Jules, be a sport, take a guess, pleeeese?"

"Carmen, you're somethin' else. What do you get for a guy who has everything?"

"I'm not tellin' until I see you." Excited, she said, "I'll get a table, see you in a few minutes...bye."

After dinner, Jules, Carmen, Smiley and Lynne Marie sipped on coffee. Carmen opened her purse and handed Jules a small box wrapped with gold paper and white ribbon.

"This is for you Jules, because you're such a nice guy."

Jules opened the gift and finds a gold money clip with his initials engraved in old English.

"Always wanted one Carmen, thank you." He leaned across the table and kissed her.

"Ok, ok, it's my turn," said Lynne Marie. She looked at Smiley, and said, "This is for you, Mr. Romantic."

"Jeez, Lynne Marie, you didn't have to do this! I must really deserve this, huh?"

"Oh shut up and just open the goddamn thing will ya lover boy!"

He ripped the paper in a million pieces and opened the gift. Smiley picked up the gold Dunhill lighter, and said, "Jules, will ya look at this! Am I a lucky guy er wha'? An, an' a box of my favorite cigars!" He reached across the table and gave Lynne Marie a big kiss.

"Thanks baby, yer beautiful, just beautiful." He looked at Jules, and said, "These ladies got class, don't ya think, Jules?"

Jules put his arm around Smiley, and said, "Whadaya think, we're messin' aroun' with chopped liver!"

They all laughed.

"OK girls," Jules said, "we have a game in the suite at nine, I have no idea how long it's gonna take. If you want, hang out in the casino, try your luck. We'll meet in Lynne Marie's room when we're done. Tomorrow, we'll go to the races. How's that sound for more fun?"

Carmen, excited said, "Sounds great."

Lynne Marie jumped right in there. "Can't wait," c'mon Carmen, let's go change into something more comfortable, with lots of pockets."

Jules gave them $500 apiece, and said, "Have fun girls."

The girls kissed the boys, and off they went.

Later, Jules and Smiley made phone calls to the players and postponed the card game until tomorrow night. Wolfgang sure would be knocking at Jules' suite by 9:00.

In Jules' suite, Jules looks at his watch, it read 8:50 PM. He is dressed in a beige silk sport jacket, black pants and a solid gold tie. Smiley is decked out in a tuxedo.

Jules said to Smiley, "OK, start rearranging the chips."

Smiley looked in the mirror, straightened his bow tie, then turned to Jules, and said, "How do I look?"

"Real sharp, lover boy—lets hear those chips clickin', he should be here any minute now."

Ten seconds after Jules stopped talking, someone knocked on the door. Jules looked through the peephole, and sure enough, it was Wolfgang. He opened the door.

Wolfgang is wearing a cowboy hat, and dressed in a maroon western suit, black shirt, string tie with a gold dollar sign ring attached to it. His red handkerchief drooped from his lapel and his matching maroon cowboy boots made him look as if he was the Best-dressed clown at the rodeo near the racetrack. "Am I to early, Jules?"

"You're just fine. C'mon in, c'mon in an' relax." Jules shook Wolfgang's hand.

"Boy oh boy, this sure is a beautiful place ya got here, Jules."

"Thanks Wolfgang. Come over here, I want you to meet Smiley."

Wolfgang hurried over to Smiley, and shakes his hand.

"Golly be Smiley, glad to meet your acquaintance." Wolfgang shook Smiley's hand as if he was pumping oil out of a drum, not letting go.

"Pleasure meeting you Wolfgang," Smiley said, enthusiastically, "indeed, yes sir-ee, yes sir-ee. Can I make you a drink?"

"Make me one too, Smiley. The other gentlemen should be here shortly." Jules said.

"Gin on the rocks fer me, Smiley." Wolfgang said.

Ten minutes later, the phone rang. Jules picked up. "Hello...that's ok, the meeting is more important. See ya around 11 or so. The boys are tied up in a meeting. Said they'd come up later, 11 – 11:30."

"Oh, gosh, Jules," Wolfgang burst out, "forgot to tell ya, Sol and Sam are still out cold at the table. A couple of bellboys brought them to their room. Never seen 'em tanked up like that before."

"Don't worry, their big boys now, why don't we play a few hands and get warmed up."

"Now yer talkin' Jules," Wolfgang said, pulling a wad of cash from inside his suit Jacket.

Jules looked at Wolfgang with a slight grin, and said, "Same stakes as earlier, Wolfgang, my man?"

"Gee whiz Jules, why don't we make it a hundred ante an' a thousand limit, that's if you're comfortable with that, my friend, whadaya say?"

Jules smiled at Wolfgang, and said, "You're not trying to get even are you?"

Wolfgang laughed, and said, "Jumpin' grasshoppers Julius, of course I am, that's why I'm here!"

Jules lay twenty-one hundred dollar bills on the table in exchange for chips. Wolfgang does the same.

Smiley said to Mr. W. "Two thousand, Mr. W, thank you, sir. Two thousand, Mr. S, thank you, sir," as he picked up the cash and gave them chips in return.

Jules allowed Wolfgang to win three thousand dollars the first hour. The more Wolfgang won, the more his avariciousness came apparent.

Smiley is the bartender as well as the chipman. Wolfgang finished his third drink, and tells Smiley to make him another. While he waits for his drink, Wolfgang counts his chips as if they were all he had in the world. He said to Jules, "Listen Jules, I'm having a great time, and I just want you to know I'm meeting my lady aroun' 12:15—why don't we raise the limit to five hundred ante, two thousand limit, can ya handle it?" Jules smiled at him, and said, "No problem my man, why don't we keep it simple and make skies the limit, at least we'll both know where were comin' from, can you handle it?"

Wolfgang laughed, and said, "Boy oh boy, oh boy, now that's the best thing I've heard since chocolate, vanilla an' strawberry ice cream was thought up." He laughed loudly, coughed his brains out, took a drag on his cigar, inhaled, then his coughing stopped.

"What a ggggreat c-c-c cigar," He said, choking. "Gotta buy more a these suckers." He coughed over and again. When he stopped, he said, "Ya know Jules, this Havana works better than the cough prescription my doctor gives me. Those goddam guys don't know what's good for ya half the time" He laughed, and took another drag. "This is my medicine, yes sir-ee."

"Your doc is only trying to help you, my good man, but I know what you mean."

Wolfgang said in a whisper, "Go ahead Jules, deal those pretty cards."

Detailing the final two hours, the last hand is played.

Wolfgang throws chips in the pot, and said, "Raise two thousand."

Jules slides chips in, and said, "See you my friend, and raise four thousand."

Wolfgang throws in more chips. "See an' raise five thousand."

"Five and call," Jules said."

Wolfgang lays down his hand, a solid two pair.

Jules turns over a royal straight flush. Wolfgang is beat.

"Tough luck, Wolfgang.

Wolfgang slurred as he stands, and said to Jules and Smiley, "Thank you gentlemen... I was on a roll fer a while there...guess I lost it. I got me a woman I never loose. What a pair a tits... an' is she mean to me. Know what I'm sayin' fellas!" Everybody laughed as Jules escorts Wolfgang to the door. "See ya later, Wolfgang—don't get in to late!" Wolfgang laughs at Jules' remark, and said, "You're too much, Jules, you're too much." He laughed and coughed his brains out on his way to the elevator.

Jules walked back in his room, and Smiley jokingly said, to Jules, "Talk about taking candy away from a baby!"

"Yeah, he dropped a little over twenty grand, plus the nineteen this afternoon, including the seventy two hundred you won, that should add up to aroun forty seven thousand. Not bad for the first day."

Jules splits fifty-fifty with Smiley. They wash their hands and faces then relax in the living room. They sip on a drink, and suddenly, Smiley starts laughing. "What's so funny, lover boy?"

Jules said. Smiley continued to laugh while telling Jules. "Jules, Jules, Jules, Jules, where do you come up with these crazy schemes?" He laughed harder, and continued to say, "I mean, you don't miss a trick...the phone rang about 9:15...w-who the fuck was that?" Tears rolled down his face. Jules said.

"Whadya do, blow yer top, er wha!"

Smiley still laughing, said, "No, no, you're jus' somethin' else, at's all. I'll call my room, the girls should be there, it's 1:15 already."

Jules is in deep thought, his one leg crossed over the other is moving up and down. Smiley talked with Lynne Marie and told her Jules and him would be down shortly. He turned to tell Jules, and noticed he was in serious thought. He said, Chris' sake Jules, I know that look, whadaya thinkin' about?"

Jules looked at him, and said, "We're gonna check out tomorrow—we'll head for Albany after the races. We did better than I predicted."

"Jesus Christ, Jules, we got six apples waitin' to be had, why don't we stay another day an' clean em out?"

"You better be content with the twenty grand you made today, pal, cause if you're not, stay. You know I play percentages, and right now, they're on our side." Smiley threw up his hands and walks away with a tight lip.

The next day at the Saratoga racetrack clubhouse, Jules, Carmen, Smiley and Lynne Marie watched the horses warming up. There are thousands of people in the Grand Stand, all over the place. The tote board shows the stats, and Jules checks his spot sheet. Carmen writes down her favorite choices. Jules looks at Carmen until she feels it, and said, "What's wrong, Jules?" He smiled, and said, "I was just thinking how lucky you were last night hitting that jackpot."

Excited, Carmen said, "I know, I now. We played the slots for hours. Lynne won, played some more, lost, then got lucky and won again...played some more, and lost it all.

I was on a roll with eight hundred dollars. I should have stopped, but we were having so much fun I put it back in the slots and lost. I had one dollar left and decided to keep it. We were on our way to Lynne's room, and we passed a large slot, and I stopped...I had a strange feeling, a lucky feeling, so I said to Lynne Marie, "Oh, what the hell," and dropped my last buck in. Pulled the handle and watched the spin. When it stopped and I seen three matching red sevens, my heart stopped, bells started ringing, smoke came out of the machine, I thought it was on fire until Lynne Marie screamed, "You won! You won! Carmen, you hit the jackpot!" I never made fifteen thousand dollars so fast in all my life."

Jules laughed, and said, "Yer Lady Luck, and you don't realize it yet."

"TWENTY MINUTES TILL POSTTIME, LADIES AND GENTLEMEN," a voice announced over the speakers. "MR.MA GOO HAS BEEN SCRATCED IN THE FIRST RACE, THANK YOU AND HAVE A WONDERFUL DAY."

"What horse do you like in the first race, Jules?" Carmen asked. "Pick one for me" Jules replied. "I like Worldly Guy." She whispered.

Jules whispered back, "Me too. Got a tip on that horse. Let's see that paper--he's a long-shot--why are we whispering?"

Carmen looked at him shocked, and said, in a whisper, "We don't want anybody to hear us!"

He held back from laughing, and said, "Here's two hundred, go to the fifty dollar window, it's to the left at the very end when you go to the top of the stairs. Tell the teller you want two hundred dollars on Worldly Guy to win, in the first. What are you playing?"

"Haven't decided yet." She said, softly.

"LADIES AND GENTLEMEN, PLEASE STAND FOR THE NATIONAL ANTHEM. ON OUR OPENING DAY AT SARATOGA SPRINGS , PLEASE WELCOME OUR SPECIAL GUEST...MAY I PRESENT, KATE SMITH!" The track announcer stated over the speakers. When the music ended, everyone roared and applauded with enthusiasm.

After placing their bets, Carmen, Lynne Marie, and Smiley come back to the table where Jules is reading the newspaper. He's not interested in what's going on around him. He knows anything to do with man, any race or anything else can easily be fixed. He usually does not bet unless it's a sure thing, and today is an exception to the rule.

Smiley sat down, and asked Jules, "Are ya playin' the ponies those owners gave ya, er wha'?" He laughed, then slapped the table like a drum several times.

Jules gave him a serious look, and said, "Why, do you think I should?"

Smiley said, in a cocky tone, "Whoever bets on that long-shot, I'll take 'em all an' leave early."

Lynne Marie punched Smiley on his arm, and said, "Why are you so cynical? We're here to have fun. Can you do that for me?"

Smiley raised his arms, as if she was holding a loaded gun at him. He looked at her with a compassionate face, and said, "OK, ok, ok, I'm sorry, honey." He gave her a kiss, and whispered in her ear, "I'm just a little kid."

The horses enter the track as the bugler blows out the traditional tune, informing the spectators the first race is about to get under way. Seven mounted horses escorted by their trainers on horses trailing behind, gait along in front of the grand stand, and back towards the starting gate.

"GOOD AFTERNOON, LADIES AND GENTLEMEN," the track announcer said over the speakers. "THE #1 HORSE, TEEN QUEEN , OWNED BY J AND D STABLES...JOCKEY, J. NEVETTO. #2 HORSE TRAILING...GALLANT KNIGHT, OWNED BY C. J. MCCALL, JOCKEY...R. RODRIGUEZ. #3...SWEET SURPRISE, OWNED AND BRED BY STELLER FARMS...RIDER, T.J. COSTILLA. IN #4 POSITION, BERRY'S TWIN, OWNED BY ELA PARKHURST. JOCKEY, CLEMENT RAMMMMOS. COMING UP AND A LITTLE JUMPY...#5...JO-EEEY'S GIRRRRRL...OWNED AND BRED BY DR. SAMUEL KING STABLES...RIDER, A. BOULANKER. OH, OH , SHE'S GETTING A LITTLE OUT OF CONTROL, FOLKS. SHE'S OK, SHE'S OK NOW. AND ON WE GOOOOO, LADIES AND GENTLEMEN. STEPPIN' FANCY, #6, GOT RHYTHM, OWNER, MR. & MRS. AoNTHONY...JOCKEY, W. HENRY HERSH. AND FINALLY LADIES AND GENTLEMEN, LOOKING LIKE HE WANTS TO GO...WORRRRLY GUYYYYY...OWNED BY WOLFGANG T. ROSEN STABLES...JOCKEY, AUDRY BAZZILLI. THE HORSES ARE APPROACHING THE GATE...OH, OH, IT APPEARS TEEN QUEEN IS HAVING A PROBLEM ENTERING ...OK, OK, LADIES AND GENTLEMEN, SHE'S SETTLED DOWN...THERE WE GO, SHE'S ALL RIGHT, AND WANT'S TO GO."

Bell rings, gate opens... "AAAAND THEY'RE OFF! IN THE..." Suddenly, the track announcer is cut off, the spectators cheer on, screaming for their horse. Just before the quarter mile, Teen Queen collides with Sweet Surprise, knocking her off balance, and she slams into the guard. The horse veered off the rail into the line of the other horses. Sweet Surprise's leg gave way and she falls. The jockey and horse get trampled. At the same time, Teen Queen tries to get away from colliding with the other horses and veers to the inside. She slammed into the guardrail and jockey and horse are air-borne over the rail and crash to the ground. In seconds, two ambulances and two pickup trucks are at the scene. The jockey riding Sweet Surprise got up and limped to a safe place as a crew of six men dragged Sweet Surprise to the side of the track. On the other side of the rail, medics place the injured jockey in the ambulance and take off. Teen Queen is on her feet and is guided on the truck, and they hurry off.

The crowd is mesmerized by the tragedy. Their faces are sad and concerned. The race is still in progress. At the quarter mile, Joey's Girl is in the lead, and Worldly Guy is gaining on the outside. Coming in the stretch their head to head. All at once, the track announcer comes back on the speakers: "CROSSING THE FINSH LINE BY A NOSE...WORRRRLDLY GUYYYYY." The crowd roars with excitement. Some are crying, others are jumping up and down, and most

are throwing their loosing tickets in the air. Three or four minutes later, the track announcer is heard again: "LADIES AND GENTLEMEN, OUR APPOLOGIES FOR CUTTING YOU OFF, WE HAD TECHNICAL DIFFICULTIES WITH OUR SPEAKER

SYSTEM. WE'RE BACK AND READY TO CONTINUE WITH THE RESULTS. AND

HERE THEY ARRRRRRRE! WINNER OF THE FIRST RACE...WORLDLY

GUYYYY...PAYING 42.80... SECOND PLACE... JOEY'S GIRL...14.20. AND

THIRD...BERRY'S TWIN...10.80.

The tote board lights up with the official results. The crowd thunders. A few minutes

pass, and the track announcer is back: "MAY I HAVE YOUR ATTENTION PLEASE.

WE JUST RECEIVED INFORMATION ON OUR TEEN QUEEN RIDDEN BY

NEVETTO. HE IS REPORTED TO BE IN GOOD CONDITION WITH A BROKEN ARM

AND TWO FRACTURED RIBS. TEEN QUEEN IS UP AND WALKING AROUND.

JOCKEY T.J. COSTILLA IS JUST SHOOK UP WITH A FEW BRUISES AND

ABRASIONS, HE'S GOING TO BE JUST FINE. I'M SORRY TO SAY, SWEET

SURPRISE RECEIVED A BROKEN LEG AND HAD TO BE PUT TO SLEEP."

Upset over the tragedy, Carmen said, "Jules, can we leave?"

"Sure honey, I know how you feel. C'mon, let's get going."

Smiley turned to Jules, "How much ya have on that pony, Jules?"

"$200."

"That's forty two hundred buckerinos, for God sake! Talk about luck!" Smiley said

laughing.

Lynne Marie put her winning ticket in front of Smiley's face, and said, "I played that

long shot too—what's it pay, lover boy?"

Smiley's eyes widened. "Wha',whad ya bet?"

"Fifty dollars," she replied. Smiley looked at the tote board again, then back to Lynne Marie, and said in her ear, "A thousand dollars Lynne Marie! A thousand buckerinos!"

"I told you to bet on that horse," she said, excited. Smiley looked at Carmen, and said, "Suppose you bet on that horse too?" "

I did just that, liked the name. Only bet ten dollars, wish I bet two hundred now."

Jules put his arm around her, and said, "You made sixty dollars, Carmen, good girl."

He turned to Smiley, and said, "If you want to stay for the rest of the race, we'll meet in Albany--"

"Where ya goin', we just got here"? Smiley said.

"Carmen is a little upset, you know." Jules said.

Smiley gave a blank look at Jules, then glanced over to Lynne Marie, and back to Jules, and said, "Oh, yeah, yeah, Lynne Marie's not taking it real good either. We'll go together, it's more fun."

After resting in Albany, they headed south to Palm Beach, Key West and ended up in Miami Beach.

It's 1951, and Mario is in his room in a nursing home. He can't understand why he was left behind so long. The phone rang:

"Hello?"

"Mario, this is Jules, how ya doin'?"

"Is this really you, Jules?"

"It's me alright. Are ya ready to get out of that joint?"

"I've been ready for three months." Mario said, excitedly.

"Has Jimmy been stopping by to visit?"

"Jeez, Jules, what a nice guy. He's here twice a week, Izzy, too. We go to the cinema 'n everything-- where are ya—I want outa here, can't wait—I'll start packin' ?"

"Start packin', kid. We're two hours away. Got some business to take of. Should be there by 7: 00 P.M. Once I pick you up you're gonna have the biggest surprise of your life. Be ready, okay?"

"No problem in that department, Jules. See ya when I see ya, bye."

CHAPTER 25

MIAMI BEACH, MARCH 7, 1951

10:00 A.M.

On Star Island, Miami Beach, an exclusive community of multimillion-dollar estates, a 28,000 square foot Mediterranean 8 bedroom mansion consisting of 8 bathrooms, a 60'x 40' den, pool and a private wall surround the estate. At the entrance, a guardhouse occupied by a watchman secured by a wrought iron gate read the paper. Jules leased the estate from an old friend he knew when he was in a gang, back in New York. His friend is known as the most intelligent gangster known to man. Jules made plans to renovate the den into an illegal casino.

Jules is in the den. He set up the apparatus from the footlocker Rocco gave him. He looked at the tablecloth and dice and cards and chips, then stared at the beautiful handcrafted abacus. After several years of mind-boggling meditation, he has finally figured out how the game was initially correlated.

If Skiafo, the so-called ghost and creator of this game is still about, he is without a shadow of a doubt, a genus. Here's to you my highbrow friend. He thought. The only ones that ever got took are long gone. They're probably in Caesar's Palace in the sky some place, still trying to get even. His face put on a twisted smile.

He lit a cigarette, and relaxed for a few minutes. The time was perfect to call Jimmy The Dealer. When he made the connection, he told him to round up his shills and luggers. Jules will be waiting inside the terminal. Jimmy, Blue Eyes, (lugger) will be the chauffeur that will drive the luggers to Jules' place. He will pick-up the luggers at 6:40 P.M. at the Miami International Airport. And later, Smiley will pick up the shills when they arrive at 3:15 P.M.

A few weeks later, Jimmy Blue Eyes chauffeur's Jules' black limousine to the entrance of the airport. Jules waits in the terminal for the arrival of his boys. He wears a black fedora with a thin brown alligator band, which is his trademark. He spots a tall good-looking man, dressed sharp, making his way through the terminal carrying a large suitcase and strutting along with a fancy walking stick. He combs the area carefully with his eyes. Finally, he catches a glimpse of Jules, and he rubs his eye as if he has an itch. This "office" sign means "OK" among con men. Jules returns the "office", and waited for the rest of his gang.

Not to far behind, Jules spots Tony Hands, Sparrow and Teddy, The Boost. As they pass Jules, the "office" is made and returned. Jimmy, Blue Eyes came in the terminal and gestures with his arm to the boys to follow him. Jules lit a smoke, and waited for the others. A gentleman with silver hair dressed in black, looking like a Catholic priest nonchalantly makes his way through the crowd. His name is Father Alisi. He once was a priest, and continues wearing the cloth; this is his trademark. He spots Jules, and gave him the "office" and continues walking out the swinging doors, and waits for Jules.

Walking and talking with a short man is Joey Tat, a thin boned sharp dresser with a consistent twitch in his neck. The short man is Fats. He's a 300-pound package of pure pasta combined with brute strength. Fats gestures Jules the "office" as the twosome walk past him. They wait outside. Jules looks around for Sol and "The Hawk". He heard a loud rasping voice. Jules thought, *who else could it be? It's big mouth Sol, all right!* As they passed Jules, the "office" is exchanged. Jimmy Blue Eyes escorts the boys into the glistening limousine, and off they go into the heavy traffic to A1A. Jimmy knows the scenic road all right; the palm trees, the ocean, the bikinis, what else is there?

That evening, Ernestine, Jules' cook poured the wine and later on brought out a special dinner. She served stuffed peppers and veal scaloppini and stuffed squid and angle hair and meatballs and sausage and finished it off with her famous rum custard pie.

Later, they went to the den and Jules is about to explain the unique card game to the luggers. The shills are not present on this occasion. The complete game is set up in the center of the den. Jules looked at his men, and said, "Gentlemen, a few days before Rocco was murdered he gave me this old footlocker." He bent over and touched it and lightly rubbed his fingers over one of the hand sculptured olive trees in the center top, and said, "Rocco could never solve this game, he only knew its purpose—to sting greedy people. I want you to listen to me good, gentlemen," He looked up at Sol, and with his acrimonious expression, said, "That means you too Sol."

Sol looked at Jules and put his finger over his lips, then with his rasping voice said, unintelligible, "Doen worfy Shluz, ah slanged ta da shpould!"

"Take the fingers outa the mouth so we can comprehend yer bullshit!" Jules said, heated.

Sol dropped his hand, and scratched his ear, and said, "Uh, huh, shit Jules, sorry. Didn't realize what I was doin', but I was sayin', 'don't worry bout me, Jules, I changed ta da good!' "

Jules gave him a twisted smile, and said, sweetly, "Changed? But Sol...that's good, at least for you!"

Everybody laughed. Somebody yelled out, "Yeah, sure, Sol, ya can take the spots offa leopard too!"

"Ahhhhh! Youz guys don't know nuttin'," Sol roared out. His arms straight up, waving and shaking to the ceiling. "Whad da fuck ya know aboud cinnamon spots anyway!" He sat down and put his cigar between his teeth, wearing a big smile as if he won the war.

The room roared with laughter.

"Yeah, sure, ya ol' hogshead," one of the boys shouted. "I assume yer right...but ya probably don't know what order there suppose ta come out!"

The room roared with laughter and cheers. The boys simply were having a great time giving Sol "The Big Tease."

They love him because he's the most lovable, know-it-all teaser of teasers of all time.

He should have been named, "The Scorch."

Jules said, "Ok, OK now, leave Sol alone...we'll hang him later...let's get down to business, we got a lot to cover." The boys calmed down like a bunch of kindergarten kids getting ready for the teacher to serve hot chocolate pudding.

"OK gentlemen, we're goin' after big time criminals. I'm gonna give you the best of the worst of the big time mobsters known to man. And, your job will be to become a best friend with him. These characters--apples as we call them are sharp enough to cut your throat if they find out you're playin' games with them. We're gonna sting these guys big time, and they will not ever find out. If you make one single slip, it can be fatal, but I'm content you will follow my directions as they are given without a flaw. You're professional enough to know the score. Why else would you be here? I'll show you how the game works first, and when I'm through I'll give you "The Story" you're gonna use on the apple after you have become his best friend. He'll beg you be his partner in the biggest game aroun'. I'll answer questions now."

Jimmy, The Dealer asked, "You did say your going to assign each of us these bloody apples, and we're to become the best of mate's with them? Is that accurate, Jules?"

"Yes. They're compulsive gamblers, and millionaires that can afford to lose."

He pointed at the next hand, moving in air. "Go ahead Sparo," Jules said, coolly.

Sparo got up, looked around the room, at the ceiling and finally looked at Jules. "Ya know Jules, this room is beautiful, a real showplace. It reminds me of the time you--"

Jules interrupted. "I know, Sparo. I want you to ask me questions that relate to what I was talking about, nothing else for now. We'll get into the room later. What's your question?" He thought, *that Sparo would never change. He has a habit of not getting to the point. He is funny though.*

Jules grinned and waited for Sparo's question. And he waited. "Well!" Jules said.

"Oh...I forgot what to ask...Oh, O-OK, I got it Jules, b-beg pardon, lost ma head, you know. I just wanna know how we gonna know what territory we're gonna cover?"

"I have a list of different parts of the country for each and every one of you...we'll get into that later."

Before Sparo sat completely down, he was halfway there, he said to Jules, "T-Thanks Jules, you're a gem, you're a real gem...I love this sting...it's the big one all right."

At that very moment, the loud voice from Sol, shouted, "Jesus Christ, Sparo, can't ya come ta da point! Shad-up will ya!"

Laughter filled the place. Father Alisi stands erect, and waves his arms about. The room is as soundless as a church. "Thank you gentlemen," He modestly said.

"Confessions will be heard when the day has ended. Sister Cecilia and I have to go over our etchings, you know."

The room filled with laughter. Father Alisi stood erect, and waited for the boys to settle down. "Sorry Julius, but my question is...well, let me put it this way...I'd like to know, if you will, can we pair up, say, if I go to Vegas, can two of us luggers be partners?"

"Yes. We'll vote later on that issue. I have a system worked out. You'll know the score later on."

"Thank you, Julius, thank you kindly," Father Alisi said, satisfied with the answer.

There weren't many questions at this time, but Jules knew there would be in due time.

Jules thought, *I think I'll tell them "The Story" first, instead of showing the game…* *…at's what I'll do. These guys aren't dummies.* He picked up one of his barstools and

…laced it next to the footlocker. He sat on it half sitting and half standing. Looking at his

…and picked boys, they were very attentive and anticipating for Jules to talk.

"Okay, gentlemen, I decided to tell you the "Story" first. We'll go over the game…"

"Excuse me Jules," Hands said. "You sayin' our goal is to find out all about this guy and

…come the best-a friends wid him an-an he's gonna get stung big time?"

"Are you with us, Hands er what?" Jules said with a dirty look smile. "We covered that

…ready. Maybe you should go out on the patio and get some air or just pay attention. Never

…ind, just sit there, you're gonna know all the details before you meet your "apple" trust

…e."

"Sorry Jules." Hands looked a bit embarrassed.

"Let me put it this way, Hands. These "apples" are going for $100,000 to $300,000, for

…e first time aroun', and will not ever, ever, not ever find out he was taken. Let me explain.

…ice the "apple" is our best friend, we know he's a millionaire, a compulsive gambler or a

…mpulsive degenerate gambler and all the other bullshit without a shadow of a doubt, we

…'e him "The Story" You'll be staying in a posh place, you will act as if you're a millionaire

…d do not ever forget, you gamble like one, act like one, live like one, think like one and live like one. You all have a bankroll, and know how spend.

Now, on one particular night, the night you've planned for, for the eight months or year you've known your best friend, will be the night you're going to tell him "The Story". That night you'll be gambling with your best friend, drinking heavy...coke, ginger ale, you know how to fake it. In the later hours, you're going to pretend you had one to many. You ask your best friend to drive you home. When he drops you off, get out of the car and fall. Play the roll of a drunk; he'll help you to your room. You're gonna feel better when you get inside your place. Invite him in for a night cap. You may have a slight problem walking, but your OK. Now, sometime during that period of time, you're going to have a slip of the tongue. As you slur and stammer, tell him "The Story"...this is it: Tell him you have a friend almost as close to you as your father--you'll go on to say, every two or three years he invites me to a millionaires club. He's the manager and head dealer there. Minimum bets are $2500. There are no maximum bets because skies the limit...biggest game aroun'. The owner has business in Europe, and he's gone for two months. He leave's my friend in charge of the whole operation. We cheat the players and split 600 grand. He pays the chip-man 5 grand, the guy is real sharp.

We've all been friends for years. I can't make it this year, my cash is tied up in Switzerland...Christ, by the time it gets here, it'll be too late, I wanna die, sonofabitch!

Now, at this point in time...shut up--the first one that talks, loses!"

Jules lit a cigarette, and looked at the boys to see their reaction. He thought, *this is a piece of cake for these guys. We're gonna get Tony Cheese, too.*

Teddy the Boost looked at Jules, and said, "So far, sounds like a winner, Jules.."

Fats interrupted. He wanted to stand, but couldn't seem to make it. "I like it Jules, where we go from there?"

Joey Tat jumped up. "Jules, how will the apple not ever know he got took?"

Jules sat on his barstool, looking content. He knew a million questions would be asked ill at once. He knew his boys all to well. He allowed them to chatter for a few minutes.

"Okay, gentlemen", he stood up and the room became quiet. "First of all, starting where left off....once you told your best friend the "story", and you've shut –up, you rush to the iathroom, just making it, and you fake a vomit...you know how to make it happen...Jesus, ou've done it a few times in your day, right Sol?"

Sol looked at Jules and smiled as he gave him "the office", by rubbing his hand across is nose, meaning, yes. "Dose days are unforgettable, huh, Jules?"

Jules smiled, nodded his head and pointed at Sol with a straight arm, as to say, yeah, yer ight, ol' buddy.

"Okay, boys, back to the "story". When you come back to the room, after you've blown our guts out...your friend is going to ask you how much will it take to make the game? Just ill him you have $150,000 available right know, but you need $300,000. We know the pple is compulsive and greedy,so he's going to want to be partners with you. You're going) of course be convincing enough to refuse the deal. Why? Because you never had a partner efore. He's gonna ask you how much the both of you make apiece if you were partners. Tell im at least $300,000 each. He will beg you to be partners. He'll ask you over again

to call your friend and ask him if it's OK. He'll give you all the reasons in the world why
you should make him tell your friend why it's right to take on a partner. When your best
friend brings you the cash, minimum $150,000, he's ready--call me. I'll tell you to make
reservations on an early flight to Miami International Airport. I will interview him. A
limousine will be waiting your arrival. The chauffeur then will bring you to the
Fountainbleu Hotel on the beach. I'll be in a penthouse suite. The chauffeur will escort
the both of you to my room. Bring cash, 50's and 100 dollar bills in a large manila
envelope with both your initials on the front. Last names are never used, never ever. You
will introduce me as Mr. S. I will call you Mr. C., the apple, Mr. T. or whatever your last
name begins with...got it?"

The room was silent. The boys looked as though they had questions to be asked.

Sol roared out with his rasp low voice, "Jules, dis is big. I heard a few "stories", but dis
one takes da cake. When we--"

Sparo cut him off, and said, I'm dyin' ta see the play (game). You gonna—"

"You're a genius, Jules." Father Alisi said. "This was all meant to be.

"Unbelievable, just unbelievable!" The Boost said, shaking his head in disbelief. "Ya
know Jules, we been waitin' for this a long time."

"I know. OK gentlemen, now, the game. Come up here, you'll get a full view.

Jules shows them how the game is played, and how the apple will make a mistake at
the actual play (game), and lose.

The boys are impressed with the game, they never seen anything so effortless, yet, there was a magic something about it that seemed too give each and everyone of the luggers a strong sense of power within. Jules had them sit back in their chairs.

"Before I draw names for who's goin' where an' when...any questions on the game?"

Suddenly, the room became completely still. The boys looked as if they were in a state of hypnosis; no movement, just sitting like statues. Jules heard a voice only he could hear.

"Jules, you know who I am...Skiatho, remember? You have chosen your luggers well. I am content you will be successful with my game. You will also find Tony Cheese, and do to him what he deserves. I am watching your every move. Don't be afraid. By the way, your boys will not ask you anything about the game—they know it well."

The voice stopped. The room, the boys, everything went back to normal again. Jules felt strange for a moment, and thought, *Jesus Christ, that fuckin' Skiatho has more power than I thought...or maybe I'm just blowin' my top...yeah, that's it.*

Jules just rubbed it off and reached for his hat on the table behind him, and said, In this hat gentlemen is your name, and where you're goin' to meet your best friend. Jimmy The Dealer walked up to the hat and had one of the boys pick the first name.

"Smiley...Vegas!"

"He's not here," Jules said. He'll be here later. I'll give him the word.

"He's going to love Vegas, lucky dog." Jimmy The Dealer said.

Pick another, Jimmy, seein' Smiley's not here." Jules said.

"Chicago...Sol."

Sol stood-up and yelled, "Dat's my town, dat's my town." You kin pick 'em Jimmy, tanks."

Sol walked to the hat, and pulled a slip, "Ya ain't gonna believe dis, but I read, Fats...New Orleans! Hey Fats, maybe you'll put some more weight on over dare, huh?"

Fats bounced his way to the hat, and said, "Eat me, moron." He picked a name. "LA...Father Alisi."

When Father Alisi walked towards the hat, he cheered-out, "The place of my heart. I can hear the angels callin' now...we're waitin', we're waitin'!"

Suddenly, the room roared with laughter and clapping.

Father Alisi pulled out a slip, and called, "The Big Apple...New York! And who's the lucky gentleman?...The Rig, himself!"

The Rig casually walked to the hat, saying, "I'll take it...love New York. She's waitin' just for me. Not only that, but I'll lay odds 10 to 1 the Statue of Liberty won't be the only lady I get into!"

Everyone yelled-out, "Boooooo."

The rest of the luggers were happy to go to where they were assigned. One week later the luggers left for their assignments. Mario learned the game, as well as learning how the business was operated. The boy is bright, and grasp's on quickly. Jules engaged him as a shill.

Later that year, Jules and Carmen were married. Six months later, they had a baby girl. They named her Tina, short for Christina. Her brown eyes resembled her father, and her red hair was similar to her mother's. Carmen wanted to raise Tina in New York. And, Jules bought a home in Forest Hills, an exclusive area in Queens, New York. He'd do anything for Carmen. Jules stayed in New York with Carmen and Tina. He was a good father and husband. They had loads of fun with the baby and all. Jules organized his business in New York temporarily, and started researching for the suitable victims (apples) for his luggers. He and his FBI contact, had made up various lists of considered candidates. When he broke them down, he made contact with his luggers, and gave them the information.

Eight months later, Jules had taken a plane to his estate in Miami. Smiley had been taking care of the 18 shills. Jules gave Smiley orders to show them the territory, including Key West, and entertain them while in New York. Jules talked to them at his estate, and wanted to know how familiar they became with the sights and places Smiley had shown them. Jules was pleased.

Before Smiley left with the shills, he said, "Jules, I'm so excited about goin' to Vegas, I can't tell ya!"

"Relax, fer Chris' sake, you're gonna be there sooner than you think. I'll give you the word when the time is right. Just keep the shills absorbed. You're doin' a good job, keep it up. By the way, get packed, you're leavin' for Las Vegas next week! Here, take your tickets!"

"You serious? Are you s-serious!" Smiley looked as if he got shot. "Jules, oh Jules, I love you." He kissed Jules on the lips. I'll call ya from Vegas, Jules." He looked at his tickets, then back at Jules, and said, "See ya later, pal."

"Wait a second," Jules shouted. "I don't want read in the papers they found a Irish male with a broad smile somewhere in the desert, know what I mean?"

"Ahhhh," at the same time, he held his arm straight out, gesturing with his fingers touching each other and shaking his hand, and said, "Whadayou tinka I am-a, a goompa er sometin?" He started toward the door, and bumped into the wall.

"Wait a second, moron!" Jules shouted again.

Smiley, overwhelmed, calmed down a bit, and listened intensely.

"Jimmy Blue Eyes will pick you up and take you to the airport, call me when you get there...good luck."

As soon as Smiley got out the door, Jules could hear him shouting.

"Hey you'z guys, ah's goin' ta Vegas...yaaa-hooooo!"

During the year, five of the luggers found their apples. They made continual phone calls to Jules. The conversations covered in detail what had been said between the apple and lugger. The luggers were doing a good job. Jules was pleased, and unceasingly advised each one. After all, the apples were criminals, the worst kind, and very intelligent. Jules made sure he and his luggers were way ahead of the game.

The phone rang, Jules picked-up.

Hello?"

"Jules, Father Alisi, callin' from Dallas. Everything in order?"

Have it altogether. You sound as though you have something important, father...talk
to me."

My best friend is ready. He has $200,000 in cash, and it's sealed in a manila envelope
as you requested. Our initials are on the front, and I'm waiting for your approval and
details."

"Did he tell you about the 200 prostitutes he owns? And the 13 year old girls he
breaks in?"

"Yes, Jules. The guy is a genuine pervert. And, I'm sure you know he's a slum lord."

"Know all about him, Father. He also has 4 million stashed all aroun' the place not
including holdings in Switzerland— do you know this?"

"Everything Jules, the whole shebang, sweetheart."

"Did he tell you he's a Russian defect? Been in Dallas 27 years?"

"Jules my son, you don't miss a trick. He's my best friend, remember?"

"You ruse your mark pretty good too, kid. OK Father, make reservations for Monday.
I'd like both of you at my suite by 7:30-8:00 Monday evening. Can you do it?"

"No problem, Jules, no problem, indeed."

"Good, good. I'll have the chauffeur pick you up. He'll escort you to my place. Any
questions?"

"This is silly to ask Jules, but how many floors up is your penthouse?"

"More than ten, why?"

"Oh, nothin'. The closer I am to heaven, the more I feel saintly. See you at the top then, Jules."

Jules knew father Alisi had motion sickness, but good old father would never admit it.

At the Miami International Airport, Monday, the chauffeur parked in his special spot and watched father Alisi's plane coming in, it was right on time. Crowds of people were everywhere. Taxis and buses and cars filled the air with carbon monoxide, making everyone high, it wasn't all that bad, it was a free ride. People walking and running every which way seemed as if they didn't know which way they were going in any event.

The chauffeur spotted father Alisi, and gave him "the office". He knew father Alisi is now referred to as Mr. A, the apple, Mr. L. He looked like the twin brother of Nikita Kruchev. His hair was colored blue black. Unkempt matching eyebrows. He wore thick black dark glasses. And had four dark brown pea size moles on the left side of his lower face. His clothes were expensive, but uncoordinated. He had no jewelry except for a Timex wristwatch. He sniffed cocaine frequently, and has no class.

The chauffeur opened the rear door. "Good evening, gentlemen."

Father Alisi said, "Delightful evening." He turned to Mr. L, touched his arm, and assisted him in the limo.

Before Mr. L. entered, he looked at Mr. A, and said, "You are special, you know?"

"I know...what are friends for!"

They laughed. While Mr.L slid across the seat, Mr. A gave the chauffeur a nod and wink with a closed mouthed smile. The chauffeur returned the wink, with a serious face, then stuck his tongue out, and said, "Thank you, gentlemen."

"Nice place," Mr. L mumbled. "I can use a drink, how about you, father?"

Mr. A grabbed his arm, and said heated, "Jesus Christ, man, no names, no fuckin' names, remember! Call me Mr. A for Chris' sake...don't disrespect the way things are done here. There's no guarantee Mr. S. is excepting you as my partner yet, goddam!"

"All right, all right, I made a mistake...I won't slip-up again, promise." Mr. L lightly slapped Mr. A on his cheek, and said, "Love ya, Mr. A."

After that, Mr. A. thought, *can't wait to see his face when he makes "the big mistake"*.

CHAPTER 26

MIAMI BEACH, MARCH 14, 1951

6:35 P.M.

On their way to the hotel, the limousine stopped for the rising bridge at the
Intracoastal Waterway. There were yachts and small craft, waiting for the open waters of
the ocean. The bridge finally went down, and the limousine headed for the Fountainbleu
Hotel. There was plenty of time. They were to be in Jules' suite between 7-8 P.M. The
chauffeur knew the route like the back of his hand, and how heavy traffic would be at
this time of year.

The black sleek limousine pulled in at the entrance of the hotel; a spectacular
horseshoe shaped edifice, equal to none. Crowds of people exiting and entering, valets,
parking and bringing cars to impatient guests, in an orderly fashion, it was a class act.

Two valets opened the doors, and asked Mr. A and Mr. L if they could assist them
with the two light suitcases they carried. The chauffeur looked at Mr. A, and Mr. a
nodded, as to say, yes, take them. The attaché case Mr. L carried contained $300,000.
He wasn't about to let go, in any event, for know, anyway.

The chauffeur escorted the twosome through the lobby, to the elevators.

In Jules' suite, he's in the bathroom combing his hair. He looked real sharp in his
white linen slacks, white silk shirt, black Italian loafer shoes and his beautiful eight-
karat blue sapphire ring on his pinky and Pateke Philipe wristwatch. He walked to the

den, and studied the card game he had set-up earlier, it was complete. Content, he walked to the living room, went out to the balcony and looked out to the vast darkness of the ocean. He had the best of both worlds, ocean view and Intracoastal. At night, on the Intracoastal side, there were lights and boats; one could see activity in motion, the whole spectrum. The ocean was black at night, but beautiful. Jules contemplated for awhile, then came back inside and read one of his favorite books, *Game of Thieves* by Robert R. Rosberg. He preferred nonfiction, overall. Once in awhile, he'd read one of Sidney Sheldon,s great ones. He lit a cigarette, and waited patiently for Mr. A , and the apple. A few minutes later, Jules heard a knock on the door. He got up, and calmly walked to the door. He was cool. One would think the bellboy was delivering his dinner.

He knew who it was all right. Jules had nerves of steel. He was a Robin Hood in disguise, which is an understatement. He opened the door, and greeted Mr. A. They hugged as if they were a father and son that met for the first time. It was a good show both incognito.

"Heyyyyy, been a long time, Mr. S. God, I'm so happy to see you!"

Jules stepped back, and placed both hands on Mr. A's shoulders. "You look terrific, you never change...same ol' face, same ol' duds--ya know what I've planned to do with you? You aren't going to be--"

"Sorry to interrupt you, Mr. S, but, I know your ingenious plan. I can't wait. There's a new Mercedes waiting just for me. And, maybe, I'll buy that old church I've always talked about, and convert it into a class poolroom."

"You're blowin' yer top, Mr. A." He laughed, and squeezed his cheek. "I miss your bullshit, I really do. But, my tailor's comin' over, and he's making you a custom-made Italian suit, regardless of whether you like it or not. I've never seen you in regular clothes."

"No thank you Mr. S, these are my threads. This is my trademark, you want me to lose my reputation?"

They laughed.

Mr. A moved aside. "Mr. S, I want you to meet Mr. L."

Mr. L shook hands with Mr. S. A vague smile appeared on Mr. L's face.

"Eet eez nice to meet you, Mr. S."

"Jules looked dead in his eyes, and said, "Come in, you must be exhausted."

The chauffeur waited outside the door. He looked at Jules. "Do you need me for anything else, sir?"

"Be here in the morning, 7:30. Thank you."

Mr. S locked the door, and calmly said, "How about a drink, boys?"

"That's my office," Mr. A said, with enthusiasm. "That bar of yours is the most beautiful piece of art I've ever seen, Mr. S. The built-in glass shelves and mirrors and the antique bar is quite unique. It's mine someday, Mr. S, you promised." On his way to the bar, he said, "Scotch on the rocks, Mr. S?"

"Thank you."

"Double Vodka on ice, with a splash of goat milk, Mr. L?"

"Appreciate it. You make good barkeeper." He reached in his pocket for a handkerchief, and sniffed. He thought, *fuck! I must try not to sniff nose to many times. Mr. S theenk I take coke.*

Mr. S kidding, said, "The chef's preparing the goat for dinner...the moron forgot the milk!"

They laughed.

"How 'bout a triple then, Mr. L?"

"No-no, double eez fine, you want Mr. S to teenk I'm alcohol addict?"

"Not at all." Mr. A laughed. "I didn't mean anything by that remark...you're a man of means, you know."

"I know, I know, my comedian friend." Mr. L told him. "What are you trying to say to me? I have known you long enough to know you give to me business. Go ahead, talk to me the punch-line!" He sniffed unconsciously, crossed his legs and clutched his handkerchief.

Mr. A laughed as he walked behind the bar. "I want you to know, my friend, you are indeed one decent sport. Sure you don't want a triple? It's only vodka."

"No-no." Mr. L smiled, and sniffed at the same time. "Double eez good. My blood eez all-weather, you must know theez, no?"

"Indeed, Mr. L, indeed."

"Why don't you just make the drinks, and stop pickin' on Mr. L." Mr. S said.

"Thezz eez good idea. Thank you, Mr. S."

Mr. A prepared the drinks. He looked at his Russian friend, and said, "Your mama must have brought you up on goat's milk. I like it, but, it gives me diarrhea."

Mr. S chuckled. "Holy Christ, remember when you had that goat milk shake?"

"Thank you Jules, you're a man of my heart. So the door to the washroom was locked...goddam, most humiliating event I ever encountered, you know."

"I remember well. Nobody aroun', no water, just the stinkin' stain you tattooed on my leather seat. I loved that car. They tried everything to get that stain out. It got worse. I ended up buying a new one, because of you."

They laughed. Now, Mr. A and Mr. L have been in Jules' place not even 15 minutes, and the interaction between Mr. S and the apple is a warm-up exercise. Interrogation is Mr. S's way to find out that Mr. L is on the up and up. Mr. S knows all there is to know about him, but want's to know if Mr. L is straight with him in person. One would not ever know Mr. S's exact method of questioning unless one studied the works of Sigmund Freud. Mr. S will grill Mr. L until he is satisfied. And, if he is, only then will the bigger games begin...

CHAPTER 27

MIAMI BEACH, MARCH 14, 1951

6:55 P.M.

Mr. L had a solemn facial cast. He was the type person one would not want to play games with or make him irritated.

Mr. S is scrupulous. He must dissect every word the apple reveals. He's not dealing with chopped liver, here.

Mr. L is getting uneasy Mr. S thought. *He should be ready to excuse himself. He's overdue for a line of nose candy. No one would stop Mr. L, would they? Of course not.*

"Mr. A, how did you meet my comedian friend?" Jules said, gravely.

"Well, I ahh--"

"I tell story, Mr. S, if you no mind—theez eez funny."

"Go ahead, Mr. L, I can imagine."

"I'm at private club, and theez priest in white collar and black suit comes to table where I play craps. I'm ahead eighteen grand, and when dice come my way, I wait for heem. He looked like he wanted to play, but faltered. I says to heem, "Theez eez not place to pray, old man. Maybe you theenk sometheeng else? He looked at me and smiled, then dropped a bankroll wrapped weeth rubber band, on table. He says to croupier, "Small percentage of the donations this week—five thousand in one-hundred dollar chips, if you will." He looked at me and smiled again, then says to me, "Sorry to hold you up, sir." To make long story shorter, theez priest was on such beeg roll, club members shouted, "Bravo Father," I have not ever known the club members, who are well-to-do degenerate gamblers act as theez. Theez man, theez priest, theez mother-fucker, he clean me out--plus table!"

"Didn't anybody question how he got in the place?" Mr. S asked.

"He bribe doorman—I talk to head-honcho, says to heem he was guest of mine. I do not know why I took liking to theez white hairdo prick, but I deed. Later, we have drinks. Next day, I invite heem to lunch. We drink vodka, and more vodka. Sometime, between drinks, he gave envelope to me. "This eez for you." He say to me. I do not understand, but I open. There eez eighteen thousand dollars inside. I do not understand. He say to me, "Easy come, easy go." Deez eez money he won from me in crap gam. He eez similar to brother to me. Theez eez end of story."

"Excuse me gentlemen," Mr. A said. "Your drinks. You forgot what I said to the head honcho when you introduced me."

Jules gave Mr. A , the "office" by winking his eye; meaning, shut up.

Mr. A returned the "office" by pulling his ear. He remained where he was standing, and waited for Mr. L to speak.

"Oh, yes. I introduce Mr. A to head-honcho as "my friend". Head-honcho says to heem, "How are you?" Mr. A says, "Wonderful." Head-honcho says to heem, "You know, sir, infrequently a table is busted. I admire the wonderful way you did it. The word, wonderful, I rarely hear anymore. Is this word special to you?"

Mr. A says to heem, "You know, we all know the word wonderful, don't we? Astonishing, amazing, marvelous? I love the word, wonderful, I say it all the time. The way I spell wonderful is one-derful. It reminds me of my wonders. With the one thought, and the one power—it does wondrous things for me when I say one-derful."

"Head honcho make handshake weeth Mr. A, and says," Wonderful. You are exceptional human being." Then he walk away. Are you satisfied now, Mr. A?

"They laughed. Mr. A said, "Thank you, Mr. L, you're indeed a gentleman."

"That's a funny story," Mr. S chuckled. He looked at Mr. A. "How did Mr. L find out about my club? Not only that," Mr. S heated, slapped the coffee table, and firmly jumped to his feet. "As long as I've known you, you've never had a partner...remember?" He waited for an answer for a moment, but Mr. A looked to shocked to answer. Mr.S continued. "Its always been you and me, Mr. A, remember? Nobody else--did you forget the pledge we made when I first figured out this deal?"

"Excuse me, don't mean to interrupt, Mr. S, but I can help you weez theez answer. I must use bathroom first, if you don't mind."

"Mr. A, show our guest to the men's room...we'll go on when you get back." Mr. S thought, *we know it's fun time, right Jules baby? He's a cocaine head, big time. To bad, I have the guy hooked too.*

"My pleasure." Mr. A replied.

Mr. A escorted Mr. L to the bathroom, and came back with Mr. S. He walked behind the bar, and arranged a few glasses, deliberately tapping them together to get Mr. S's attention.

Mr. S came in from the balcony. He looked at him, and at the same time he gave the "office", by scratching his chin, meaning, good job. Then, with another "office", he rubbed his nose, meaning, shut-up.

Mr. A winked at Mr. S, as if to say, "OK." Mr. S remained focused on details.

A few minutes later, Mr. L came back. He laughed, and said, "I am ready to tell you how Mr. A make known to me about you."

Mr. S looked in his eyes, and thought, *Jesus Christ, if his pupils dilate any faster, virtigo and confusion may blow him away. Look at him, he's not too observant, he overlooked some of that white lady on his tie, fer Chris' sake. He's going to be easier than I had anticipated.* "Go ahead, Mr. L, I want to know."

What Mr. L is about to make known to Mr. S, is known as "The Story". He dreamed it up, mostly used in sales procedures, among other things. In life, the term "take away" is referred to as offering something to somebody, then taking it away. Everyone wants what he or she can't have. The apple, Mr. L, tells Jules "the story" Mr. A, Father Alisi had told him.

"Tank you, I tell you precisely. Almost twelve months I know Mr. A. One night we score on crap table beeg. Mr. A, he drink heavy an' could not drive car. I take home my friend. He can not walk, talk, he was, how you say...smashed...destroyed is better word. I help heem to heez apartment. After he heaves guts out, he made drink for me, an' had balls to make drink for heemself. He make toast, an' says, from Frank Seenatra, to us, one for my baby, and one more for the road. I deed not understand theez toast. As of theez moment, I steel do not understand."

Mr. S, and Mr. A laughed. Mr. L was totally unaware what the toast meant, for sure.

Mr. S asked Mr. A, "You're a Sinatra fan, tell Mr. L the lyrics to the last verse or about."

"My pleasure. I'll even sing the last line. Who knows, somebody may hear me, and sign me up. Ready? Here goes...one for my baby, and one more for the road."

Mr. A had a nice singing voice. After all, his experience came from all the masses he gave before the church ousted him for embezzling donations, twenty some odd years ago.

"Yes-yes," Mr. L said, "that eez it! I like deez singer, Seenatra. Theez eez what my friend meant...one for me, baby, and one for heem...one for road...eez good line. Seenatra Rat Pac lingo says charlies, wheech eez noun, meaning, sexy breasts. And, gasoline as booze—I like jargon of Rat Pac. Eeet eez cool."

They laughed.

Mr. S said, "You gonna finish the story, Mr. L, or maybe you would like a handful of charles?"

"Maybe Mr. A make me more gasoline, no?

They laughed.

"Double Vodka coming up!" Mr. A shouted. "How about yours, Mr. S?"

"Thank you, less water this time."

"Ring-a-ding!" Mr. A shouted.

Mr. S gave him a blank look, and said, "What the fuck is that suppose to mean?"

"Terrific! Rat Pac Lingo, Mr. S, forget?"

"He chuckled at Mr. A's remark, and said, "Knock it off with the bullshit, for Chris' sake--you're startin' to act like a harve! Can't you see Mr. L wants to finish the story!"

A harve is Rat Pac Lingo, meaning; harve (n.): a square. Mr. S was hip with the jargon.

They laughed. Mr. L didn't know why he was laughing--he just joined in.

"Mr. S shook his head looking at Mr. L, and said, "Finish the story, Mr. L."

"You know," He unconsciously sniffed again, at the same time, loosening his tie. "I am relieved to know what Mr. A meant when he make toast on that night." He looked at Mr. A, smiled and gestured with a nodding of his head.

"I feeneesh story. My friend says to me, heez friend eez like father to heem, an' he eez dealer of millionaire club. He says to me, he cannot make game theez year because heez money eez tied u i Sweetzerland bank. By time money arrives to heem, eet would be much too late. He eez best friend, so I ask heem how much cash eez needed to make game? He says to me, he has one hundred feefty thousand cash, but, what eez needed for game eez total of three hundred thousand. And, eef he had theez amount, he weel ween seex hundred thousand--you make same an', twenty five hundred apiece pays for cheepmans expertise. Mr. A says to me, no way can he have partner. But, I am avaricious man. I make to heem many reasons to call you. All of sudden, my friend goes een coma—theez eez not accurate word—unconscious, that eez correct word. My apologies, sometime I say wrong word."

"That's okay," Mr. S said, "I understand what you're saying, please continue."

"Well, I cover heem weeth blanket, and leave. Next day I call heem, no answer. I call every day for three days, maybe four, no answer. I theenk to myself, where eez theez fuck, why he not call? So, I rush to heez place theenking maybe friend eez dead. So, I make double time to heez place. My anxiety was overwhelming. The door eez locked, curtains in weendow closed--I break door open--he eez not there. Apartment was same as I left—half-feeled glasses of vodka where I leave them, blanket on floor--eet looked to me like somebody abduct heem. Each day I call, five days, maybe six, knotting, zero. At last, he call me. He says to me, he had emergency. He make apology, an' told to me he had conversation weeth you. He says to me, he does not want another partner. My excessive self-indulgence could not stop theenking of theez game. I am like leech. I theenk to myself, eez good idea to take one hundred fifty grand from safe, and go to my friend's place, an' maybe I throw deez money in heez face. I deed theez to heem, eet work every time. I leave heem weeth cash, an' next day he wake me at 3:00 A.M. to tell me we are going to Miami so you can have conference weeth me. I theenk theez 'money-throw-een-face treek has much influence. Money eez not necessarily root to all evil. As you well know, we all have weak moments, no?"

Jules gave him a smirk, then looked at Mr. A. "Look at him, elbows on the bar, red face, unemotional-- anyone knowing him would think he was about to break in Sister Grace in one of the church bench's."

Laughter broke out.

Mr. A just stayed in the same position taking it easy. He knew Jules was checking to make sure the apple was telling him the truth. At the same time, making sure Mr. A had "the story" down pat.

"Go ahead Mr. L, finish." *This cokehead has a photographic memory. He told "the story" almost as accurate as I made it up.*

"Well, Mr. A, says to me, we must place een manila envelope, 300,000 thousand dollars een manila envelope. Feefty an' one hundred dollar beels eez what you approve. Maybe now you make me partner?"

Mr. S raised to his feet, pissed. "I've been manager and dealer for several years, Mr. A, you never needed or had a partner before! Jesus Christ, it was always you an' me! Ya tryin' to blow my gold mine! What the fuck you flappin' yer mouth for! Sonofabitch! He walked out to the balcony looking as if he was in deep thought. He was faking it, of course. His angry remarks are referred to as "a take-away." The more he takes away what the apple wants, the more the apple wants it.

Five minutes later, Mr. S came back. He had a serious look painted on his face. He looked at Mr.L. "If you get in on the deal, you have to promise me that you will never divulge this to a soul, do you understand?"

"I pledge to make known to no one whatever I master weeth theez business venture, weez you. I make deez promise, Mr. S."

"OK, come with me, you too, Mr. A."

The three go into the den where the card table is set up.

Mr. S sat in the dealer's position. To Mr. S's left, at the end of the table is where the chipman is positioned. There are red, white, blue, yellow and black chips stacked in an orderly fashion. To the left, Mr. A and Mr. L were directed to sit in the two chairs at the end, facing the other end of the table. These two chairs are assigned to Mr. A and Mr. L when "the play" (game) takes place. They are facing the 6, 7 and 8 of spades. The abacus is in front of Mr. A. At Mr. L's left, on the opposite side of the dealer, are three empty chairs reserved for players. The five, four, three, two and ace of spades appear here. To the left, one empty chair, by itself on the end, facing Mr. A and Mr. L, the king of spades is displayed here. The queen, jack, ten and nine follow to the right completing the rectangular sequence.

"The chairs you're sitting in gentlemen are your assigned chairs. They will be reserved for you when you come to the table. Mr. A is familiar with the set up. The game starts at 7:30 sharp. Tuesday night at 6:30, the chauffeur will pick you up. He'll drive you to the club, the escort you to the private card room. A security guard will escort you to the private card room by 7:20. When you enter the room, I'll be shuffling the cards. There will be four players, and the chipman getting ready for the game to start. Sit down as soon as you enter. Mr. A will guide you to your chair. I'll say, good evening, gentlemen, and ask Mr. A for the manila envelope. Mr. A will hand it to the chipman, and will ask for $300,000 thousand in chips; $150,000 for Mr. A and $150,000 for you, Mr. L. The abacus keeper starts with Mr. A, and with each new game, is passed to his left. I'll show you how the abacus works. After I shuffle the cards, I'll have one of the players cut the deck. I'll draw a card." A ten come into sight. "This first card is a cue card. It means nothing in the first game. It's a cue card. Don't forget it. You'll understand this cue card in the second game, when the abacus is passed on to you, Mr. L. I'll ask Mr. A if he recorded the ten. He'll reply, ten recorded, sir. I'll place the card in this white square behind the Win/Lose squares, face down. Then place the rest of the cards in the shu. I'll call, place your bets, gentlemen, look around to make sure all bets are placed, then call, bets down, and draw the second card. This card is a Win card." He pulled a two. "I'll call, two wins, place it face up in the Win square, then draw the third card," He pulled a six. "Six loses. The six is placed in the Lose square face up. The chipman picks up the losers, and pays off the winners. He will call to each player after he picks up, place your bet, sir, thank you. This is a courtesy call during the excitement. It makes the game move on at a smooth pace. At this point, I'll look at the abacus keeper, and ask him if he recorded the two and six."

"Two and six recorded, sir." Mr. A, responded assuredly.

"Ya got that, Mr. L?"

"Eez piece of cake."

"OK. Now, this is what happens next. I pick up the win/lose cards, as you can see, place them face down in the square here. They are placed on top of the first three cards drawn. I'll continue where I left off. This time, at the traditional pace. Place your bets, gentlemen. Mr. A, bet twenty-five hundred on the eight—Mr. L, twenty-five hundred on the seven. These cards you will place your bets on, and lay twenty-five black chips which is equal to twenty-five hundred dollars in the first game. No other cards are to be played, is that clear? When we are at the actual game, this is what you will do, flawlessly—is that clear?"

"First game, I bet on the eight—twenty-five hundred, that's it." Mr. A said.

"For first game, I put twenty-five black cheeps on seven of spades, only."

"Good. Bets are down, gentlemen." Mr. S pulled the next card. "Ace wins--five loses. Chipman would be picking up and paying off. Seeing he's not here, pretend he is. Did you record the ace and five, Mr. A?"

"Ace and five recorded, sir."

Mr. S went through forty-eight cards, and four remained in the shu.

"This is the procedure, gentlemen—piece of cake. There are four cards left. I will call, bet your cards, gentlemen. As you can see, a pad and pencil is in front of each player. Mark the four cards you think will be drawn in sequence, fold the paper in half, and the players will bet whatever they wish. I want the both of you to print on that slip, 7 – 8 – jack – queen—bet ten thousand—write them down, memorize them. You're going to win one hundred thousand apiece with these cards, for starters. When the chipman pays you both, be cool, don't show any excitement. The members will show a little resentment, but they'll get over it. They're a bunch of greedy degenerates, and they don't know how much is enough. When all bets are down, I will draw the last four cards, and lay them across the table. These last four cards pays 10 to 1—I repeat, you both will win a hundred grand apiece. I will pick up the cards, and place them face down on the deck.

Now, the second game will begin. Mr. A will pass the abacus to you, Mr. L. He'll have each row of beads in their right place. Are you ready, Mr. L?"

"Deez eez like geeving girl feefty, an' she geev me blow job." He sniffed, and looked at the abacus. "Go ahead, you draw cards, I keep record."

"In this game, we're going to score big time. I'll shuffle a new deck, have one of the players cut, and I'll draw the first card." He pulled the first card, a jack appeared. "This jack is the cue card. I'll ask you, Mr. L, did you record the jack?"

"Jack eez recorded, sir."

"Good. Now, there are three jacks left to play in the deck." Mr. S lay the jack where the rest of the cards will be placed, and put the fifty-one remaining cards in the shu." Place your bets, gentlemen."

He watched Mr. A and Mr. L bet twenty-five hundred on their assigned cards. They did exactly what Mr. S had told them.

"Good. Mr. L, when you see the third jack I had drawn, and has been recorded, the next card will be the fourth jack. You and Mr. A will bet $150,000 apiece on the jack. Tell the chipman, and he'll place the $300,000 on the jack. It's too far for you to reach, as you can see. Remember, when the third jack is recorded, the next card I pull, will be the win card, the jack. When the chipman pays you off, Mr. A will tell him you're both cashing out. He'll give you a marker for $900,000, your total winnings for two games. You both get up, and the security guard will escort you to the cashier. He will give Mr.A an attaché case filled with our cash. The chauffeur will take you both to your hotel, and around 9:00 P.M. bring you over to my place. We'll split the cash, and you both will depart from Miami International Airport around 11:20 or about. Now, Mr. A, practice with Mr. L for awhile, I have business to take care of. When you leave, lock the place up, the chauffeur s' downstairs. He'll take you to the Diplomat Hotel, your room is taken care of. Be ready by 5:00 P.M. tomorrow for the game. You know the routine, Mr. A. See you at the club 7:20 sharp. Any questions?"

"No, Mr. S, everything is under control, am I accurate, Mr. L?"

"I know exactly what I must do, Mr. S." He wiped his nose with a handkerchief, trying to silence his chronic nose sniffling.

"Good." *He has everything under control, all right, the nose too. Wait until tomorrow night. I can't wait to see his face when he makes a mistake, and goes into mild shock. He'll beg to get even, just like all greedy gamblers do.* "Good night, gentlemen."

CHAPTER 28

MIAMI BEACH, MARCH 15 1951

6:45 A.M.

Jules is studying his list of apples (criminals) for future "plays". There are fifty he had picked. His friend, the CIA agent had given him more than two hundred names. Each one is notorious for criminal acts and is gangsters, film directors and producers, senators, three congressmen and many other classifications. The bottom line is each one has something in common, they are degenerate gamblers, compulsive thieves, avarice and can afford to lose. Jules, having nerves of steel, will sting these rebels simply because they can afford to lose, and he needed the bankroll to avenge Tony Cheese, the killer of Rocco.

The phone rang. "Hello."

"Hey meatball, how ya doin'?"

"Why haven't you called? Jesus Christ, haven't heard from you. What the fuck ya doin' besides shackin' up with all those show girls?"

"Jules-Jules, my name is Smiley O' Brian, not "Lucky" Luciano or "Bugsy" Siegel!"

"Yeah, sure, lover boy. Now, what's goin' on? And, don't break my balls."

"Jules, Jules, I wouldn't do a thing like that, I love ya, fer Chris' sake. But, I finally snagged me my apple. He's not my best friend yet, but I'm getting there. Looked all over Vegas for the renegade. You aren't gonna believe where I found him."

"I can imagine."

"You know the photo an' data you gave me on him?"

"Yeah, what about it—get to the point, Smiley." *Jesus Christ! What a moron.*

"I'm in this a la mode club, right—I'm waiting for one of the call girls, and who walks in the spot—my apple. We rapped for 10-15 minutes. He asked me if I wanted a drink, and later he'd show me a few casinos. We had a great time. I won $7,000 grand, and he liked how I handled the dice and blackjack table—the broads too. He's everything you told me about him—I mean, the only thing you left out was he's an asshole from abyss, especially when he drinks that Jose Cuervo 80 proof Tequila."

"Good. Did he like how you handled the 'dice and blackjack tables and broads' in that order, or are you on the square?"

"Funny, Jules. I miss the bullshit games we play. Fuck you, OK?"

"You know, if you had a cock like a telephone pole, and your hands were sandpaper, you'd have a dick like a toothpick!"

"OK , Milton, that's cute, is there anything else, I'm meeting my apple in 10 minutes, we're gonna hit one of casinos."

Just do your thing, make nice-nice with the guy and call me every night after 11, my time, got that?"

"OK-OK-OK. Are you gonna wish me luck n make my day?"

"Good luck, Smiley. "Get a job you want and you'll never have to work.""

"Like that line, Jules, where did ya pick it up?"

"Confucius."

"Hey, Jules-Jules, didn't he also quote, "The safe one once in a while can miscalculate?"

"Jules laughed. "You're beautiful, Smiley. Confucius would have given you a passing grade if he were your teacher. But, he also would have scorched yer ass for twisting his exact quotation, too, moron!"

He was giving Smiley the big tease, as usual. After all, he loved the knucklehead.

"W-Whataya talkin' about, Jules?"

"I don't mean anything by that, except, Confucius quoted, "The cautious seldom err"--that's how he phrased it—four simple words—right to the point, moron!"

"Well, excooz-em-wah, Sigmund, maybe in your other life, you should assist Mr. Freud, huh? I mean, you got the medulla oblongata, right?"

"Don't say 'you got, it's, **you have**, how many times do I have to tell you, Christ! You're suppose to be a millionaire, have a little class and have street smarts, you know, the whole worldly bullshit! Don't go blowin' your top over this, wise guy. Christ, I'm just tryin' to help you in the culture department—goddam you, Smiley."

There was a pause. Jules knew Smiley was lost for words...suddenly, they both broke apart laughing at the same time. Smiley played along as he would always do. He loved Jules as a brother. Every once in a while, he'd lose it, but all in all, he respected Jules.

"OK Smiley, call me every night, after 11, my time. I want to know everything, everything that transpires between you and the apple, got it, pal?"

"Loud and clear, Jules. Talk to ya later."

"Wait! Wait a minute!" He looked at the phone, and thought, *the moron hung up, couldn't wait, had to go--ahhh, it wasn't a big deal. I only wanted to tell him to be extra careful. He's dealin' with death. Why am I so concerned, Jesus Christ, ya think I was his mother. He'll be all right.*

CHAPTER 29

MIAMI BEACH, MARCH 15, 1951

7:15 P.M.

That evening, Ernestine, the maid, was removing the after dinner dishes from the table. When she returned from the kitchen, she placed a large bowl of assorted fruit in the center of the table. There were bananas and oranges and peaches and red and yellow grapes and strawberries and tangerines and plums. They were arranged on a bed of red cherries and shelled walnuts. It looked beautiful. Ernestine had an aptitude for doing things with class. Her African complexion had darkness about it comparable to a burnished black opal. She pranced about carrying her 300-pound body as if she were a young girl going on a first date. A guest was sitting with Jules at the table, his name is Felini. He is a craftsman carpenter, born in Cuba. He is a short thin man with black wavy hair, dark complexion and speaks broken English. He is in Florida illegally trying to earn enough money to bring his family here, and to live in freedom. Jules wants to get an estimate on the cost for the special casino he intends to build in the 60 X 40-foot den.

"In our conversation," Jules said, "you mentioned, while living in Cuba, like your father, your forte was making game tables and whatever game devices a casino may need, is that right?"

"This I do very well. What is it you have in mind?"

Jules unrolled a large sheet of paper, showing Felini the layout he had designed.

"I want the blackjack table here. Crap table, roughly in this area. The roulette table about here--and along this wall, we're going to enclose eight slot machines. The unique part, we're going to build the tables so they fold into the floor. The slots as well. I want to play it safe, just in case there's a raid, know what I mean, Felini?"

"Gambling is illegal here, I am here unauthorized. In Havana, my father and I, we make casinos for big Jewish gangster, nice guy. When he propose to my father and me to make certain tables, he said, he will make us an offer we can't refuse, but they have to be adaptable to win or lose."

"I don't do those things. To each, his own, right Felini?"

"I agree. So, my friend, I must first look at the room, and then we go to basement to inspect crossbeams, bottom surface of room, columns and so on. The making of these structures on this Island are constructed to survive the most violent storm. I know. I have had six properties nearby; my crew has worked on. I think the phrase, "Built like a brick shithouse", comes from the well-to-do people who built these admirable fortresses."

Felini had a serious face mostly all the time, a sad expression, and tone of voice Jules knew so well. One who met him for the first time, and had a bit of mentality and sentiment would notice his thoughts were of his wife and family in Cuba. Jules knew, and felt sorry for him. Jules also knew there was only one Felini, he who was the finest mechanic around, and as loyal as they come.

Jules smiled, and said, "When do you want to start diggin' aroun' in this shithouse, Felini, my man?"

A grin came across his face. "You are also a humorist like me, I see. I will be available Monday morning at 7:30, if it is good for you?"

"Good. See you at sunrise."

Felini got up, and shook Jules' hand. "Thank you for the wonderful dinner, my friend."

"It wasn't like the cookin' your wife prepares, but, Ernestine is pretty good." He gave a wink at Felini, knowing Ernestine was nearby.

Ernestine heard Jules' remark as she brought Felini's fedora to him. She bumped into Jules intentionally. "What do you mean, 'Ernestine is pretty good'! There are no such words in this house--shame on you, Mr. Jules. No coffee or favorite desert for you later—and get yer own carrot juice, too!"

Jules gave her a smirk behind her back.

She handed Felini his fedora, and said, "He thinks he can get away with making funny faces behind my back. Lordy, Lordy, I know him all to well." She giggled. "Hope you enjoyed your dinner, Mr. Felini."

"It was the finest I ever had, thank you."

When Ernestine turned, her giggle turned into a sophisticated woman, her chin up, eyes to the ceiling, then she bolted back, and with a spring to her step made a rebound to the other room, mumbling, "I never heard such a disgraceful thing in all my life!"

Jules thought, *I'm in trouble. Ahhh, she'll get over it. She's had plenty of my teasing. She' a bright servant, doesn't miss a trick.*

Later, Jules is on the phone talking to Red, manager of the shills. Red is 6'4". Stocky. A solid 265 pound Hercules. Black hair. Thin black mustache. Sharp dresser. Talks with a deformed upper lip.

"And make sure Murray, Billy Joe, Moe, Joey Clams and Lucky are at my place by 3:00 P.M. sharp." Jules said.

"All taken care of, Jules. They'll be in two cars. BoBo, Arny, Joey Dee, Tommy Chips, Lou the Twitch, Monty, Theo, Mugs an' me are comin' in three cars; I'll be with deez guys all day. We'll be at your place at 4:00 sharp. The other guys should be on their way to the club by the time we get to your place, right?"

"Yeah, they know what to do."

Jules has set the shills in their proper positions for the "play" tomorrow. They know what to do. Jules will get to the club at 6:15 P.M. to make sure everything is the way it's suppose to be. Each of the shills will be dressed in a conservative suit and tie.

"I picked up the four security uniforms at the cleaners," Red said, "you want me to bring the four?"

"No. Just bring yours."

Red laughed. "Ya know Jules, I can't wait to see Monty and Theo standin' in an at ease position durin' the game."

"That's gonna be a challenge, all right, they'll be fine, you'll see."

"Tell the boys not to give them to much of the tease. They're a little sensitive in that department, know what I mean, Red?"

"OK, Jules, see ya at 4:00 sharp."

The voice of the guard at the front gate can be heard over one of the speakers of the central intercom system: "The chauffeur is here, Ernestine."

She pressed a button, and the gate opened. The limousine pulled up to the entrance, and Jimmy Blue Eyes (shill & chauffeur) opens the car door for Mario. Blue Eyes assisted him into his wheelchair.

Ernestine came running out of the house with her usual big smile. "Well, well, well, you two white boys look like your afternoon was enjoyable." She wrapped her arms around Mario, and kissed him. "Was the movie as good as they all said?"

"It was better than that, Ernestine. I'm gonna see it again next week—an' you're comin' with us, OK?"

She combed her fingers through his black wavy hair. "If it's all right with Mr. Jules, I'd love to go, especially with a handsome white boy like you! They laughed. "Mr. Jules is waiting in the Florida room. He told me to tell you to get your butt in their tout-de-suite as soon as you get home, important. And after that, I made your favorite chocolate pudding."

"Oh, boy! You are special, Ernestine. But what is 'tout-de-suite', whipped cream or something?"

She laughed. "Lordy, Lordy, you're so funny. Tout-de-suite means, without delay, you know, pronto?"

I thought so, thanks. Jeez, I forgot to tell you something."

"Shoot, honey, I'm all ears."

"Promise you won't get mad?"

"Good Lord, son, how can anybody get mad at a boy in a wheelchair, and smell like a rose garden at the same time? Did you help yourself to some of my rose grease paint?"

"Well, kinda. I found it on the floor. It smelled so good, I put some on my face n hair."

She laughed. As she did, her belly moved unsteadily like ready to eat Jell-O.

"Good Lord in heaven! Mario! We better get that washed off at once! That cream, boy, has bleach and other chemicals that makes the skin lighter, and it removes hair. You sure would look silly with no hair. And with that dark complexion of yours, you'd surly be lookin' like a real white boy!"

"Are you serious?"

"As the Lord above!" She stroked Mario's hair and face. "Today, the Lord is making an exception. I'm not serious, son, just pullin' off one of Mr. Jules' big tease exercises— getting' pretty good, huh?"

"Ernestine! You had me fooled. Jeez, you're getting good, real good."

C'mon now," Ernestine said, "we don't want Mr. Jules blowin' his top, you know."

Jimmy Blue Eyes wheeled Mario into the Florida room. Jules was reading the paper, and smoking a cigarette.

Jules looked up. "Hey boys, come over here. Have a good time?"

Jimmy Blue Eyes laughed. "This kid's a riot. He wanted to stay and watch a second round of that movie. We stopped and had a banana split instead."

"What a movie, Jules. Gotta see it—right up your alley." Mario said, excited.

Jules gave him a questionable look. "What movie are you talkin' about?"

"Casablanca. Love that Bogart. He reminds me of you—but you're better lookin'.

They laughed.

Jules looked at Jimmy Blue Eyes. "Tomorrow, be at the Diplomat Hotel by 5:00 P.M. At 5:45, call room 1204 and tell Mr. A you're waiting. They'll be down within 10 minutes. You've been through the practice run enough, right?"

"Down pat, Jules."

"Make sure you stay within the speed limit. You know the procedure from there. Here, take these passes, clip them on your lapels or the guards won't let you enter. You should be knocking on our special marked door by 7:20. You didn't see the plaque yet. It reads: Millionaires Club, VIP Only. It's solid brass, 15 by 7-inchs, engraved in Old English, framed in dark mahogany. Real class. When you boys enter the barroom, a security guard will escort Mr. A and the apple from there. Wait in the limo until I come out. Mr. A and the apple will be coming out first. They aren't going to be looking to good. Mr. A will throw up a few times, he's good at faking it. When I come out, I'm going to be pissed. I'll tell them off, and go back in. By the time you first bring in Mr. A and the apple, and they come out, figure on 20 to 25 minutes. Take them back to the Diplomat.

They'll change and you'll bring them to the Foutainblue, and will escort them to my

suite. Be there by 9. Everything clear, Blue Eyes?"

"Clear as ice. Have a nice evening, I'm hittin' the sack early tonight." He started

walking out of the room, then stopped and turned to Mario. "Hey, kid, save me some of

that chocolate pudding, will ya?"

"I'll do better than that, I'll bring a big bowl right to the guest house, how's that?"

"Now, who couldn't love a kid like that. I'll be waiting—whipped cream, too." He

walked out the door rubbing his hands together, as if to say, boy-oh-boy, my favorite

desert, chocolate pudding and whipped cream!

"OK, Mario, do you have your job down pat for tomorrow's play?"

"I bet on the ace and king. I'll be betting $15,000 to $20,000. On the 48the card, I'll

bet $100,000 and print on the pad, 10-ace-2-3, and lose. I get a little upset, and kinda

moan and groan, then I hit the table kinda light, and have a pissed off look on my face,

but keep my composer. In the second game, I bet $100,000 on the third card, the ace. I

lose. Before the 4the card comes up, I bet another $100,000 on the king, and lose again.

How'd I do, Jules?"

Jules smiled, and patted his head, then grabbed his neck muscle, and squeezed. Mario

didn't flinch. "Didn't that hurt!"

"Can't get me, Jules. Maybe you can get Smiley and Jimmy The Dealer, but not me.

I'm tougher than you think."

"I guess so. *This kid has what it takes. Takes after his father, for sure.* "You did a great job, perfect. Just do everything exactly like you just did, and you'll be all right. Before you leave tomorrow, Red is going to disguise your face with a little makeup. He will glue a mustache and beard to your kisser, this will make you look much older, know what I mean?"

"Do ya think I can leave it on for a couple weeks?"

"Why?"

"Well, the girls around here kinda like older boys, if ya know what I'm sayin'.

"Hey, I don't see why not. After two days without washing, their gonna turn you down anyway. So, your gonna have to be the judge in that department."

"Jules, you're a basket case, did you know that?"

"Sure. My mother told me I was the only baby in Italy that had a pink bassinet."

"Boy, Jules, how corney can ya get."

"You better take care of that chocolate pudding, and promise to Blue Eyes before I get a hold of it. And when you're through, your bed is waiting, we have a big day tomorrow, know what I mean?"

Mario rolled his wheelchair close to Jules and gave him a hug. "Good night, Bogey."

They laughed.

Ernestine wheeled Mario to the kitchen, and they filled up on chocolate pudding and homemade whipped cream with cherries.

The phone rang.

CHAPTER 30

MIAMI BEACH, MARCH 16, 1951

10:40 P.M.

"Hello."

"Jules? Smiley. The weather is fabulous. The food is great, the tables are hot and so
are the broads. Got my apple wrapped aroun' my finger and his balls are bigger than
mine—now, what's goin' on in your neck of the woods?"

"Seein' you're doin' all the tellin', and yer wrapped up in you, go ahead, go ahead, Mr.
Unethical, just continue with your preliminary layout—I'll get pissed, later!"

"Aww, jeez, Jules. I'm sorry, I'm sorry, to much excitement happenin' to fast aroun'
here."

"You taken on a number—maryjane, you know!"

"I'll get a rush once in a while, why?"

"Whatever yer smokin," Jules said heated, "Acapulco gold, aunt mary, bomb, boo,
bush, hemp or ganja, get the fuck off it! Get a rush on your apple! Go over the hump,
goddam it!"

"But, Jules, I-I--"

Jules is heated and furious to the highest. "But, Jules, I-I what, moron?" Do you have
any idea who you're dealin' with!? Do you know the apple you're getting to know is one
of the most dangerous criminals on the fuckin' universe!? Don't you realize if you say or
do or make the wrong move, you'll be history—dead—the curtains!? No. You would

rather whore aroun', play Mr. big shot, and stick me and the luggers holdin' the bag. Get your--"

"W-Wait, wait a minute, J-Jules--"

Jules thought, *I'm gonna put the scare on him, ya, that will straighten the Irish fuck.* "You wait a minute, you moron bastard. Get your ass outa Vegas, keep the fuckin' bankroll I gave you, and don't show your face around either. I'm tired of your disfigured face, expression and your moronic attitude!" He hung up, and looked at his watch. *10:48. I'll give him 12 minutes. Guaranteed, he'll call back. He going to dream up an exclusive story, I can't wait.* Jules put on a wry face as he slipped off his shoes. He lit a cigarette, then looked at him in the mirror. *Jules baby, why do you tolerate with that Irish moron? Is it because you think he has potential, and you want to see him straighten out? Or maybe you just like the way he has always wanted to be like you. Well, I do like the guy, we've been friends since we been kids. So what if he never changes, I like to insult him. Some of it rubs off—oh, sheeit, I'll give him another chance, but, make him think its over, finiee, end of our relationship. He's gonna be all right.* Jules lay on his bed. He rearranged three goose down pillows, and looked at the time. Ten minutes had passed. He thought, *two more minutes. I know the moron to well.*

He closed his eyes for sixty seconds. He knew, saying five Hail Mary's and one Our Father would take up one minute. Looking at his watch, he counted off the remaining sixty seconds. When the second hand hit the ten-second mark, he counted in a sympathetic mode.

"Ten, nine, eight, seven, six, five, four, three, two, one." The phone didn't ring. *The moron didn't get his story straight. The blockhead is reevaluating his story, I'll lay odds, 100 to 1. This is crazy. My bladder is crying for freedom. I'm not waitin'.*

He went into the bathroom, and started to do his duty, and the phone rang.

"Doesn't it figure, sonofabitch! I'm gonna finish. I don't care if the goddam phone rings fifty times!"

After ten rings, it stopped.

"Good. He'll call and wake me at 3:00 A.M., watch."

Ernestine knocked on his bedroom door. Mr. Jules, I have some chocolate pudding for you."

"Come on in, Ernestine. You tryin' to fatten me up?"

She giggled. "I wouldn't think of doing that, Mr. Jules, but there is a phone call for you."

"Who is it?" *I know goddam well who it is. Do I know that moron or wha'?*

"Smiley. He's such a nice person. I told him you were tied up. Shall I tell him you're involved?"

"Involved in what?"

"Well, hmmmmm, I guess I could tell him you're involved in contemplating over that chocolate pudding? Lordy, I don't know, Mr. Jules."

He laughed, saying, "You're the best, Ernestine, what would I do without you?"

"Lordy, Lordy, Mr. Jules, I have to know if there is a period after that remark or a question you want me to answer?"

"Question."

She turned to the door, stopped and turned her head to Jules, and said, in a biting voice, "Starve. Answering phone calls, and cleanin' da house, for starters. Night, Mr. Jules. She closed the door, turned around, and opened it. Her big black eyes pierced into Jules'. "Don't forget your phone call, Mr. Jules." And off she went.

Jules gazed at the phone for a moment, and thought, *I should make him wait all night. On second thought, better not. One of the boys may want to get through. OK, Jules, get ready for the big Oscar--Endurance of the year is not easy to achieve.*

He picked up the receiver. "Hello. Can I help you, please."

"H-Hello. May I speak to Jules, please?"

"Who is this?" Jules said, perplexed."

"Jules, this you?"

"Who do you think it is ?"

"N-No. It didn't sound like--"

"How can it sound like me, for Chris' sake. I can smell that grass from here. I told you before, and I'll tell you again, 'Get your ass outa Vegas, keep the fuckin' bankroll I gave you, and don't show your face around either.' And if your brain is not burnt out, you should recall, 'I'm tired of your disfigured face, expression and your moronic attitude.' Can you comprehend what I said, and what I am telling you now?"

"Jules, Jules, Jules, I don't know why you exaggerate my well being. Once in a while I'll take a poke, that's all. If it'll make you feel better, I promise you the shit is outa my life. I got me an apple with so much loot, he lights his cigars with hundred dollar bills, don't matter where we go, the immoral fuck thrives on observance. The guy's a magnum opus from the word go. He's mine, I mean, he's ours Jules, big time. I'm begging you, please, give me another chance, you will not regret it, promise."

"Hang on a minute." Jules lay the receiver on the bed, and walked to the mirror. He looked at him, and thought, *Jesus Christ, I don't know whether to cry or laugh. I'd rather laugh. Smiley can be a bright guy if he want's to. I'll play around with him for a few minutes then make his day.*

Jules picked up the receiver. "OK, what else have you figured out what to make things emend. Knowing you, you probably tried to think out what you were going to say to me. But no, you needed something to print on. You found some paper or a white sheet some place and printed out exactly what you had to recount to me. Then, you did the perfect edit to make the bait complete so Jules will forgive you, right, Smiley?"

"I-I d-don't believe my ears." Smiley hesitated. "I don't know how you knew that. How do you do that, Jules?"

"You're an open book—always have been—always will be."

"Do you think I'll ever change?"

"No."

Jules' intentions were not negative when he said to him, 'no'. He used reverse psychology on him in hope Smiley would change. This technique had always been fruitful, and worked out well for both parties. Jules has had an immense amount of patience with Smiley through the years, and Jules knows what he has to do to make him a better person. The bottom line is Jules want's Smiley to feel indignant about his attitude. Smiley will change, just to proof to Jules, he can. That fellow, Jules, has always had a good relationship with Smiley, and he knows Smiley will eventually have what it takes to be round.

"I'll turn to the virtuous guy I know I am. Ya know Jules, I never told you about the dream I have every night, I don't know why, maybe I was too much in me."

"I've always told you, 'best friends keep nothing from each other', remember?"

"How can I not forget? I mean, it distressed me to the point that I had to go to that shrink Shrap told me about."

"I know. Best thing you ever did for yourself. What about the dream?"

"Well, I'll tell ya under one condition."

"What's that?"

"Don't laugh or have a joyous bout with me with derogatory remarks. In other words, no big tease."

"You should be one of those short story writer's--better yet--a theme writer!"

"Whadaya mean?"

"Don't get me wrong, but, why didn't you simply say, 'Don't laugh or have a joyous bout with me with derogatory remarks. In other words, no big tease.' " But, no, you have to make a long short outa a short one."

"I'll work--"

"I know, you'll work on it—and you will. I want to interrupt you for a moment. This example may help you understand better. Bruno Bettelheim wrote the theme of "Jack and the Beanstalk", whom most people would consider a competent psychologist (or at least not stupid), the story is about penis envy--surely a minority opinion. Some might say that the story is about the victory of childish innocence; some might say other things. The point is you should definitely have a session with this guy, who knows, you both may discover you have something in common!"

They laughed like old times. Slowly, Jules wanted Smiley to continue to be his best friend, and say it the way it is.

"OK, wise guy, can't let go, right? At this point, seein' you like givin' me the business, maybe I'll tell the dream at a more convenient time."

"Awww, fer Chris' sake, are we gonna have a nice relationship or wha' "? *He'll open up with that line, guaranteed.* He told himself.

"Well, when ya put it that way, how the hell can I trash it. OK, OK, OK, I have this dream, had it ever since we met. It's of me in a beautiful emerald-green cloak , sitting on a high seat. This guy dressed in a knee-high kilt is playin' a bagpipe. On his belt, he has this thing-uma-jig, you know, a round branch of olive leaves? Whadaya call--"

"A caput—headpiece—the olive branch--symbol of peace. Let me interrupt you again, I have ta tell ya this. Caesar got pissed off one day and demanded the caput-keeper to cut branches with fresh black olives attached, you know, he liked a change in headdress. The guy was versatile, wanted a change, keep up with his image. One of his counselors questioned his change. Caesar told him it was an isolated alteration. His counselor said, but it would look fatuous. Caesar said, look, I'm the honcho around here, I favor a nibble or two while frolicing with the maidens, ya mind! Thought I'd tell you that story--good reminder for the 'thing-uma-jig'? Caput? Sorry. Go ahead."

"Funny. What's the point? Jesus, Jules, you baffle me at the most solemn times."

"Just a reminder. Maybe you'll remember the thing-um-a-jig? Caput? Get it?"

"Ohhh, sheeeit! I guess I'm not with it. I'll remember that one. It's witty, Jules, waggish, even. OK, let me get back to story time. Anyway, a pretty servant takes the ca-caput, and places it on around my forehead. In the background, I can hear bagpipes play this beautiful melody. Suddenly, clouds are all over the place, can't see nothin'. Then, they slowly disappear. Before my eyes I can see a long table with eleven thugs sitting down. Their faces are all the same. I mean, like Attila the Hun. A-And they're passin' a joint aroun' givin' me the look of death. I can see a b-bulge in their pin stripped suits. I jump to my feet, and yell out, "What da fuck ya want!" They get up, pull out the heat, and drill me. I fall on my thrown, and see myself as a block of Swiss cheese. Feel no pain, just taste whipped cream—vanilla whipped cream. When I open my eyes, t-there's this pink whipped cream gurglin' all over my body. The bastards shot me with p-pink whipped cream. Gradually, the room fills with clouds again--couldn't see, but deranged laughter from those gangsters filled the room. That's the dream!"

"Absorbing dream. I recognize the olive branch. That is interpreted as peace. The emerald-green cloak means, you're from Irish blood, a strong breed of people. Sitting on a thrown represents a baby sitting in a high chair, and you have the mentality of one. But, the throne you sit on is of great importance. It represents the desire you have to be successful. It's telling you to read, and make sure it's seen and understood. And, listen to people close to you, for your mastery. The gangsters are what you always wanted to be. When you stand up to them and yell. 'What the fuck you want', you're showing them your still immature. Your ego allows you to have no emotion, no patients, no empathy; a wise guy attitude, you know. The Attila faces on the gangsters, symbolize how people see you and talk behind your back, you know, when you carry on like a fervent devotee. When the goons stand and blast you away, those shots are telling you to shut the fuckin' mouth. The whipped cream is telling you, ignorance is bliss—do this, and nobody will hurt you. Pursue your old image, and suffer in meditation, as you are now--a psychotic case. And the deranged laughter you hear from those bad guys--is exactly what people do behind your back—by the way, those bad guys are really good guys, you have to learn to read between the lines. That's my rendition, kid, hope the dream dies, now."

"Jesus Christ, Jules! You left me speechless. I c-can't tell you w-wha..." He started to cry out loud. His hand covered the receiver so Jules couldn't hear him.

CHAPTER 31

MIAMI BEACH, MARCH 17, 1951

3:00P.M.

In Jules' estate the next day, the first crew of shills were sitting and listening to

Jules. There was, Murray, Billy Joe, Zig, Moe, Lucky and Mario. Tony Gallo, the

the phenomenal chipman, (professionally known as the croupier) came in ten minutes

later. This is admissible. Tony had a self-assured job, and he was a pro. He snorted

cocaine frequently. He was the life of the party. His humor is second to none. And, at the

card table, his super fast hands handle the chips with unique moves. His attributes are

expeditious, wrapped up with charisma and gusto. Also, a Don Juan, ever since he

discovered girls was not boys.

Tony came in the room with a big smile. He's handsome. Black wavy hair. Full

matching mustache, well trimmed. His custom made tuxedo combined with his dark

olive–drab coloration gave him the appearance of a professional getting ready for an

opulent get together. When he came in the den, he greeted the shills, then Jules.

They gave a close embrace, and Tony said, "You never change. Not only that, Jules, but

also this place is more impressive than the White House. One thing money cannot buy is

poverty?"

Laughing, Jules said, "Most times the anticipation is greater than the realization." He patted Tony on his shoulder, and said, "Nice to see you, Tony--lookin' sharp."

"Thank you, sir. Another thing, that silk sport jacket you have on is inept on you—what I'm tryin' to say without hurting your feelings is--"

"I know, it's not my style, and it would look better on you."

They laughed. Jules knew Tony's excerpts all to well.

"I better sit down," Tony said, laughing, "people do odd things to get even."

Jules smiled. "Yeah, the basis of friendship is trust."

"Like that, sweetheart--oh, one more thing and I'll get out of our emotional closeness. My job is a piece of cake, Jules, and I appreciate it with a passion beyond expectation, beyond penance, but ever since you called me for this play, I've been taken over with a uncertain feeling.

"Maybe you're having to much ejaculation, know what I mean?"

"No-no, no-no, it's more like, wait, I'll tell it to you in a humble way--playing with dice is a insecure business." They laughed. "Thought I'd throw that one in for ol' times, know what I mean, Julius, darling?"

Tony embraced Jules, then he sat down like a gentleman waiting for him to start the meeting.

Jules stepped back, and lit a cigarette. He casually exhaled waiting for the boys to calm down. They realized he was about to talk, and respectfully became attentive.

"Thank you, boys. I heard you're having a good time here in Miami. Your accommodations are okay, weather's great, how sweet it is. Before I get started, I have to tell you something about the Hollywood Beach Hotel. I knew it was perfect for each one of you, so I booked you there. The place was built in the early 1920's. It was a haven for well-to-do people, con men and big-time smugglers. There are tunnels beneath the basement, and they still lead to the ocean; they're blocked off now. That's how the pirates got away with bootlegging and other action we know so well. These boys were clever. The secret doors in the grand ballroom are how they got down there. They're sealed off now. They say the place has ghosts of the thugs who were killed, and they appear as phantoms. Nobody talks about it in the place unless you come across an old timer. Now that you know the joint you're stayin' in. If ya hear eerie sounds and precarious happenings goin' on, don't lose it, chances are ya just had one to many."

The boys laughed, and applauded as if they expected Jules to tell them something ghostly.

"OK, gentlemen, let's review the play again, timing is critical. Red, you stand on the inside door at the bar entrance. When Mr. A. and the apple get there, the chauffeur will escort them in the door. They'll be there at 7:20. He'll knock three times, pause, and knock twice more, let them in. Lucky is the other guard, he all ready has his uniform. He'll be at the card table standing in the background. Mugs and Theo, sit at one of the round tables away from the bar in the center room. This looks like your waiting to get in the game. The tables are in the next room. Louie and Monty, you're also sitting at one of the tables waiting. You're talking softly and smoking. When you see Lucky, the guard escorting Mr. A and the apple, don't look at them, just continue talking and minding your own business, got it?"

They nodded their heads and listened.

"Tommy, Joey Dee and Arny. You'll be sitting at the bar, drinking and talking softly. When Mr. A and the apple come in, the first thing they see is you. In their mind, you are players waiting to get in the game, understand?"

The three nodded their heads, and smiled.

"Mario, Ace, Murray and Billy Joe," Jules said, "You all know your assigned cards, and the amount to bet. Just remember not to bet more than fifteen thousand on each card." They nodded their heads in approval.

"Murray, you and Mario set the table up as soon as you get there. Moe, set the bar up, you know what to do. When Mr. A and the apple come in, wait 5 minutes or just before the game begins, and come in the card room and ask the apple and Mr. A if they would like a drink—simple as that, got it?

"No brain twister, Jules."

Jules looked for Billy Joe. "Billy Joe, you with us?"

He was bent over in a chair looking for something.

"I'm right here, Jules, dropped a few chocolate covered nuts on the carpet. Didn't want anybody makin' mush on yer gorgeous oriental. Sorry."

Jules gave him a look everybody knows when he's angry. "Jesus Christ! Did you ask anybody if they wanted some?"

Billy Joe gave Jules a look as if he was going to get the dark room for a month.

"S-sure, they didn't want any. The rug's okay, Jules."

"No big deal. Don't do it again!"

The boys broke apart laughing. Jules was giving him the big tease. They all played on each other. It was a game like hide 'n seek, but this game was around-the-clock.

"OK, Billy Joe, make sure you secure the plaque on the outside door. Find yourself a partner and bullshit with him at one of the round tables. Do you have a question?"

"No-no, I look like that at times. Oh, by the way, the plaque in the locker?"

Laughter filled the room. Two of the boys picked him up and turned him upside down. "It's all there, Billy Joe," Jules yelled out, "everything. The only thing missing are those chocolate covered nuts!"

Another session of laughter split the room up from the outer world.

"Good. OK, help yourself to a drink while Murray is fixin' up Mario. Oh, Murray, the footlocker's in the closet. Make the felt table clothe nice n tight. Thumb tacks, pads, pens, everything is in the locker. I'm expecting the other shills by 4. OK, Murray, glue the beard on Mario—try to make look like you. Leave all together, I want all of you outa here by 3:40. The rest of the boys will be here in about twenty minutes. Red, your security uniform is hangin' on the closet door where the locker is, dress when you get there." I'll be there between 6-6:15.

The first section of shills left as the second shift arrived. Theo, Louie The Twitch, Arny, BoBo, Tommy Chips, Joey Dee, Monty, Mugs and Albert looked as if they were bankers, stock brokers, the ruling class.

Ernestine welcomed them in. They sat in the den waiting for Jules to give them their last minute instructions. When Jules came in the room, the shills greeted him warmly. They chitchat for a while, talking about old times and what's new. In a serious tone, Jules reviewed their assignments. Their job was to sit in the bar room and in the other room at the round tables acting as if they are waiting to play in the game. The shills left for the club aware of what they had to do.

Jules relaxed on his favorite chair, smoking and thinking. *The time is drawing near. The first play will be in the making pretty soon. I feel the whole deal is faultless.* Jules looked at the time. *OK Jules baby, it's 5:29, in three hours Mr. L will be out $150,000 for the first round. He'll want to get even, they all do. The scoundrel will beg Mr. A to convince me to arrange another game, they all do. The Russian bastard thinks nothin' of money, just his egotism. I'll get to that part when the time comes,* he told himself.

Jules knew when Rocco was alive, he found and hired the best luggers and shills around. When Jules came in the picture, and Rocco murdered by Tony Cheese, the luggers and shills remained as loyal and respectful to Jules. They are not the brightest boosters around, on the other hand, no particular person could match the street smarts and professionalism of the entire group. Jules now will instate his theater of operations. He is determined to even the score with Tony Cheese. Only then, will Mr. Cheese become the victim of circumstance.

CHAPTER 32

MIAMI BEACH, MARCH 18, 1951

6:35 P.M.

The chauffeur picked up Mr. A and Mr. L. On their way to the club, Mr. L tried to snort some cocaine. Mr. A caught him in the act and tried to stop him. Before he did, he thought, *I'll pretend I don't see him. When he's finished I'll fake it and tell him off, the Mephistopheles that he is. He's making things easier for me, thank you Lord. When he finds out he made a mistake in the game, Jules will have an extra motive to chew his fucking ass out. After all, he's not Jules' and my partner because he has a pretty face. Partners don't blow away nine hundred grand snorting gold dust, ya know.* He laughed to himself then put on the black hat ("bad guy").

With a serious face, he slapped the drug and small gizmo from his hand, and whispered very roughly, "What the fuck you doin'! You tryin' to blow my mutual esteem with Mr. S!"

"Why should you care? I only take small wheef, it make me like razor blade."

"Jesus Christ, you Russian fuck! I-I don't want you doin' that shit! Do you comprehend what I'm saying!? Jesus, Mary 'n Joey—fuck!"

"I am very sorry. I am not only ashamed, I am remorseful also. How can I make deez trivial incident healthier for you? Deez eez not time to be unsettled, my friend."

"Just do me a favor, Mr. A said, "Don't talk to me until we get to the club."

"If you weesh. I be like saint."

Meanwhile, Jules just entered the club, and one of the guards let him in the Millionaires VIP room. The shills had their positions and everything was to Jules' liking. They listened to what Jules had to say.

"When you see Mr. A and the apple leave, stay in your positions just as you would if you were waiting to be called for the next game. About three minutes later, you'll see me come out looking real pissed—relax, all show. I'll be outside chewin' the living shit outa both of them for fuckin up. I should be back in five or six minutes. While I'm out there, get the place cleaned up, rearrange the tables and chairs, put the scotch, whiskey and the rest in the cases you brought them in and break the table down, make sure you put everything back in the locker the same way you found it. Make sure your security guard uniforms are put on hangars and covered the way you found them. When I come back in, I'll pay you off. We'll meet at Joe Sonkas Stone Crab Restaurant, on Hollywood Boulevard and A1A at 10:00 P.M., bring your ladies. Any questions?"

Red asked," Can I have the hundred bucks instead of the dinner, Jules?"

"You have ta have the dinner, Red."

"What's the catch, Jules? I can't resist?"

"I invite. You come. You eat. We celebrate. You stay. I pay."

Jules looked around and rechecked the card table to make everything was in its right place. He seated himself in his dealer position, and pulled five decks of sealed cards out of his attaché case, and lay them on a small knee high table on his right side. He relaxed and lit a cigarette. He looked at Mario, and thought, *I'd never recognize the kid. He looks as if he were forty-forty-five years old. The rest of the boys look good. I'll loosen up and enjoy my smoke.*

Tony Gallo, the chipman said to Jules, Ya know sweetheart, An ol' timer once told me, as you climb the ladder of success there are more people interested in your possible fall than in your further ascent."

"Ya know Tony, I wonder what this world would be like if Noah had missed the ARK."

"Ya, know, I know you know what I know, but I don't think you know what pisses me off the most."

"I give up." Jules replied. He had a controversial look painted across his face.

"What I mean is, ya never, never, ever, ever, never, never heard a huckster shout,

"Rotten vegetables!"

"Tony."

"Name it darling, I have a lifetime."

"I heard through the grapevine, you're haulin' aroun' a small penis, that right?"

"Love, I'm average—when unfrequented of course."

They were just killing time. Corny stuff, but it kept their mind off the seriousness of what they had to do soon. Everything was right, and the shills were in their positions. Now, the waiting game begins.

CHAPTER 33

COUNTRY CLUB, MARCH 17, 1951

7:10 P.M.

Back in the limousine, the chauffeur opened the private window separating the driver from the rear passenger area, and said, "Five minutes, gentlemen."

The chauffeur turned onto a private cobblestone road boarded with lush landscaping. There were rows of palm trees and lakes and gorgeous plants and flowers of every kind along the way. They were scattered everywhere in the perfect setting. As they drove along the winding road, they could nearly see the greens and fairways to a golf course. Mr. A opened the window. There were sounds of birds and splashing waterfalls. And infrequently, the blow of a golfer hitting a ball off the tee and yelling, "Fore"!

They advance toward a stone guardhouse. The chauffeur stopped, identified himself, and is allowed to pass. A wrought iron gate ten or twelve feet high opened. It appeared as if they were entering a highly restricted area. As the limousine approached the clubhouse, its architectural design is reminiscent of the earlier Spanish style with an ambiance of California flair. The limousine pulled up to the entrance. A valet opened the door and greeted Mr. A and Mr. L. The chauffeur escorted them through a quiet lounge where two female singers were rehearsing with a guitarist, drummer and pianist. The chauffeur looked at the time, it was 7:15. Within 4 to 5 minutes, they will be at the place they have been waiting for.

Finally, they walk through a spacious columnar building, and reached a secluded area. As they turn a corner, unexpectedly, two large mahogany doors come into sight. A solid brass plaque read:

Millionaires Club

VIP Members Only

The chauffeur rapped on the door three times, paused then rapped two more. The door was opened by a security guard. Another guard escorted Mr. A and Mr. L through a room with eighteen or twenty round tables. Ten or twelve gentlemen were sitting and smoking, talking over their drinks. A sliding accordion partition in two sections left an opening for two people to enter the card room. Mr. A and Mr. L followed the guard into the room to two empty chairs. The sound of the chipman stacking chips against each other and fumes from burning cigarettes and cigars was in the air. The guard went on the other side of the room and stayed in his special spot guarding the room; he looked as if he was a Gestapo with the state secret police of Nazi Germany.

Mr. S was shuffling cards. The chipman's passing chips to the players and collecting manila envelopes. Four of the players were counting their chips and talking softly to one another.

Mr. A and his partner settle down and study the room.

Mr. A whispers in Mr. L's ear. "This is it, baby. These guys have so much dough, they even smell good, can you get a whiff of it?"

"Eet eez so. Deez dough eez more suitable een pocket, than breadbasket, no?"

"Is right, eez right—don't make me laugh, I'll blow my cover. You--"

"Good evening, gentlemen." The dealer said to the twosome.

"Good evening, sir." Replied Mr. A and Mr. L.

"Are you ready to cash in?" The dealer said, with a solemn utterance.

"Yes sir." Mr. A replied. He handed the manila envelope to the chipman.

"Thank you, sir. What would you like?"

"A hundred fifty thousand my way and the same for Mr.L, here."

"Very good, sir." He lay the chips in front of Mr. A and said, "Hundred fifty thousand. thank you sir,"

"And--one hundred fifty big ones for you sir. Good luck. Thank you very much, sir."

The chipman handed Mr. A's and Mr.L's manila envelope to the dealer, and said, "The two gentlemen on the end are ready, sir."

"Thank you." The dealer replied. He placed the manila envelope on top of the four others the players had turned in and handed them to the guard. The guard left the room for a moment, and came back to his spot.

The dealer opened a new deck of cards, shuffled and a player cut them. He looked at Mr. A. "You're in charge of the abacus this game, Mr. A."

Mr. A said, "Thank you , sir."

The dealer pulled the first card out of the deck. "Queen, gentlemen."

He looked at Mr. A. "Did you record the queen, Mr. A?"

"Queen recorded, sir."

The dealer put the queen back in the deck then put the deck in the shu.

"Place your bets, gentlemen." He looked to make sure all bets were down. They were. He called, "Bets down." Pulled the second card in the deck. "Five wins." Placed it face up in the Win square, then pulled the third card. "Eight loses." He placed it in the Lose square.

The chipman enthusiastically paid off the winners and picked up from the losers, and said in high speed, "Five wins-thank you-sir-eight loses-thank you in countless ways- sir."

The chipman had an idiosyncrasy of communicating at a rapid pace. He talked effectual, however, his words propelled through the air like bullets exploding out of a machine-gun.

When the players are paid off and the table is clear, the next card is drawn.

The chipman calls, "Place your bets, gentlemen."

Dealer calls, "Bets down." Pulls the next card. "Ten wins—deuce loses."

Chipman's eager, paying off, picking up. "Ten wins-gentlemen-deuce loses-thank you-thank you-gentlemen-place your bets."

The dealer asked Mr. A, "How many cards have been played, Mr. A?"

Mr. A looked at the abacus, and counted. "Forty eight cards, sir."

"OK gentlemen, "Sky's The Limit" game is drawing near. Print on your pads the last four cards you think will be the winners. Remember, the numbers have to be in sequence to what I draw. Thank you."

When the players were finished, they folded their picks, and placed their bets in the center of the table.

The dealer called. "Bets placed, gentlemen." Then he pulled the forty-eighth card through the fifty-second consecutively, from the shu. "King—eight—jack—six! King, eight, jack, gentlemen—the noble house is looking forward to the fortunate heavyweight."

The chipman looked over each slip—no winner. Each player scrunched their paper, and the chipman picked up a hundred thousand from Mario and twenty-five thousand from another player and fifteen thousand from the other two players and twenty-five hundred apiece from Mr. A and his partner.

Mario did a good job faking his bit part. He moaned and groaned and slapped the table easily, as if he actually lost the $100,000. The other players acted fitting also. They were calm, cool and collected. There likeness of the perfect man of means was genuine, as if they lit a cigar or gave a hooker a $100 tip. Just to cover my butt, statistically speaking 89% of the "authentic" 'man of means', do act this way, on the outside, chiefly, when they gamble. They have accumulated excessive self-indulgence, self-centeredness and carry on a notable dramatic performance for the naïve, that is. The other 11% are the good guys.

The click clacking of chips steadily sounded off as the bizarre chipman stacked and kept the bank organized.

The dealer looked at Mr. L. "Mr. L, you're in charge of the abacus this game."

Mr. A moved the abacus to the center of the pair to oversee, just in case.

"Are you set for the next game, Mr. L?" The dealer said.

He hesitated, looked at the dealer, and said, "O-One moment please." Then pushed the quarter size beads into their official place.

Mr. A leaned over and whispered. "Relax, you Russian piece a sauerkraut-- relax fer Chris' sake—this is our game. You all right?"

Mr. L turned to Mr. A's ear, and humbly replied, "Theez Russian guy for your eenformation meester Irish fuck eez fine. I am completely een control-- now, leeson to me; I must tell you something more—urgent."

"Jesus Christ!" Mr. A said sternly, in a soft whisper, "What! Come on, the dealer's waiting!"

"Maybe later we get hot dog weeth abundance of sauerkraut, no?"

Mr. A coughed, to prevent from laughing. At the same time, he gave the dealer the "office" by rubbing his ear, meaning , everything's OK. Then he sniffed twice in order, another "office" sign, meaning, hold off a bit. Mr. A thought, *I know this fuck better than his ol' lady—he's chokin' up, just holding back. I can hear his ticker pounding a mile a minute, for Chris' sake, the lyin' rogue.*

Jules thought, *this kraut is chokin' up—I find it hard to believe, but it's true.*
He can use a little toot (cocaine) about now. In five minutes he'll be busted.
Then, he can toot, shoot, do miss morph (morphine) or crash, I'll have his cash.
OK Jules baby, blow him away.

He turned to Mr. L for the second time. "Are you all set for the second game,
Mr. L?"

"My apology, please. I am now ready. Thank you, sir."

The dealer has to make sure all the players are conscious of each and every
move he makes. Professionalism and suavity is the name of the game at Mr. S's
table.

The dealer opened a new deck, shuffles them, and a player cuts the deck.

He pulled the first card (queue card). "Jack, gentlemen." He looked at Mr. L.

"Did you record the jack, Mr. L?"

"Jack recorded, sir."

"Place your bets, gentlemen." He looks at the table to make sure all bets have
been placed. "Bets down—jack wins—9 loses."

Chipman pays off, picks up. "Big-jack-wins-poor-niner-loses—sorry-my-well-
to-do-sweethearts--get-those-bets-down-please-gentlemen--thank you-thank
you-very-much—last call—bets down." He looked at the dealer, and said," All-
bets-down-sir."

"Jack wins—6 loses" (second jack recorded. Queue card counts as one).

Eagerly, the chipman paid off, picked up. "Jack-wins-six loses—thank you-gentlemen." He noticed a player didn't place his bet. He put off with his charismatic talking. "Place your bet, Mr. C. Thank you. I see you're doubling up, sir, is that correct?"

"I'm betting $15,000 on this card—need a change of luck."

"No-problem-sir." He continued with his machine-gun way of verbalizing. He looked at the dealer. "Bets-down-sir."

"Next card, gentlemen. Ten wins—five loses."

The chips are picked up and paid off. "Ten-wins—five-loses--place-your-bets-gentlemen-place-your-bets—you're-doing- fine—so-divine—wish-I-had-a-glass-a-wine--thank you-gentlemen." He looked at the dealer. "Bets-in-place-sir."

The chipman was a bit enthusiastic. Far out would be a better choice of words. A cokehead he is. He apparently had a sniff too many.

Jules looked at the table to make sure all bets were in place. As he did, he slapped his head once, as if a fly was annoying him. This "slap on the head" symbolized the "office", meaning: "slow down with the mouth."

The chipman got the drift.

"OK, gentlemen, bets are down. Seven wins—four loses." He looked at Mr. L.

"Did you record the seven and four, Mr. L?"

"Seveen end four, recorded, sir."

Chipman : "Seven-wins—four-loses." Picked up. Paid off. "Thank-you-gentlemen—pleasure-kind-sirs." He glimpsed at the dealer to assure him. "Bets-are-down—dealer—sir."

The chipman was getting smart with the dealer. He gave him "The **small** tease," when he said, 'dealer—sir.' What he really meant was, "eat me, sweetheart." This was a joke, of course. On the other hand, of all the luggers and shills, the croupier, our machine-gunin' chipman, was the only crazy who could get away with a sly remark like that. In a serious game such as this, Jules didn't mind, getting even was more fun. Moreover, 'The **small** tease' relieved the tension at this stage of the game.

The dealer looked at Mr. L. "Did you record the seven and four, Mr. L?"

"Jack end four recorded, sir."

Dealer : Nine wins—nine loses."

Mr. L : "Nine—nine, recorded, sir."

Chipman: Picked up, paid off. "Thank you, thank you, sir, thank you very much...

Dealer : "Jack wins—deuce loses."

Mr. L : "Jack end two, recorded, sir."

Mr. A leaned into Mr. L's ear, and whispered, "Three jacks are out, this is it. Know what to do?"

Mr. L turned to Mr. A's ear, and whispered harshly, "You teenk I am dummy? We put $300,000 on jack—an' we go home weed collection, maybe bundle of coins. I teenk sometimes you look over me like mama."

Mr. A turned to his ear. "Undeniably. Lets do it, pop."

Mr. A slides his $150,000 and his partners in front of him, and looked at the chipman. "I want $300,000 on the jack, please."

"Three hundred thousand on the jack. My pleasure, sir--thank you." With his left hand, his fingers encircled one stack of chips. He tossed them in the air landing in perfect order into his right hand, as if they were attached to an invisible string. Then, firmly positioning them neatly in his bank. He continued with his performance until the six hundred chips were obtained; each chip was worth five hundred dollars. He exchanged them for a marker honored at three hundred thousand, and placed it on the jack. His motions were fast, precise and confident; as fast as one shake of a lamb tail. His stunt was outstanding; 600 chips relocated in less than 12 seconds—without a mishap.

When completed, the chipman looked at Mr. A, and the apple. "Three hundred thousand big ones on the jack, gentlemen--thank you, good luck."

The dealer looked around the table.

"Bets down—ten wins—three loses."

Mr. L bolted back in his chair in mild shock. He was perplexed. He looked as if someone had shot him. In a soft cry of distress, he moaned, buoyantly.

"Huh...WHA...what een fuck hap–"

Mr. A grabbed his arm, and abruptly pulled him in his direction. In an enraged whisper, he said, "Snap out of it! What the fuck's wrong with you! Get yourself together, goddam it!"

The chipman stared at him for a moment. He looked disillusioned (faking it). Immediately, he started picking up chips from the players. "No winners, gentlemen," Picking up from each player, he moved like lighting with his routine, and whisked them away, and said, "Thank you, sir--thank you. Thank you, very much." A few seconds later, his bank orderly, he said, "Place your bets, gentlemen, thank you. He looked at the dealer. "Bets in place, sir."

The dealer looked dissatisfied. "Hold all bets, gentlemen. Something is wrong, gentlemen." He picked up the thirty-nine cards he had pulled from the shu, and counted them under his breath. When finished, he recounted them close-mouthed. When completed, he turned to Mr. L. "Give me the card count recorded, Mr. L"

"I-I...cannot–"

Mr. L was still in mild shock. Mr. A looked ambiguous. One could see he was trying to hold on to his composure. He grabbed his partner's arm without looking obvious to the other players. "Relax, I'll cover for you." Mr. L watched his partner.

The dealer was discontent. His eyes rolled over to Mr. A. "Mr. A, would you please give me the number of cards recorded."

"Yes sir." Mr. A said, stiffly. He counted the buttons that were pushed down underneath each miniature card on the abacus, and replied, "Thirteen cards, recorded, sir."

The dealer looked displeased. "Recount the cards to me, Mr. A."

Mr. A looked at the abacus, and read off the cards. "Three jacks, two tens, two nines, one seven, one six, one three, one five, one four, and one deuce, sir."

As Mr. A read off the recorded cards to the dealer, he placed each card bordering each other in sequence, face up, in view of the players. He removed the remaining thirty-nine cards from the shu, and lay them on the table separate from the recorded thirteen. One by one, he placed them corresponding, in view of the players. As he did so, he read them above a whisper. Everyone could ascertain the identity, clearly.

The dealer looked incensed. "I count thirty-nine cards, gentlemen. Recorded on the abacus–thirteen. According to my count, thirteen cards were attended to. I show one jack left to be played. According to the recorded jacks, there are three." He looked at Mr.A and Mr. L. "How many jacks are you accounted for, gentlemen"?

Mr. A looked at the abacus. Mr. L, still a bit shook up, leaned over and looked also. "Mr. A replied, "Three jacks recorded, sir!
The dealer had a slight trace of uncertainty. He picked up the cards, put them on his knee high table then lay a new deck on the table.

"Misdeal, gentlemen."

Without delay, the players started to grumble, coolly. The hubbub carried on for seven or eight seconds.

Mr. A leaned into his partner's ear, and whispered, "Let's get outa here." He guided him to his feet, and they walked out of the room. The security guard at the bar entrance graciously opened the door. As the twosome walked through the spacious columnar building, they could faintly hear music.

They approached the lounge, the music was clearer now. The music stopped, applause could be heard, and a new song had begun. The piano, guitarist and drummer started off playing a few bars. The duo walked in the lounge, and the place was crammed.

Suddenly, two attractive young females in matching red sequence gowns came prancing out.

The blond with blue eyes said, "Hi, I'm Cannon--this is--"

"Her sister, Dee." Her hair was short and red. "Don't call me red—I'll let ya have it! We're sisters--don't think of putting the make on her—she's married." The crowd applauded. "Thank you, you're very kin--"

"Can I talk!" Cannon said, in a quick shout?"

"Sure, go ahead, they have your number." Dee replied as if it wasn't a big deal.

" We have a favorite of ours, sit back and dream. We want you to come along with us on a journey." Cannon said, romantically.

The sisters melted into the tune: "Gonna take a *Sentimental Journey,* gonna set my mind at ease...

Jules paid the girls to sing this tune as soon as Mr. A and the apple entered the lounge. This is known as "The Big Tease". The apple was going on an *Arty-crafty Journey,* all right. No one caught on except Mr. A. It took a lot of doing on his part to stop from breaking apart laughing.

Mr. A and the apple continued walking through the lounge, to the lobby. As soon as they stepped outside, the chauffeur immediately jumped out and opened the door. Mr. A hurried to get in first. As Mr. L entered, he paused.

"You look like ghost. I teenk we should go to lounge for dreenk, no?"

The apple, halfway in the limousine rested one hand on the seat, and waited for an answer.

"Get in...close t-th." Mr. A started to gag. "You...god...da...agggg-ahh-gaaaaaa" He tried to open the door but didn't quite make it. He upchucked over the window, door, and you name it (put his finger down his throat).

Meanwhile, back in the card room, the dealer looked heated. "Excuse me, gentlemen." He looked at the chipman. "Start a new game."

"Yes sir," He opened a new deck, and started his new position, as the dealer walked out.

He left the clubroom and went out to the limousine. The chauffeur was about to get in the car. "Hold on!" The dealer called out." The chauffeur stood there looking as if something was wrong.

"Get in the car, I won't be long!" Jules said, pissed.

He opened the door, looked at the combo, and shouted, "What the fuck happened!"

Mr. A suddenly felt sick again. He pulled the door handle to open the door, but there wasn't enough time, so, he kicked the door open, and heaved his guts out again, over the door, flowers and driveway. "I-I do...got to... gaaaaaa-ughhhhhhh...sonofabitch! The onl--yuccccccccock suckerrrrrohhhhh...

"Jesus Christ! What about you!" Jules yelled out. "You, you Russian fuck! How could you screw up! Goddam it, a fourteen year old kid coulda pulled it off!"

"I do not know what went wrong. Eet eez unknown to me what happened. I-I am seek to my stomach. Before I kn--"

"Never mind! This is it! Last time! He shouted. "Last fuckin' time. Get outa my sight! Nine hundred thousand blown away!" He looked at the chauffeur. "Take them back to their hotel. "He looked at the duo, and said, "We'll straighten this matter later—9 sharp, my suite! Better have good answers—fuckin' morons." He slammed the door, and the limo took off.

Mr. S walked back and stopped a moment in the lounge. The sisters were singing, *I'm Looking Over A Four Leaf Clover*. When they seen him, they gave a big wave, and added new lyrics: ...a four leaf clover that Jules gave to me before...

He winked at them and continued walking to the card room. The solid brass

plaque had been taken down from the double doors. He knocked a different code

this time, the guard let him in. The barroom was quite different. The shelves were

empty, and there were no barstools. The waiting room no longer had thirty two

round tables, there were only ten, and rearranged contrarily. As he walked to the

card room, the sliding dividing wall was no longer in sight, or any sign that the

room had one. One could see the card room was no longer there. Where the

sliding wood partition was, were now two rows of chairs facing where the card

table was, now a part of the waiting area. The dark paneled mahogany wall

behind the dealer position had a 5' X 8' built-in silver screen, and the light

fixtures were different (false walls, light fixtures and sliding dividing wall

controlled in secret room). It was now a conference room also consisting of a long

table and eighteen chairs.

The shills went out through a secret door to a storage area with the footlocker

and liquor, and were waiting to get paid off.

Why the quick change you may ask? Jules did not take anything for granted.

It was a long shot if the apple decided to come back in the heat of anger. And,

there was no way he could prove a card game took place. This particular room has

been arrogated for dignitaries only. As far as the guard inside, a completely different knock would be a sign of danger. He would simply leave, and join the rest via the secret back door.

Jules paid off the shills. They received five hundred-fifty dollars apiece.

"Red, you drive with me. Carry my attaché case." Jules said. "Mario, you and Murray bring the locker to my place. Put it where you found it. The rest of you can leave—see you tonight—Joe Sonka's—10 sharp."

He paid the chipman fifteen hundred. "That was a cute tease you gave me at the table, Tony."

"Couldn't resist."

"By the way, My brother Joe is gonna take your place for awhile, I hope you don't mind."

His mouth fell. "Joe? I don't mind Jules. What can I do to help out?"

"I want you to follow him for a week, and find out what he's up too. If you find out, good—if you don't--shoot him!"

"Jesus Christ! You had me freaking out there for a minute! OK, OK, ya got me good—but, did you really like my 'dealer—sir' pressure healer, love?"

"You couldn't have picked a better time. Beautiful Tony, beautiful."

"I knew I was good for something around here." He lit cigarette, and blew smoke rings.

"I have a feeling we're gonna have a busy schedule. Get your butt outa here. Oh, are you comin' tonight?"

"Ten sharp. I'm coming, my lady's coming too. Later, we'll both be coming or going—if she comes before--"

"Get outa here!"

"OK, love. See you later. Oh, shit, forgot to tell ya, I'll come up with a few pressure breakers—thanks love."

Jules and Red walk in his home. Ernestine greets them. "Mr. Jules, Mario and another gentleman dropped off the footlocker."

"OK, thank you. You look cheerful, did your sister call?"

She giggled. "I haven't seen or heard from her in twenty years. You're puttin' me on, Mr. Jules, you always do. Maybe you both would like some coffee, real strong?"

"Took the words right out of my mouth. We'll be on the patio."

"A's feels just fine, just fine, comin right up, Mr. Jules. Mario, he said for me to tell you, he's in his room writing a letter."

"When you get a chance, tell him we'll talk later. Make sure he gets dressed, we have reservations at 9 for dinner at Joe Sonka's."

"I don't know if I could remember all that!" She giggled, and went off.

Jules and Red walked out to the patio, and relaxed. They talked about the play.

"Jules, that play was a masterpiece, an absolute magnum opus. I wouldn't want to meet the apple in a dark alley."

"He defected Russia with a ton of stolen money. He's a big time pimp, pervert and an executioner. I'll lay odds he'll want to get even."

"They all want to get even, Jules. Do you have a second play, should this happen?"

Jules laughed. "Red, when you see the second play, you're not going to have the desire for sex for at least a week.!"

Red laughed. Don't do this to me, Jules. You can tell me—I won't be able to sleep if you don't."

"I can't right now, it's not perfected to detail yet. You'll know about it soon enough, promise. You coming to dinner with us?"

"I can't wait." He slapped his forehead. "Sonofabitch! I almost forgot—your brother Peter told me to tell you he and JoJo are at the top of their class in collage. He said, they owe it all to you. They're bright boys, positively."

"I haven't had time to talk with them. Tell them I love them. Listen, Red, I have to shower and get dressed, I'll see you later."

Ernestine came with the coffee. "You don't want coffee, Mr. Jules?"

"Sure I do. Set it on the table, I'll help myself."

"Im-immm, that man is gonna get sick. Oh Lordy, save his soul—mercy-mercy." She muttered under her breath.

Jules went to his room. He applied a couple of hot towels to his face, and looked in the mirror. *OK sweetheart, when you go to your suite, take it away from that Russian bastard as if you were the greatest actor around. Make him beg to get in another game,* He told himself. He threw a kiss at his image, and left to chew and spit out Mr. A, and the apple.

A black Cadillac convertible pulled in the entrance of the Fountain Blue Hotel. A valet drove it off and parked it in front of the entrance. Jules walked through the lobby and waited for the elevator. When he got to his suite, he unlocked the door and entered. Mr. A jumped to his feet.

"Mr. S, I don't know what to say. My--"

"Never mind!" He was pissed. "I can't seem to understand for the life of me how this fuckin' mistake was made—a $900,000 dollar fuck up!"

Mr. A started to gag. "I don't know wha...wh...gaaaaa...ughhhhhh" He vomited on the side of the couch and oriental carpet. "Aww Jesus, I'm sorry. I'll clea- clean it up."

Leave it, stay right there, dummy. What do have to say, Mr. L?"

He was coked up. His eyes were blood shot and dilating. He looked as if he was feeling no pain.

"I be perfectly straight weez you. I snort leetle cocaine, so leetle, eef a fly snorted theez amount, maybe he fly a leetle beet higher, that eez all--just before game. My friend deed not know until too late. Please except my deepest apologies."

"What would you do if you were in my shoes? You lost $150,000 of your cash, a $150,000 of your partners, and everything else! Nine hundred grand— gone, disappeared, vanished, all because of a move that shouldn't have been made."

"I ask of you, Mr. S, give second change to me, and Mr. A. Eef it were not for heem, I would not be here, I beg of you."

Mr. S gave the apple a look that would scare a rattlesnake. He walked out to the balcony, and pretended to think about it, and cool off. *He's easier than I thought. Now, I have to find out how much cash he can afford to lose. I'll play Russian roulette with the bl'adki (fuck),* he thought.

A few minutes later, Jules came back. "I'll think about it. Mr. A, leave the lights on when you go. I have an appointment. Call me tomorrow morning at 9- 9:15." He walked out, and slammed the door behind him.

CHAPTER 34

JOE SONKA'S RESTAURANT, MARCH 17, 1951

12:45 A.M.

The party was just breaking up. The shills thanked him for the great dinner. When they go out for a get together such as this, Jules does the ordering of the food. The chef knows him well enough to prepare the meal fresh. Before he told the waiter what everyone wanted, he would ask them if they liked it first. There was no problem in that department. They knew their meal would be the finest. They started off with a toast of wine. Then they talked and talked and laughed and laughed until the appetizers were placed on the table. They had green and red stuffed peppers and an assortment of olives and celery and raw clams and bread and shrimp and scallops and Caesar salad. For the main course, veal and wine, stuffed veal breast, London broil marinade Lobster Newburg and snails ala Romano and chicken breasts flambe and stuffed pork chops and Baccala (cod) Alla Veneta. For dessert, Ricotta pie, Rum cream pie and Italian Rum cake and cheese cake and cheese cake a la Sonka and lemon rice pudding and finally hot wined melba, with their coffee and expresso.

At 7:30 the next morning, Felini, the carpenter and Jules checked out the basement ceiling to make sure the blackjack and crap tables can be hidden in the upper floor. There was no problem. The next day his crew started work.

Later, on the patio, Smiley was talking to Jules.

"Big game last night. The Colonel n me had a great time."

" Knowing you, ya probably picked up a dame and haven't had a good night sleep, you horny bastard."

"Jules, Jules, Jules, I may be horny, at least I'm a steady dude doin' it right!"

"I know. Now listen, the apple is all what he told you except he still sells stolen guns with an inside CIA agent. They're partners, and both are very dangerous. When buyers are interested in their merchandise, they're known to successfully pull off a double cross. Be careful. Stay with him, he's hot."

"No problem in that department, my man. By the way, what happened with the first play, everything work out as you anticipated?"

"Everything worked out as planned. Right now I'm waiting for the apple to beg to get even. OK, Smiley, I have business to take care of, call later to fill me in, good luck."

"Will do, Jules, talk later. Smiley replied.

The phone rang five or six minutes later. "Hello?"

"Hey, Jules, Fast Eddy, how ya doin'?"

"Good, good. What do you have for me?"

"This apple of mine looks older than twenty-eight. The little prick steals from one of his old man's manufacturing plants. He's the CEO, the bastard. He's a drug lord and has 30 or 33 runners that sell the shit. He deals in marijuana exclusively."

"Did he tell you he's a "reef runner" and his take off point is Key West and he and his boys pick up in the Bahamas?"

"Yes. The information you gave me is accurate and up to date, Jules."

"How about his name, did he tell you, you know, what they call him?"

"Reef. He's known as Reef. Last week I had my first experience out to sea. Talk about fast, he's got the fastest speed boat, that sucker skims over the water at 140 mph, and the other eighteen follow in a arrow formation about a hundred yards apart. I was sicker than a dog. Heaved my guts out five minutes after we took off. The waves musta been at least four to six feet, and the wind and speed almost blew me sky high. Jesus Christ, Jules, I didn't think I was gonna make it, no shit!"

"Have you gambled with him?"

"Yeah. He's a good loser. Loves the crap table—no question about it, he's a high roller. I showed him a few pointers--he appreciated it. We're getting to know each other. In a few more months, we'll be best of friends."

"OK, stay with him. Give me your number."

"Hang on, Jules. Let's see, (312) 246-7144."

"Good work, Fast Eddy. OK, I'll talk with you later."

In the background Jules heard sawing and hammering from Felini's crew. He went downstairs, and a rectangular opening had all ready been cut out for the crap table. Felini and three other men were measuring the second rectangle for the blackjack table.

"You don't waist any time." Jules said to Felini.

"Time is valuable, Mr. Jules, do you not agree?" Felini replied, smiling.

"No question about it. Looks good." Jules said, looking down into the basement.

"You have not seen anything yet. The best is yet to come." Felini said, as he started to saw.

Ernestine came in the den. "Lordy, Lordy, Mr. Jules, it looks to me they're makin' a hole there for a casket!"

Jules laughed. "In a few days you'll see what goes there. Bring the boys some lemonade after. Maybe some of your fantastic tuna sandwiches too,"

"OK, Mr. Jules. I got my eyes on that good lookin' black man wearin' the red plaid shirt over there."

"He is a good looking fellow. Ya better watch out, woman, he's been staring at you."

"Now Mr. Jules, what you think I is, anyway, a Jezebel?"

"I didn't say that. You're more of a nun type, if anything, know what I mean?"

She gave him a dirty look. "Hmm!" And walked away.

Later that evening, Jules was talking to Sol on the phone.

"...this weekend will work out perfect. Take the afternoon flight. The chauffeur will pick you up at the front entrance. Talk to ya later.

Father Alisi's partner, Mr. L , begged for a second chance. Jules gave him a run for his money, but eventually allowed him to sit in on the second play. The apple is going for $200,000.

In Jules' suite, Mr. A and Mr. L are sitting waiting for the chauffeur to bring them to the club. The phone rang.

Jules picked up. "Hello? What! What do you mean they can't find the keys! He's pissed. "Get up here right away." He slammed down the phone. Heated, said to Mr. A, "The fuckin' limousine is blocked in. They can't find the keys to the car that blocked in the limo—and the best part, a goddam concrete column is in front of the fuckin' limo! Jesus Christ!"

There was a knock on the door. Jules let in the chauffeur.

"Sir," the chauffeur said, "there's no way I can get the limousine out."

Jules paused for a moment. "I have to get going. Mr. A, take a cab when your ready to leave. Mr. L, stay here with the chauffeur till the moron finds the keys. I'll delay the game as long as possible."

"Theez eez okay weez me." Mr. L said, looking perplexed.

"OK gentlemen, I have to leave. Game starts 7:30 sharp—I'll delay it as long as possible. See you there." He left.

At 5:45 P.M., no keys were found. Mr. A called a cab and left with his attaché case containing a manila envelope with $400,000 in cash.

At 7:30 P.M., Jules and Mr. A met at the theater and watched *Casablanca,* staring Humphry Bogart and Ingrid Bergman. (This was the second play.)

"Mario wanted me to see this movie. Couldn't have picked a better time, wouldn't you say Father?"

"Indeed, Jules, indeed." Father Alisi said, delighted.

"Ya want some popcorn, Father?"

"I'll go get some Coke and popcorn and my favorite, chocolate covered peanuts. You too, Jules?"

"Hey, let's go for it. Here, take this twenty dollar bill."

"I got it Jules, don't be absurd."

After the movie, Jules went home, and Mr. A waited until 10:15, and called a cab. In the lobby of the Fountain Blue, Mr. A entered the elevator and went to Jules' Penthouse suite. Before he knocked on the door, he took a few deep breaths and knocked.

The chauffeur opened the door. "Good evening , sir."

"Evening." Mr. A said, in disorder.

Mr. L looked at him, and said, "You do not look so well. Why do you walk so slowly?"

"I made a mistake! I made a fucking boner, sonofabitch!"

Mr. A had looked as though he was about to vomit. "I-I'm gonna puke... aggggg." He put his hands over his mouth, and ran to the bathroom. "Ohhhh noagggg." He vomited in the toilet, making sure he wouldn't have to clean up after himself this time. He did a convincing performance. "Putting the finger down the throat ruse" was all part of the performance.

Mr. L laughed. Sure, he was disappointed he "thought" he made a mistake in the first game. And, sure, he could afford to lose. His covetousness was the worst there was. Believe it or not, he felt relieved his partner, Mr. A made a mistake. Now they were even, and a good sport is the name of the game.

Mr. A flushed the toilet, and came out with a towel wrapped around his neck.

"You aren't going to believe what I'm about to te...tel...aggggg...awwwww..." He did it again, this time in the towel. "Ohhh, Jesus Christ, I'm sorry. I made a fuckin' mistake! I can't beli...agggg...God, I'm dyin'...

Mr. L laughed ecstatically. "I cannot believe what I hear an' see. My friend make mistake, like me? I do not feel so bad now—we get even weez each udder!"

Detailing the plays throughout the year and a half, each of the apples bolted back in mild shock, and the lugger assisted them out to the limousine. We begin with: Fast Eddy (lugger) Mr. R (apple) 28 years old. Black hair. Pock face. 5'9". 185 pounds. Drug dealer.

Tony Hands (lugger) Mr. JT (apple) 50 years old. Shaved head, with scared face. 210 pounds. 6'2". Oil Baron. Women abuser.

Smiley (lugger). Mr. C (apple). 55 years old. 190 pounds. 6' 1". Light blond hair. Brush cut. Handlebar mustache. Thief and pervert. Lost $300,000.

Sparrow (lugger). Dr. Z (apple). 48 years old. 180 pounds. 5' 6". black wavy hair. Psychologist. Lost $425,000.

Gunner (lugger). Mr. C (apple). 44 years old. 5' 10". 200 pounds. Red hair. Movie Producer. Lost $950,000.

Sully (lugger). Mr. D (apple). 37 years old. 5' 11". 220 pounds. Dark brown hair. Senator. Lost $750,000.

Tony Hands (lugger). Mr. B (apple). 49 years old. 5' 7". 210 pounds. Balding. Blond & reddish beard. Manufacturer. Lost $900,000.

Sol (lugger). Mr. T (apple). 63 years old. 6' 1". 205 pounds. Black hair. Thin rat tail mustache. Movie Director. Lost $985,000.

There were several other plays totaling more than $5,000,000. Jules donated all of it to the church and the needy. Now he was ready to track down Tony Cheese, to even the score.

CHAPTER 35

NEW YORK, APRIL 16, 1952

10:00 A.M.

Jules became the father of another girl. They named her Michelle and called her Micki for short. Her facial features are her mothers, and have her father's light brown hair and dark brown eyes. Jules, Carman and the two girls spent fun time together. They strolled through the park and zoo and climbed trees and went to the seaside and had a grand time. For two months Jules tried to make up the lost time he never gave them. His nights were restless and he couldn't sleep. Tony Cheese haunted his dreams.

He incessantly gave generously to the needy and unskilled worker; he was a show-off when he had to be but a class act under different conditions.

In 1954, Jules heard through the grapevine that Cuba would be a hot spot to do business. Meyer Lansky, a friend of Jules' wanted to turn Havana into the Monte Carlo of the Caribbean. The legal casinos would make it a great gambling and tourist Mecca. Lansky knew how to promote to get the right names, and sent invitations to all the high rollers all over the world. Jules thought it would be a good opportunity to run the Tropicana Casino until his casino is completed in

Miami Beach. At the same time he passed the word for the whereabouts of Tony Cheese.

Jules and his family departed for Havana. Meyer Lansky introduced Jules to President Fulgencio Batista, and they talked about percentages of the take that would be disbursed to Batista and the State from all casinos owned and operated by Mr. Lansky.

President Batista asked Jules for his opinion pertaining to the new proposal on gambling under his presidential term.

There were only sixteen words that came out of Jules' mouth for the entire meeting. "Mr. President, I heard through the grapevine, honest high stake gambling will prevail here in Havana."

Those sixteen words brought President Batista, Jules and his family a close relationship. The girls had the finest education tutored by Batista's selected teachers.

Before the casinos opened, Batista asked Jules if he could get first-class seasoned mechanics.

Jules said, "My friend Smiley is the best. In fact, when we were kids we made a mint off of dead rats."

Batista smiled. "Well, Meester Jules, our wear ties ena suites. They smoke hand-rolled Habana cigars. If you can take them, I weel give you 50% of what you ween. These people are undesirable, and I do not want them in Cuba. Castro

is a troublemaker; he made hees own rules. Hees tyranny made Havana what eet

ees today. That ees why I have been elected. Castro weel not stop, and chances

are he weel want control sometime in the future. I want clean and fair

casinos here. My friend Meyer and I have agreed to such an operation. Weel you

do thees for Habana, Jules?"

"My dear Mr. Fulgencio, you are a fair man, and I realize what you are trying

to do. I'll bust out these rats, but I need to know who they are."

"I have photos of each one, I weel deliver them to you personally, how does

that sound?" Batista said.

"Like music to my ears, Mr. President."

"Then, we agree." They shook hands, and had a toast. "To Habana and all the

goood peoples—my apologies—I should say, goood people, my English must be

polished much more. Hear! Hear!"

Batista knew Jules was a loyal person, not only to his wife, but to his family

as well. Jules operated the Tropicana Hotel Casino for four years. At the same

time, Meyer Lansky owned and operated the Riviera Hotel and Casino (1958).

Jules wanted to be on his own. His casino had been completed two years ago

in Miami. He had a 70' yacht, and his captain sailed Jules, Carmen and the girls

to his dock on Star Island on weekends. The only reason Jules stayed in Havana

was his wife loved it there and the two girls were getting an excellent education.

The thought of Tony Cheese troubled Jules at times. He knew deep down he'd find him sooner or later, he was sure of that. He would not allow himself to get obsessed. His individuality knew patience is a virtue, and he controlled his emotions conformably.

Jules avoided Lansky as much as possible. He did what he had to do and made the Tropicana Hotel Casino an opulent spot. As time goes by, the undesirables and degenerates disappeared as Jules had promised Batista.

Smiley mellowed down, and had a position as pit boss at the Tropicana.

Many weekends, Batista invited Jules, Carmen and the two girls to his mountain retreat.

On one weekend, Jules and Smiley went to Star Island, at Jules' estate. He had made an appointment with Felini to show him how the equipment worked. Felini walked Jules to the fireplace, and pushed on a certain brick. Suddenly, the blackjack, crap and roulette tables lowered silently under the floor. The floor closed and locked in place. The casino was once again a beautiful den. On the opposite wall where ten slot machines were positioned, the wall slid closed. To bring the tables and slots back into view, the brick was simply pushed again, and the den turned into a casino, in less than a minute. Jules was impressed. Felini brought Jules and Smiley to the basement. The tables were concealed with partitions that looked as if they were a part of the existing structure. If the place was raided, there was no way one could detect if a casino existed here.

The following weekend, the captain sailed Jules, Carmen, Tina, and Micki
and Smiley back home to Star Island, and Felini was their guest. After dinner,
Ernestine brought out a large bowl of fresh fruit. She poured expresso, then
refilled the wineglasses. Jules raised his wineglass. "I want to make a toast to my
good friend, Felini." Everyone raised their glass, and waited for Jules to make the
toast.

"Here's to you, as good as you are,

And here's to me, as bad as I am;

As bad as I am, as good as you are,

I'm as good as you are

as bad as I am.

Salutea!"

They laughed as Jules handed Felini an envelope. "This is for you, Felini."

Felini opened the envelope. "Meester Jules, there are eight teekeets to New
York, here!"

"That's right. Here's something else." He handed Felini eight legal passports.
"These go with them, my good man."

Felini's eyes filled with tears. He wiped his eyes, at the same time, his wife
and six children walked in the room and wrapped their arms around him.

"I-I do not know what to say, Meester J-Jules."

"There is nothing you have to say, my friend."

Jules looked at Felini and his family. "When you get to New York, a job is waiting . This is between you and me. No one must ever know how you got there or how you received those passports. You did it on your own, do you understand?"

"I understand. Thank you. Thank you from the bottom of our hearts, Meester Jules. You are a Godsend. God bless you. You will always be in our prayers."

Back in Havana, Jules convinced Smiley to leave, and go back to Las Vegas and find an apple. Meanwhile, the other luggers were working on their apples. Jules had a friend that owned a private plane, and would fly to Miami when a play was made official.

One month later, Smiley rambled around in Caesar's Palace. He studied the tables, and spotted a crammed crap table. At his height, 6' 1", he was able to see the table and players. His eyes caught a fat slob who was winning heavy. It appeared to Smiley he had more than fifty thousand dollars in black, gold and red chips. He hovered over his chips as if someone was about to steal them. Without warning, someone slapped him on the back. He turned around and it was an old friend, Lucky Luciazzo.

Smiley was surprised. "Hey, Lucky! What's goin' on?" They shook hands. The three-karat diamond on Smiley's pinkie glittered from the bright lights.

"Ahh, ya can't be doin' to shabby wid dat rock on da feelers, huh, Smiley baby?"

"It's not real, somebody in the jon passed it. I found it stickin' on the wall."

"Ya, ya, sure, sure, my mudder's havin' twins, too, she's only eighty-tree."

"Hey Lucky, who's the heavy winner over there." Smiley asked.

"Dat asshole? Dat's Tony, Tony Capillano, you know, the fuckin' pervert who owns all the prostitutes in New Yoik? I hoid he butchered Rocco, ya know--Rocco D'Lucca—ya know, ya know, Rocco's joint--da restaurant? It was a front for ahhh da casino, ya, dats right, he had da joint up the steps--ya know who I mean?"

"Yeah, sure, sweetheart. Looks to me the fat slob is up fifty-sixty grand." Smiley said, watching his moves.

Lucky jabbed Smiley a couple of times on his side to get his attention. "Small change Smiley, small change. He's got a yellow streak down his back an' he's a mudder fucker, too, believe me, I know whad I'm talkin' abou'."

A waitress came by and Smiley ordered a martini, extra, extra dry. He studied Tony Cheese, and thought, *Jesus Christ! Wait till Jules hears about this. He won't waist any time getting here. He'll plan the whole deal out, bet your ass he will. I'm hangin' around a while. I'm gonna fondle with Cheese. Hope I don't gag with his garlic breath. That's what I'm doin', gettin' in the game—maybe I'll wipe the wop out. He's not going to recognize me, not by a long shot. I'll worm my way to the table. Call Jules later.*

Smiley made an effort to get to the table. "Excuse me. Excuse me, sir." Person by person he easily shoved them aside or grabbed there arm or shoulder. "Excuse me, sweetheart. Move aside, please." He did this until he reached the table. With the luck of the Irish, a player dropped out of the game due to a losing roll. Smiley moved to a player next to Cheese. He squeezed his slender body next to him, at the same time he gave Cheese a serious nod. Smiley turned away as if Cheese wasn't there and dropped fifty-one hundred-dollar bills on the table as if it was a pea in the bucket. Smiley made this move while one of the players rolled the dice and won, and the crowd carried on as if they had a piece of the action. Smiley waited for the croupier to give him chips. When Cheese seen Smiley's cash, he jabbed him.

"Beeg spender, huh, pal?" His raspy voice and garlic breath almost knocked Smiley off his feet.

The waitress brought Smiley's martini, and the croupier gave him five thousand in chips. Smiley nodded his head to the croupier as to say, thank you, and ignored Cheese's cheap remark. He stacked his chips neatly in rows of one thousand and piled them exceptionally high. Not to high to be noticed by the croupier, but high enough for Smiley's screen, when the time was right to be applied. He learned this move from Jules.

Cheese jabbed Smiley again. "I see you are high roller, no, my friend?"

Smiley gave him a dubious look. "Looks to me you're the high roller around here, my gamester friend."

"And, eet ees not over." He motioned to his blond girlfriend. She was attractive, tall and just about naked. She was a typical hooker playing nice-nice.

Smiley licked his lips and turned to study the croupier's actions as he pushed the dice with his stick to the next roller. He studied his routine until he had it down pat. When it was time for his roll, he switched the dice, bet five hundred and threw a seven. He continued on a roll until he thought it was time to replace his dice with the house bones. When the croupier pushed the dice in front of Cheese, Smiley made the perfect switch. He intentionally knocked over his chips, some landing on the dice, bet a thousand on the lose line and in a lightening fast move, he palmed the house dice for another pair of Smiley's losing dice in one swift motion.

Cheese bet twenty thousand, threw the dice—crap. He lost. "Sonofabitch!" He shouted out, "My luck ees getting sour!" He turned red, and slapped the table, then looked at Smiley. "I teenk you bring to me bad luck! Maybe you move to udder side of table, gabeesha, boy?"

"I'm sorry you feel that way. Maybe you should roll the dice again!"

"How can I roll again? I am not allowed to do thees theeng--I just lost--dice move forward to you?" He said, roughly.

Smiley raised his arms. "Ladies and gentlemen, do you mind if this gentleman throws the dice again? He feels I have brought bad luck to him. What do you say? Is it OK or not? Mr. croupier, do you mind?"

The croupier looked at the pit boss, was approved. He looked at Smiley, and gave him approval with a nod of the head. Then pushed the dice in front of him.

"Your roll, sir. If you want someone else to throw your dice, that's fine."

Smiley made a swift switch of his dice in his palm, and sliding the house dice in front of Cheese.

"There you are, my friend. Please, roll a winner, my baby needs a new pair of shoes."

The crowd applauded and carried on as if a teacher was bringing them ice cream for good behavior.

Cheese looked at Smiley with a confused look painted across his face. "I have never seen thees before. Thank you."

Cheese bet everything he had (eighteen thousand dollars). He snaked the dice, shook them and threw them across the table. They bounced off the end of the table and settled with two fours. Cheese made six attempts, and on the seventh roll, he made his point.

While Cheese counted his chips, Smiley said to him, "Ya see, Irish people don't bring bad luck to anybody. They may drink pretty good, and steal a wife or two, but never, ever, ever, never, never, would they steal your four leaf clover."

Smiley threw two one hundred-dollar chips to the croupier. "Thanks pal."

The croupier thanked him.

At the same time, the waitress went up to Cheese, she said, "Sir, that gentleman (Smiley) says you're an ass. But, he wants to buy you a drink, anyway."

Cheese, the cheeseparer that he is, never tipped the waitress or the croupier. He only had won more than eighty-four thousand in hard cash. The pimp didn't even thank Smiley. Cheese was a nice guy. His only problem was he wasn't a human being. A pariah with garlic running through his veins may be letting it go lightly.

Smiley held up his racks of chips and smiled over and above his incessant smile. He cashed out and sat at the bar gazing at Tony Cheese, the man who killed Rocco. If his friend Lucky had not told him, he would not have recognized the cutthroat. The once handsome Italian is now bald, and tipping the scale at 385 pounds. His voice was an octave higher and he smelled like burnt garlic ceaselessly. Cheese was sitting at a table not far from Smiley. His long legged lady in red was soothing him by massaging his neck and levator scapulae areas.

Smiley thought he'd be a deranged wise guy for little gag he thought to pull off on Cheese. He gestured to the barmaid wearing a tuxedo. "How can I help you gorgeous?" She said.

"Hey love, do you have any of those beef jerky sticks?" He said, looking at her up and down.

"Darlin', I got 'em. You want one?"

"No-no. I want you to put ten or twelve in a tall glass, on ice, and have one of the girls bring them to that table over there. Big order, huh?"

"OK, Mr. Nice guy, you're sayin' you want a glass full of beef jerky, on ice, and if I heard you correctly, you want one of my choice bunnies to bring it to Mr. Tony's reserved table?"

"That is correct, you ravishing little bitch!"

She gave him a sensual look. "You're turning me on, love."

"Oh, God, I didn't mean to do that. Jesus, you must put in some heavy hours here. You seemingly must get horny at this late hour—no offense pretty face, just givin' ya a hearty word or two, you know--considering you're here--I'm here--we're both near feelin' queer, I make a toast to you dear." He raised his martini glass. "Hear! Hear!"

"Yer funny, blue eyes, and the martini wasn't that stiff." She laughed. "Heavy hours? My day requires twelve-fourteen hours, six days a week."

"Holy sheeeit! What time do you usually get outa here?"

"Oh, honey—2:00-2:15 A.M. Long hours wearin' the tux, is how I make the big bucks."

"You're a poet and don't know it—that is definitely settled. I'll pick you up at 2:00—wait-wait-wait, if you're too tired for breakfast, we'll go directly to my room and I'll show you how the TV works, whadaya say?"

She walked away, and made him another martini. As she placed it near his hand, her voice dropped to a whisper.

"On the house, gorgeous one. First, you have to tell me your name."

"Smiley, Smiley O' Brian. I can see on your brass ID, your name is Heather, pretty name."

She leaned over and lightly fondled with his fingers. "Will you show me how to draw a mockingbird too, Smiley?"

"Probably not." He said troubled.

"Why not, love?"

"To tell you the truth, I never seen a mockingbird. I can show you how to draw a female chicken and a dog and a sparrow. And if you're good at observing, maybe, just maybe, I'll draw my pet dog, Asti, and my other special friend, Hardy, my cock. He cock-a-doodle-do's every sunrise without fail. You'll love that little sucker.

"OK, Mr. Wonderful, you sold me—you're on!"

"Do you spell wonderful, w o n d e r f u l?"

"No, love. I spell it, o n e d e r f u l—because I count my wonders."

"No question about it, you are a special lady—an angle would be more fitting. Before noon tomorrow, you're going to be a connoisseur of penipeepeedoo cacciatore ala pastenea, guaranteed."

Heather gave Smiley a look of certainty. "I like it. Sounds to me like we're gonna eat rather than draw!"

They laughed. She took care of a customer, and said, "Later, handsome."

Smiley noticed Cheese whispering something in his lady's ear. She got up and wiggled her butt to Smiley. "Hi honey, Tony wants to talk to you."

"Well, I--"

She grabbed his arm. "C'mon, love, I won't bite you."

"W-Wait, my drin--"

"Fuck the drink, blue eyes, we have a overkill at our table."

"Not for anything, doll, but you're a gorgeous hunk." Smiley said, softly.

"Thanks. You're not bad yourself." Cheese's lady said, touching his butt.

Cheese puts his hand out to Smiley. "Hey, my friend, you were on roll. When you steal my luck, I teenk you are motherfucker. But when you geev me extra roll, I say to myself, dees guy ees OK—he no thees name, no way."

"Glad you're taking it so well. I didn't get your name."

"Tony, justa call me Tony. What ees yours?"

"Smiley, every body calls me Smiley."

"I can see why. You face has smile alla time."

They talked for nearly an hour. One of Cheese's henchmen came to the table and whispered something in his ear.

Cheese looked at his aide. "Go ahead," Cheese said to him, tell Smiley what you say to me."

The henchman looked at Smiley, looking irate. "You work for Jules Salarno, Mr. hot shot, da fast hand dude—"

"Jesu Chreest!" Cheese yelled out. "Get to fucking point!"

"Sorry, boss. Rocco's crony, you know. He taught him da ropes? Poor Rocco got sliced wid a knife in self-defense abou' 7-8 years ago. Heard he didn't make it. His kid got caught in da middle an' was killed fallin' down the stairs. Terrible thing to happen. Whadayou do--"

"Yeah, yeah, yeah, he's a has been. What else ees new?" Cheese said, as if it was nothing. The story was highly fabricated, but that's the myth Cheese brainwashed into his mobster's heads.

"J-Just keeping you up on things, boss, at's all-at's all."

"Awright, you stay here for two minootes, I geev you note."

Cheese looked at Smiley, and said politly, "My friend, Smiley, I do not want you to theenk I am getting personal, but are you staying in dees hotel?"

"As a matter of fact I was checking in as soon as I leave you, why do you ask, Tony?"

"I would like to have discussion weeth you, maybe later or tomorrow. I weel call your room and let you know what the score ees—time, place, ees thees all right weeth you?"

"Sure, Tony, call anytime. If I'm not in, I'll be at the crap table."

"Good-good, I see you then. Have a gooda rest tonight, huh?"

"No problem in that department. The left side of my bed will be nice n warm. Good night. Good night, lady in red."

Cheese looked at his henchman. "You find hees room number and send heem a magnum of Dom Peringnon. You do job well, I geev you surprise, later. "

In his raspy baritone voice, the henchman looked timorous of Cheese, he said, "No problem, boss, I'll take care a tings, boss—good as done, bet on it."

The faithful follower intensely walked off, as if he had earned a bonus check for twenty-five dollars and a two-day supply of fresh garlic.

In his penthouse suite, Smiley counted twenty-eight thousand dollars he had won at the crap table. He gazed at the magnum of Dom Peringnon Cheese had sent him, he thought, *I know the garlic breath rat is up to something, I'll invite him for a drink to show my appreciation. I'll clue Jules in on Mr. fuck face when I get more details. I can't wait to tell him, Jesus Christ, he's gonna be ecstatic, exhilarated—I'll lay odds 5 ta 1, he won't be able to get a hard-on till he sees the murderin' rat, slob face, motherfuckin' Cheese, the sleaze, in the kisser.* He looked in the ceiling mirror, and winked, then laughed at him.

Later, Cheese took advantage of Smiley's invitation. He brought two of his bodyguards with him. The name of one was Thorn, the other, Trif "The Bush".

Cheese and Smiley sat and had a drink for around fifteen or eighteen minutes making small talk.

Cheese finally broke the ice. "I have heard through grapevine, your friend Jules ees holdeen reins to one of beegest games in country, thees ees so?"

Smiley laughed. "Yeah, sure, Tony. I don't know what grapevine you been scoopin' out--I only heard Lansky, Murder, Inc. and Donald Duck paid off Castro to leave Cuba. And further more, Batitsta took over to make sure the casino percentages were fair for all the people. And the ones owned by Lansky were contracted to be painted the color, Tope."

Cheese laughed like a hyena in heat. "You are comedian. I teenk the--"

"Oh, almost forgot. Lansky leaves Jules alone because he doesn't try to weasel in on anyone. Would you believe that?"

Cheese developed a smirk on his scared face Rocco had given him. "And a rat saves eet's own fleas from exteenction."

They laughed. "One of thees days I am takin' down Jules. Smiley, you seem like nice guy. You have been good friend weeth that fuck for long time. Maybe eet ees time to cut apron string and have much more in one's favor, no?"

"Why? What did Jules do to you?" Smiley played dumb. He is planing to set Cheese up.

"Dat motherfucker, Rocco took me for seven grand. Da only bitch I ever had left me weeth my bambino inside her. Bank takes away my home, also. Eef Jules was not at restaurant at time we fight, theengs would have been contrary, you see." He leaned forward into Smiley's face. "What ees eet you are lookin' for, Smiley my friend? You want--money ana power? I canna geev you dees theengs."

Smiley looked into Cheese's eyes. "We can get it from one of Jules' games.

One of the shills at the table could go either way. I can get him to throw in with
us. A cool three hundred grand each isn't bad for openers, right?"

Cheese gave Smiley a squinty-eyed curious look. "Why would **you** turn on
Jules, yooza sideakick?"

"Smiley leaned into Cheese's ear, and whispered, "Between you an' me, he
would fuck his own mother—all right!"

Cheese throws up his arms. "Cuta my tongue out ana use to fuck pussy ala
veneta. Now, you leeson to me. Eef you want een weeda Tony Cheese, you musta
show me somea guts, gabeesha? C'mona-c-mona, spilla da beans to me . . .

Smiley dropped his head, and muttered, "Only woman I cared about ... Jules
stole her--nice fuckin' friend." His eyes filled with tears.

Cheese patted Smiley on his shoulder. "At'sa awright, sona, everytinga ees
meant to be for reason. Okay now, tings gonna work outa for da besta, you see.
We talka later. Letsa go boys, we gotta tings to do."

Smiley called Jules and told him about Tony Cheese. Jules gave orders to
bring him to Havana, Riviera Hotel, penthouse suite 2100 ASAP.

Smiley took Heather, the barmaid to breakfast at The Desert Inn Resort &
Casino. That was it. Is not like Smiley, but he could be a gentleman on rare
occasions. He apparently had his first play. Besides, Jules pay back time was
about to happen.

CHAPTER 36

HAVANA CUBA, MAY 3, 1958

7:15 A.M.

Smiley and Cheese arrived in Havana and kept a low profile. This was the first time Cheese's bodyguards weren't with him. They shared the same luxurious suite on the twentieth floor.

In the meantime, Cuba's political scene changed fast ...

One day Batista is in charge, another day Castro and his men swarm down from the hills promising Democracy.

On Jules' yacht that evening, Jules told Smiley the "play" is set up for Sunday, three days away. Jules has always been superstitious to never have more than three plays with one apple. Apples are very greedy people.

Jules, Smiley and Cheese get together in Jules' suite. Jules pretends he does not recognize Cheese; he really didn't if Smiley hadn't told him. Jules went through the routine showing Cheese exactly what to do; betting his and Smiley's $300,000 on the fourth jack.

"OK, Mr. C," Jules said. "In the second game, you understand you'll be in charge of the abacus?"

"I understand." Cheese replied, with a smirk painted across his fleshy face.

Jules carried on saying, "Your partner, Mr. O will be on top of you to guide you if need be. Just be cool and everything will work out fine. Any questions?"

Mr. O chuckled and sniffed a few times. "How much we takin' the House down for?" He sniffed again. "And, what's our cut, sir?"

We're grabbin' the House for 900,000 grand, maybe 75 or 80 more. Keepin' it simple, 900,000 will get you 300,000 thousand apiece—forget the small change for now, If I can get it, we split three ways. And another thing, Mr. O, you snort that shit before the game, I'll tell ya right now, I'll have one of the guards boot your ass out of the game so fast, Castro will chew you up and spit you out, ya got that?"

"S-Sure, Mr. S. we don't want that to happen. You have my word."

"I'm holding you responsible, Mr. C, understood?"

"I cut off hees hands eef he fuck weed lady snow, mark my words!" He said pissed. He turned to Smiley, in a sweet tone. "Do you gabeecha, my handsome comrade?" He leaned over to Smiley, and pulled his ear lobe, roughly.

It's Sunday, 7:20 P.M. In 10 minutes Jules will exonerate the killer of Rocco and his son Mario, who will be in a wheelchair for the rest of his life.

Smiley knocks the code on the door and a security guard admits them. Another guard escorts the twosome past the bar, where Joey Dee, Arny Roth and BoBo are having a drink. As they continue, six gentlemen are sitting at tables, as if they were waiting to get in the game behind the almost closed sliding accordion wooden partition. The six shills waiting were Tony Chips, Louie The Twitch, Monty, Theo and Mugs. Fat Vinnie was taking drink orders in the card room.

The guard escorted Smiley and the apple directly to there assign seats.

Jules (the dealer) was opening a new deck of cards. When he seen Smiley and the apple, he lay the cards on the table, and looked at Mr. O.

"Good evening, gentlemen. Are you ready to cash in for chips?"

Mr. O hands his manila envelope containing $300,000 to the chipman.

"Would you like this split up two ways, sir?"

"Please." Mr. O replied.

The chipman swiftly placed the stacks of chips in front of Mr. C. "Twenty red—50 thousand—20 black—100 thousand—total—150 thousand--thank you, sir."

Chipman stacked chips at Mr. O's position. "Twenty red— 50 thousand--20 black—100,000 thousand—total—150 thousand. Thank you, sir."

The chipman handed 6 manila envelopes to the dealer. The dealer handed them to the guard. The guard brought them into another room.

First game went as usual. Second game, Mr. C was in charge of the abacus.

Dealer opened a new deck. He shuffles them, had a player cut, and then drew the first card. "A jack, gentlemen. Did you record the jack Mr. C?"

"Jack recorded, sir."

The dealer placed the jack in the deck, then placed the deck in the shu.

The twenty-ninth card was drawn.

The thirtieth.

Thirty-first.

And, thirty-second.

Three jacks had been drawn and recorded.

Mr. O whispered to Mr. C. "This is it, sweetheart." Mr. O pushed 150 thousand in front of him, and Mr. C followed suit. Mr. O looked at the chipman.

"Sir, my partner and I wish to bet 300 big ones on the jack, please."

"My pleasure, gentlemen." He placed a 300 thousand dollar marker on the jack and lay a 300 thousand marker in the middle of Mr. O and Mr. C.

"Thank you gentlemen, good luck."

The dealer called, "All bets down, gentlemen... 7 wins—10 loses.

The dealer looked perplexed.

Cheese bolted back in mild shock.

Smiley slapped the table, firmly and cringed back, groaning.

The chipman enthusiastically picked up and paid off the players in less than 30 seconds; he nodded his head at the dealer, and said, "Bets down, sir."

The dealer looked dumbfounded. "Hold on, gentlemen, something is not right." He counted the drawn cards, and asked Cheese to count the recorded cards aloud. Cheese was lost for words—he was in a mild trauma. He tried to say something. Between the trauma, greed and garlic breath, he said, "I-I canno--"

"The dealer interrupted the apple because he knew he was in deeper mild shock than he had foreseen. The dealer, looked as if he were bothered. He turned to Mr. O. "Give me the count, Mr. O. Seems your confidant is preoccupied."

"Sorry, sir." He interpreted each card, above a whisper.

At the same time, the dealer placed each card face up to prove the abacus keeper made a serious mistake. When he was through, he firmly slapped the deck on the table, looking disgusted. He put the complete deck of cards together, and called, "Misdeal, gentlemen."

The players moaned and groaned while the dealer opened a new deck of cards. This second game up to the third jack was over in seventeen minutes.

Mr. O guided his partner to his feet, and said, "You okay, Mr. C?"

"W-Wha' da fuck h-happen to jack!" He almost fell, but Mr. O held on to him tightly. "Lets get outa this joint--come-come on."

As they walked away, the guard escorted them out the door.

When the guard came back to the card room, the dealer knew it was safe to give the new game to the dealer, and go out to the limousine and have a big time showdown.

Jules thought, *Cheese was a lay down (easy). Wait till I chew his ass out, he's gonna feel lower than a snake in a cesspool.* He laughed within, and prepared in thought for his grand performance outside. which will take place within four minutes.

The dealer looked at the chipman. "Start a new game, I'll be back in eight minutes."

"Yes sir. Take your time, sir."

The dealer hurried out of the room. He looked heated when he got to the limousine. It appeared that the chauffeur was about to get in the limo and leave.

The dealer shouted. "Wait! Wait!"

The chauffeur's expression was perplexed. "Yes sir, how can I help you."

Jules said, "Wait near the valet stand over there. I'll call you in a few minutes."

"Yes sir." The chauffeur replied.

The rear door was open, and Jules could see the pair clearly. He no sooner leaned over to chew them out when Mr. O vomited over his window, door and you name it.

"Ohhhh, sheeeit. Ohhhh gaaaa ah ahh Godd gaaaaa. He happened to kick the door open on that "put-the-finger-down-the-throat trick.

Jules began to shout. "Go ahead, go ahead, ya wanna spill your guts out too, Mr. C! What the fuck you do with the abacus! Maybe ya had an itch in yer groin and your arm pushed one of the buttons an' you didn't realize it!

Mr. C's head was looking at the floor of the limo. He was totally ashamed.

"I-I don't—we don't kn--"

"Never mind! You just blew 900 grand down the tubes! You both are fuckin' morons! Get outa my sight. Be at my suite by 9 tonight, I'll discuss this matter with the two a ya then." He gestured to the chauffeur to leave. "Take them where you picked them up and bring them to my suite by 9 sharp."

"Yes sir, sir."

And off they went onto the winding cobblestone road.

The threesome met at Jules' place, and he got down on Cheese and Smiley like as if they lost 900 thousand dollars three times. Cheese begged to get even, but Jules kept taking it away. He threw the two out after he told them he needed time to think it over. Smiley made several attempts by phone to persuade Jules to allow Cheese and him to play in another game. Jules finally gave in because Cheese had a million dollars he wanted to bet. In turn, he would win three million and Smiley and Jules' share would be 800 thousand apiece.

On the forth night, Smiley said to Cheese, "This is my lucky night. I got a call from Jules. He told me we're suppose to get to a big crap game tonight."

"Ees dees da game I breeng my million, and ween back tree times?"

"You got it sweetheart, but maybe you should stay here, and I'll go and play with my 200 grand. You n me can wait till next week and cash in big time."

"You are fucking crazy. Eef you tink I wait till nexta week, you are mistaken. We go tonight or else ...

"OK-OK-OK. Don't get mad. Christ, I like the cash just as much as you."

"Then eet ees settled?" Cheese asked.

Smiley and Cheese walked in the Tropicana Hotel & Casino. A hotel guard escorted them to a large double door. A solid brass plaque read:

MILLIONAIRES CLUB
VIP MEMBERS ONLY

A Cuban police officer was standing at the entrance. Smiley knocked the code, and a guard escorted them to a room filled with chattering, clamoring people. Three crap tables were occupied with heavy rollers. One of the three tables, on the end, Jules was winning big time. The crowd was growing larger as they watched him stacking his last win of fifty thousand. He's on a roll and skies the limit. He has 500 thousand dollars in chips in front of him. Jules had arranged Smiley to be on his right, and Cheese to Smiley's right. A long unlit cigar protruded from his mouth. He coolly looked about and dropped 5 thousand in 100 dollar bills on the table, and waited for chips. Cheese also had a spot reserved, he lay 50 thousand in cash on the table and waited for the croupier to give him chips.

Forty-five minutes later, Cheese was hovering over his winnings. He won more than forty thousand. Plus the fifty thousand he came in with equals a lot of chips.

All eyes were on Jules and Cheese. They were the only two betting big bucks. The watchers waited impatiently, and cheered and clapped, waiting for Jules to roll for his point.

Cheese played the same as Jules, but had not bet large amounts, except for the next roll.

Jules looked at the pit boss, then at Cheese, and back again to the pit boss. Jules studied both of them. He casually pushed 500 thousand near the center of the table. He looked at the pit boss. "Goin' all the way—let it ride.

Cheese pushed 50 thousand on the come line, and gave the pit boss a dirty look. Cheese leaned over and picked up his suitcase and dumped one million more on top of his 50. He looked at the pit boss with intense dislike, and said, "Make eet dees million, plus 50 granda more—I wanna see how mucha guts you got, boy!

The arrogant pit boss paused a second, stared at Jules, then at Cheese then at the cash and looked at the pit boss for approval. The pit boss put his fingers on his chin and thought deeply. Within 80 seconds he made a decision. He looked at the croupier, and said, "Clear the table and give the gentleman a mark for the million, and another for 50 thousand."

The croupier looked at Cheese. "Your markers, sir. Thank you."

A larger crowd gathered around Jules' table. One could feel the power, the glory, and the guts, to bet that amount on a single roll.

Jules snaked up the dice, rolled them around his palm once, and threw them in the air. They hit the backboard, and slowly turned over—two sixes appeared—

craps. Jules lost, Cheese lost--they looked as if they were shot. The crowd awed and ahd in grief.

Cheese looked as if he was ready to shoot everyone in the place. He happened to glance at Smiley and Jules who looked at each other with barely contained grins.

Cheese was frenzied. He looked at Jules. "Ya got me good, deedn't you! Fuckin' wop bastard."

Cheese drew a gun, but Smiley slapped it out of hid hand. The gun bounced on the table toward Jules. The crowd scrambled to get out of the way. Jules grabbed the gun and pointed it at Tony Cheese. "This is how you did in my friend—by surprise? Those the same hands that kill innocent kids?"

Cheese looked as if he cracked up. "I do not know what you fuckin' talk aboud. He lunged at Jules, who accidentally pulled the trigger. A shot, Smiley hit the floor. Cheese yanked the gun from Jules' hand. Everyone in the place dove for cover and hit the floor. Cheese pulled the trigger, a shot, another shot. Jules hung on to the table for a moment. "Awwww, sonofabitch, he got me g-good...who'd ever think I'd go this w-way... Jesus Chri... he fell to the floor. Immediately, as Jules hit the floor, the double door smashed open. Two of Castro's soldiers pointed their automatic machine guns at Cheese, yelling PARE! PARE! (STOP! STOP!).

One soldier yelled out to Cheese. "What eez going on here? You, drop pistola on fl...

Cheese blew the guy away with three shots.

The other soldier pumped 15 or 20 rounds into Cheese, blasting him against the wall. He slowly sank to the floor in a pool of blood.

One of the shills whacked the soldier's head off with a baseball bat.

Jules tried to get up, but he fell back down. Two shills helped him to his feet.

"Theo, Red." He yelled out. "Get Smiley outa here. Get to the hospital ASAP. Pick up those two soldiers, and drop them in the secret basement under that crap table. The rest of you, clean up the blood and throw the towels down in the basement too. Let's move it, we got three minutes to get outa here. One of the shills came running in the room, yelling, "Castro's combat squad is a minute away! Better get the fuck out, or no bacon an' eggs in the mornin', their burnin' everything in sight and blowin' people away like ther' outa style.

Everything was cleaned except for the cash on the table. Jules motioned to one of his shills to come over to him. "Fats," He said, "Put the cash in my suitcase over there. Drive with me."

"OK-OK. I'll be packed in less than a minute."

Not a soul would have known what took place in that room. They all slipped out a secret door, and went their way.

Soldiers were everywhere. Jules and Fats made it to his place in one piece.

When Jules arrived in his driveway, Smiley was talking to Arny and BoBo who brought him to a doctor friend of Jules.

Jules looked at Smiley in amazement. "Thought you were a goner, Irish."

"Just a flesh wound, no big deal."

Fats said, "We gotta get Jules to a doc, like right now. He lost a lot of blood."

CHAPTER 37

HAVANA, JULES' HOME, MAY 8, 1958

11:32 P.M.

Jules was telling Carmen and the girls to pack quickly. Castro and his soldiers were taking over. He stood there with his left arm in a sling. When Cheese shot him, one bullet hit his gold Dunhill lighter Carmen gave him in Saratoga, and it ricochet leaving a .38 caliber hole in it as a reminder. The second shot pierced his upper left shoulder, and he will recover with no permanent damage.

It apparently was not meant to be for the curtains to fall upon Jules yet. The Boss upstairs didn't think it was Jules' time for everlastingness.

Smiley came in carrying his suitcase. Shirtsleeves and underwear dangled and his white suit were stained with blood and dirt.

He shouted. "Jesus Christ, Jules! Are ya coming, goin', stayin' or prayin'?"

One of Batista's men pounded on the door, it opened and he entered, shouting. "You people must leave NOW! IMMEDIATELY! Castro's soldiers are coming thees way. They weel not hesitate to keel all of you on thee spot! Presidanty Batista weeshes you and your family the best of luck. HURRY-HURRY!" He swiftly left the house.

Jules told Smiley to round up as many shills as he can and to meet at the wharf no later than 11:55. Smiley only had eighteen minutes. And, if they're not there, they would have to stay.

"Oh, sheeeit--Jules-Jules, I forgot to tell ya something." Smiley said.

"What! What! Hurry up!"

"On my way over here, I seen all these Castro soldiers draggin' the goddam slot machines, crap tables—everything, out in the street and-and throwin' 'em in a pile and doin' a torch job--I couldn't believe my ey--"

"Get the fuck outa here--Jesus Christ!"

"Lets go, Carmen" Jules shouted. "He picked up his personal phone and called his captain. "Hello, skipper?"

"It's me, sir."

Prepare to sail in ten-fifteen minutes, we're gettin' the hell outa here! Can you do it?"

She's all fueled up and ready to sail, sir. I'll warm her up. We ain't got much time, ya know, sir. I kin see the bastards right now, ther' burnin' everathin in sight!"

"Don't worry, skipper, we're all goin' together—just put the coffee on!"

Jules went in the girls room. "C'mon, my little ladies, I see your all packed and ready to go. We're going fishing. And if your especially good, Daddy will give you some coffee with those chocolate chip cookies, you like."

Micki said, "Can we have two, daddy?"

"You and Tina can have the whole box. How's that?"

Tina went up to her daddy. "Ya know, I know that you know, that's a no-no."

"Your right, angel, but sometimes, there's an exception to the rule."

He picked up Micki, and moaned quietly in pain. Carmen and Tina walked out with the chauffeur carrying the luggage. They jumped in the limousine and the chauffeur drove cautiously to the wharf. As they passed the Riviera Hotel & Casino, it had been overrun with troops. There were four or five enormous fires burning. They looked as if the fingers of the out of control flames were reaching for the stars. The red and yellow and orange inferno looked as though a Fourth of July celebration had launched its fire works. The reek of burnt mahogany and walnut and admixture of metals filled the air. They reached the private dock where Jules' yacht was waiting. All the shills were patiently waiting on the deck. Carmen and the girls, climbed aboard, and the Captain assisted them. Jules studied the crew before boarding.

"Where's Smiley, Red?"

"I dunno!" He told me he had to take a dump. His stomach was actin' up— diarrhea—said he musta ate a bad clam err somethin, know whadimean, Jules?"

"You mean to tell me the sonofabitch isn't here!"

Red looked at the shills, raising his arms. "SMILEY HERE?"

They all shook their heads and a few shouted, "NOOO!"

Jules' right hand clutched his left arm so as to hinder movement. He started to climb aboard on his own, but the Captain and Red jumped out to help him.

"Thanks boys. OK Captain, take off—real slow. That Irish bastard is full of surprises. Leave at least fifty feet of anchor line adrift. It may be a good idea to tie one end to the aft, just in case." They laughed.

The yacht slowly moved away from the dock, around forty-five or fifty yards off shore.

"OK, idle about here--good-good, Jules said to the Captain. "We're pretty safe out here, never know who's gonna take a pop shot at us. Ya know Captain, that fuckin' Irish moron can sometimes be a goddam pai—"

A car careened into the dirt next to the wharf. Smiley raced out naked with two females in their panties. He ran faster than Jules had ever seen him.

"Wait! Wait for me!" Smiley shouted.

Jules said to the Captain, "I can't believe that moron. But on the other hand, why shouldn't I. You wouldn't believe what I've done for that sex maniac." He shouted to Smiley. "Hey, lover boy, stay with the broads or swim--alone!"

Smiley turned and through kisses at his ecstasy. While running backward, he stumbled and dropped four feet doing the perfect belly smacker. He hit the water so hard, the yacht headed skyward a bit, then came down and slammed against the water like a whale leaping from the sea and smacking its reverse, just for fun.

"Help! Help!" Smiley cried out. "I can't swim! I c-can't swim!"

"What do you want me to do, sir?" The Captain asked, Jules.

"Go to him. Give him just enough rope so he can grab it. I'll fix his ass."

The Captain swung around, and he maneuvered the yacht like a true seaman. He dragged the line and positioned it in Smiley's reach. Smiley just made it. He grabbed the line and held it for dear life.

Jules told the Captain to pull Smiley for two more minutes. Fats and Red started reeling him in.

"Hold it, boys, let him get a taste of Cuban water." Jules shouted to Smiley, "Great opportune for you to learn the new sexual stroke!" Everyone broke apart laughing.

The shills never laughed so hard. Fats shouted, "Ahhh, drown-drown-drown, ya big baby! Castro don't give a shit!" The shills laughed harder than before.

"Jes-pi-pi-us Chri-ghaa-st," He was spitting and blowing out water like a hunchback whale. "I'm drowning, gasp, aggggg."

"OK Captain, let's pull him in."

The Captain put the engines in neutral.

Jules shouted, "OK, Fats, Red, get him in here. We can't leave a good Irishman to Castro! Know what I mean?"

The boys had more laughs than the three-week stay in Havana. They were having a good time.

Fats and Red pulled Smiley aboard. He looked like the last rose of summer.

" Let's get outa here, Captain." Jules shouted.

The yacht sailed off and disappeared into the mist of the night.

CHAPTER 38

NEW YORK, JULES' OLD NEIGHBORHOOD, DECEMBER 11, 1972

6:16 A.M.

It's a windy, snowy morning, the kind that clears the streets of all but the snow removal gang of four young men with long hair. They're having their morning high, smoking a joint. The wino leaning on the telephone pole carried heat of his own liking.

Jules gazed at the old isolated grocery store where he first paid Izzy, to get him dead rats for the "Mickey Mouse" scam, he dreamed up. He paused a moment, and shook the snow off his boots. An aura of wealth surrounded him. He knocked on the door and Izzy appeared. He looked at Jules recognizing him immediately, and smiled.

"Jules, long time. You made it real big—always knew you would. As you can see, nothing has changed. I'm so glad you stopped by. Please, come in."

"I have to go, Izzy. Just wanted to drop by and give you a gift. This envelope is for the little things you did for me when we were kids."

Izzy opened the envelope and counted fifteen thousand dollars. He looked at Jules tearing and speechless.

"Jules, I-I--"

"There's nothing to say. Only one catch. Don't ever tell anyone. Maybe someday I may need a pack of cigarettes or a meal. See you my friend."

Jules headed toward his old tenement. Nothing had changed. There still was over-filled trashcans and debris everywhere. There were cats feasting on rats, a stray dog tearing at garbage bags. The stench was disgusting. His old building had graffiti painted far and near. The front door was still half-open. He walked away and a black limousine slowly followed him. He turned and gestured with his hand to pick him up. The chauffeur opened the door and Jules stepped in. He lit a cigarette taking a long drag, then sat back in a comfortable position. His face revealed a sense of contentment. As the limousine slowly moved along, Jules had a flashback.

Images from the mind were clear, as two sets of men's legs from the knees down, carried his footlocker up a flight of stairs, with total recall. When they reached the landing, they set the locker down and unlock the door. The hand turned the white ceramic doorknob, and opened it. As the door opened, it squeaked in a scary sort of way. The men picked up the locker and continued up the rickety stairs. They got to the top floor and an arm pulled on a long string to turn on the light, it didn't turn on. The only light in the attic was from an octagonal stained glass window at the far end of the room. The attic consisted of three slot machines, a crap table with no legs, two blackjack tables, countless number of boxes neatly stacked, magazines crammed in grape cartons and several oil paintings piled on top of each other, covered with red, leopard, and green quilted bedspreads. The hands are carrying the locker to the back corner. As the hands and legs move forward, he dreamed of seeing his high gloss wood floor, it is immaculately clean. The long oriental area rug leads to the spot where the locker is placed. Just above the locker is a 4' X 5' landscape painting hanging. It's an original painting of an olive grove on a hilltop in Sicily. Rocco had it on the wall behind his desk in his office, as well as covering his safe. All things are neatly in its place, and covered with dust and cobwebs. A rocking chair slightly rocks from a current of air coming from an opening near the window. The legs walk away. Out of the clear blue sky, a beam of light pierced its way through the octagonal stained glass window. It beamed its blinding white rays upon the footlocker. The legs stopped walking at the stairway. They turn to the unexpected illumination, but they're blinded from the glare. Suddenly, the entire room is in complete darkness. The only sound heard are footsteps going down the rickety stairs, and the squeaky door closing. Then, a small noise...clicks.

Unexpectedly, Jules heard a voice.

"Sir! Sir!" The chauffeur called out—"Sir?" He reached his arm on Jules' leg and shook it. Jules flinched, then his eyes opened. His cigarette was still between his lips. He noticed ashes had dropped on his silk scarf and burned a small hole directly through it.

The chauffeur turned in Jules' direction. "Sir, we're home."

Christ, all ready? I was out cold. Went to the Elysian fields, Max. I don't know why I'm so tired lately."

"You're entitled, sir." The chauffeur said, opening the rear door.

"Said a mouthful, Max, yer right-yer right. I not going to be using you until 9:00-9:15. Go, relax, I'll call."

"I'll benefit from that, sir. The special home made wine, you know? A half filled glass will indeed take me on a journey to Arcadia, don't you agree, sir?"

"Nice place, Max. When you arrive, check the Nether Regions Men Haberdashery, the place will knock your socks off."

"Thank you, sir. I may not be fitted for that."

Jules laughed, and patted Max on his shoulder. "Funny, Max. Have a good trip!"

He smiled. "Thank you, sir."

Jules lived in a Victorian style home. It was a historic masterpiece. He went inside, and Ernestine greeted him.

"Lordy, Lordy, what a surprise! Can I make you coffee and, Mr. Jules?"

" How about coffee and, and?"

"Mr. Jules, either yooz is err either yooz ain't, if ah's don't make da coffee real soon, ah's' may sit right down n faint. So's, just in case yooz didn't know, ah's jus' back from Lake Mapawkapaw, n learned from Chief Pawkeekateetee ta make coffeetoopee. So's, yooz be nimble n yooz be quick cause yooz'll be jumpin' inside da stick!"

A half an hour later he sipped his coffee and wine and decided to go to the attic. This place was where Jules "treasure" was. He walked up the stairs in his slippers, and when he got to the landing, he stared at the white ceramic doorknob once attached to the wine cellar door in Rocco's basement. He unlocked the door and it squeaked as it always has. He went up the rickety stairs to the landing. Then he reached up and pulled the long string to turn on the light. The light burnt out as in Rocco's basement. He paused a moment, he could hear his heart beat pounding at a fast rhythmic pace. He relaxed momentarily. His heartbeat lowered.

He studied the place. It was the same as it always had been. The only light was from the octagonal stained glass window. He paused to brush away cobwebs in his path. As he walked along, he touched and stroked his first crap table Rocco had in the back room of Jules' first apartment, in the restaurant. It rested at the top portion of his bed.

Jules spotted his footlocker and his eyes filled with tears. He studied the painting once behind Rocco's desk, then at the locker. His walk was very slow as he approached his rocking chair. He dusted off the chair with his scarf, and sat down looking at the footlocker near his feet. The bright piercing rays of the sun intensified as they beamed through the stained glass window. The glare of the light made the cobwebs attached to the locker seem as if a goast was leaning over the footlocker and attempting to open it.

Jules' heartbeat began to lower, and gradually got slower and slower. He said to the footlocker, in complete contentment, "Is there any...anyone out there dare...have..." He was losing it. "I-Is there anyone out there ...that dare open you, with passion such as...you have given to me...

His eye's closed.

In Memory Of

Jules S.

Made in the USA